continued ...

Also Available in the Killer Instincts Series

MIDNIGHT ACTION

A KILLER INSTINCTS NOVEL

ELLE KENNEDY

A SIGNET ECLIPSE BOOK

SIGNET ECLIPSE
Published by the Penguin Group
Penguin Group (USA) LLC, 375 Hudson Street,
New York, New York 10014

USA | Canada | UK | Ireland | Australia | New Zealand | India | South Africa | China
penguin.com
A Penguin Random House Company

First published by Signet Eclipse, an imprint of New American Library,
a division of Penguin Group (USA) LLC

First Printing, November 2014

ISBN 978-0-451-46570-2

Printed in the United States of America
10 9 8 7 6 5 4 3 2 1

To Jesse, for convincing me that these
two had to be together!

ACKNOWLEDGMENTS

I couldn't have written this book without the usual suspects:

My incredible editor, Laura Fazio, for her invaluable input and sheer enthusiasm for this series.

Travis White for his superior research skills and finding answers to all the strange questions I lob his way.

The incomparable Vivian Arend for her early feedback and endless cheerleading.

My proofreader, Sharon Muha, for her eagle eye and, more important, her friendship and support.

My agent, Don Fehr, for his career advice and assistance.

My friends and family for putting up with me when I'm in my deadline cave and still talking to me when I come out of it!

And of course, all the fans of the series for their e-mail, support, and love—I adore each and every one of you.

Prologue

Nineteen years ago

The overcast sky and turbulent gray clouds rolling in from the east made for a miserable afternoon. Rain was imminent, and the chill in the air had already sent all of the café's patrons inside. Only Noelle remained on the cobblestone patio, her gloved hands wrapped around a cup of hot English breakfast tea. She wished she'd brought a scarf, but she'd forgotten it back at the elegant town house in the heart of Saint Germain-des-Pres, the prestigious neighborhood she'd been calling home for the past ten years. Except the nineteenth-century property where she lived, with its soaring ceilings and sweeping gardens, was not a real home.

It was a prison.

She'd come to the Marais district today to escape, but deep down she knew there was no such thing. The numbing pain in her left hand confirmed it—she was trapped. Forced to endure René's torment, at least for another two months. But once she turned eighteen? She'd be out of that house like a bat out of hell. For good. Forever.

She wasn't foolish enough to think she could convince her mother to join her. No, Colette had made her choice. She would never leave René, but Noelle was past caring. Past begging her mother to see the light.

Pushing away her bitterness, she took a long sip of her tea. The hot liquid instantly warmed her insides, but it didn't ease the relentless throb in her fingers. At least two were broken—the index and middle—but her thumb ached too, so perhaps it hadn't been spared in René's vicious attack either.

I'm going to kill you.

She silently transmitted the message to her stepfather, willing his subconscious to hear it. And it was no longer wishful thinking—she *would* kill him. She didn't know when, couldn't even begin to figure out how, but René Laurent was going to die at her hands. She would make sure of it.

"Is this seat taken?"

The deep, gravelly voice jolted Noelle from her blood-thirsty thoughts. When she laid eyes on the man it belonged to, her breath caught in her throat.

She blinked, wondering if maybe she'd dreamed him, but then he flashed her a captivating grin and she realized that he *must* be real—her mind wasn't capable of conjuring up a smile this heart-stoppingly gorgeous.

A pair of vivid blue eyes watched her expectantly as she searched for her voice.

"There are lots of other seats available," she finally replied, gesturing to the deserted tables all around them.

He shrugged. "I don't want to sit anywhere but here."

She moistened her suddenly dry lips. "Why?"

"Because none of those other seats are across from you," he said simply.

Her heart skipped a beat, and her gaze . . . Well, her gaze couldn't seem to leave his face. He was the most handsome man she'd ever seen in her life. His features were perfectly chiseled, his jaw strong and clean-shaven, his mouth far too sensual. And those eyes . . . midnight blue and utterly endless. A girl could lose herself in his eyes.

And this girl nearly did, until the beautiful stranger chuckled softly, alerting her to the embarrassing fact that she'd fallen into a trance.

Noelle cleared her throat, feeling her cheeks heat up. "I guess you can join me." She put on an indifferent voice, but she could tell he saw right through it.

He was studying her intently as he lowered his tall, lean body into the chair opposite hers. As he set his coffee cup in front of him, her gaze landed on his hands. Big and strong, with long fingers and short, blunt fingernails.

"You're shivering," he said gruffly.

"It's cold out."

"Yes, it is."

Noelle took a hasty sip of tea, shifting awkwardly in her chair. She watched as he ran one large hand through his dark brown hair. So short it was nearly shaved off. She wondered if he was a soldier. His bulky hunter green sweater and faded blue jeans weren't exactly military-issue, but something about the way he carried himself, something in his shrewd blue eyes, told her he was much more than a tourist or local college student.

He was also a foreigner—she definitely hadn't missed the distinct American accent lining his flawless French words.

"You're from the States," she remarked in perfect English.

He nodded in confirmation. "Virginia, born and raised. And from the sound of it, you're American yourself."

"My father is."

"Did you ever live in the States?"

"Yes. We were in D.C. for eight years."

"But now you live in Paris?"

She offered a quick nod. "My mother is French. She and I moved here after my parents got divorced."

"I see." He reached into his pocket and pulled out a pack of cigarettes.

The hiss of a lighter cut through the air as he lit up, bringing a frown to Noelle's lips.

"Smoking is very bad for you," she said frankly.

"What can I say? I like to live on the edge."

He grinned again, and her heart began to pound.

As she tried to control the butterflies in her stomach, his mesmerizing eyes swept over her once more and a thoughtful expression flitted across his face. "You're beautiful. Has anyone ever told you that?"

Her cheeks scorched again. There was nothing lewd or creepy about the compliment, but the intensity with which he said it made her pulse race. Something about this man affected her in a strange, confusing way she'd never experienced before. She found herself wanting to reach across the table and touch him. Hold his hand, stroke his jaw, place her palm on his broad, muscular chest. The urge only confused her further, and so she avoided his gaze by peering down at her teacup.

"What's your name?"

Swallowing, she lifted her head to meet his eyes.

And was stunned by the odd combination of heat and desperation she saw in them.

"Noelle," she murmured.

"Noelle." His voice came out hoarse. "I'm James Morgan, but everyone calls me Jim, or Morgan."

Jim. What an ordinary name for a man who was anything but.

"What brings you to Paris?" She was incredibly proud of herself for managing to speak in a steady voice when her entire body was consumed with erratic jolts of heat.

"I'm here on vacation. I have three weeks' leave so I thought I'd travel until I had to report back to the base."

"The base . . . Are you in the army?"

"Yeah. Doing my second tour now."

"That's nice. Do you enjoy it?"

His blue eyes flickered with . . . a glimmer she couldn't quite decipher. "I do. I enjoy it a lot, actually."

"Good. It's important to love what you do."

"It is," he agreed, before slanting his head pensively. "What about you? What keeps you busy?"

"School." Noelle shrugged. "I graduate from *high school* in the spring."

She'd purposely emphasized the words so he would be aware of her age, but he didn't seem distressed by it. She knew he was older—she would pin him down at twenty-one, maybe twenty-two—but the age difference didn't bother her either.

Waves of tension moved between them. Or maybe it was awareness. She couldn't be sure, couldn't quite understand it, but she knew she wasn't the only one feeling it. Jim's pulse visibly throbbed in his throat, as if his heartbeat was as irregular as hers. And his eyes . . . they never left hers, not even once.

"And afterward?" he prompted. "What will you do then?"

Run.

Run and never come back.

"I don't know," she said.

Before she could blink, his hand breached the space between them and found hers. The burst of excitement that went off inside her was immediately replaced by the ripples of pain that seized her injured fingers.

Jim must have noticed her agitation, because his eyes narrowed. "You're hurt," he said flatly.

Surprise filtered through her. "I—"

He was peeling off her brown leather glove before she could protest, and when her hand was exposed, a deep frown puckered his mouth.

She saw exactly what he did—two black-and-blue fingers swollen to twice their size, and unpolished fingernails that had broken and bled beneath René's heavy boot.

"Who did this to you?"

His low growl startled her, as did his astute assumption that her injury was no accident. When he gently ran one callused fingertip over her thumb, tears pricked her eyes, but she desperately fought them off. She refused to cry. Crying was a show of weakness, and Noelle was not weak. She would never be weak.

"You need to see a doctor," Jim said hoarsely.

"No! No doctors," she blurted out. "I'm fine, honestly. It was a clean break. I'll just tape them up when I get home."

His eyes flickered with surprise, and she could have sworn she glimpsed a gleam of admiration.

But he didn't capitulate, just spoke again, sternly this time. "Your hand needs to be X-rayed at the hospital. There might be damage you're not aware of."

"No doctors," she repeated.

"Noelle—"

She set her jaw. *"No."*

The lump of panic jamming her throat doubled in size. He couldn't force her to see a doctor, could he? Hospitals and doctors left paper trails, and she couldn't risk leaving a trail that her father might find. Douglas Phillips had raised her to be strong. He'd passed his warrior genes on to her, made sure she could take care of herself.

What would he think if he knew she'd allowed René to have power over her? How ashamed would he be?

Jim released a heavy breath. "Fine. If you won't go to the hospital, at least let me take you to see a friend of mine."

She eyed him suspiciously. "What friend?"

"An old army buddy. He runs a small medical practice in Seine-Saint-Denis," Jim explained, naming one of the more run-down neighborhoods of the city. "He'll keep the visit off the books if I ask him to."

Uneasiness swam in her gut, making her hesitate.

"Nobody will ever know you saw him. I promise."

The total assurance in his tone was impossible to ignore. God, she believed him. She believed that when this man made a promise, he kept it.

"All right," she whispered. "I'll go."

"Thank you."

Their gazes collided and locked, and that unsettling and thrilling sizzle of connection traveled between them again.

Noelle couldn't tear her eyes away from his. Her surroundings faded. The wind died into utter silence. She'd never felt this way before. Ever. And she couldn't even begin to put into words why she was so drawn to this man.

All she knew, right here, right now, on this cold and cloudy autumn afternoon, was that her entire life was about to change.

Chapter 1

Present day

Noelle raised her cigarette to her lips and took a deep drag, sucking the smoke and chemicals into her lungs before exhaling a plume of gray into the night air. The apartment across the street was dark, save for the one light shining in the study where Gilles Girard was currently sipping on a cup of espresso. She'd been watching the Parisian barrister for three days, and she knew that after he indulged his caffeine fix, he'd move on to the bottle of Rémy Martin on the mahogany bar. The guy had expensive taste in cognac. That was for sure.

The lawyer's west end private residence was located in the 16th District, one of the most prestigious areas in the city. That told her he had the required cash to procure the services of someone like her, or, at the very least, represented clients who could afford her. But she didn't trust the man. Granted, she didn't trust anyone, but Girard's out-of-the-blue request was definitely fishier than most.

He'd contacted her via several middlemen, though that alone wasn't unusual, considering her number wasn't exactly listed in any phone books. No, what made her uneasy was the urgency she'd detected in his voice. *The job must be done as soon as possible. There's no room for delay.* The harried plea had rung with desperation, and in Noelle's experience, desperate men spelled nothing but trouble.

Which was why she now lay on the dark roof opposite

Girard's, flat on her stomach with a rifle at her side and binoculars zoomed in on her prey. Watching, waiting.

Girard lived alone. No wife or kids, no household staff. He was in his late fifties, and his choice of attire told her he was an old-school, aristocratic kind of guy. Anyone who wore perfectly pressed slacks, a cashmere Burberry sweater, and a Gucci scarf around his neck, in the privacy of his own home, was someone who valued luxurious items.

Noelle adjusted the zoom on the binoculars and studied Girard's handsome features and groomed salt-and-pepper hair. There was something very . . . jaunty about him. And honorable—he seemed like a man with a moral code.

So why was he trying to hire a contract killer?

Frowning, she snuffed out her cigarette on the pavement and extracted her cell phone from the pocket of her tight-fitting leather coat. A moment later, her field glasses revealed Girard reaching for his own phone.

"Bonjour?" came his baritone voice in her ear.

"It's me," she answered in French. "It's time to continue our little discussion."

She clearly saw the man's face stiffen through her zoom lens. "You ended our last call very abruptly," he said in annoyance. "It was quite rude."

"I told you, I had to check out a few details."

"You had to dig into my background, you mean."

"Yes."

"And are you satisfied with what you found?"

"For the most part." She lazily ran her free hand over the barrel of her rifle. "Who is your client?"

"I already told you, I can't reveal that. But I can assure you, my client has no shortage of funds. He is more than capable of paying your fee."

"Good to know," she said lightly. "But I don't like working for shadows, Mr. Girard."

"Then I'm afraid we've got nothing more to discuss. The identity of my client will not be disclosed, mademoiselle. This is nonnegotiable."

Irritation flared inside her. Christ, sometimes she wished she'd gone into a different line of work. Secretive men were so goddamn infuriating. And yet she didn't disconnect the call—her curiosity had been piqued the moment Gilles Girard had contacted her, and she wasn't the kind of woman who walked away from a puzzle. Or a challenge.

"All right," she conceded. "I can live with that."

"Good. Shall we discuss the details, then?"

"Not over the phone."

"Fine. We will meet tomorrow?"

"Tonight," she said briskly. "We'll meet tonight."

"I'm afraid I've already retired for the night."

"No, you haven't." Chuckling, she zoomed in closer and saw the flicker of alarm in his dark eyes.

"What makes you say that?" he asked carefully.

"Well, I'm looking at you as we speak, Gilles, and your fancy-pants clothes don't look like pajamas to me."

Noelle got great satisfaction from seeing his gaze dart around wildly, as if he expected her to pop out of a closet and ambush him.

She laughed again. "Don't worry, *monsieur*. I'm not inside your house. Yet."

She tossed the binoculars into the sleek black duffel by her side. As she gracefully rose to her feet, the warm August breeze lifted her blond ponytail and heated the back of her neck.

"I'll see you shortly, Gilles," she told the panicked man. She paused in afterthought. "Oh, and I suggest you don't reach for that pricey cognac of yours."

Suspicion floated over the line. "Why not?"

"Because I poisoned it."

His startled curse brought a smile to her lips. "Y-you . . . h-how . . ."

"Don't you worry about that, honey," she answered as she quickly disassembled her rifle, while balancing the cell on her shoulder. "It was just a precaution, in case I didn't like the outcome of this phone call."

When he made an outraged noise, she fought a laugh and said, "Out of curiosity, who's the target?"

There was a pause. "I thought you didn't want details over the phone."

"Not about money or method. Names are fine."

She zipped up the rifle case, then tucked it next to the duffel—she'd leave both on the roof and collect them after her little tête-à-tête with the good lawyer.

"Ah. All right, then." Girard hesitated. "The target is a soldier. Well, a former soldier. He now works as a private military contractor."

"A mercenary."

"Yes."

Shifting the phone to her other shoulder, she patted her jacket to make sure the weapons beneath it were secure, and then she walked across the gravel-littered rooftop toward the wrought-iron ladder at its edge.

"He's used various aliases over the years," Girard continued, "but he's currently operating under the name James Morgan."

Noelle froze. "What did you say?"

"Morgan," Girard repeated. "The target's name is James Morgan."

"I met someone else."

The slender brunette kept her back to him as she snapped the clasp of her bra into place. Her long, straight hair fell down to her panty-clad ass, shimmering in the pale glow of the bedside lamp.

Morgan zipped up his cargo pants and waited for Maya to continue, which she did, with great regret in her throaty voice.

"I should have ended it sooner, but I was ... waiting ... hoping, I guess." She turned to face him, her bottomless brown eyes flickering with unhappiness. "I suppose I was silly to think that we might have a future."

When he didn't argue, her expression grew even more pained. "I know. You made yourself clear from the start."

Morgan cleared his throat. "Maya—"

She held up her hand to silence him. "No. Don't apologize. Like I said, it was silly of me. But Cruz ... he's willing to give me everything you can't. And he adores Diego ..."

Whom you have never even met, was the unspoken implication.

And damned if it didn't make him feel like a total dick. In the two months they'd been sleeping together, he'd gone out of his way to avoid Maya's seven-year-old son. Not out of malice or dislike, but, well, he knew how attached kids could get, especially young boys without a father figure in their lives, and he hadn't wanted to take any risks. He'd known from the onset that his affair with Maya would be a temporary one.

She was a wonderful woman—he couldn't deny that. Smart, beautiful, hardworking. But relationships didn't interest him. Sex was all he'd ever wanted out of the arrangement, and Maya had always been more than happy to provide it.

"I want to give my son a good life, Morgan."

"I know," he said gruffly, his Spanish coming out stilted even though he normally spoke it impeccably.

Maya slipped into a pale blue tank top and a pair of denim shorts, then walked over and kissed him. She was a tall woman, didn't even have to stand on her tiptoes to bring her mouth to his, and he kissed her back with more tenderness than he'd ever shown her before.

She blinked in surprise as she pulled back, but the resolve in her eyes didn't falter. "I had a lot of fun."

"Me too." He dragged his thumb over her soft jaw before taking a step back. "But it was bound to end, sweetheart."

She nodded sadly. "I'll walk you out."

They moved through the dark bungalow in silence, with Maya ahead of him, her expression shielded from his view. Although she'd known the score from the get-go, Morgan knew she was disappointed he hadn't put up a fight about ending it. He could see that disappointment in the slight slump of her shoulders and the weariness in her long strides.

But he wasn't going to give her false hope or make empty promises. He wasn't the man she wanted him to be. Husband, daddy—that wasn't him, and never would be.

"Will you at least tell me about her?"

Maya's quiet plea made him frown. As they paused in the shadow-ridden front hall, he searched her gaze, trying to make sense of the request.

"Tell you about who?"

"The woman who broke your heart."

A harsh laugh slipped out. "Oh, sweetheart, I've never had my heart broken."

"I see." Maya hesitated. "She died, then?"

A thread of discomfort knotted around his insides.

Christ. Why did women always assume he belonged to the *loved and lost* camp? Why did they always feel the need to analyze him, to discover what his demons were?

"I know I'm right," she murmured. "And I'm never going to see you again after tonight, so what's the harm? Tell me about her, Morgan. What was she like?"

Morgan stifled a sigh. He didn't have time for this. Didn't *want* this.

But when he opened his mouth, the words that popped out surprised them both.

"She was sweet."

Maya's eyebrows shot up to her hairline. "Sweet," she echoed. "What else?"

"Strong." He swallowed. "She was very, very strong. And innocent. And when she laughed . . ." The lump in his throat made it difficult to go on. "Her laughter was . . . Fuck, I can't even describe it. And she always knew what I was thinking. She could read my mind, and it was damn infuriating."

Maya bit her lower lip. "She's dead, isn't she?"

An ache tightened his chest. "Yes. She's dead."

"I'm sorry, Morgan."

He managed a shrug. "Yeah, so am I." Before she could question him again, he dipped his head and brushed his lips over hers. "Take care of yourself, Maya. Maybe I'll see you around in town sometime."

"Maybe." She sounded noncommittal, and he could feel her retreating from him as she flicked the dead bolt and opened the front door to let him out.

He stepped into the night air without another word, and headed for his SUV without looking back. The soft click that met his ears told him she'd closed and relocked the door.

The moment he slid into the driver's seat, he popped open the glove compartment to retrieve the nine-millimeter Sig Sauer stashed there. He never brought a weapon into Maya's little bungalow—he didn't want to scare her—but he felt naked without his trusty Sig. Even now, just sitting in his car, he didn't feel fully comfortable until he placed the gun next to his thigh, within reach of his right hand.

Letting out a breath, he started the engine and reversed out the dirt driveway. He didn't glance in the rearview mirror to get a final glimpse of the house. Their time together was over, which meant it was time to move forward.

And if there was one thing Jim Morgan excelled at, it was never looking back.

Still, his heart felt heavy as he drove down the darkened street toward the intersection that would lead him into town. He hadn't wanted to hurt Maya, but he suspected that he had. He just hoped this new man of hers could give her everything she needed. Everything she deserved.

He reached the heart of town a few minutes later, found himself easing his foot off the gas pedal. The sleepy village of Turtle Cove didn't offer many options in terms of night-life, but it did boast a tiny dive bar that Morgan and his team of mercenaries often frequented. He headed toward it, and then parked in front of the narrow strip of dusty, crumbling storefronts.

It was just past eleven, but he wasn't in the mood to go back to the compound yet. Nearly every member of his team was a night owl, and Morgan didn't feel like seeing anyone right now. He'd been restless lately, itching to continue the search he'd embarked on so many years ago, but he couldn't skip town on a whim anymore, not after his last spontaneous trip.

In his absence, his compound had been ambushed by a private hit squad, two of his employees had lost their lives, and one of his men, Holden McCall, had suffered a crushing loss. Morgan knew the attack couldn't have been foreseen, but he still felt responsible for Beth McCall's death. He wondered whether Holden blamed him for it too. Probably. Fuck, it'd be rightfully so.

Sighing, he hopped out of the SUV and strode into the deserted bar. Ernesto, the owner and sole bartender, stood behind the counter chatting on a cell phone, but he nodded in greeting when he spotted Morgan.

"Tequila?" the bald man said briskly.

Morgan nodded back and slid onto one of the rickety wooden stools. He chose a seat that provided him with a perfect view of the door and corridor leading to the rest-rooms, and his gun was tucked in his waistband, a reassuring bulge beneath his shirt that allowed him to relax.

A moment later, Ernesto deposited a shot glass of Jose Cuervo in front of him, then wandered back to the other end of the counter, his phone glued to his ear. From the sound of it, Ernesto was trying to convince his wife that he had indeed cleaned the rain gutters like she'd requested, but clearly the woman wasn't buying it.

Tuning out the other man's conversation, Morgan thought about all the shit he needed to take care of tomorrow. The CIA was on his ass about a potential extraction of an agent who'd gotten himself captured in Angola, but government jobs were always such a pain in the ass. Too much red tape and peanuts for pay. But he supposed he could send Castle and a few members of his B-Team to get the job done.

He'd also just accepted a security gig, which he'd probably assign to Luke and Trevor, since the client had requested trained snipers. That meant he and the rest of his A-Team would have to handle the Ecuador job also in the pipeline. The government officials down there wanted a particularly delicate rebel situation handled, and were trying to avoid military involvement.

Man, so many jobs on the go, which gave new meaning to the words *soldier of fortune*. But even though the team would make a killing this month, Morgan had never been in it for the money. It was the action he craved, the rush of adrenaline and the surge of triumph he received after a successfully executed mission.

"Another one?" Ernesto's voice drew him out of his thoughts.

Morgan glanced down to see that he'd slugged back his shot without even realizing it, but he shook his head at the bartender's inquiry. Instead, he dropped a few US bills on the counter and rose from his stool. "Have a good night, Ernesto."

"You too, Mr. Morgan."

He left the bar feeling as unsettled as he'd entered it. What the fuck was up with him tonight? Yeah, he and Maya were done, but he knew that wasn't the reason for the persistent edginess he was feeling. Inexplicable unease continued to crawl up his spine like a colony of ants, and it stuck with him during the entire drive home.

The new compound was about twenty miles outside of

town, bordered by dense jungle on one side and rolling hills on the other. And it was isolated and hidden, just the way he liked it.

It had belonged to a drug kingpin whose empire had recently been crushed by the DEA, and Morgan had bought the place for a song at a government auction. Surrounded by a twelve-foot electric fence, the hundred-acre property consisted of an enormous main house, several outbuildings, and a Playboy Mansion–esque backyard with a swimming pool, grotto, and ten-person hot tub that his men were fucking gaga over.

He found it ironic—for a group of hardened soldiers, the men in his employ sure enjoyed their luxuries. Sullivan couldn't go a day without talking about his prized sailboat. Liam owned more designer clothes than a male celebrity. And as no-nonsense as Kane and Abby were, they sure spent a helluva lot of time in the sixteen-seat movie theater down in the basement. Yup, the house had an honest-to-God movie theater. Not to mention a game room, gym, indoor and outdoor target range, and a dozen other decadent goodies.

But Morgan didn't give a shit about the frills. He cared about the tunnels running beneath the house. The armory. The top-notch security system and each strategically placed block of C4 in every corner of the house. After last year's attack, he was taking security even more seriously than before, especially since this latest place seemed to pick up new residents like a damn boardinghouse.

Ethan had moved his girlfriend, Juliet, into the compound a few months ago, and even though Luke and Trevor were living off-site these days, Sullivan and Liam had swiftly moved in to take their place. Plus, the recent addition of Ash, their newest rookie, meant there was yet another person to bump into every other second.

Sometimes he felt like a goddamn babysitter, with all these younger, sexed-up soldiers running amok. For a man who'd been on his own since the age of eighteen, living with so many people was kind of unnerving, but Morgan ran a tight ship. And truth be told, he preferred having his team close by where he could keep an eye on them.

It took him five minutes to drive through the three enormous gates that blocked off the compound from the road. Each one required a different access code for the security panel, and a glance at the cameras mounted on the chain-link fences. One of the two security men who worked around the clock buzzed him in each time, and when he finally reached the large courtyard in front of the main house, he was starting to wonder whether this new security protocol of his might be overkill.

The thought died the second he spotted the out-of-place Mercedes parked next to Kane's silver Escalade.

His eyes narrowed as he stared at the sleek black car. Almost instantly, wariness flooded his gut and stiffened his shoulders.

Son of a bitch. Either Sully and Liam had brought a late-night visitor onto the property, or . . .

His hands curled into fists over the steering wheel. Fuck. The alternative was grating as hell, and he suddenly found himself praying that his boys had broken the rules and invited a woman over. But he knew better.

And the ominous feeling that had been prickling his spine ever since he'd left Maya's made sense now.

Perfect fucking sense.

Squaring his jaw, he stalked into the three-story house, paused in the cavernous parlor to rearm the alarm, then strode purposefully toward the living room. Light spilled out from beneath the heavy oak doors, and the soft murmur of voices reached his ears.

He pushed open the doors, paying no attention to the three chocolate brown Labrador retrievers that scurried up to him.

"Where is she?" he demanded.

Abby Sinclair and Kane Woodland glanced up from their perch on the couch. The couple was snuggled together under a red afghan, looking too damn calm, considering the toxic presence they'd allowed into the house. The blanket hid Abby's growing baby bump, which, if he were being honest, was a relief not to see. Abby was almost five months pregnant, and each time Morgan noticed the rounded curve of her belly, he was unsettled as hell.

He couldn't imagine a baby living in this house amid a group of highly skilled operatives, but Abby and Kane hadn't discussed their plans with him yet. He wasn't sure if they planned to raise the kid here or find a place of their own. Though he was kinda hoping they'd choose the latter.

"You're home earlier than usual," Kane remarked.

He repeated himself. "Where is she?"

Abby ran a hand through her long red hair, her voice quiet and composed. "Out back."

Without another word, Morgan ignored the excited dogs still nipping at his heels and marched off. The massive screened-in porch at the back of the house offered access to the backyard, and when he emerged onto the endless stone terrace and approached the railing, he instantly spotted their unwelcome visitor.

She wasn't alone. Derek "D" Pratt was with her, the two of them standing side by side near the kidney-shaped swimming pool. Although a foot of distance separated them and neither one was talking, their body language didn't reveal an ounce of aggression. If anything, they seemed utterly relaxed standing there together.

The anger that flooded Morgan's insides was both expected and infuriating.

Had she come here to see D?

It hadn't even occurred to him that she might be here for someone other than him, and the strange vise of possessiveness that squeezed his throat only pissed him off even more.

"Evening, Jim. Are you going to join us, or just lurk there in the shadows?"

Her mocking voice wafted toward him in the balmy night air. She hadn't even glanced his way, yet she'd known he was up at the railing, and the evidence of her razor-sharp senses was a reminder that he couldn't let his guard down around this woman. Ever. She was a threat. Had been for years, and probably always would be.

As he descended the stone steps, he steeled himself for this latest reunion. Each time they crossed paths, he went through the same old routine. Stayed on the alert, masked his emotions, armed himself for the inevitable showdown. He never knew what to expect with Noelle, except for one constant—her unceasing attempts to unnerve him.

If he were being honest, she succeeded more often than not.

Damned if he'd ever admit it to her, though.

"Why are you here?" he muttered when he reached the couple.

Couple. Goddamn it. The thought made him want to . . . Fuck, he didn't even know. Throw up? Shoot them down like rabid dogs? Laugh?

D seemed to be reading his mind as the two men locked eyes. The big, tattooed mercenary took a quick drag of his cigarette before breaking eye contact, then headed over to the poolside table to put out his smoke.

"Nice catching up with you, honey," Noelle drawled to D's retreating back.

The other man didn't turn around, just kept walking, but Morgan noticed those broad shoulders stiffen for a beat. He watched as D went up to the terrace, noting the power and confidence in the man's stride. D was a warrior, a terrifying force to be reckoned with, and for a moment, the image of that muscular body tangled with Noelle's petite one between the sheets flashed in Morgan's head.

His hands involuntarily curled into fists, but he tamped down the anger and resentment that rose in his throat, and finally turned to face Noelle.

"Why are you here?" he asked again.

Her pale blue eyes gleamed in the light glowing from the pool. "Just stopped by to say hello to an old lover, but you seem to have scared him off."

Morgan jerked his thumb in the direction D had gone. "He went thataway."

She threw her head back and laughed. "Aw, I'm just messing with you, Jim. You know exactly which ex-lover I came to see."

Her laughter was like a razor blade scraping a chalkboard. Cold, humorless, deadly.

"What do you want, Noelle?"

"You look good, Jim."

"What do you want, Noelle?"

She blinked innocently. "You're not going to return the compliment?"

He kept his gaze locked with hers, despite the fact that looking at her took a major toll on him. She was too beautiful. Too fucking beautiful, with her exquisite face, those big blue eyes, the perfect rosy lips. Her long hair was the color of spun gold, and he knew firsthand that it was silky to the touch.

And her body . . . it was goddamn sin. Endless curves hugged by black leather pants and a bloodred tank top, a body designed to make a man think of pure, carnal fucking.

Noelle's beauty was beyond compare, and that only stoked the hatred burning like lava in his gut. She looked like an angel, but she had a devil's heart. She was poison, and he refused to utter a single complimentary word to her, even as his hard-on strained against his zipper in salute to all her splendor.

"Fine." She gave a mock pout. "I guess pleasantries aren't really our style, huh? Let's get right to business."

He shot her a pointed look. "What favor do you need this time?"

She was positively beaming now. "Oh, baby, this time the favor's all yours."

As a cloud of suspicion floated through him, he reached for the bottom of his shirt and yanked it right over his head.

Noelle's gaze fastened on his bare chest, her head tilting to the side. "What are you doing?"

He unzipped his pants and let them drop to the concrete pool deck. "Going for a swim," he answered in a bored tone.

His boxers came off next, and Noelle's slight hitch of breath confirmed that she noticed his raging hard-on.

It was kind of hard to miss.

"You don't want to know what I mean by that?" Those blue eyes remained glued to his cock, but she didn't comment on his state of arousal.

Probably because she knew damn well the erection had nothing to do with lust. This was an anger-fueled boner, pure and simple.

He arched a brow at her. "I'll hear you out when I'm good and ready. Right now, I feel like a swim."

Brushing past her, Morgan headed for the deep end, hopped on the diving board, and dove cleanly into the warm water. The moment he was fully submerged, his head began to clear. Soon the volatile emotions Noelle always managed to elicit in him had reduced to a manageable degree.

When he finally poked his head out, he saw that she'd sat

down on one of the lounge chairs. Her annoyed expression brought a surge of satisfaction to his blood and a burst of energy that had him doing laps.

He'd do twenty-five, just to stir up her irritation. Make her wait, watch her stew. It was the same old game they always played. See who could piss off the other one more. Who could inflict more pain, cause more destruction.

Morgan sliced through the water in a clean crawl stroke, wishing he could see her face. But no biggie, because he could clearly envision her displeasure, picture the scowl twisting her lips.

Except . . . bad idea, thinking about her lips. That only triggered the unwelcome memory of what he'd done the last time they'd been alone together. Not two months ago, when she'd helped the team out in Cairo, but on the job in Belarus earlier that year, when he'd . . .

Kissed her.

Goddamn it, he'd *kissed* the bitch.

You felt nothing.

Right, he'd felt nothing. Nada. Zip. It had just been a test, a need to confirm that there was nothing between them.

Absolutely frickin' nothing.

He forced the memory away and concentrated on counting out his laps. Six. Seven. Ten. Fourteen. His arms burned from the brisk pace he'd set, but he preferred the pain to the other burn he felt around Noelle.

Another glance at the deck revealed the bitter grimace on her face. Good. Let her sulk. He'd spent years thinking of ways to punish her and make her suffer, but the woman was a block of ice, totally impenetrable. Unless she was being ignored—that was when the wall of indifference crumbled, her desire for power and recognition trumping her need to conceal her emotions.

And so he kept swimming, knowing the longer he made her wait, the faster her carefully composed mask would unravel.

Times like these, when he was imagining new ways of hurting her, it was impossible to believe that he'd ever loved this woman with all his heart.

Chapter 2

"Why is Morgan skinny-dipping in our pool?" was the first thing Sullivan Port demanded after he'd strolled into the room without knocking.

Liam Macgregor glanced up from the computer screen. "That's news to me. But please tell me he's not in there alone, 'cause that's just weird."

Sullivan collapsed in the armchair across from the bed as if his long legs could no longer support his weight. "He's in the pool alone, but he's got an audience. She kinda looks like she wants to murder him, though."

Closing the laptop, Liam leaned his head back on the mountain of decorative pillows their housekeeper liked to pile on his bed. No matter how many times he told Inna that he despised all those damn pillows, every night when he entered his bedroom, the Mount Everest of fluffiness was back on the king-size. Damn Russian females—they were a stubborn lot—that was for sure.

He placed the computer on the end table and raked a hand through his hair, all the while fighting a yawn. It was almost midnight, and he'd had a long day. Spent most of it in the gym working out with D, and then he, Ethan, and Juliet had gone for a hike in the mountains bordering the compound. Sullivan had been out all night, and even if he hadn't sent Liam a text with a heads-up about his plans, it would've been easy to figure out how he'd passed the time.

Liam could always tell when his buddy had gotten good

and laid, and at the moment, the guy was exhibiting some serious post-fucking symptoms. Rumpled blond hair, sated gray eyes, and a hundred and eighty pounds of sheer laziness. Sully's six-foot-three frame had practically melted into the chair, as if he didn't have the energy to move a single muscle.

It didn't escape Liam that he could've been feeling the same sexual satisfaction right about now, if only he'd accepted Sully's invitation to partake in the fun. In the year and a half since he'd joined Jim Morgan's team, he and Sully had been joined at the hip, indulging in more threesomes than he could keep track of.

Not lately, though. They hadn't shared a woman in more than a month. Not because Sully didn't ask him anymore—he did, every damn time—but lately Liam found himself reluctant to join in on the sexual escapades.

Ever since that last time, when . . .

When nothing.

He swiftly banished the thought, focusing instead on the curious look Sullivan shot him.

"You really didn't know she was here?"

Liam frowned at his teammate. "Who?"

"Noelle. I ran into Abby in the hall and she said her former boss showed up about an hour ago."

"I've been up here all night. I had no clue the Queen of Assassins was visiting."

"Well, she is. And trust me, mate, Morgan's not happy about it. He's doing a real angry-looking crawl."

Liam snickered. "Yeah, I'm sure you could tell his mood based on his swimming stroke."

"Trust me," Sully repeated.

"So what does she want?"

"Fuck if I know. Maybe one of her crazy operatives needs rescuing again."

"Doubt it. Most of her chameleons live with us now," Liam grumbled. "Or in Isabel's case, with Trev in Vermont."

"Good point." Sully released an exaggerated sigh. "Why do those blokes get all the breaks? I'd kill to sleep with one of her girls."

Liam couldn't disagree. Sometimes he wondered if Noelle's employment contracts contained a clause that said all her assassins had to be drop-dead gorgeous. Because so far, the ones Liam had met absolutely fit that bill. Abby, Isabel, and Juliet were so hot it was almost criminal, and from what Juliet had told him, the others were easy on the eyes too. Of course they were all deadly as hell too, so maybe it was a good thing he wasn't getting jiggy with one of Noelle's operatives.

Who wanted to sleep with a woman who was capable of murdering you in your sleep?

He'd much rather stick to the nonlethal chicks he met at the bars, thank you very much.

"You say that as if you're not getting any," Liam said mockingly. "And yet we both know you didn't spend the night alone. Or the day. What—are you practicing for a marathon?"

Sullivan's silver eyes twinkled. "Bloody right. Stella and I beat my record today—seven times."

"Stella . . . Have I met her?"

His buddy snorted. "We hooked up with her sister a few months ago."

"Shit. Right." A laugh flew out. "You're such a whore, bro. Just *had* to make a move on the sister, huh?"

"Uh-uh, *she* made the move," Sully said smugly. "What was I s'posed to do, turn her down? That'd break her heart."

Liam couldn't help but laugh again. Truth was, he appreciated Sullivan's open attitude toward sex. Until he'd become friends with the cocky Australian, he'd never known anyone with that reckless anything-goes mentality.

"Anyway, it's a bloody shame you bailed today. You woulda had fun."

Liam didn't doubt it. He always had fun with Sullivan.

But . . . maybe it was *too* much fun.

Their sexual antics had begun to distract him lately, even confuse him, if he were being honest. And he valued their friendship way too much to watch it crash and burn because of some weird, complicated tension he couldn't even explain.

Liam's eight-year stint in the DEA had made it impossible to form any lasting friendships. He'd been in deep cover for most of his career, cozying up to slimebag drug dealers and kingpins in order to take them down. A damn lonely way to live, but the extent of his loneliness hadn't truly sunk in until after he'd gone private and hooked up with Morgan. The easy camaraderie he'd witnessed among Morgan's men had been a major reason why he'd joined the crew full-time, and once he'd become ingrained in a team, he'd realized just how much it sucked to work alone.

To *be* alone.

His friendship with Sullivan Port, girly as it sounded, meant a lot to him. He'd never connected with another guy the way he connected with Sully. The two of them could read each other's minds, and with the rest of Morgan's men dropping like flies into commitment territory, Liam and Sully were among the few remaining hound dogs of the bunch.

"Yeah . . . sorry," he told Sullivan, keeping his tone vague. "I had a shit ton of e-mail to answer."

"Your family's on your case again, eh?"

He sighed. "Yup. But that's what happens when you come from an Irish Catholic clan. Eight kids, for fuck's sake. I don't know what my folks were thinking."

"Ah, mate, you're lucky. You'd hate being an only child, not to mention an orphan."

Liam gulped at the wistful note in Sullivan's voice, suddenly feeling like a total ass for complaining about his family. He'd been raised by parents who adored him, and surrounded by seven boisterous siblings who always had his back, while Sully had spent his entire childhood in foster homes. Sometimes he forgot that, especially since Sullivan didn't talk about his upbringing often.

"Anyhoo," his teammate hurried on before Liam could say another word, "wanna go downstairs and spy on the boss?"

"Nah. I don't feel like being murdered tonight."

That got him a loud laugh. "Another good point. Fine. Let's watch a movie, then. I don't feel like going to bed yet."

He hesitated, then said, "Pass. I'm frickin' exhausted."

"Jeez, Boston, you're such a bloody pansy." Rolling his eyes, Sullivan heaved himself out of the chair and rose to his full height. "If you change your mind, I'm down in the theater."

"I won't. I'm ready to collapse."

The blond man headed for the door, then paused to toss a quick taunt over his broad shoulder. "Night, Princess."

"Fuck off."

With a laugh, Sullivan left the room and closed the door behind him.

The moment he was alone again, Liam leaned back against the pillows and released an unsteady breath. Shit. Sooner or later, Sully would start noticing the distance Liam kept placing between them, which meant it was definitely time to try to get his head on straight.

Before he screwed up the one friendship that meant the most to him.

His body was magnificent.

Not an ounce of fat on it, just a solid mass of muscle and raw masculine power. Noelle eyed Jim's molded biceps and triceps as those strong arms propelled his body forward. Long legs kicking through the water, tight buttocks flexing with each commanding stroke.

She hadn't seen him naked in years, and she was intrigued by the scars—both old and new—that marred his sleek, tanned skin. She wondered how he'd gotten each one. A big part of her wished she had been the one who'd inflicted them on him, but alas, she hadn't laid a hand on the man since they'd parted ways in Paris all those years ago.

Her hands suddenly tingled with the urge to alter that. To pound into his flesh and administer pain, bruises, any kind of mark to serve as proof that she could cause him damage.

God, he deserved to die for what he'd done to her. So why did she continue to let him live? She used to tell herself it was because she wanted to torment him first, but lately she'd been questioning her motives. Wondering if maybe the reason she hadn't killed him was because she simply didn't want to see him dead.

But why not, damn it? All she'd ever dreamed of was wiping him out of existence, out of her life and her thoughts.

And clearly she wasn't the only one. Someone else wanted Jim terminated, someone who was willing to pay a small fortune to make it happen, and instead of acting like the professional she was and getting the job done, she'd come here to warn him.

To *warn* him, for fuck's sake.

A soft splash recaptured her attention, and she lifted her head in time to see Jim hop onto the deck. Water dripped from his warrior form, rivulets gathering between his heavy pecs, running down his rock-hard chest and clinging to his washboard abs. He was unconcerned with his nudity, unfazed by the erection jutting from his groin.

His arms rose in a lazy stretch, roped muscles bulging as his gaze found hers. His cobalt blue eyes gleamed mockingly.

"Say your piece and leave, Noelle."

She rose from the deck chair with a careless shrug. "Someone wants you dead. Offered me five million big ones to eliminate you."

Jim slanted his head. "Who?"

"Not sure. The client is using a middleman."

"Interesting." He swiped a towel from the stack on one of the lounge chairs and wrapped it around his trim hips.

The second his erection was out of sight, Noelle was able to breathe again. It sickened her that her body was capable of responding to his aroused state; her heart had actually skipped a beat and her core had ached with need.

She wasn't allowed to get turned on by Jim Morgan. It was a weakness she refused to possess.

"He gave me five days to get the job done," she added. "After that, the contract hits the open market—two million bucks for your head on a silver platter. It'll be an assassin free-for-all."

"Thanks for the heads-up," he said gruffly. "Any idea who the client might be?"

"No, but I can give you his associate's information. Gilles Girard, a lawyer in Paris." She took a step toward the flagstone path that led to the terrace. "Happy hunting, Jim."

"Did you take the job?"

She kept her back to him. "Of course. Turning it down might have raised a red flag."

"You planning on following through on it?"

"Nope."

His husky laughter grated. "Why not?"

"Why do you think? I'll kill you on my own terms, not under orders from some anonymous asshole."

"Right. You've still deluded yourself into thinking you're actually gonna off me."

She slowly turned around. The amused glimmer in his eyes made her want to reach for the pistol at the small of her back and shoot him right in that mocking mouth of his.

"Right back atcha, baby," she said softly.

"Oh, I already explained why I haven't killed you. I'm not done making you suffer."

"Whatever you say, Jim."

She took off walking again, but he came up beside her, matching her hurried strides.

"Where you headed?" he asked.

"What do you care?"

He ignored the question. "Back to Paris?"

"Yes," she said grudgingly.

"Good. I'll catch a ride with you, then. Give me twenty minutes to gather my gear."

He was on the terrace and marching inside before she could protest, leaving her standing there in annoyance. Presumptuous ass. She'd rather slit her wrists than let him board her jet.

So why are you still here?

The snide voice raised a valid point. Jim couldn't force her to give him a ride. All she had to do was walk out of the house, get into her car, and drive to the airstrip. Without him.

Or she could put a bullet in his brain and finally be done with him.

But Noelle chose neither of those options.

Instead, she lit up a cigarette, took a deep drag, and waited for Jim.

"You really think it's a good idea to handle this alone?" D's gravelly voice sounded from the doorway, where the tattooed mercenary stood with his arms crossed over his broad chest.

Morgan tossed a couple pairs of pants into his large black duffel, followed by a few T-shirts and a handful of rolled-up socks.

"No other choice," he muttered as he packed. "I need my A-Team in Ecuador, and the rest of the men on other gigs."

"Sully, Liam, and Ash are all off rotation," D pointed out. "Take them with you."

"No."

"Morgan—"

"No," he repeated. "I have no idea what I'll find in Paris, and I'm not dragging anyone else into this until I know for sure what I'm up against. I'd rather they stay at the compound—you can call them in for backup if the rebel job gets too hairy."

D scowled. "They'd be of better use serving as backup for *you*."

"They stay here." He spoke in a firm voice, refusing to yield to D's menacing expression. No way was he endangering any of his men in what could very likely be a dangerous wild-goose chase.

As if reading his mind, D stepped into the room and closed the door behind him. "She could be fucking with you."

Although Morgan had been entertaining the same notion, his brain kept dismissing it. He knew Noelle better than he knew himself, and he believed with absolute certainty that she'd told him the truth.

But what were her motives for sharing the information? The cynic in him assumed she'd come to gloat, but that didn't sit right with him. As crazy as it was, he suspected she might have actually come to warn him.

Figure that one out.

"Nah, she's on the up-and-up." He checked the clip of his semiautomatic, shoved the weapon in a smaller canvas case, then stowed the gun bag in the big duffel. "Question is— who was stupid enough to hire an assassin to take me out?"

"Speaking of stupid, don't go teaming up with her," D said curtly. "If you don't want to bring the boys, fine—that idiocy is on you. But at least work it solo, then. You can't trust that woman."

"No kidding." Stifling a rush of resentment, he straightened up and met D's coal black eyes. "Though I'm surprised to hear *you* dispensing the advice. Weren't you the one cozying up to her for the better part of a year?"

As usual, D's expression remained shuttered. "Doesn't mean I trust her." There was a pause. "It's over now, in case you were wondering."

"Already knew that—never cared either way."

"If you say so."

Morgan could have sworn he glimpsed a flicker of amusement in the other mercenary's deadly eyes, but if he had, it was gone now. Still, the idea that D didn't believe him—no, even worse, that D was *challenging* him—made his blood boil.

As far as he knew, out of all the men in his employment, D was the only one who'd made use of previous connections to dig into Morgan's past with Noelle, and it pissed him off that the man might've gained even a smidgen of insight about their turbulent history. Fortunately, D had raised the subject only once, never to mention it again.

But it still fucking grated.

"Anyway, if you need backup, just say the word." With a shrug, D opened the door and disappeared into the hall.

Morgan finished packing his gear and left the room a moment later. He strode down the long hardwood corridor toward the east wing of the house, where Kane and Abby's suite of rooms was situated. He'd heard them come upstairs a few minutes ago, and sure enough, they were in their bedroom when he knocked on the door.

"I'm taking off," he said once Kane appeared in the doorway. "D's got the details about the rebel job. Call if you run into any trouble."

"Yes, sir." Kane's green eyes took on an irritated light. "Would you please consider taking backup? Sully and Liam are—"

"Staying here," he finished, swallowing his own irritation. "I just had this same argument with D, and I'm not in the mood for a repeat performance. If I need help, I'll call 'em. Until then, they stay here."

"Fine." Kane sighed. "Keep in contact, all right? Don't go AWOL on us again."

"I'll try not to." He peered past the man's shoulders and nodded at Abby, who was perched on the edge of the bed. "Don't even think about joining them in Ecuador, Sinclair." He shot a pointed look at her stomach. "You're grounded for at least another six months."

"Don't remind me." The redhead sighed, her hand absently lowering to rub the slight bulge. "Christ, what am I going to do with myself? I've never had this much time off in my life. Is there such a thing as knife withdrawal?"

Morgan had to grin. Abby was probably the most skilled operative he'd ever worked with, but she was definitely way too fond of her knives. He wouldn't be surprised if her and Kane's kid popped out with an immediate case of bloodlust.

"I'm sure you'll find ways to occupy yourself." He glanced at Kane. "And you, don't screw up this job. The pay is too good."

"Like you need any more money," Kane cracked.

Chuckling, Morgan carted his duffel down the hall again. His scuffed-up combat boots didn't make a sound as he descended one of the twin spiral staircases and stepped into the parlor.

When he slid out the front door, he found Noelle waiting on the pillared porch, a cigarette in her hand and a frown on her face.

"Let's go," he muttered.

She rolled her eyes disparagingly. "Yes, sir."

They walked toward her Mercedes. The three feet of distance between them was nowhere near vast enough to reduce the tension surrounding them like a dark cloud. If anything, Morgan was even more on edge than before. They had a twelve-hour flight ahead of them, and he wasn't looking forward to it in the slightest.

It suddenly occurred to him that for the first time in years, they were about to be alone together for more than five minutes.

Just the two of them. On a small jet. Tens of thousands of feet in the air.

Christ.

Maybe he should've packed a parachute, just in case.

Chapter 3

Nineteen years ago

She was so beautiful, it hurt to look at her. The pictures in her file didn't even come close to doing her justice, and Morgan was becoming far too distracted by her angelic looks.

Remember the objective. Get the intel. Get out.

Should've been easy as fuckin' pie. As far as missions went, this one was considerably less bloody. No guns, no death—all he had to do was tap into his innate charm and seduce the information out of the girl. He'd done it a dozen times before.

So why couldn't he seem to focus on the goal this time around?

"You really don't act rich," Noelle remarked.

"Tell me, baby, how does one *act* rich?"

The two of them were lying on the thick blanket he'd laid out in front of the fireplace. She'd joined him for dinner in his two-bedroom suite at the Lancaster Hotel, and after the room service staff had whisked their dishes away, Morgan had suggested they light a fire, one thing led to another, and now here they were. He on his back, Noelle stretched out beside him with her head nestled against his chest.

The sweet scent of her strawberry shampoo was driving him crazy. She smelled so damn good, felt so damn delicate in his arms. And he felt the need to kiss her so strongly that his lips were actually trembling.

Christ.

What the hell was wrong with him?

She was a tool and nothing more. A means to an end.

He had to remember that, for fuck's sake.

"All the rich people I know like to show off their wealth," Noelle murmured. "They dress wealthy, talk wealthy, go to wealthy places. But you don't seem at all interested in money."

"That's because I'm not," he said gruffly. "My parents left me a huge inheritance, but that doesn't mean I need to blow every dime, or wave my cash around so other people will think I'm important. At the end of the day, money is just paper. It means nothing."

"Maybe." She paused. "But power doesn't. Power means everything."

"Nah, power's overrated too."

His hand, of its own volition, began stroking her silky hair. He lazily twined one thick strand around his fingers, noting that in the light of the fire, the soft golden tresses almost seemed to be glowing.

"You only say that because you have it." Her voice grew strained. "I bet you've never let anyone have power over you, Jim. You'd never let anyone hurt you, would you?"

"I'd kill anyone who tried."

She fell silent, and her uneven breathing told him that she was troubled. The topic at hand didn't surprise him. Going into this mission, he'd already known everything about Noelle Phillips, including the abuse she endured at the hands of her stepfather. The information hadn't affected him before—simply another tool at his disposal—but when he'd seen her broken fingers the day they'd officially met . . . Christ, in that moment, his vision had turned into a red haze, and his rage had been so visceral he could feel it burning his throat even now.

The thought of anyone hurting her made him want to go on a shooting spree.

"I used to think that too. I was sure I'd never let anyone hurt me. I thought I was strong." Her voice wobbled. "But lately . . . I'm beginning to wonder."

He knew she was thinking about Laurent. The sadistic creep had been on Morgan's mind too. He didn't understand men like that. Men who beat up women, men who got off on victimizing what they perceived to be the weaker sex.

Needless to say, Morgan wouldn't mind it one bit if René Laurent accidentally took a fall down a flight of stairs one of these days.

But that was a different objective for a different day. Right now, there was only one man he needed to be concerned with: Douglas Phillips.

Noelle's biological father.

Unfortunately, she hadn't mentioned dear old Dad even once tonight, though Morgan had subtly coaxed her to talk. Then again, it was only their first date. He still had lots of time to gain the necessary intel.

If he could quit stroking her hair and actually concentrate on the damn job.

"You *are* strong," he said huskily. "Your strength was what drew me to you."

She laughed softly. "Bull. You just thought I was pretty."

Pretty. Ha. Biggest understatement of the year.

The girl was stunning.

For his own peace of mind, he found it necessary to keep referring to her as that—a *girl*. Otherwise he might do something stupid.

Like fuck her gorgeous brains out.

He couldn't sleep with her, though. She was seventeen years old, for Christ's sake. Too young and innocent for a man as jaded as him.

She'll be eighteen in two months . . .

He silenced the eager reminder. It didn't matter that she would be legal soon. He wasn't going to take advantage of Noelle Phillips any more than he had to.

"No," he corrected, "I thought you were *spectacular*."

"And what do you think now?"

She was teasing him, and damned if his heart didn't do a childish little somersault.

"I think you're perfect." His voice came out thick and gravelly.

"I'm not perfect, Jim. Nobody is." Her warm breath heated his neck as she sighed. "I try to be . . . I don't know . . . *good*, I guess. I try to be the person I know I should be. But sometimes, when I'm lying in bed, late at night . . . I think very bad thoughts."

His fingers tangled in her hair, tilting her head so he could see her eyes. The fierce look in those pale blue depths startled him.

"What kind of thoughts?"

"I fantasize about all the ways I would kill my stepfather." Guilt flashed on her face. "Isn't that sick?"

"No."

"No?"

"It's human nature to want to strike back against the people who've hurt you." Morgan hesitated. "He hurts you, doesn't he, baby?"

Her bottom lip quivered ever so slightly. "Yes."

"What does he do to you?" Although he voiced the question, he wasn't sure he wanted to know the answer.

"Everything," she whispered. "He does everything."

Anger torpedoed into his chest, and if he hadn't been lying down, the force of it would have knocked him right off his feet.

Head in the game, man. You're not here to protect her from Laurent. Focus.

He choked down his rage, took a deep breath. Enough. He had to quit letting his emotions rule him. Otherwise he'd blow this entire mission.

"He'll get what's coming to him," Morgan said quietly. "Evil men always do."

Noelle's loose red sweater rustled as she disentangled herself from his arms. "I don't want to talk about René anymore. He'll be out of my life soon enough." She checked the expensive silver watch around her delicate wrist. "Actually, I should probably go. My mother doesn't like it when I stay out late on school nights."

"I'll drive you home," he said immediately, and the surprise that filled her gaze made him chuckle. "What?"

"You'll drive me home, just like that?"

"Of course. Did you think I'd make you walk?"

"No, but . . ." She looked sweet and innocent as she nibbled on her lower lip. "I thought you'd be upset that I'm not . . . that we won't . . ."

"Have sex?" he said knowingly.

She nodded.

"This is our first date." He grinned at her. "I don't put out on the first date, baby."

Her melodic laughter wrapped around him like a warm blanket. "I didn't expect you to be such a gentleman."

"No?"

"You told me I was beautiful. And then you invited me to have dinner at your hotel." A cynical note crept into her voice. "Other men would have tried to seduce me."

Shrugging, he hopped to his feet and held out his hand. "I'm not other men," he said lightly.

"No, I guess you're not." After a beat of hesitation, she took his hand and stood up. "You're one of the good ones, aren't you, Jim?"

This time, it was impossible not to have an emotional response—and the emotion that seized his chest was pure and total guilt.

You're one of the good ones.

God. Fuck. No, he certainly wasn't. He was not a good man at all.

And Noelle Phillips would discover it much sooner than later.

Chapter 4

Present day

They'd been in the air for eight hours. Eight long hours and not a single word had been exchanged. Granted, Noelle had been asleep for most of that time, but Morgan had stayed awake, checking databases on his laptop and calling various contacts for intel on Gilles Girard, the lawyer who'd solicited Noelle's services. He'd struck out at every turn, and his frustration had grown with each dead end.

All he'd managed to glean was that Girard was an estate and tax lawyer, an upstanding citizen, and a lover of eighteenth-century architecture. He wasn't linked to any shady characters, hadn't been red-flagged by any government agencies, and had never been arrested for a crime.

So why the hell was he hiring an assassin?

Fuck. Where was Holden McCall when you needed him? Morgan could've really used the man's technological wizardry at the moment. Holden was capable of plucking information out of thin air, but ever since he'd lost his wife in the attack on their compound last year, he'd pulled a disappearing act. Quit the team via text message, and Morgan hadn't heard from him since.

He knew that Holden needed to grieve in peace for the time being, but Morgan had every intention of tracking down his former soldier if he didn't hear from him by the end of the month.

He wasn't just worried about him, but Holden's absence also made Morgan's life damn difficult, which was why he marched across the cabin to finally address Noelle.

Her blue eyes slitted open at his approach. "I'm sleeping. Go away."

"I need Sean Reilly's new number. The one I have for him isn't in service," he said curtly. "Otherwise, give me Oliver's number. Either brother will do."

She chuckled. "What's the matter, Jim? Couldn't figure out how to type the name 'Girard' into Google?"

"Girard is clean. On paper, anyway. Which means I need to dig deeper."

"Well, find your own information dealers." Noelle adjusted the thin blanket covering her body and promptly ignored him.

Gritting his teeth, he plopped down in the seat across from hers. "Fine. I'll just get it from Isabel."

"You do that, honey," she murmured without opening her eyes.

He felt like tearing his own hair out. "You'll actually make me jump through hoops instead of giving me the number?"

Her eyelids snapped open. "Yes. Want to know why? Because we're not friends, and we're not colleagues. Therefore, I don't owe you a damn thing."

"Yet you flew all the way to Costa Rica to warn me," he said dryly.

"And that's as far as I'm willing to go. You've been warned. Now you're on your own."

Silence settled between them, and his frustration deepened. He hated spending even a modicum of time with this woman. They'd been enemies for so long. Too long. Truth be told, he was sick and tired of it.

Kill her and be done with it.

The flare of anger behind the thought faded rapidly because he knew he couldn't act on the threat. Not now, anyway. Not when he might still need to make use of her vast network of resources.

"Go back to your side of the plane, Jim," she muttered in annoyance.

"What—you don't want to make small talk?"

"Not in the slightest."

When he didn't budge, her lips tightened in a thin line. After a beat, one slender arm emerged from beneath the blanket, and she pressed a button on the arm of her seat.

Not a second later, the all-black-clad attendant who'd greeted them upon boarding appeared in front of Noelle.

"What can I do for you?" he asked instantly, ready to serve his mistress.

Morgan frowned as Noelle's blue eyes swept over the steward's tall, muscular frame.

"You can do *a lot* of things for me, Joachim," she cooed. "But for now, I'll settle for a coffee."

"And for you, Mr. Morgan?"

He coolly met Joachim's light green eyes. "Coffee. Black."

After the man disappeared behind the blue curtain on the other side of the cabin, Morgan flashed Noelle a sardonic smile.

"Let me guess. You didn't hire Mr. Sweden for his serving skills alone."

"Of course not. I hired him because he's a great lay."

She licked her bottom lip seductively, which drew his attention to her pouty Cupid's bow of a mouth. She never wore lipstick because her lips were naturally red—he remembered that little tidbit now as he stared at her mouth.

When he moved his gaze to hers, he didn't miss the flicker of challenge in her eyes.

"I'm sure he fucks you real nice," Morgan drawled.

"But you couldn't care less, right?" Her tone became mocking. "Same way you don't care that D and I were sleeping together for months."

"If you're under the impression that I give you much thought in my day-to-day life, then you're dead wrong, baby. You're not even a blip on my radar."

"Uh-huh. Of course I'm not. I'm sure you didn't think about me and D at all." She absently toyed with a strand of her golden hair. "You didn't picture us naked together, didn't imagine how I looked when your soldier made me come. Right, Jim?"

His jaw clenched.

"Say what you want about that man, but he knows how

to make a woman scream." Noelle's lips curved in a secretive smile. "He's cold as ice outside the bedroom, but between the sheets? Molten lava."

Morgan didn't respond. He refused to give her the satisfaction. Refused to let her get to him.

"Does it make you hard? Thinking about me coming?"

His groin stirred.

And damn it, he knew she noticed it.

Cursing his body's betrayal, he offered a careless shrug. "You want to know what gets me hard, Noelle?"

She eyed him thoughtfully. "What?"

"The thought of wrapping my hands around your throat and squeezing."

Her laughter danced between them. "Bring it on, baby."

Joachim chose that moment to return with their drinks. He served Morgan first, then leaned over to hand Noelle a steaming cup of coffee, his blond hair falling onto his forehead as he did so.

"Joachim," she said in a throaty voice. "My friend has expressed some interest in watching you fuck me. How do you feel about that?"

Morgan nearly crushed the ceramic mug between his stiff fingers.

Joachim straightened up with an intrigued smile. "I'm here to do your bidding. You know that, *älskling*."

Noelle glanced at Morgan, then released a delighted laugh before turning back to the young Swede. "Ah, another time, honey. I see that our guest has changed his mind."

"As you wish." Without another word, Joachim left them alone again.

"You're a real piece of work," Morgan said flatly.

With a sweet smile, she took a sip of coffee.

He did the same, the hot liquid burning a path down his throat and joining the anger and bitterness bubbling in his stomach. It was mostly self-directed anger, though. As unaffected as he tried to be around Noelle, she always succeeded in riling him up.

But why did he let her? He knew exactly what kind of woman she was—cold, cruel, self-serving. So why wasn't his carefully constructed armor ever enough to fully shield himself from her poison?

Because she wasn't always this way.

He stifled a sigh. No, she hadn't always been like this, and though it pained him to admit it, he knew he was wholly responsible for the woman she'd become.

The reminder brought a flash of guilt, quickly followed by the burn of resentment. Fine, so maybe he'd stolen her innocence, but she'd taken something from him too, something far more important than girlhood fuckin' purity.

And one of these days, he was going to make her pay for it.

"She's been asking questions again."

The man at the window didn't turn around, but Nikolaus Bauer saw his shoulders stiffen beneath his black cashmere Valentino blazer.

Nik walked into the library and paused near a bookshelf with rows and rows of German classics. He waited for his boss to respond, but as the silence dragged on, he felt compelled to repeat himself.

"Did you hear me? She's asking questions."

"I heard you, Nikolaus."

The fair-haired man moved away from the floor-to-ceiling glass panels and went to the bar to pour a drink. He only drank German whiskey, no matter how many times Nik reminded him there were much finer brands of liquor available to him. But Walther Dietrich was a nationalist to the core. He'd been living in France for the past decade, went by a French name, and wore French designer clothes, yet the man would always be a German at heart.

Sipping on his glass of Höhler whiskey, Dietrich turned to Nik with slightly annoyed brown eyes. "I already told you, it's being handled."

It was difficult to hide his frustration. "He should have been eliminated the moment we uncovered his true identity. That was months ago, Walther—" When his employer's eyes flashed, Nik quickly corrected himself. "Maurice."

"These matters can't be rushed," Dietrich answered. "We've taken great pains to secure our new position. If this leads back to me, it will destroy everything we've worked so hard for."

Nik knew the other man was right, but it was hard to see

reason when his thirst for vengeance still burned strong. Seventeen years of hatred and bitterness had left him weary, but now that weariness had transformed into eagerness. James Hathaway—no, James *Morgan*—was finally within his reach. All Nik had to do was reach out and grab him. Eliminate his enemy once and for all.

"If she finds out where he is, she'll want to see him," Nik said, a lump of anger rising in his throat.

"She won't find out. How could she? She doesn't even know his real name." Dietrich took another sip of his drink. "You're worrying yourself for nothing, Nikolaus. Girard did careful research before choosing the assassin—this woman will get the job done immediately."

He bristled, but forced himself to bite his tongue. It was pointless to rehash his feelings on the subject. From the start, he'd maintained the argument that killing James Morgan was *his* right, but Dietrich had strictly forbidden it. Nik was an integral cog in the running of Dietrich's empire, and his boss insisted that Nik needed to concentrate on taking care of business rather than chasing old ghosts.

Nik had agreed to stand down out of loyalty and respect for the man, but if it were up to him, *he'd* be the one putting that bullet in James Morgan's head.

"She'd better get it done," he muttered. "Morgan can't go unpunished for what he did, Wal—Maurice."

Dietrich polished off his whiskey and slammed the glass on the walnut bar counter. "He won't, my boy. He won't. Now . . ." An indulgent smile crossed the older man's face. "Tell Bertrand to bring the car around. I'd like to go and visit my daughter."

Chapter 5

"Why are you still here?"

Morgan tensed at the sound of Noelle's voice, but didn't glance up from his laptop screen. Her question didn't surprise him—it was one he'd asked himself countless times today, while he'd been holed up in the living room of Noelle's elegant town house. There was nothing stopping him from checking into a hotel, yet instead of doing that, he'd parked his ass on her white leather couch and had been digging up intel on Gilles Girard ever since they'd arrived in Paris.

Slowly, he lifted his head, but no words left his mouth when he laid eyes on her.

She was dressed for seduction.

From head to fuckin' toe.

A skimpy red dress clung to her curvy body, hugging her full, braless breasts and barely covering her firm thighs. Silver stilettos added four inches to her petite frame, and her blond hair was artfully twisted atop her head, pulled back to emphasize her high cheekbones and timeless features. She rarely wore her hair up, and it annoyed him to realize that he preferred it down.

Goddamn it. He shouldn't have a fucking preference.

Swallowing his irritation, he pasted on an indifferent look. "Aw, baby, is that all for me?"

"Absolutely not," she said cheerfully.

"Hot date?"

She ignored him. "I want you out of my house. Your gear is already in the car, and my driver will drop you off at a hotel on our way."

"On your way where?"

Again he didn't get a response, just the sharp clap of her hands. "Get off your ass. I've got somewhere to be."

Smirking, Morgan leaned back against the couch cushions and got comfortable.

"I mean it, Jim. It's time for you to go."

When he still didn't budge, she reached for the hem of her dress and slid it up a few inches.

His mouth went arid when a lacy black garter was revealed. But it was no ordinary garter—this one was custommade to secure a silver derringer to her thigh.

"Please don't make me use this," she said coolly. "My decorator insisted on an all-white color scheme in this room, and poor Miles will have a bitch of a time scrubbing your blood off the carpet."

He supposed he could've argued some more, but truth was, he was feeling stir-crazy from being cooped up indoors all day. He had no intention of going to a hotel, though. Nah. A night on the town might do him some good.

With a shrug, he leaned forward and shoved his laptop in its case. "You win. Let's go."

When he reached the doorway, Noelle spoke through gritted teeth. "Your laptop."

He glanced at the black case on the glass coffee table, then hid a grin and went over to retrieve it. Fine. Looked like the computer would join his gear in the car. But it was damn well coming back here, just like he was.

As he followed Noelle down the wide corridor, he had to wonder why he was so determined to stick close to her, when normally he couldn't get away from her fast enough.

Then again, normally he wasn't the target of a faceless enemy who wanted him dead.

He might not trust Noelle, but he couldn't deny that she was a good ally to have in hairy situations. Besides, until her story checked out and he received confirmation that Girard had actually hired her to eliminate him, he wasn't letting the woman out of his sight.

The town house boasted its own elevator, which they

rode down to the spacious garage in the basement. When they stepped onto the concrete floor, Morgan couldn't help but admire the collection of vehicles Noelle kept stashed there. A sleek silver Ferrari, a cherry red Lamborghini, a yellow Ducati motorcycle whose model hadn't even hit the market yet. The woman had expensive taste in cars; that much was obvious. But she ignored all of them and headed for the black Lincoln Town Car parked in front of the automatic steel door.

Noelle's driver, a bulky man with a shaved head, instantly hopped out of the sedan to open the back door for his mistress.

Morgan had noticed that every member of Noelle's staff just happened to be a handsome male. Her driver, her flight staff, her housekeeper. But since one of her favorite pastimes was toying with men, it didn't surprise him that she surrounded herself with an army of them.

They settled in the back of the Lincoln on opposite ends of the leather seat. As the car engine hummed to life, the partition between them and the front seat rolled down.

"Which hotel should I take him to?" the driver asked in a disinterested voice.

Morgan spoke up before Noelle could. "No need for a hotel. I'll be staying here with your employer. Just take us to—" He glanced at Noelle. "Where are we going again?"

Her lips went so tight they nearly disappeared off her pretty face. But just as he expected, she didn't challenge him. Noelle would never allow herself to appear undermined in front of her staff.

"The Nuit Rouge, Frédéric. Thank you." Then she pressed a button on the door and the partition swooped right back up.

"What the fuck kind of game are you playing?" she demanded.

"No game. I just think your house is super-duper cozy and I sure don't want to leave it," he replied with saccharine sarcasm. "Got a problem with that?"

She glowered at him. "Yes."

"Tough cookies. Because I'm not going anywhere."

Her hand played with the bottom of her dress again, as if she were contemplating pulling out her pistol and using it on him, but after a beat, she laid her hand flat on her thigh and turned to him with a thoughtful expression.

"If you want my help, just ask for it."

He arched a brow. "Who says that's what I want?"

"Why else are you forcing yourself into my life?"

"Maybe I just like spending time with you."

A genuine laugh popped out of her mouth. "Bullshit. You hate being around me as much as I hate being around you."

His lips twitched. "You're right. That was a load of bull."

"So then man up and ask me to help you find the person who hired me."

"Are you offering?"

"Nope. But I might consider it."

Son of a bitch. Nothing was ever easy with this woman.

Morgan spoke through clenched teeth. "Will you help me track him down?"

"I'll think about it." She shrugged. "Maybe if you ask me nicely next time and say please."

Whatever. That was good enough for now. At the moment, he was more interested to know why she'd gotten dolled up and was apparently hitting a club.

"So why are we going to the Nuit Rouge? You tracking a target?"

"Just feel like dancing."

He narrowed his eyes. "That's it? You just want to go dancing?"

"I happen to enjoy it. I do have interests outside of killing scumbags, you know."

A thread of discomfort coiled around his throat. She *did* like to dance—he remembered that now. All those little details about her were stored in a deep abyss in his brain, banished from thought and locked down tight, but they'd started floating to the surface ever since Noelle and her operatives had gotten entangled with his team.

He wondered if she still liked watching old black-and-white movies late at night. Or if she still liked her steaks rare. If she still added a shit ton of salt to everything she ate. Did she still go for a run every time it rained?

He could never ask her, of course. Noelle would take any interest on his part as a sign of weakness. And it would be.

Christ, it'd be so much easier if he didn't have those memories. That way he could just hate her, destroy her, end her life without ever having known the taste of her lips, or the way she felt naked and writhing beneath him.

They didn't speak for the rest of the car ride, and when the Lincoln came to a stop twenty minutes later, Noelle was out of the car in the blink of an eye. He suspected she was trying to ditch him, but Morgan was a trained soldier, which meant he was capable of moving just as fast. He stayed on her six as she brazenly bypassed the mile-long line of hopeful clubgoers, and marched right up to the red steel door.

A monstrous bouncer with a deep scowl manned the entrance, but his meaty hand immediately unclipped the velvet rope at Noelle's approach.

"Est-il avec vous?" the bouncer barked.

She glanced over her shoulder, her expression flickering with aggravation when she realized Morgan was directly behind her.

"Oui," she said tersely, then strode through the door.

Morgan followed her into the club and let his eyes adjust to the sudden darkness. A heavy bass line pounded in the shadowy corridor, and the intermittent flash of strobe lights illuminated the path to the main floor. This time, Noelle did manage to lose him—before he could even blink, she darted toward the red-and-white-checkered floor and was swallowed up by the crowd of dancers.

Ah well. He knew he'd spot her again sooner or later. In that boner-inducing dress of hers, she'd be hard to miss.

Morgan drifted over to the bar spanning one black-painted wall. He ordered a beer, then turned to face the dance floor, his gaze seeking out his prey.

And there she was. Dancing, just like she'd claimed she came here to do. Her curvy hips undulated as she moved to the music, slender arms raised, firm ass rolling sensually. The techno beat blasting out of the speakers made it impossible to hear anything but the relentless drum and bass and the shrill synthesizers. It wasn't Morgan's kind of music—he preferred classic rock or easy blues, not this headache-inducing bullshit.

Noelle didn't seem to mind it. She stayed on the floor while he leaned against the counter and sipped his beer.

And he wasn't the only one watching her. Every male gaze seemed to be glued to the beautiful blonde. She drew men to her like a flame luring a moth. A hot flame of seduction, igniting every libido in the club.

But she didn't accept any offers to dance; she simply turned from the flock of men who approached her, spinning around and flitting away each time a new bachelor joined the fold.

Morgan kept watching as one song ended and another began. She was up to something. He could feel it in his bones.

Sure enough, the suspicion was confirmed a minute later, when a tall, muscular man stepped onto the floor and moved with purpose toward Noelle.

The newcomer came up behind her—and she let him. She ground her ass against the man's groin, allowing his hands to slide down her body and grip her hips.

Morgan's nostrils flared with derision as he studied Noelle's dance partner. Dude looked like a total creep with his slicked-back hair, sharp features, and lips that were far too pouty to belong on a man's face. His getup consisted of tight leather pants and a black wifebeater, and only added to the slimebag vibe he was broadcasting.

What was the damn woman up to?

It pissed him off that he couldn't figure it out. He usually had no trouble getting inside Noelle's head and intuiting her next move, but tonight he was drawing a blank.

"Danse?"

The shrill female voice had him jerking his head to the side. He glanced at the dark-haired woman who'd sidled up to him, then gave a brisk shake of the head.

As the brunette slunk off in disappointment, he refocused his attention on the dance floor, but Noelle and her slimebag were gone.

Shit.

Where the hell were they?

His shoulders went rigid as he scanned the crowded club. He didn't spot them in the throng of dancers. Didn't see them near the DJ platform. They weren't in the bar area, and they wouldn't have been able to head out the door without crossing his line of sight, which left only one option—the shadowy corridor leading to the restrooms.

Setting his jaw, Morgan left his beer on the counter and marched toward the rear of the club. He dodged a group of inebriated young men, waved off several offers to dance from eager women. When he finally ducked into the back hallway, he discovered two long lines leading into each of the restrooms, but no sign of Noelle and the creep.

He assessed the narrow space, catching sight of the closed door with a succinct French sign: SUPPLIES—KEEP OUT.

His right hand tingled with the urge to reach for the Sig tucked into his waistband, but he kept his arms at his sides as he approached the closet. A test of the handle revealed the door was unlocked. Hmmm. Noelle had gotten sloppy.

Or not, he discovered a moment later, after he'd opened the door a crack and noted that the padlock on the interior handle was broken.

He quietly slid into a room that was bathed in darkness and much larger than he'd anticipated. As his eyes adjusted, he could see rows and rows of metal racks that took up the space, shelves lined with cleaning supplies, bags of cocktail napkins, and random storage items.

The hairs on the back of his neck stood on end when he heard a low male groan. Followed by a female purr of pleasure that hardened his veins to ice.

For fuck's sake, was she screwing the loser in a goddamn supply closet?

A rustling noise broke the silence, the unmistakable sound of a zipper dragging down, and then a metal clatter and a soft giggle, as if someone—a curvy female body, perhaps—had been backed into a rack by an overeager lover.

Morgan's jaw was so tense his teeth started to hurt. He took a step forward, then stopped, forcing his scuffed-up boots to remain planted in place. Fuck it. If Noelle wanted to get drilled by a creep who didn't know how to use hair gel in moderation, then fine. It was none of his damn business.

He had just taken two steps back to the door when the horrified male expletive echoed in the darkness.

This time he didn't hesitate—he drew his weapon and crept down one of the aisles, just as a loud thump reached his ears. When he turned the corner and reached his targets, the sight he encountered made him gape.

"You really don't know how to mind your own business, do you?" Noelle said in a dry voice.

Morgan stared at the dead body lying on the cement floor, then focused on the woman kneeling beside it. Without waiting for a response, Noelle stuck her hand in the stiff's front pocket and pulled out a ziplocked plastic Baggie full of white powder.

"Hold on to this for me? I didn't bring a purse and this needs to look like a robbery."

The bag came sailing in his direction. Morgan caught it on instinct, all the while blinking at the macabre scene before him.

A puddle of blood pooled around the dead man's head, courtesy of the sharp blade that had pierced his jugular. Noelle must have had that deadly six-incher stashed on her other thigh, the crazy bitch. And evidently she wasn't overly attached to the knife, because she gracefully rose to her feet, leaving the blade lodged in her prey's throat.

Morgan finally found his voice. "Should I even ask?"

She shrugged. "Marcel here was pissing off some very important people by dealing coke in their territory. He really should have known better."

"So tonight was a job after all."

"Obviously." She brushed past him, fixing the bottom of her dress as she walked.

When she realized he hadn't moved, she halted in her stiletto tracks and tossed a mild look over her shoulder. "You coming, Jim?"

Swallowing, he spared one last look at the lifeless body sprawled on the ground, then followed Noelle to the door.

Chapter 6

Nineteen years ago

With a bored look, René zipped up his pants and glanced at the bed. "Say one word to your mother about this and I'll kill you both. Understand?"

"Yes," Noelle whispered.

She waited until her stepfather had left the bedroom before allowing the anger to surface. She'd learned not to reveal her fury during their encounters. That only made the beatings worse.

Now, with the door closed, the impotent rage bubbled over. It burned her throat, tingled in her palms, surged through her blood.

She was going to kill the bastard. Goddamn it, she was. But not until she came up with a foolproof plan, one that didn't result in her behind bars.

Dad can help.

She immediately banished the thought and stumbled off the sweat-soaked mattress. No, she would never go to her father for help. He couldn't know about René. Ever.

She ran into her private bath, bare feet slapping the white marble floor. Like the rest of the house, the bathroom was the epitome of elegance. Noelle ignored the raised bathtub and hurried into the enormous glass shower stall, where she cranked all four showerheads and adjusted the faucet not to warm, but scalding.

It didn't take long for the blistering hot water to soak her naked body and wash away all traces of René, but it still wasn't enough. She still had to scrub her skin raw with a scratchy loofah, scouring off the sweat and semen, the sickening scent of his cinnamon-flavored aftershave.

When she finally emerged from the steamy stall, her flesh was red and sore, and the rage sizzling inside her was just as potent as before. Soon, she reminded herself. Soon she'd be out of this hellhole.

But God, a month and a half seemed like a lifetime. A goddamn eternity.

In her bedroom, she grabbed random items of clothing from the antique mahogany armoire, dressing on autopilot, the frantic need to flee taking over. Breathing hard, she swiped her red leather Louis Vuitton purse from the white-upholstered Bergere chair in the corner of the room, then fumbled inside it for her phone and dialed Jim's number with trembling fingers.

When his husky voice filled her ear, she almost keeled over with relief.

"Can I see you?" she blurted out.

He replied with no hesitation. "Of course. Come to my hotel?"

"I'll be there soon."

Noelle hung up and raced out the door, and fifteen minutes later, she was hurrying into the lobby of the Lancaster. The fierce jumble of emotions in her chest hadn't dulled during the taxi ride over. She was just as mad, just as bitter, and just as ashamed.

She'd run into René and her mother on her way out. The happy couple was going to a charity dinner for the police department, and René had been decked out in full police regalia. The nerve of it made her want to vomit. Two minutes after raping his wife's daughter, he'd donned his dress uniform and was about to spend the rest of his evening strutting around like a hero and charming rich suckers out of their money so his department could have more tools to catch criminals.

But *he* was the criminal.

Worse than a criminal. He was a *monster*.

Noelle's breathing went shallow, her vision wavering as she ducked into the elevator. She was near tears, and that only made her madder. Her real father didn't condone tears. He considered them a sign of weakness.

I'm trying, Dad. I'm really trying to be strong.

She choked on the lump in her throat, wishing she could be as tough as her dad, but knowing she wasn't. Because if she was, she never would have let René lay his revolting hands on her. She would have fought harder and kept him off.

The elevator doors dinged open and she rushed down the carpeted corridor, her gaze homing in on the door of Jim's suite. The gold-plated numbers were like a shining beacon of salvation. *Jim* was her salvation. They'd been seeing each other for only two weeks, but she was already dreading the day he had to go back to America. She didn't want him to leave. She wasn't sure she'd survive saying good-bye to the gruff, intense soldier she'd come to rely on.

When he opened the door, Noelle launched herself into his arms and buried her face in the crook of his corded neck. She inhaled his spicy, masculine scent, drawing warmth and comfort from his embrace.

"You okay?" He closed the door and led her inside.

She nodded weakly. "I'm fine."

Jim's sharp blue eyes searched her face. "No, you're not. What happened?"

"Nothing." Averting her gaze, she shrugged out of her peacoat and set it on the arm of the beige sofa.

"Noelle."

She sighed. "Nothing out of the ordinary," she amended. "René was in one of his moods tonight."

"C'mere."

He opened his arms and she stepped into them once more.

"Will you do something for me?" she asked softly.

"Anything."

"Will you . . ." She tipped her head so she could meet his eyes, feeling her cheeks flush with embarrassment. "Will you kiss me?"

His expression flickered with reluctance.

"I know you said you wanted to take it slow," she went on hastily, "but please, Jim, I need this. I need you to make me forget."

He stayed quiet, but his eyes never left hers. What she saw there only added to her muddled, emotion-ridden state. Reluctance again, but also tenderness. And desperation. Heat. Lots and lots of heat.

"Please," she whispered.

His Adam's apple bobbed. "Noelle . . ."

She held her breath, watching his expression go from hesitant to tortured to . . . defeated.

"Okay," he murmured. "Okay."

Her pulse sped up when he touched her chin. His hand was big and warm, his fingers gentle as he dragged them along the curve of her jaw. She parted her lips, anticipation building inside her, but when his mouth finally covered hers, it was like nothing she could have ever imagined.

His lips brushed hers with infinite care, soft and sweet and so thrilling her heart stopped beating for one crazy moment. Then the pressure increased, the tip of his tongue slid inside her mouth, and the kiss went from gentle to downright *possessive*. She'd kissed boys before, but not like this. Never like this.

Jim's lips teased and coaxed, his tongue so skillful and demanding she forgot how to breathe. His mouth, hot and wicked, moved over hers, and each brush of his lips and stroke of his tongue stirred the fire inside her, until her entire body felt consumed by flames. His stubble scraped her cheeks in the most delicious way, and when he drew her closer so that their chests were flush against each other, she could feel his heart hammering against her breasts.

She kissed him back like a woman starved, taking every ounce of pleasure he had to offer. When her tongue slipped into his mouth so she could do some exploring of her own, Jim's low groan of approval vibrated between them and made every inch of her melt.

"Christ. Noelle." He pulled back only to whisper those two passion-laced words, and then he was kissing her again, while his hands traveled down the length of her back and settled over her bottom.

He cupped her buttocks and thrust his lower body into hers, and a moan escaped her lips at the feel of his erection pressing into her belly.

So this was desire. This was lust. She'd feared that René

had destroyed her ability to experience such powerful sexual emotions, and triumph soared through her when she realized that he hadn't. He hadn't stolen this from her.

As a wave of liberation crested inside her, Noelle dug her fingers into Jim's shoulders and kissed him back hungrily. She didn't care that he wanted to take things slow. She wanted him. She *needed* him.

With frantic hands, she tugged on the hem of his T-shirt, desperately trying to lift it up, but he stopped her by stumbling backward.

"No," he said hoarsely. "We can't."

Determination hardened her features. "We *can*. I want to."

"Not yet." He practically choked out the words, as if he didn't want to say them but was forcing himself to.

She could see in his eyes that he didn't want to stop. His gaze burned with need, and his cheeks were flushed from passion. He kept his hands at his sides, curled into tight fists, like he was trying not to reach out and touch her.

"Why not?" she pressed.

"Because I don't want to rush it. You're special—don't you get that? You deserve more than . . . than *me*, damn it."

She furrowed her brows in surprise. "Don't say that. I'm lucky to have you—don't *you* get that?"

His expression went shuttered, but not before she glimpsed a flash of anguish.

"You really want us to wait?" she said slowly.

He released a ragged breath. "I do. I know it doesn't make much sense to you, but I can't just rush you into my bed. I need to earn it."

He was right—his cryptic words didn't make a lick of sense to her, but he sounded so tormented and looked so upset that she decided not to push him.

"Okay," she murmured. "We'll go back to taking it slow."

The relief that flooded his face was unmistakable. "Thank you." He cleared his throat. "Do you want to go out for dinner?"

Dinner? Uh, yeah, right. What she wanted to do was kiss him again. To lose herself in those incredible sensations and never leave his side.

But after a beat, she simply nodded. "Sure."

"Okay, cool. Let me just grab my coat and wallet."

He took several steps toward the bedroom, but stopped before he reached the door. "Noelle?"

"Yeah?"

When he turned to face her, her breath lodged in her lungs.

He swallowed, looking more vulnerable than she'd ever seen him. "That was the best kiss of my life."

Chapter 7

Present day

The second she and Jim got back to the town house, Noelle made a beeline for the living room bar and poured herself a glass of brandy. She heard him come up behind her, and his proximity raised her hackles. For some inexplicable reason the man seemed determined to stick to her like glue—and she didn't like it one damn bit. Bad enough that he'd joined her at the club, but now he was crowding her in her own home?

She spun around and scowled at him. "Quit shadowing me. It's annoying."

"Why couldn't you just say you were working a job back there?" he said gruffly. "Why all the subterfuge?"

"What subterfuge? I said I wanted to go dancing—I went dancing." She sipped the expensive alcohol, hoping it would ease her high-strung nerves. "I also happened to eliminate a slimebag and make a million bucks. What's it to you? In fact, why the hell are you still here?"

His long fingers hooked into the belt loops of his olive green cargo pants. She saw a muscle in his jaw twitch, and then his throat dipped, as if he was fighting the words that finally left his mouth.

"I want you to help me find the person who hired Girard." When he met her eyes, she'd never seen him so ill at ease. "So . . . I'll ask you again. Will you, please"—he blanched at the word—"help me?"

A smug smile stretched across her face. "Aw, was that so hard?"

"Yes or no, Noelle."

"Yes." Her grin widened. "But only because it means you'll owe me one."

"Nothing comes from the goodness of your heart, huh?"

"Of course not. Generosity gets you nowhere." She slugged back the rest of her brandy and slammed the glass on the bar top. "I'm turning in now. We'll do some digging in the morning."

As she stepped forward, she deliberately allowed her bare arm to brush his, and enjoyed his intake of breath.

Before she could blink, his hand curled over her wrist to keep her in place.

"This teasing bullshit needs to stop," he snapped.

"Let go of me," she said coolly.

His fingers only dug harder into her flesh. "And your pretense of indifference is getting old, baby. Go ahead and flaunt your body, rub up against me, try to get me going, but don't pretend it doesn't affect you too." He pressed his thumb on the pulse point in her wrist. "You want to fuck me."

She let out an incredulous laugh. "Oh really?"

Jim's answering laugh was dark and sensual. "You. Want. To. Fuck. Me." Each word came out in a slow, infuriating rasp.

Noelle tilted her head, and the look on his face sent her pulse careening. Hot and feral, with raw resentment thrown into the mix.

He hated this as much as she did. The tension thickening the air, the volatile emotions whipping between them like unsecured cables in a windstorm.

As she peered up at him, signs of arousal bloomed in her body. Her breasts grew achy. Her core throbbed. Her heart pounded. And in the center of the carnal storm raging inside her was her own hefty dose of resentment. She hated him for having the power to do this to her. To ignite her body this way.

"Not gonna try to deny it?" he taunted.

Noelle sucked in a shaky breath.

"Nah, didn't think you would."

Keeping her wrist in a death grip, he brought his other hand to his groin and cupped his package. Hard.

Her sex clenched as she watched him stroke the hard ridge of arousal beneath his pants.

"You want this, don't you?"

"Fuck off," she managed to squeeze out.

Jim wasn't finished tormenting her. "Baby, we both know you want my cock inside you. Remember how deep it filled you? Remember the way I made you moan?"

Oh God. She did. She remembered it like it was yesterday. Their naked bodies entwined on crisp linen sheets, her pussy stretching to accommodate him, her inner muscles clasping his thick shaft.

Moisture pooled between her legs, while the saliva in her mouth turned to dust.

"Do you remember?"

She swallowed before responding. "No."

"Yes, you do." He stroked the inside of her wrist with the pad of his thumb. "You remember every second of it."

She yanked her hand away as a spike of anger pierced her chest. "No, what I remember is your lies. I remember your betrayal. I remember *that*. So I repeat, *fuck off*. Fuck off and don't ever touch me again—"

His mouth came down on hers without warning, his kiss hot and demanding, a greedy domination that almost knocked her off her feet. She had no choice but to grab on to him, bunching his T-shirt between her fingers as his tongue plunged inside her mouth.

The taste of him sent her mind spinning. His rock-hard abs quivered beneath her fingers, neck muscles straining as he angled his head to drive the kiss deeper.

When their tongues touched, it was like an incredible drug had been injected into her system. A moan of desperation slipped out before she could stop it, which only triggered a low growl from Jim's throat.

He thrust his hand in her updo, tugging at the pins that kept it up. They fell to the carpet as her hair came free, and then he fisted the loose strands, pulling to the point of pain. All the while his mouth continued to devour hers, depriving her of much-needed oxygen, a never-ending kiss that exhilarated her senses and stole her sanity.

God, she had to regain control. She couldn't let him draw her in again, not after everything he'd done to her.

The memory of his betrayal was all it took for her to find her footing. It was all it took to bring a flash of clarity to her mind.

With a growl of her own, she captured his lower lip between her teeth and bit him.

Hard.

Jim's angry curse delivered her back to the welcome realm of reality. Gasping for air, she wrenched herself out of his grasp. She saw his blood glistening on his lips, and she basked in the satisfaction of knowing she'd caused him pain.

Aggravation burned in his midnight blue eyes as he lifted a hand to his mouth and touched the puncture. But he didn't say a word. Just gazed at her, thoughtfully almost, which only fueled her growing rage.

"Don't ever do that again," she hissed out.

Jim wiped his hand on the front of his shirt, leaving a streak of red against the white fabric.

"I let it slide at the airport back in February, but I'm done with this shit. You understand?" Her features hardened as she glowered at him. "Kiss me again without my permission and I'll slit your throat."

Fighting the uncontrollable beating of her heart, Noelle bulldozed past him and stormed out of the room, leaving him in the same state he'd left her all those years ago.

Bloody and alone.

Chapter 8

"I hate this." Sullivan's gray eyes flashed as he voiced the bitter complaint to the other men. "We should be helping the boss."

It was rare to see Sully so distressed, though Liam didn't blame him one bit. Their boss's order for them to stay put didn't sit right with him either. He'd been trying not to think about it, had even suggested a night of poker to distract himself and the others, but nobody had bothered dealing the cards yet; the unshuffled deck sat in the center of the table, along with the men's unopened beer bottles.

"But your girl is helping them, right?" asked David "Ash" Ashton, the newest member of their team.

The question was directed at Ethan Hayes, who shook his head. "Juliet left this morning for South Africa. She's on another job." He rolled his eyes. "Besides, can you really see Jules enjoying herself on a fact-finding mission with Noelle and Morgan? The woman is built for action. She'd go nuts."

From his seat across the table, Sullivan finally seemed to relax, casting Ethan a grin. "Action, huh? I hope you've been giving her all the action she needs. If not, I'm perfectly happy to step in and take over."

Ethan flipped up his middle finger. "In your dreams, dude."

"Oh, for real. I dream about Juliet every night, mate."

"Remember what I told you in Belarus?" Ethan's hazel eyes took on a deadly glint. "Touch her and you're dead."

Sullivan sighed. "You're so possessive, rookie. Jeez. Share the wealth."

Now the other man looked smug. "I ain't the rookie anymore, Aussie. You get to pick on Ash now."

"Hey, don't go bringing li'l ole me into this." Ash's Tennessee drawl always seemed to thicken when he was pulling his aw-shucks, good-old-boy shtick.

Ash had been around for only three months, but Liam already loved Morgan's newest recruit. Ash was young—twenty-three or so—but he was smart, highly trained, and damn good at following orders. The kid also had *ladies' man* written all over that chiseled face of his, and Liam had no doubt that Ash's messy dark hair, laughing green eyes, and crooked grin had charmed the panties off numerous ladies.

"Hey," Ash suddenly said. "So what exactly *is* the deal with Morgan and that Noelle woman? Did they date or something?"

The other men snickered.

"Morgan doesn't 'date,'" Liam answered with a grin. "I'm pretty sure he just fucks and runs."

"So he used to fuck her?" Ash pressed.

Sullivan shrugged. "Sure seems like it, mate, but he's never confirmed or denied it."

"He hates her guts," Ethan spoke up. "We know that much."

Ash sounded thoughtful. "If he hates her, why did he fly off to Paris with her?"

"You ask us this as if we're in the loop," Liam said dryly. "But trust me, we're the last people to know the important stuff. If you want details, go upstairs and ask Abby. I bet she knows."

"Dude, I'm not going anywhere near her unless I have pickles or ice cream on hand, and we're out of both because she ate them all." Ash sighed. "Pregnant women are scary."

"Well, then you're shit out of luck, because we never know shit."

"Aw, Boston, are you jealous about not being part of the inner circle?" Sully taunted.

"Damn straight," Liam retorted. "'Cause you know what happens when you're in the inner circle? You get to hook up with a hot chick. Case in point—Kane. Second-in-command and he lands a hot redhead. Trevor—team leader for most gigs, marries a hot blonde. Former rookie over here"—he hooked a thumb at Ethan—"gets to lead an op in Belarus and winds up with a hot brunette. I rest my case."

"And don't forget about D," Ethan said in response to Liam's theory. "Also in the inner circle, and hooked up with Noelle. So . . . you might be onto something."

"Wait—what?" Liam blinked in surprise.

Ethan rolled his eyes. "Oh come on, like you didn't suspect."

"You're messing with us," Sullivan piped up. "No way is D screwing around with Morgan's archenemy."

"I'm pretty sure he is," Ethan replied, shrugging. "Or at least he was at one point in time."

"Bullshit," Liam argued. He didn't know much about D's background, but he knew the guy's *personality*, and, well, he couldn't imagine that prickly asshole getting involved with a woman. Or a man. Or pretty much anyone, really. The tight-lipped merc didn't form attachments. Hell, he barely spoke more than five words at a time.

On the other hand, unless D was living a life of celibacy, he had to get his rocks off sometimes, and Liam realized Noelle was probably the best candidate for that. She was smokin' hot, but not a woman you'd ever want as a permanent fixture in your life. For a man like D, that must be a damn good arrangement.

"Well, if he's doing her, he's one lucky bastard," Sully muttered.

"No way," Ethan disagreed. "That woman is terrifying."

"Yeah, but she's also the hottest chick on the planet. I'd do her."

Liam had to sigh. "You'd do anyone."

Sullivan, of course, didn't refute that. The man made no secret of the fact that he enjoyed sex. A lot.

Liam had witnessed and participated in his fair share of Sully's hookups, and those he hadn't experienced firsthand had been recounted to him in excruciating detail by the cocky Australian. Which meant he knew damn well that Sullivan wasn't picky when it came to sex, and yeah, he also knew that Sullivan swung both ways, but he honestly didn't care who the guy slept with. Men, women—Liam wasn't one to judge.

Except . . . Aw hell, *bad* idea thinking about Sullivan with another man right now. Bad fucking idea.

"I'm gonna take a walk." He rose abruptly from his chair, averting the men's gazes. "If we're not playing poker, I might as well get some exercise."

From the corner of his eye, he saw Ethan stand up too. "Yeah, I should go in and gather my gear. We're heading out soon."

Liam headed for the stairs on the other side of the terrace, all the while wishing the boss hadn't inflicted this mandatory downtime on them. He would've killed to join Ethan and the others in Ecuador, to have a mission to concentrate on, but Morgan's orders were set in stone, so Liam had to suck it up and stay on the compound.

"Wait up," he heard Sullivan call from behind him. "I could use a walk too."

He hesitated on the bottom step. But for the life of him, he couldn't think of a single excuse for why Sully couldn't join him.

The two of them fell into step with each other, heading away from the pool area toward the cluster of ceiba trees at the edge of the backyard. Tangled vines and thick undergrowth spanned the ground beneath their boots, which didn't make a sound as they walked through the brush.

Liam breathed in the familiar scents of the jungle, the damp earth and acrid rot and sweet flora. A gap in the sweeping canopy of trees allowed a sliver of moonlight to light their path, and that same shard of white light also illuminated Sully's features, those rugged good looks that never failed to make women swoon.

"Being around those two makes me feel old," Liam remarked in a glum voice.

"Ethan and Ash?"

"Yeah. They make me wish I was still in my twenties."

"You're only thirty-two. That's closer to your twenties than you think. Besides, thirty is the new twenty."

"I don't get why people say that," he grumbled. "It doesn't make any sense. Twenty is twenty. Thirty is thirty. End of story."

"You really need to stop thinking in black and white, mate," Sullivan said with a chuckle.

It wasn't the first time his buddy had accused him of that, but Liam didn't know how to think any other way. Right and wrong, good and bad—that was how his brain worked. He operated on logic, thought things through, weighed each and every action before carrying it out.

Sullivan was the impulsive one in the friendship, the one who jumped first and asked questions later. His spontaneity had led him into a shit ton of precarious situations over the years, and lately it was Liam who'd taken on the role of keeping Sully in check, forcing his friend to consider the consequences before he went off half-cocked.

"Why do you want to be twenty so badly?" Sullivan asked curiously. "You feeling unfulfilled? Wishing you could go back and redo shit?"

"Nah. I'm happy enough with where I am." Liam pushed a low-hanging branch out of his way and moved deeper into the lush vegetation. "But sometimes I miss my younger, optimistic self. You know, the guy who saw the world as sunshine and rainbows and all that crap." A twinge of embarrassment crept into his voice. "I always figured I'd be married by the time I was twenty-five. Have a couple of kids by the time I turned thirty. You know, normal life stuff."

Sullivan sounded amused. "Is that what you want? Marriage, kids, normalcy?"

"One day, I guess." Liam paused. "You?"

"Fucked if I know. I don't think ahead, remember? I live for the moment. Besides, I'd make a terrible husband, and an even worse father."

Liam stopped walking, shifting his head so he could meet Sullivan's eyes. The moonlight danced over his friend's face, emphasizing a strong jaw and vivid gray eyes.

He swallowed a groan. Now was not the time to be staring at his teammate's pretty mug. The time for that was . . . never. He should *never* be checking out the man.

"Bullshit," Liam said gruffly. "I think you'd be a great father."

"Doubt it, mate. I'm just a shallow playboy who travels the world on his boat, remember? Besides, with my ADD? I'd be the dad who forgets his kid at the grocery store."

Liam laughed. "Nah. You'd be the coolest dad on the

block. Husband, though? I dunno. You'd have to learn to keep your pants zipped first."

"Hey, if my pants stayed zipped, your sex life would plummet into obscurity, Boston." His friend smirked. "I've gotten you more ass than you could ever get on your own."

"Bull-fucking-shit. I don't need your help getting laid. The ladies are *all* over me."

Sullivan heaved out a sigh. "Yeah, of course they are. With your Black Irish good looks and million-dollar smile? Chicks don't stand a chance."

Discomfort rolled through him like tumbleweed, forming into a knot at the pit of Liam's stomach. Sullivan was such a natural flirt that it was impossible to know when he was actually flirting, and when he was just fucking around.

"Let's head back," Liam said awkwardly. He took off walking again, not checking to see whether his friend was following.

High up in the trees, a monkey screeched, reminding him that they weren't alone in the jungle. Nocturnal creatures scampered along the branches over their heads, and the hum of insects echoed in the humid night air. The low buzz was almost soothing, and Liam felt the tension draining out of him as he listened to the familiar sounds.

They were halfway to their destination when he abruptly stopped by the massive trunk of a tree whose roots started aboveground and were nearly as tall as he was.

"You really think you're nothing but a shallow playboy?" He drew his brows together pensively. For some reason, it bugged him that Sullivan viewed himself that way.

The other man wrinkled his forehead. "What? No, of course not. I was just talking stupid."

Liam's lips twitched. "You tend to do that a lot."

"Yeah, I guess I do."

The tension returned in full force when he realized his friend was studying his face, almost like he was trying to burrow his way into Liam's mind. Those gray eyes narrowed, lips parting slightly as their gazes locked.

Liam's breath caught. "C'mon, let's go back to—"

"Don't move," Sullivan murmured.

He froze, unease washing over him.

Ever so slowly, Sullivan took several silent steps closer, until their bodies were nearly touching.

When he lowered his hand to his waistband, Liam's blue eyes widened.

"Sully . . ." One hoarse word, laced with confusion.

"Don't. Move."

With lightning-fast accuracy, Sullivan whipped out his KA-BAR and stabbed the blade five inches to the left of Liam's head.

Right between the eyes of the reddish pink pit viper that had slithered out of the thick foliage.

"Fuckin' hell!" Liam started to laugh as Sullivan grabbed the highly poisonous snake by the tail and held it up. "Thanks, man."

"No prob." Sullivan tossed the dead snake on the thick vines beneath their feet. "Happy to save your bacon, Boston. C'mon, let's go." Then, seemingly oblivious to Liam's current state of emotional turmoil, he sauntered off.

Christ.

Liam watched the other man's back for a moment, then let out a breath and trailed after him, all the while trying not to think about what had just happened. Right before his teammate had reached for that knife, Liam had thought . . .

Nothing. He'd thought nothing.

You thought something.

Fine. Okay. So maybe, just maybe, for one teeny moment, he'd thought his best friend was going to . . .

Well, kiss him.

But that was crazy. They were just *friends*, for fuck's sake. Neither one of them was interested in . . . something more. It was stupid of him to think Sullivan had been making a pass at him. Or that the inexplicable gleam that for one brief second had crossed Sully's eyes had actually been *lust*.

For *him*.

Gulping, Liam banished every crazy thought from his head and followed his teammate back home.

Early the next morning, Morgan dunked his head under the shower spray and let the cold water soak his body. It didn't help. He was still hot and edgy and as primed for sex as he'd been last night.

He really had to stop kissing the woman. He'd done it twice in less than a year, and both times his mouth landed on hers, his brain screamed betrayal.

He shouldn't let her get to him, but she did.

He shouldn't want to fuck her.

But he did.

The rush of water muffled his aggravated groan. He braced both hands on the white-tiled wall and tried to banish all thoughts of Noelle's warm, pliant lips from his mind. Tried to ignore the raging hard-on that not even the cool water could get rid of.

Eventually he just gave up. The rock between his legs wasn't going anywhere, not unless he gave it some relief.

Wrapping his fingers around his stiff shaft felt like an even bigger betrayal, but he couldn't stop himself. Couldn't stop the dirty images that swarmed his brain, all of which featured Noelle. Her naked golden skin, her red fingernails scraping his bare back, her pussy clutching his cock in a tight vise.

He'd never jerked off in a rage before, and yet here he was, pumping his cock as lust and anger warred inside him.

It took no time at all before he was coming all over his hand. The orgasm was quick, unsatisfying, and only made him angrier, and after he'd rinsed off the evidence and stepped out of the shower, he felt utterly exhausted.

Christ, he was so tired of keeping his guard up all the time, fighting the carnal need that hit him whenever he saw Noelle. He harbored so much hatred but, at the same time, held on to memories of a woman who no longer existed.

He toweled off wearily, wishing like hell that he could just hop on a plane and get far, far away from here. From *her*.

But until he figured out who wanted him dead, he wasn't going anywhere.

When he entered the lavish guest bedroom he was currently calling home, he found Noelle sitting on the king-size bed. She wore black leggings and a tight red tank, and her blond hair was arranged in one long braid that hung over her shoulder.

The hairstyle threw him for a loop. It made her look younger and more approachable, reminding him of the girl he'd known almost twenty years ago.

But then her cold blue eyes locked with his, and the girl of yesterday vanished, replaced by the detached woman she'd become.

"Paige got her hands on Girard's client list," Noelle told him, holding up a paper-thin Apple tablet as if to prove her claim. "I figured we could go through it and see if any of these names ring a bell for you."

He nodded. "Sounds good. Let me just get dressed."

Rather than give him some privacy, she set the tablet beside her, leaned back on her elbows, and smirked. "Nobody's stopping you."

Morgan battled another rush of fatigue. Fuck, he was so sick of these games.

With a sigh, he dropped his towel and strode naked toward his duffel. "I have a proposition for you," he said as he grabbed some clothes.

Noelle's intrigued voice wafted from the bed. "Yeah?"

He yanked on a pair of boxer-briefs and cargo pants, then turned to look at her as he zipped up. "I propose a cease-fire."

"A cease-fire."

"If we're going to be working together to find out who hired Girard, we can't afford to be distracted by all the baggage between us. The games. The constant battles." He let out a breath. "Let's just do this job without letting all our old crap get in the way."

"You think that's possible?" She sounded both curious and unconvinced.

"We can make it possible." He put on a clean white T-shirt and met her eyes again. "And not just a temporary cease-fire. I'm talking permanent here. After we find Girard's client and take care of him, we'll go our separate ways. For good, this time. No more professional team-ups, no more death threats. We just . . . walk away."

Noelle sat up, placing both hands on her thighs as she bit her bottom lip. "We walk away," she echoed.

He nodded.

"Can we really do that?"

"I can, if you can."

It took a lot out of him to say that. He'd spent years hating her, keeping tabs on her, dreaming of ways to inflict pain. Walking away now was ... unimaginable.

But it was also cathartic in a way. Ending this war between them and finally being free of the destructive emotions she summoned from him? Sounded like music to his ears.

"Well ... all right, then," she said, her voice thoughtful.

His eyes narrowed. "Just like that?"

She looked like she was fighting a laugh. "Yes, just like that. What's the problem?"

He honestly didn't know. There shouldn't be a problem. There *wasn't* a problem.

Except ... Shit, what was that strange pang tugging at his gut?

Was it *disappointment*?

Which was fuckin' nuts, considering that severing their sick bond had been *his* idea. He should be thrilled that she'd acquiesced so easily.

"So are we going over this list or what?" Noelle asked impatiently.

Morgan snapped out of his messed-up thoughts and went to get his laptop. "Sure. Let's do it."

Her sweet, feminine scent ensnared his senses the second he joined her on the bed. It was as intoxicating as it'd always been, and just as difficult to label. She smelled like the ocean, vanilla, a garden in full bloom. Such a peculiar combination of fragrances, as complicated as the woman herself.

He forced himself not to breathe her in, instead focusing on the tablet she handed him.

"Recognize any of them?" she said briskly.

Morgan scrolled through the list of sixty or so names. "I recognize a lot of them," he admitted, "but not through any personal connections. Girard represents some serious bigwigs."

Media moguls, high-powered executives, descendants of long-ago French royalty. The list went on and on, and the sole element that tied most of the names together was that Morgan had never crossed paths with any of them. Nor could he think of a single reason why they'd want him dead.

"Oh shit, look. He represents Jacques Moreau," Noelle spoke up, her blue eyes dancing with amusement. "That's the cabinet member who was outed last year for using government funds to pay for his butt implants."

Grinning, she swiped Morgan's computer from his lap and quickly typed Moreau's name into the search engine. A second later, she leaned closer to show him the image on the screen.

"Check out that ass. Can you imagine the pancake butt he must have had before? I mean, to resort to *implants*?"

A laugh flew out of Morgan's mouth, startling him into abrupt silence.

Shit. He couldn't remember the last time he'd genuinely laughed in this woman's company.

Noelle looked as surprised as he felt, but she didn't comment on the aberration. She simply shot him a puzzled look before clearing her throat and refocusing her attention on the screen.

Shifting awkwardly, Morgan reached for the tablet and spoke in a gruff voice. "Let's go through these names again and see if anything jumps out."

Chapter 9

Nineteen years ago

"How come you never talk about your parents?"

Morgan shifted on the wrought-iron park bench so he could see Noelle better. She looked genuinely curious as she sat there tracing the rim of her foam coffee cup with the tip of her finger.

"How come you never talk about yours?" he countered.

"I do it all the time," she protested. "You know everything about my mom." Her expression darkened. "And about René."

"Yeah, but you never mention your father . . ."

He let the remark hang, then held his breath as he awaited her reply. Although they'd been seeing each other for more than a month, she still hadn't opened up about her father, and Morgan's supervisors were growing impatient. When he'd checked in earlier, Commander Jeremy Thomas had even hinted that they were considering pulling him out if he didn't produce some information soon.

He refused to let that happen, and not just because he'd never failed to meet an objective before. If they called him in, his CO would send another intelligence officer to take his place, and then Morgan wouldn't be there to protect Noelle from getting caught in the cross fire.

Just thinking about her being hurt unleashed a flurry of panic, causing his fingers to tighten around his coffee cup.

"You're right. I don't," she said. "But that's because it hurts to talk about him. God, I miss him so much. I try not to think about him when he's gone. Otherwise I miss him even more."

He spoke in a careful tone. "Does he ever come to visit you?"

"Usually a few times a year, but I haven't seen him in a while. He's been away on business."

Morgan's body tensed. "What does he do?"

Noelle wagged a finger at him. "Nope, you're not getting any more details from me. Not until you answer *my* questions. Tell me about your parents."

A thread of discomfort wrapped around him. "There's not much to tell. My folks weren't around much."

"Why not?"

"My father was busy running his business, and my mother was busy running their charity foundation. Which means I saw them every morning for about five minutes, and then again at dinner, if I was lucky. Usually they didn't leave their respective offices before nine or ten at night."

"What about the weekends?"

"I spent those with my nanny. And when I got older, I hung out with friends."

"Weren't you upset that your parents didn't have time for you?"

He shrugged. "I had a lot of freedom growing up. Can't complain about that."

"You don't have to do that with me."

"Do what?"

Noelle's voice softened. "Pretend that nothing hurts you."

She reached out and took his hand, lightly stroking his knuckles.

Morgan stared at her fingers, his gaze zeroing in on the two she'd broken the day they'd met. They were no longer splinted, but still looked stiff, with a hint of bruising on her creamy skin. He knew they bothered her—he saw her wince whenever she moved them—but she never commented on the lingering pain. She continued to floor him with her strength.

"It's okay to admit that your parents not being there was hard on you," she said quietly.

He wanted to dismiss the claim, but as usual, Noelle summoned an emotional response from him.

"I guess it was," he said hoarsely. "Just a little bit."

Still gripping his hand, she leaned close and brushed her lips over his. The addictive scent of her filled his nostrils, made it difficult to think clearly.

Her lips left his far too soon, and he was tempted to yank her back for another kiss. Not a peck this time, but a deep, passionate one. They'd been sharing a lot of those since that first explosive kiss at the hotel. He couldn't help himself, couldn't seem to break the spell he'd fallen under.

His CO had accused him of dragging his feet and losing focus on the objective, but even though Morgan had denied the accusation, he was beginning to suspect his commander might be right. Every second he spent with Noelle was . . . God, he couldn't even describe it. All he knew was that the girl had gotten under his skin. Big-time.

"What about you?" he asked her. "How do you feel about your father not being there for you?"

"He *is* there for me."

Her reply was so swift and so ferocious that it caught him off guard.

"My father loves me." Her expression grew even more determined, almost like she was trying to convince herself. "I know he feels bad about not being here, but it was my mother's decision to move back to Paris. He didn't have a say in the matter. She got custody in the divorce."

Morgan quickly jotted down a mental note—*never* say a negative word about Douglas Phillips to his daughter. Clearly she was protective of the man, if even the slightest indictment against him could set her off.

He decided to change course. "So your dad stayed in the States after you and your mother came to Paris?"

Noelle's expression lost some of its ferocity. "Yeah, but he travels a lot, so he's not home very often."

"What does he do?"

"He works for the government."

"That's vague."

She bit her bottom lip, looking uncertain. "Well, if I'm being honest, I'm not a hundred percent clear on what he actually does. He's a consultant. I know that much. He works with the CIA and NSA and some other defense agencies, but I'm not really sure what he does for them. I think it has something to do with defense strategies. My dad was in the military, and he's a genius, so of course all those agencies would want his help."

Her naïveté made him stifle a sigh, but at the same time, he wasn't surprised that Douglas Phillips hadn't told his daughter what he actually did for a living. Phillips was a CIA spy. Legendary in the espionage community, possessing one of the highest levels of security clearance an agent could reach. With all the secrets he knew, he could destroy every politician and intelligence agent in the country, topple foreign governments, blow apart a hundred conspiracies, and start World War Three if he chose to.

And that made him a threat. A very dangerous threat, and one that Morgan needed to neutralize.

"When was the last time you saw him?" he said lightly.

Noelle had to think about it. "About six months ago. He came to Paris to visit me."

Six months . . . Phillips had still been a patriotic member of the intelligence community back then; he hadn't gone AWOL until three months ago.

The powers that be had been certain the man would want to see his daughter before he permanently went off the grid. Maybe they were wrong, though. He'd had three months to contact Noelle, yet he hadn't tried to arrange a single meeting, so chances were he'd already skipped town and—

"But he called me last month." Noelle's admission interrupted his thoughts.

Morgan instantly masked his eagerness. "What did he say?"

"Not much. He told me he's finishing up a job and that he's going to try and visit before he starts his next assignment."

Jackpot.

So Morgan's superiors were right, after all. Douglas Phillips *would* attempt to say good-bye to his kid before he disappeared.

"Well, that tells me he misses you as much as you miss him," Morgan said, forcing a smile.

"I guess." Noelle put down her coffee cup and glanced around the deserted park. "I like this place. It's so pretty."

Her blue eyes had focused on the huge circular fountain,

which remained illuminated even though it was nearly midnight. Morgan knew the fountain would be drained for winter soon, but at the moment, the two feet of water in its base bubbled away, and the graceful arches shooting from all around the circle shimmered in the darkness.

He was startled to realize how late it was—time flew by when he was with Noelle. They'd already spent the whole day strolling along the Champs-Élysées, and the evening having dinner in Montmartre. Afterward, he hadn't been ready to say good-bye to her, and somehow they'd wound up in this beautiful park two blocks from his hotel.

He liked this place too. It was quiet. Peaceful. And the air was surprisingly warm for autumn. Neither one of them was even wearing a coat tonight.

"What do you want to do after you leave the army?" Noelle's gaze left the fountain and focused on his face.

"I haven't given it much thought," he admitted.

"Okay. Well, what do you like to do in your spare time?"

"I don't know."

She laughed. "You don't know what you like to do?" Now she rolled her eyes. "What are you good at?"

"Following orders. Shooting things. Saving lives. Protecting my country." He paused. "I'll probably just end up being career army."

"And if that wasn't an option?"

"I don't know. Maybe start a security company?"

Noelle heaved out an exaggerated sigh. "How boring. You lack vision."

"What would *you* have me do?" He arched a brow in challenge.

"Anything. Everything." She shrugged. "You inherited a fortune from your parents. That opens up a world of possibilities."

He flashed her a crooked grin. "I'm a simple man, baby. I don't need a world of possibilities. I'd be perfectly happy living in a cabin in the middle of the woods. Hunting, fishing, living off the land. Sitting on the porch and smoking cigarettes and listening to the blues."

"Where's your sense of adventure?" Her tone was playful. "Don't you ever do anything crazy? Step out of your comfort zone?"

"In my line of work, crazy gets you killed," he said ruefully.

"Fine. I'll give you that. But you're not in the army right this second, are you? Nope, you're on leave. Which means you're allowed to have fun and be crazy." Her blue eyes shone in the yellow glow of the lamppost next to their bench. "So do something crazy already."

"Like what?"

Her expression grew even more impish. "I don't know ... Hmmm ... All right, I've got it." As a mischievous smile tugged on her lips, she pointed to the fountain. "Take off your clothes and run around in the fountain."

He snorted. "Sorry, babe. I'm not much of an exhibitionist."

That got him a haughty look. "See? You're no fun."

"I'm cool with that. You can be the fun one in the relationship."

Relationship?

Jesus Christ, what was he saying?

He quickly tried to backpedal, but Noelle spoke before he could.

"You know what, Jim? I think it's time you stopped being such a control freak. I *dare* you to strip to your underwear and run in the fountain."

"You dare me? What is this, middle school?"

"It's an exercise in letting go." She hopped to her feet with the agility of a gymnast. "Come on, *babe*, I dare you to let go."

He stayed seated.

"I'll tell you what—if you do it, so will I."

The smile she shot him was the most beautiful thing he'd ever seen. Brighter than the lights sparkling in the water, more luminous than the full moon shining above them.

"Come on, it'll be great," she coaxed. "Unless ... You're not scared, are you, Jim?"

She blinked innocently, triggering that macho-man switch inside him that made it impossible to ever back down from a challenge.

He promptly stood up. "Oh, trust me, I'm not too scared to do it. I just don't think *you* will."

A delighted laugh flew out of her mouth. "Oh, Jim. Clearly you don't know me *at all*."

The next thing he knew, she was unbuttoning her cardigan sweater.

Morgan's breath jammed in his throat as she began removing items of clothing. Sweet Jesus. Why had he opened this can of worms? Why had he—oh fuck. She'd stripped down to her bra. A pink, lacy bra that was so thin he couldn't *not* notice the puckered nipples beneath the dainty cups.

His mouth went bone dry, all common sense and propriety draining away as his cock hardened beneath his pants. His gaze was only capable of registering the endless expanse of creamy skin. The way her long blond hair gleamed in the moonlight. The full breasts practically pouring out of that skimpy bra.

He was on sensory overload. Frozen in place as Noelle unzipped her dark blue jeans and wiggled out of them, leaving her in a pair of panties that matched her bra.

She was incredible. Smooth skin and supple curves, a golden goddess standing before him.

"And look who's still dressed. Wimp."

Her teasing snapped him out of his lust-filled stupor.

"Who you calling a wimp?" He whipped his shirt over his head, then shot her a cocky look.

He didn't miss the way her eyes widened at the sight of his bare chest, or the rosy flush that bloomed in her cheeks. His erection throbbed painfully, and it dawned on him that there was no way of hiding his arousal once he took off his pants.

He tried to come up with an excuse to leave the pants on, but Noelle squashed the notion by pointing to his lower body.

"Down to your underwear," she ordered.

Shit. This woman was going to be the death of him.

Reluctantly, he kicked off his combat boots and peeled off his socks, trying to prolong the inevitable.

The second his cargo pants hit the ground, Noelle's breath hitched, but she didn't comment on the erection trying to tunnel its way out of his boxers.

Instead, she gave him a wide smile, then darted off in a mad sprint toward the fountain.

Laughing despite himself, Morgan chased after her. He caught up just in time to hear her high-pitched shriek as the cold water doused her bare flesh.

Definitely wasn't swimming weather—that was for sure. Goose bumps popped out on his skin when he got in the path of one of the spouting arches. Water dripped down his chest and soaked his boxers, which only made him curse, because damn it, now there was the distinct outline of his cock in the wet cotton.

He couldn't believe he was actually doing this. Noelle's observation hadn't been too far off the mark—he *was* always in control. Fun didn't play much of a role in his life.

And yet Noelle managed to bring out a side in him that he hadn't known existed. A side that was light and tender and . . . *insane.*

For fuck's sake, this was total insanity, he decided as the cold water had him breaking out in shivers.

Noelle's squeal made him grin.

"God, Jim, it's so cold!" But the temperature didn't stop her from running through the spraying arches.

Her feet kicked up water, arms raised high above her head, and her hair grew darker the wetter it got. But her eyes remained as pale as ever, sparkling ice blue, full of joy and laughter and *life.*

Morgan halted in his tracks. He could hardly breathe, barely move. He simply stood there, gazing at her with wonder.

She was the most beautiful girl he'd ever seen, but there was so much more to her than just looks. She was smart, exciting, so quick to laugh despite the hardships she'd faced. The fact that she could even smile after what she'd suffered at the hands of Laurent was utterly astonishing.

As her carefree smile and laughing eyes ensnared his gaze, Morgan suddenly realized that Noelle Phillips was a helluva lot stronger than he could ever hope to be.

"Come here!" she called out, holding her hands out to him.

Like a lovesick fool, he went to her. He felt dazed, confused, and more contented than he'd ever been in his life. The sensation of soothing satisfaction only heightened as Noelle twined her arms around his neck, and then she stood on her tiptoes and kissed him, and a moan of longing slipped from his throat.

"Told you this would be fun," she murmured. "Now dance with me."

"I don't like to dance," he murmured back.

"Tough, because I love it." Her tone brooked no argument, her grip forceful as she grabbed his hands and dragged them down to her hips.

"There's no music." He gulped uneasily, feeling completely out of his element.

"We don't need music."

And then she started to sway, and he had no choice but to follow suit.

He held her close as they danced beneath the arches of water, and when she peered up at him with so much trust in her eyes, his heart squeezed painfully in his chest.

Oh God.

He was a terrible man. He deserved to rot in hell for what he was doing.

"Kiss me," she whispered.

Despite his misgivings, despite the shards of self-loathing slicing his heart, he lowered his head and captured her lips, kissing her so passionately he caught not just her, but *himself*, off guard.

When they breathlessly broke apart, she looked stunned.

"Wow," she gasped

He swallowed hard. "Noelle—"

"Hey, you two! Get out of there!"

Their heads swiveled in alarm just as a uniformed security guard appeared by the row of benches behind them.

They looked at each other for a beat.

And took off running.

They stopped only to swipe their clothing from the bench, and then they were streaking down the path that led to the street like a pair of convicts escaping from prison.

It was hard to run when you were overcome with laughter, but somehow Morgan managed to get one foot in front of the other. He was laughing so hard his side hurt. Noelle's melodic laughter mingled with his, and he reached for her hand as they emerged onto the sidewalk, where they nearly plowed down a group of late-night pedestrians.

"Oh my God, do you think he's chasing us?" Noelle asked as she frantically slipped into her shirt.

Morgan donned his own shirt. Inside out, but he didn't

care at that moment. "Do you really want to wait around and find out?"

"No, thanks."

They kept moving, stopping every few feet in order to put on another item of clothing.

When they burst into the Lancaster five minutes later, soaking wet and with their clothing in total disarray, they drew startled looks from every single person in the lobby.

Swallowing a laugh, Morgan greeted the night clerk with a brisk nod, then strode toward the elevator bank, still clutching Noelle's hand. He knew the hotel staff wouldn't throw a hissy fit—he was paying an arm and a leg for his lavish suite, and there was no way the Lancaster would be willing to lose his business over a minor infraction like wet hair and inside-out clothes.

Two minutes later, he and Noelle entered the suite, and he turned to her with a grin. "Let me grab you a towel so you can dry your hair."

He made a beeline for the private bath in the bedroom and popped inside to grab a couple of fluffy white towels from the rack. He tucked them under his arm and strode out, intending on going back to the living room.

Except Noelle wasn't in the living room.

She was on the bed.

Naked.

The sight stopped him cold. Or maybe *hot* was the more accurate description. Flames engulfed his body, a red haze of lust clouding his vision as nothing but endless curves and golden skin assaulted his gaze. His breath came out in a fast swoosh as he focused on her bare breasts, round and perky and tipped by the palest pink nipples he'd ever seen.

Her sex was also bare.

Sweet Jesus.

Morgan's brain quit working. All he could do was stare at the goddess lying on his bed.

"Don't you dare tell me to get dressed," she said in a warning tone. "We've waited long enough."

Okay, now his heart wasn't working either. It had stopped beating, lodged itself in his throat so he couldn't get a single word out.

"Take off your clothes, Jim." Her expression turned fierce.

He must have entered a hypnotic trance. There was no other explanation for why he was unbuttoning his pants.

One by one, pieces of clothing dropped to the carpet, until he was standing there totally nude and fully erect.

Noelle's eyes roamed his naked flesh, approval and heat burning in those beautiful blue orbs.

"Come here," she ordered.

As he approached the bed, he found that his hands were trembling. Desire continued to wreak havoc on his motor functions, and he felt like an awkward oaf as he stretched out on the mattress beside her, his muscles and limbs unable to remember their individual roles.

Noelle took pity on him by grasping his hand and placing it directly over one full breast.

His heart abruptly started beating again, a fast, pounding rhythm that drummed in his ears and surged through his blood. He squeezed that perfect breast, groaning when her rigid nipple brushed the center of his palm. God, he didn't even know where to begin. Which gorgeous part of her to kiss first. To touch. Lick. Devour.

In the back of his mind, he knew he should stop this before it was too late.

But who was he kidding?

It was already too late.

He'd been a goner from the moment he'd laid eyes on her.

Those big blue eyes peered up at him, shining with trust, anticipation, and need. "Make love to me, Jim."

His pulse kicked up another notch.

His hands started shaking again.

And then he did exactly what she asked.

Chapter 10

Present day

They poréd over Girard's client list for more than an hour, flagging names and calling up their respective contacts to gather information. But by the time Noelle closed the laptop, they were no closer to narrowing in on the mystery man who'd hired her.

Being in such close quarters with Jim was unbearable. She couldn't remember the last time they'd shared the same space for more than ten minutes, and she'd been so infuriatingly aware of him this past hour.

His crisp masculine aftershave, with a hint of sage and leather, had suffocated her lungs. The roped muscles of his arms, bare beneath his white T-shirt, had captured her gaze more than once. Equally captivating was the bristly stubble that shadowed his jaw, and the long callused fingers moving over the computer keyboard, and the faded white scar at the side of his neck . . .

He was one of those annoying men who only got better-looking with age, which made her want to slug him. But they'd called a cease-fire, so going violent on him was no longer an option.

Still, it was definitely time to wrap this up and take a much-needed break from the man.

"All right, I say we focus on the six names you didn't recognize," she said in an authoritative voice, rising from the bed. "I'll get Paige to do a more thorough background search."

"We might be able to vet at least one of them ourselves." Jim spoke absently as he studied the tablet. "I'm looking at the appointment calendar your girl copied when she hacked into Girard's office computer. It says there's a shareholders function at Maurice Durand's house tonight. Girard made a note to send his regrets about not being able to attend."

Noelle frowned. Durand was one of the clients they hadn't been able to get much intelligence on. All they'd managed to find was that he owned a major pharmaceutical company and was somewhat of a recluse. He rarely left his country estate, which might have seemed suspicious if not for the fact that the other five wild cards on their list were equally reclusive.

"Feel like crashing a party?" Jim arched his dark eyebrows at her.

"Why not?" she said with a shrug. "I'll make some calls and see if I can get us in the proper way. Otherwise we'll have to be creative."

She tossed her long braid over her shoulder and headed for the door, only to stop when Jim said her name.

"What?" Irritable, she glanced over at him.

His eyes locked with hers.

And then he said, "Wanna fuck?"

A genuine laugh flew out, but it died in her throat when she saw the look on his face.

Noelle's mouth fell open. "You're serious."

With a tired breath, he dragged a hand over his close-cropped hair before crossing his arms over his broad chest. "I figure it might benefit both of us if we just get it out of our systems."

Noelle wasn't speechless often, but at the moment, she couldn't think of a solitary thing to say.

Her gaze stayed glued to Jim's, while her brain sped through every implication, ran through every detail in order to determine whether this was a test. A trap. A joke.

Nothing about his expression or body language corroborated her suspicions. He just stood there watching her, waiting for a response. Cold and emotionless, like a damn robot.

Her gaze lowered to his groin. To the bulge beneath his pants, the proof of his arousal. Clearly he was as defeated by the physical attraction between them as she was, and that only made her angrier.

Gritting her teeth, she got up into his personal space and stared into his veiled blue eyes. "I don't want this," she snapped.

Only her hands were already fisted in the front of his shirt, pulling the material from his pants.

"Neither do I." His voice was equally tense.

Her jaw tightened.

So did his.

"This won't change how I feel about you," he muttered.

"Never," she muttered back.

There was a beat of silence. For a moment she thought he'd back down. Walk away, end the insanity.

For a moment *she* nearly walked away. Ended the insanity.

But then their eyes collided again.

And the knot of awareness sizzling between them detonated the air and unleashed a firestorm.

Noelle gasped as she suddenly found herself up against the dresser. Jim thrust his thigh between her legs and ground against her, so violently the dresser shook and smacked the wall, and the decorative candles sitting on the chest of drawers clattered to the hardwood. The glass candleholders shattered, sharp pieces littering the floor beneath their feet, but Noelle paid them no attention.

She yanked his shirt over his head, leaving his chest bare to her touch, his skin prey to her fingernails as she gouged them into his sinewy back. He jerked from the assault, growling with pain, and then his mouth came crashing down on her neck and sharp teeth sank into her flesh.

Noelle flinched from the sting, but she didn't slap his head away. She simply raked her nails down his back, so hard she knew she'd drawn blood.

"Fucking *hell*," Jim rasped, his voice tinged with anger and thick with passion.

His mouth closed in on hers, but she wrenched her head to the side at the last second, denying him her lips.

The rejection didn't faze him. He simply kissed her

everywhere but on her mouth. Her jaw, her earlobes, the column of her throat. Those wicked lips devoured every available inch of skin, and when he'd run out of exposed places, he stripped off her clothes and hauled her naked body into his arms.

Noelle swore when he unceremoniously dumped her on the bed, but the curse turned into a greedy moan when the wet heat of his mouth surrounded her nipple. He sucked hard, the pressure so intense that her hips shot off the bed.

"This. Changes. Nothing." He squeezed out the words even as he feasted on her breasts, his breath warming her already feverish skin.

"Nothing," she retorted in angry, breathless agreement.

He pushed her breasts together and flicked his tongue over her nipples, alternating between each one, licking and sucking and tormenting her with his lips.

God, she didn't want to feel any pleasure. She didn't want to bring *him* pleasure, yet she couldn't stop herself from unzipping his pants. From shoving her hand inside his boxer-briefs and wrapping her fist around his shaft. His cock was massive, as long and thick as she remembered, and harder than steel.

She gave it a lazy stroke, and the groan that escaped his lips was like a knife to the chest. When she pumped him faster and saw the fiery lust in his eyes, she fought a wave of self-loathing.

"I hate you," she whispered.

Jim snaked his hand between her legs. "Hate me all you want, baby."

Then he pushed one long finger inside her sopping wet channel and she moaned so loudly that everyone in a five-mile radius must have heard her.

Jim let out a dark, satisfied laugh. "You like that?"

"Go to hell," she spat out. "Just go to hell and fuck me already."

He shoved his pants and boxers down his trim hips, using only one hand because his other one was busy cupping her breast, squeezing to the point of pain.

Noelle lay there on her back, her heart pounding, her gaze eating up Jim's magnificent chest and washboard abs. And his cock. He was hung like a stallion, so big and hard that her mouth watered and her core clenched with anticipation.

She spread her legs wider, her lips forming a smirk when she saw the flare of heat in his eyes.

"You like that?" she mocked.

He didn't answer. Just whipped his clothing aside, covered her with his heavy naked body, and drove his cock inside her.

The penetration was deep and unexpected, summoning a wild cry from both their throats.

Son of a bitch. Fuck. Hell. *Shit*.

She'd hoped it would be different.

Prayed if they ever slept together again, that feeling of completion would have vanished.

But they still fit together so goddamn perfectly and it made her want to scream. It brought the sting of tears to her eyes, the crushing, hopeless realization that she might never be free of this man.

She shut her eyes, hoping that if she didn't see his face, she might be able to pretend he was someone else, anyone else, but Jim forcibly grabbed her chin and hissed in disapproval.

"Open your eyes, Noelle," he commanded. "I want you to look at me while I fuck you."

When she didn't obey, he curled his fingers around her thick braid and yanked hard. "Look. At. Me."

Anger jolted through her, but not enough to stop the encounter, and not nearly enough to quell the electric shocks of pleasure crackling in her system. She reluctantly opened her eyes, and a gleam of triumph joined the inferno of need lighting Jim's gaze.

"Now wrap your legs around my ass," he said thickly.

Her legs followed his order of their own volition, deepening the contact between them.

Jim drew his hips back, then plunged in again. He set a brutal rhythm. Hard, fast, and deep. So goddamn deep.

And Noelle's body betrayed her. Her pelvis rose off the mattress to meet each punishing thrust; her fingers dug into his shoulders; her inner muscles bore down on his cock to intensify the friction.

She'd never felt more helpless in her life, and she would

have been more furious about it, if Jim's expression hadn't revealed that same powerless emotion.

"Why . . . How is it still so . . ." He trailed off with a groan, then snaked his hands under her ass and lifted her up so he could drive his cock even deeper.

His desperation fascinated her. He was coming undone right in front of her. The cords of muscle in his neck popped out from the strain. His warm, male flesh took on a sheen of sweat. The pistoning of his hips grew erratic, frenzied.

The mattress squeaked in protest and the headboard whacked against the wall, but Jim didn't slow down. Didn't show mercy. He pummeled into her, over and over again, flesh slapping flesh, his slick chest crushing her breasts.

Noelle couldn't breathe. She felt the telltale signs of orgasm tingling in her core, but coming felt like another betrayal. If she let this man bring her to climax, that was something she'd never be able to undo. It would be a permanent show of weakness.

"I know you're close," he taunted. "I can feel your pussy throbbing around my cock."

She inhaled deeply, hoping to curb the impending orgasm, but all she succeeded in doing was breathing in his addictive scent, which only sent another jolt of desire straight to her core.

"You don't get to avoid this, Noelle," he said hoarsely. "If I come, then you come."

She clamped her teeth over her lower lip, fighting the rising waves of release, desperately trying to stop that coil of pressure from blowing apart.

"Damn it, *come*," Jim ground out.

Then he stole her choice in the matter by shoving his hand to where their bodies were joined and pressing his thumb directly on her clit.

And Noelle exploded.

"That's it, baby," he muttered. "There you go."

A cry flew out of her mouth as the orgasm ripped through her body. Wave after wave of pleasure crashed into her, tingling in her breasts, pounding in her core. Her body shook so hard she had no option but to cling to Jim's broad shoulders. If she hadn't been lying down, she would have toppled right over, and she hated him for having this power over her.

Except . . . well, she had the same power over *him*, a realization that became evident as she caught her breath and watched him orgasm. His powerful body shuddered from the force of it and the surrender in his eyes was both thrilling and terrifying. He went still, his cock jerking inside her, flooding her channel with hot jets of release. That was when another dose of comprehension dawned on her.

No condom. Damn it. She'd just realized it now, but she wasn't worried about pregnancy or diseases. One, she was on the pill, and two, she knew without a doubt that Jim was clean as a whistle—and not just because she'd been spying on him for years and had gotten her hands on all his medical reports. Jim Morgan considered himself a man of honor; she knew he'd never keep something as important as a sexually transmitted disease from the woman in his bed.

With a low groan, he withdrew from her core and rolled onto his back. Crooked his arm and rested it on his forehead, almost as if he were trying to shield himself from her view.

Noelle stared up at the ceiling and waited for her heartbeat to regulate. Her thighs were sticky, her sex still throbbing from the mind-shattering orgasm.

It took a while to find her voice, and once she did, it came out as dejected as ever. "Did this get me out of your system?"

He didn't speak for one long beat, until finally he muttered, "No." Another pause. "Did it get me out of yours?"

She kept her gaze on the ceiling. "No."

The mattress shifted as Jim sat up. He didn't try to touch her. Didn't try to kiss her. He simply slid off the bed and stood at the foot of it, still naked, still impressively erect.

After a moment, Noelle shifted her head and looked at him.

He looked back, his cheeks hollowing as his stubble-covered jaw went rigid. "Then I guess we'll just have to try again later."

Chapter 11

The encounter with Jim left Noelle shaken and confused. The second their clothes were back on, she'd retreated to the master bedroom, where she'd remained all day to avoid any further interaction with him.

As much as it annoyed her, it was impossible to deny that the sex had been explosive. Violent and terrifying and passionate to a degree she hadn't anticipated. Not only that, but she knew it would happen again. She wasn't fooling herself into believing it was a onetime deal, but she had every intention of gaining the upper hand next time. Oh no. Next time she wouldn't lie there gasping and writhing beneath him. *She* would be in charge.

But first, they needed to investigate Maurice Durand, which meant banishing all thoughts of sex, and perfecting her party face.

She'd put painstaking effort into her appearance. Her black Esteban Cortázar gown was elegant enough to blend in among the corporate folks attending Durand's event, and the neckline was low enough that it provided plenty of cleavage to keep Jim's gaze on her breasts. She wanted him hot and needy tonight, so that the next time they came together, he'd be the one lying there in a panting puddle of mindless need.

"You ready?" Jim opened the door without knocking and strode into the bedroom.

She opened her mouth to scold him for his rudeness, but

it snapped shut when she noticed his appearance. A designer tuxedo was molded to his muscular frame, the slim fit emphasizing his long legs and broad shoulders. It was all black, from the wool-blend jacket to the crisp shirt beneath it. A silk tie and patent leather dress shoes finished it off, and with his clean-shaven jaw and cropped dark hair, he looked suave as hell and sexier than sin.

It took a second to recover from the sight of him, and his slight smirk confirmed that he knew she'd been checking him out.

Noelle quickly pasted on an indifferent look. "Dolce and Gabbana?"

"Good eye."

"You keep a tux in your travel bag just in case?"

He ignored the question. "Are you ready or what?"

"Just one more sec."

She lifted the bottom of her dress, slipped her bare feet into a pair of sexy Louboutin heels with red-lacquered soles, then strode toward him.

He didn't compliment her as they left the bedroom together. Didn't comment on her dress, her fuck-me shoes, her sweeping updo. And not even a single remark about her smoky eye makeup and the uncharacteristic red lipstick she wore.

She would have been insulted, except the hard set of his mouth and the way he painfully avoided looking at her were more telling than any compliment he could give her. Yep, her outfit was definitely having the desired effect.

Her heels clicked on the hardwood floor on the way to the private elevator that led to the garage. In the front parlor, she collected her black satin clutch from the credenza, but didn't bother with the coat closet. It was too humid out for a coat, which she'd discovered when she'd had a cigarette on her private terrace earlier. Normally she adored summer in Paris, but it was hard to enjoy it when Jim was around. His presence meant she was forever on guard and therefore unable to appreciate even the simplest things like a sultry summer night.

"How many weapons do you have stashed under that dress?" he asked after they stepped into the elevator.

She shrugged. "Enough."

His lips twitched ever so slightly, but she didn't know whether it was from irritation or amusement. "Anticipating trouble?"

"Always. But I think this is going to be a pretty tame evening. As long as the real Eloise Lambert doesn't show up, we'll be fine."

"You sure Lambert is taken care of?"

"If Bailey does her job, then yes."

Noelle had to chuckle as she thought about her phone call with her prized chameleon. Other operatives might question a last-minute assignment that entailed impersonating a federal officer and detaining an innocent French executive for hours on end, but the request hadn't fazed Bailey in the slightest.

"Did you have to pull your girl off another job?"

Noelle shook her head. "She was already in the city. She's got some downtime before the next assignment."

"And she's capable of keeping Lambert away from the party?"

"Bailey is more than capable. Trust me. Eloise Lambert is about to have a real shitty evening."

"Let me guess. You don't feel at all bad about that."

Exasperation washed over her. "Why should I? Bailey keeps the woman occupied, and we get to use her invite and stroll into the party without any trouble. Which, by the way, we wouldn't have to do if it weren't for the target on *your* back, remember?"

He didn't look thrilled by the reminder, but he didn't argue either.

The elevator doors slid open and they entered the spacious garage, where Noelle's car and driver awaited.

Maurice Durand's estate was forty-five minutes outside of the city, a fifty-acre property enclosed by a tall stone fence that ensured privacy. Frédéric drove through the imposing wrought-iron gateway, then continued along a winding driveway bordered on one side by majestic oaks and a cluster of olive trees that must have been transplanted from the south of France, because Noelle had never seen them growing in the north before.

When they reached the end of the driveway, even she

had to raise her eyebrows. The main house was spectacular—three stories high with a stone and stucco facade, featuring multiple peaked gables and an arched front entryway with massive French doors and round stone columns.

"Nice digs," Jim remarked.

The back door opened courtesy of Frédéric, and Noelle slid out of the car with ease, her heels connecting with the paved driveway. Jim stepped out next, his shrewd gaze taking in their surroundings with military precision.

She blinked in surprise when he offered her his arm. After a beat, she tucked her hand in the crook of his arm and allowed him to lead her toward the pillared entrance. They climbed the stone steps, then paused to greet the bulky suit-clad attendant with a clipboard in his hand.

"Eloise Lambert and guest," Noelle said coolly.

Neither she nor Jim spoke as the man checked his list. They remained relaxed albeit aloof, and when they received a satisfied nod, they wasted no time strolling through the front doors.

"Enjoy your evening," the man said woodenly.

Once the door closed behind them, Noelle glanced at her date and murmured, "Easy as pie."

His tone was grim. "Let's hope it stays that way."

The foyer was as impressive as she suspected the rest of the house would be. The cathedral ceiling was thirty feet high at least, and the white-and-gray-veined marble beneath their feet gleamed from the light of the crystal chandelier. The walls boasted several expensive pieces of art, including a much-sought-after van Gogh, if Noelle wasn't mistaken.

Another tuxedoed man appeared from a wide doorway to their right, greeting them with a warm smile. "Right this way, sir, madam."

They followed him down a spacious hallway adorned with more eyebrow-raising art. No family photos in sight, Noelle noted. Just canvas after canvas, painted by some of the most iconic artists in history. Renoir, Gauguin, Monet, a handful of Rembrandts, a rare Dalí, and a piece from German painter Max Ernst that seemed oddly out of place. Durand clearly had eclectic tastes when it came to art, and his collection was enough to make other private collectors die of envy.

"Where is Mr. Durand?" Noelle inquired politely. "I'd like to say hello and thank him for hosting such a lovely event."

"He hasn't arrived yet," their guide answered. "He had an appointment in Paris this afternoon and he was delayed, but I assure you, he'll be here as soon as he can."

They reached another set of French doors. A murmur of voices and strains of classical music reached Noelle's ears, and she had to stifle a sigh. She was so not in the mood for a party.

"Until then," Durand's employee went on, "I urge you to enjoy the finest champagne our country has to offer and sample the delicious food our chef has prepared."

She flashed him a sweet smile. *"Merci, monsieur."*

The man opened the doors with a flourish, revealing the magnificent ballroom that lay beyond. From the corner of her eye, Noelle saw Jim's mouth fall open, and she didn't blame him one bit. A soaring ceiling, cherry flooring, and pale yellow walls made up the space, and Noelle had never seen so many chandeliers in her life. They hung from the ceiling in all their lighted glory, sparkling like diamonds and reflecting off the expansive display of windows on the north wall.

The music they'd heard was coming from the eight-piece orchestra situated in one corner of the room, strings and brass accompanied by a handsome man behind a white grand piano. Waitstaff in black-and-white uniforms floated through the vast room with trays of champagne flutes and gourmet hors d'oeuvres that made Noelle's mouth water. She'd skipped dinner because she'd been hiding from Jim, and her stomach rumbled from the heady aromas filling the air.

"So all these folks are shareholders in Durand Enterprises, huh?" Jim mused, assessing the three dozen or so guests milling in the ballroom. "Nice of their boss to host such a fancy-pants party for them."

Noelle was doing her own examination of the crowd. Most of the guests were older gentlemen, accompanied by much younger women decked out in expensive cocktail gowns. A few women in their thirties lingered near the orchestra, and several younger males with an ambitious air to them were drifting from group to group, mingling with the older executives.

Whenever she went out, Noelle was usually the one who stood out in the crowd—her golden hair and flawless features made it that way—but the number of beautiful women in attendance tonight was reassuring. Noelle might be able to slip under the radar after all.

She continued to scope out the room, her eyes resting on the elegant spiral staircase in the corner of the room, leading up to an honest-to-God opera box suspended twenty feet above them.

Beside her, Jim's gaze had rested on the massive ice sculpture near a set of doors leading out to the terrace. The sculpture was shaped like an elaborate dragon, posed as if it were about to take flight.

"Our host went all out," Jim said dryly.

"I imagine he can afford it. This house is incredible."

A petite redhead approached with a tray of champagne, and both Noelle and Jim readily accepted the glasses she offered them. Once the waitress was gone, Noelle took a delicate sip of the sparkling Dom Perignon, savoring the crisp taste of it. Jim did the same, only he didn't seem to be savoring a damn thing.

She had to smile when she glimpsed the look of distaste on his face.

"So it's still only beer and tequila for you, huh, Jim?"

"Yup."

"I don't get it. You grew up loaded—you should be used to guzzling down Dom. Your parents probably put it in your baby bottle instead of formula."

"My parents preferred Merlot," he corrected. "You, on the other hand, were always into the expensive bubbly." He paused for a beat. "Remember when I made you order a beer at that pub in the Left Bank? I still remember how horrified you looked after you took a sip."

"Because it tasted like sewer water," she protested. "My reaction had nothing to do with the price, or the fact that it wasn't champagne. It's not my fault you have terrible taste in beer, James."

He grinned, and her pulse promptly sped up.

Damn it. She hated seeing that crooked smile on his sexy

mouth. She hated her body for responding to it. And she hated being reminded of how easy it used to be between them. Once upon a time, they'd never run out of things to say to each other.

She suppressed a curse, annoyed with herself for letting the past surface. "I wonder what's keeping our host."

"No clue, but I wouldn't be surprised if he hasn't gotten held up at all." Jim used his glass to gesture around the lavish ballroom. "Men this rich know how to play the game, and making people wait is a great way to make you look important and mysterious. It adds to the allure."

"You're probably right."

"I'm always right."

"Aw. Your modesty is *so* endearing."

Another waiter walked up to them, this one carrying a tray of hors d'oeuvres. "Would you like to try some salmon-trout tartare?" the dark-haired man inquired in crisp French.

Noelle accepted the square linen napkin he handed her and picked up one of the delicate hors d'oeuvres. She took a bite, then moaned.

"This is amazing. Here, try some."

Without thinking, she brought the delicious pastry to Jim's lips.

He stiffened, his blue eyes flickering with surprise.

And then to *her* surprise, he opened his mouth.

Noelle's fingers quivered ever so slightly as she fed him. Jesus. What was wrong with her? What was she *doing*?

Her gaze fixed on his lips, the way his strong jaw worked as he chewed.

After he'd swallowed, his eyes rolled to the top of his head. "Motherfucker. That's good."

Noelle laughed before she could stop herself. "Told you. Come on, let's go find another waiter. I want to try everything here."

"Women," she heard him mutter under his breath.

Yet he didn't protest. He just followed her on her food quest, and even though he acted like he was humoring her, she knew he enjoyed every second of it. Not only did he taste every item they came across, he raved about each one afterward. They sampled everything they could find, from the tasty pork rillettes to the adorable mini tart flambés, from the incredible wild mushroom and chicken fricassee to the sweetest chocolate-covered strawberries she'd ever tasted.

Noelle found herself relaxing. Her naturally suspicious mind warned her that she shouldn't lower her guard, but for the first time in years, she wasn't overcome by tension in Jim's company. Her shoulders weren't stiffer than two-by-fours, her chest wasn't plagued by resentment, and her jaw didn't feel like a toy car that had been wound up to its limit.

As they wandered around the ballroom, she noted that Jim's body language also conveyed a serious lack of hostility. And it was impossible not to miss the way his magnetic blue eyes kept fastening on her cleavage.

After she'd caught him ogling her for the tenth time, Noelle raised her eyebrows. "You're being very rude, you know. You keep leering at my dress, yet you still haven't bothered to compliment it."

He shrugged. "Your dress is all right, I guess. Nothing to write home about."

"Bullshit. I'll have you know it cost me three grand—that makes it more than *all right*."

"I don't care about designer clothes."

"Says the man in the D and G tux."

"Says the woman who knew the correct label of a man's tuxedo by sight."

"Would it really kill you to admit this dress is sexy?"

"Sexy, huh?" Looking thoughtful, he appraised her from head to toe. "Nah, it would have to be way shorter and cut much lower for that."

"Bullshit," she said again.

He just smirked.

"Fine. Well, how about this?" She raised herself up even higher on her Louboutins and brought her lips dangerously close to his ear. "Picture me wearing this dress—except I'm on my knees sucking your cock."

He stiffened.

"What do you think of the dress now?" she prompted.

His nostrils flared, and she tried not to laugh at his lustful expression.

"That's what I thought," she said sweetly.

A waiter walked up just then to collect their empty champagne flutes, but they both declined another drink. Instead, they wandered closer to the orchestra, which was playing a Viennese waltz.

As they paused to listen, Noelle felt several curious gazes on her and Jim. They hadn't spoken to anyone since their arrival, and even though nobody had approached them when they'd been making their hors d'oeuvres rounds, now that they were standing in one place they had big fat targets on their heads.

She wasn't wrong—as if on cue, two couples who had been chatting about ten feet away were starting to make their way over.

Noelle quickly touched Jim's arm. "Let's dance."

"I don't like to dance," he grumbled.

"I don't care. We're about to have some company, and trust me, neither one of us wants to get drawn into a conversation about a pharmaceutical empire we know nothing about."

Jim nodded in resignation. "Fine."

They swiftly moved toward the center of the room, where only a few other couples had decided to make use of the dance floor. Noelle and Jim joined them just as the tempo changed into an even slower waltz.

Reluctance creased Jim's forehead as he roughly placed his hand at the small of her back, so low he was almost touching her ass. "I fucking hate the waltz," he muttered.

Fighting a grin, Noelle corrected his pose by shifting his hand higher up her back, then rested one hand on his shoulder and tucked her other one into his. When another grumbling sound left his lips, her grin finally breached the surface, because there was truly nothing she enjoyed more than seeing Jim Morgan out of his element. He fit that tux to perfection, moved with grace you wouldn't expect from a man so big, and yet despite all that, she'd never seen him look more uncomfortable.

"I think I'm going to lick your pussy when we get back to your place."

The raspy declaration caught her by complete surprise, which, she realized, was exactly what he'd intended.

As her pulse raced and her sex clenched, she stared into

his eyes and was unprepared for the sensual glint she saw in them. He no longer looked ill at ease, but confident as hell, and incredibly arrogant.

"What do you think about that?" he murmured, dipping his head close to her ear. "You think I should?"

She recovered from her shock and smiled sweetly. "Only if you've been working on your technique. I remember you weren't very good at it."

"Bullshit." His white teeth gleamed in a wicked smile. "I always knew how to make you scream. There was this one spot—I'd flick my tongue over it, and you'd come all over my face. Remember that?"

Then he spun her around and led her around the floor in a carefree waltz, acting as if he hadn't just sent her arousal levels soaring right out of the atmosphere.

Bastard.

Noelle clenched her teeth and tried to focus on not tripping or stepping on his feet. But it was hard. She was so wet her thighs were actually slippery and sticking to each other, and she had to curse herself for not wearing panties tonight. She'd wanted to avoid panty lines, but now, as desire pooled between her legs, she wished she'd chosen comfort over ego.

She was acutely aware of him as they continued to dance. The pressure of his hand on her back, his heady aftershave, the sexy curve of his lips. His clean-shaven face was almost startling—she was so used to seeing stubble slashing that hard jaw—and his skin was so smooth she was tempted to stroke it and find out if it was as soft as it looked.

She suddenly heard herself speak in a faraway tone. "Remember when I made you dance in the fountain?"

For one brief moment, tenderness softened his eyes before the cocky sparkle returned. "Remember when you sucked me off in the shower that one time? It was the first time you ever swallowed, as I recall."

"It was," she said grudgingly.

Then she inched closer, rotated her hips, and rubbed up against his crotch, but just as his breath caught, she backed off and resumed the waltz.

"You loved every second of it," she added in a throaty voice. "My mouth wrapped around the head of your cock, sucking you dry. You looked real wobbly after that. Could barely stay upright." She proceeded to mimic his casual words. "As I recall."

His eyes went heavy-lidded, his sharp cheekbones taking on a bit of a flush.

"You all right, Jim? Or is all this teasing too much for you?"

She stroked the inside of his palm, and he gave another sharp intake of breath.

"Because you're the one who took us down this path," she reminded him, coyly batting her eyelashes.

"Trust me, I'm beginning to regret it." Sounding rueful, he shot a pointed look at his crotch.

She laughed.

He did too.

As always, the sound was downright astounding. She wasn't used to seeing the rough edges of his face smooth away like that. Or hearing gruff laughter escape his mouth. Scowls and glares were all she'd come to expect from him these days.

"Don't worry. You're a supersoldier, remember?" Her mouth curved mockingly. "I'm sure the army taught you how to dance with a hard-on."

She ground her pelvis into his again, just because she could.

With a tortured noise, Jim lowered his head, his warm breath tickling her earlobe as he murmured one word.

"Cocktease."

Her grin widened. "Hey, it's not my fault you can't enjoy a nice waltz without springing a boner."

"Right, because *you're* not turned on in the slightest."

"Of course I am. I'm just better at ignoring it than you are."

"Uh-huh." He tightened his grip and pulled her against his muscular chest, deliberately brushing his very noticeable erection over her belly. "You can ignore it, huh?"

"Yep."

An evil flash lit his midnight blue eyes. "Interesting. So you're not thinking about my cock inside you at all."

Her pussy spasmed. "Nope."

"Liar."

Fortunately, the orchestra chose that precise moment to end the waltz, bringing a rush of relief to her chest. Except then the bastards proceeded to slow down the tempo even more, effectively wiping away her relief and yet again turning her body into a lightning rod, helpless to stop the heat Jim was channeling into it.

Their dance might have seemed innocent to the people around them, but each brush of their bodies heightened her arousal. Each time his palm grazed her tailbone, her skin sizzled. Each time his cheek brushed hers, her breathing grew more labored.

Still, no matter what Jim thought, she *was* a pro, and thus perfectly capable of suppressing her desire.

Of course, that didn't mean she had to stop testing *his* ability to remain professional.

With a mischievous smile, she looked into his eyes and said, "By the way, the shower blow job you mentioned before? I orgasmed the second I swallowed that first drop."

A strangled growl left his mouth.

And suddenly they weren't dancing anymore. But still moving. Moving very, very fast, in fact, as Jim dragged her toward the staircase on the other side of the ballroom.

Morgan had no idea where he was going or what he was thinking. He ignored the inquisitive eyes boring into his back as he gripped Noelle's hand and led her up the spiral staircase. He didn't know where it led, or where they'd end up—all he knew was that if he didn't get inside this woman right fucking now, he was going to pass out.

"Jim," she said uneasily. "This isn't the time to . . ."

She didn't finish and he didn't care. His lower body was aching, his cock so stiff he could barely walk. He was a man on a mission, his gaze focused straight ahead like a missile homing in on a target.

At the top of the stairs was a small landing opening into a wide hallway with half a dozen doors, but the red velvet curtain to their left was what caught his eye. Gripping Noelle's forearm, he pushed open the thick velvet and immediately liked what he saw—a shadowy space the size of an opera box. No, it *was* an opera box, Morgan noted when he spotted the curved railing at the edge and the row of plush, red-upholstered seats.

He turned to Noelle. "Come here," he ordered.

She stayed put. "I don't take orders from cavemen, thank you very much."

His gaze swept over her. He'd lied before. He was *totally* digging the dress. And the hairdo. The shoes. The vixen-red lipstick. Christ, he wanted to kiss those fuck-me lips more than he wanted his next breath.

"Come. Here," he growled.

"Make me."

Just like that, his control snapped like a bungee cord. Forget breathing—his brain stopped working right along with his lungs, his vision nothing but a thick haze of lust as he grabbed her by the arm and yanked her toward the railing. He spun her around so she was against it, then moved in behind her and ground his aching groin over her ass.

Noelle's moan cut the air, soft enough that he doubted anyone down below had heard it. And if they did, he didn't give a fuck. He'd turned into an animal, a desperate, hungry animal with one thought on his mind.

He scrunched up her dress and shoved the material all the way up to her waist. She was still covered in the front, but naked from the lower back down, and when he glimpsed her bare ass, a groan left his lips.

"Oh Jesus." He stroked her tight buttocks with his palm, then undid the button of his trousers.

Letting out a ragged breath, he reached inside his boxer-briefs and pulled out his granite-hard cock. With Noelle in front of him, he wasn't worried about anyone catching a glimpse of the little soldier, but there was nothing shielding *her*. If anyone in the ballroom so much as craned their neck, they'd get a hell of an eyeful: Noelle bent over the railing, fingers curled over the cool steel, cleavage spilling out of her dress.

Cursing softly, he wrapped his arms around her and drew her backward, repositioning them so they were against the wall, several feet back and out of view of any guests.

The second he rubbed the head of his cock along the crease of her ass cheeks, she gasped in pleasure. "Oh God. *Please*."

The quiet plea was enough to make him shudder.

Holding her dress up with one hand, he gripped her hip with the other and drove into her from behind.

Fuuuuuck.

It felt so criminally good he literally saw stars. Heat and moisture surrounded his erection, her inner muscles clamping around him like a hot, pulsing glove. The sexual excitement burning in his blood was stronger than any burst of desire he'd ever felt in his life.

But no, that wasn't true. He'd experienced this same blast of need before. Earlier today, when he'd been balls deep in Noelle. Nineteen years ago, when he'd been buried inside the most beautiful girl in the world.

It was her. It was always *her.*

The realization spurred his emotions, propelled his hips forward. He slammed into her, struggling for breath, desperately trying to hold on to his crumbling restraint. But there was nothing controlled about this.

With Noelle, it was impossible to hold back.

His chin rested on her shoulder as his hips pistoned hard, his cock furiously thrusting into her tight channel, over and over again. Her unique scent drugged his senses, and the fine hairs at the nape of her neck tickled his cheek and made him shiver.

A moan slipped out when his next thrust hit deep. "Oh God," she whispered. "More. Faster."

The tempo went from fast to frantic, as he relinquished all common sense and gave in to raw, primal need. His balls slapped Noelle's perfect ass with each demanding stroke, and he knew from her little mewls of pleasure that she was getting close.

When she threw her head back and trembled in orgasm, it was like stepping into a room engulfed in flames. His heart stopped and his body burned, and triumph blinded his vision, because it was so rare to watch this woman come apart. So rare to hear her throaty cry of surrender and see the sated slump of her delicate shoulders.

"Coming," he ground out. "Oh *fuck.*"

The hot waves of pleasure started deep in his balls and shot out in every direction, turning his limbs to jelly and his mind to mush. His release filled her, dripped down his still-hard shaft, and even as he tried to catch his breath, he reached into his pocket for a black silk handkerchief and hastily cleaned them up before their clothes got ruined.

The climax had been so intense he still saw black spots, still had trouble breathing. With a hoarse groan, he withdrew from her tight sheath and tucked his semierect cock back in his pants. As he zipped up his trousers, the hem of Noelle's dress slipped from his fingers, the silky material floating to the floor with a soft rustle.

"How about now?" Her voice shook slightly as she turned to face him. "Out of your system?"

"No," he said thickly. "You?"

She opened her mouth, but was cut off by a sudden buzz of voices from the ballroom. Frowning, she tucked a strand of hair behind her ear and approached the railing.

Morgan followed her, resting both hands on the steel rail as he gazed below.

He immediately pinpointed the source of commotion. A small crowd had formed near the ice sculpture he'd been admiring earlier, and holding court in the center of the group was a man in a black tuxedo jacket and white dress shirt.

"I think our host is here," he said.

Noelle nodded. "Looks like it."

They watched from the box, but the new arrival was blocked from their view, surrounded by several taller men who didn't seem inclined to move out of the way. Morgan glimpsed a head of dark blond hair, an aristocratic profile, and a flash of straight white teeth, but it wasn't enough.

Annoyance filtered through him. "Let's go downstairs. I can't see shit from here."

No sooner had the words left his mouth than the crowd parted to reveal the center of attention. Maurice Durand. The man was in his late sixties. Medium height, fair complexion, handsome face . . . that *face*.

Morgan couldn't quite place the man, but he knew him. He wasn't sure how, but—*son of a bitch*.

At that moment, Durand turned to speak to someone, offering Morgan a perfect view of his eyes.

He froze, unable to fathom what he was seeing.

Those eyes.

The color of dark roast coffee, deep and intense and completely unsuited for that lily-white skin and light hair.

In his lifetime, Morgan had come across only two people with that particular combination of chocolate eyes and pale skin.

All the air seeped out of his lungs as his brain made the connection.

"Ariana," he breathed.

Chapter 12

One word. Four syllables.

That was all it took for the color to drain from Noelle's face, for her heart to stop midbeat and her knees to buckle. Hearing that name, now, when her body was still exhibiting the lingering effects of her orgasm . . . It was like a splash of icy water to the face. God, she still felt the evidence of her and Jim's coupling sticking to her thighs.

How could he *say* that *goddamn* name?

She gripped the railing to steady herself, while her gaze frantically scanned the crowd below, searching it for a tiny blonde with dark, petulant eyes. She came up empty-handed at every turn.

Ariana wasn't here.

Maybe she'd misheard him and he hadn't spoken Ariana's name at all. Or maybe he'd said it to hurt her. Waited for her to drop her guard, to give in to desire again, only to twist the knife deep by saying the one thing he knew would hurt her the most. Maybe he—*shit.* Her train of thought came to an abrupt standstill as her gaze landed on a familiar face.

Walther Dietrich.

Noelle wasn't taken aback often, but there was no mistaking his face. It was older now, boasting new wrinkles around the mouth and eyes, but aside from that, Dietrich hadn't changed.

Beside her, Jim was frozen in place. Blue eyes glued to Dietrich, his face pale and stricken.

In all the years she'd known him, this was the first time she'd seen Jim Morgan look . . . powerless. Honest-to-God powerless, as if he had no answers, no master plan, no idea what to do next. He remained paralyzed with shock, prompting Noelle to snap into action.

She grabbed his arm and forcibly moved him away from the railing, using her other hand to fish her phone out of her clutch.

"Frédéric," she snapped once her driver answered. "Bring the car around. Now."

Her command snapped Jim out of his trance. "What are you doing?" he demanded.

"We have to go."

The color slowly returned to his face. He blinked wildly, as if still trying to make sense of what he'd seen. "Are you kidding me? We can't go! Didn't you see him? That's Walther fucking Dietrich down there!"

The desperation flashing in his eyes brought a rush of bitterness to her throat. She swallowed through the acidic burn and fixed him with a grave look.

"We have to go," she repeated. "We're not equipped to deal with this right now. What if he recognizes you?"

His cheeks hollowed in dismay. "We can't leave. What if she's here? Ariana . . . What if she's here in this house?"

A wave of fury crested inside her, so strong she nearly launched her fist into his jaw. Goddamn him. *Goddamn* him. How could he even say that?

"I don't give a shit if she's here," Noelle hissed out. "If Dietrich sees either one of us, we could both lose our lives. If you want to die tonight, then by all means, stay. But I'm getting the hell out of here."

She bulldozed past him, flinging aside the velvet curtain and stumbling into the brightly lit corridor. It took every ounce of willpower not to pick up the antique brass candelabra on a nearby Louis XV–era credenza to hurl it into the wall. The rage she'd been harboring for so many years had bubbled to the surface, threatening to blaze everything in its path, but somehow she managed to tamp it down. She needed to keep a clear head.

She halted at the top of the stairs, realizing she couldn't risk going back to the ballroom. No, she had to find another way out of the mansion, an escape route that wouldn't place her in Dietrich's path.

Walther Dietrich. Here, in Paris. She still couldn't wrap her head around it.

But she forced herself to banish the slew of questions that arose. She didn't have time to think about what had happened between her, Jim, and Dietrich all those years ago. She didn't have time to dwell on that moment that had made Jim Morgan hate her as much as she hated him. She just had to get out of this house unseen. End of story.

Drawing an even breath, Noelle headed in the other direction, marching past closed doors and walls adorned with more expensive artwork. She'd just discovered a second staircase at the end of the corridor when she sensed Jim's presence.

Setting her jaw, she turned her head and said, "Finally saw reason, huh?"

His jaw was equally tight, twitching from the rigid posture. "Let's go. We can't afford to be seen."

"No shit, Sherlock."

They didn't speak as they descended the stairs. Noelle took the lead, not trusting Jim to follow through on the exit plan. If that bitch Ariana popped out during their escape, she had no doubt Jim would freeze again, and that only enraged her further.

At the bottom of the stairs they found themselves in another hallway, this one with bare walls and tiled flooring instead of marble. Most likely part of the servants' quarters, which meant there had to be a service exit nearby. A flurry of voices drifted out of an open doorway up ahead. The kitchen, Noelle realized, as a medley of mouthwatering aromas floated in their direction.

"Quick," she murmured.

They bypassed the kitchen with lightning speed, and suddenly they were in another hallway. A narrower one, without a single door on either side. Jesus. The house was a damn maze.

Fighting a burst of frustration, she hurried to the end of the hall, took a right, and wound up in a new corridor that contained a wall of rear-facing windows.

She peered out, taking a moment to orient herself. She

glimpsed the hedge maze to the left, a rectangle-shaped swimming pool to the right, each landmark bordered by the beautiful gardens that surrounded the mansion.

"There should be a way out over there." She took off in a brisk walk, turned another corner, and breathed in relief.

The enormous sunroom they'd stumbled into offered comfortable-looking wicker chairs, an endless amount of leafy green plants, and French doors that led outside.

Neither of them said a word as they exited through the doors. Noelle felt Jim's warm breath on the back of her neck, heard his unsteady exhales, but she didn't glance over her shoulder. She didn't want to see his expression.

She was worried it could actually cause her to kill him.

They emerged onto a stone patio. The sweet fragrance of the garden filled Noelle's nostrils, but she didn't take the time to admire the scenery. She stepped onto the cobble-stone path winding through the property and followed it to the edge of the house, her hand instinctively moving to her thigh as they crept along the exterior wall toward the front of the mansion. She paused to peer around the corner, ready to go for her knife if she had to, but the circular drive-way was deserted.

Except for her Town Car waiting near the arched entryway.

"Come on," she muttered to Jim.

She didn't turn to check whether he was following her. Frankly, she didn't give a shit if he was. All she knew was that she had to get out of here, and her self-preservation mattered more to her than Jim Morgan's emotional state.

Ten feet from the car, she risked a glance at the front entrance, and spotted the same tuxedo-clad attendant who'd granted them entry before. He had company now, in the form of a tall, blond man who looked vaguely familiar. Noelle couldn't place him, and she didn't stick around to try.

Keeping her gait as casual as possible, she headed for the Town Car and opened the back door before Frédéric could come out to do it for her.

"Get in," she said when Jim appeared beside her.

He had the nerve to hesitate, so she swallowed a curse and nudged him into the car. She'd just slid in after him when the blond man by the door took a distrustful step forward.

Their eyes locked for one brief moment, and the last

thing Noelle saw before she slammed the door shut was the deep frown creasing his mouth.

A second later, Frédéric stepped on the gas and sped off, leaving the blond stranger and the Durand estate in their proverbial dust.

The moment they drove through the gate, Noelle allowed herself to relax, but her breathing remained unsteady, thanks to the emotions clogging her chest.

Beside her, Jim wore a vacant expression and his broad shoulders were slumped over. He hadn't uttered a word since they'd fled the house, but now those dark blue eyes focused on her.

"Seventeen years," he said dully. "I've been searching for her for seventeen years."

The confession stabbed Noelle like a knife to the heart. She'd known he was still looking for Ariana, but hearing him say it out loud ...

She clenched her teeth and gazed out the tinted window, watching the countryside whiz by as Frédéric delivered them to safety.

Ariana Dietrich. Jim had been searching for that spoiled, awful girl for seventeen years.

It shouldn't hurt this bad, but God, it did. Knowing that he'd loved Ariana *that* much, that he'd invested so much time in his search ... It ripped Noelle apart.

And that, right there, encapsulated her entire history with the man sitting beside her. Ripping her apart—it was what he always did. He'd ravaged her heart. He'd ruined her life, stolen the only person who'd ever given a damn about her. He'd made her believe he truly loved her, and then he'd snatched that love away, leaving her broken and alone.

He'd used her. Discarded her like a piece of garbage. Destroyed her.

She'd thought he was the man of her dreams, only to find out that he'd faked their entire romance. And then, two years later, he'd done the same damn thing to another unsuspecting female.

At least that was what Noelle had thought. But what do you know—turned out she was wrong. Yep, because although he'd pretended to love the young and foolish Noelle Phillips, he hadn't been pretending with Ariana Dietrich.

The symbolic knife in her chest twisted harder, causing her fingers to tighten over the very real one strapped to her thigh. It wouldn't take much to slide her hand beneath her dress and unsheathe the blade. She could end it now. Shove the deadly tip directly into his carotid artery. Be done with him forever.

But her hand stayed put.

It was a long and agonizing drive back to the city. When they finally got to her town house, Noelle was out of the car before it even came to a complete stop. She had to get away from Jim. Had to collect her thoughts, control the dangerous emotions running through her. If she didn't get a handle on herself and these impulsive urges, she might do something she'd regret, and for a woman who prided herself on self-control, her current state just pissed her off more.

"Noelle." Jim's gruff voice sounded from behind her.

She'd just reached the elevator on the other side of the cavernous garage, but she forced herself to look over at him. "I want you gone. Right now."

He frowned.

Her hands began to shake again. She spun around, jammed a finger on the elevator button, and kept her back to him.

"You have no reason to be here anymore," she said stiffly. "You know who wants to kill you now, and it's not much of a stretch to figure out why. So get back in the car and tell Frédéric where you want to go. I'll have your things delivered to you."

Rather than heed her order, he followed her into the elevator.

Uncharacteristic panic clawed at her throat. "I mean it. You need to go."

"I'm not going anywhere."

The moment of weakness he'd succumbed to earlier had vanished. His face was no longer slack with shock, but hard with fortitude. And his voice was steady again, ringing with determination.

Noelle slowly met his eyes, not bothering to mask her expression. Let him see her anger. Her pain. She didn't give a fuck.

"I'm not helping you find that woman. Do you understand?"

"You owe me."

A harsh laugh flew out, tainting the air between them. "You really are a heartless son of a bitch, aren't you? Do you actually think I'm going to stand around and watch you reunite with the love of your life? Do you expect me to applaud and hold the train of her fucking wedding gown as you whisk her down the aisle? Fuck you, Jim. Fuck. You."

"You owe me," he repeated. "You're the reason she disappeared in the first place."

Fists of disbelief pounded into her, and her breathing went shallow as she tried to collect the splintered fragments of her composure and dignity. Her eyes stung, and she was horrified to realize she was close to tears.

"You deserve to rot in hell," she spat out.

Perfect timing—the doors slid open and Noelle stumbled out of the elevator. Her wobbly legs miraculously carried her to the living room bar. Her numb fingers managed to pour some brandy without spilling it all over the carpet.

She drank the entire contents of the glass in one desperate gulp, and the alcohol seared her throat and joined the volatile emotions churning in her gut.

Jim entered the room and approached the bar, where he poured himself a drink of his own. As she watched him, she suddenly felt like vomiting, her stomach revolting against the copious amounts of alcohol she'd dumped into it.

Beside her, Jim sipped his drink, staring at her with an impenetrable expression. He didn't say a word.

Noelle's legs still felt weak, so she kicked off her heels and staggered to the sofa. She sat down and took a deep breath, trying to ignore the dull ache in her heart.

Her heart. God, she was surprised to discover she even still had one, and that it was still capable of aching this way. She'd hardened after Jim's betrayal, closed herself off to the world and refused to let herself feel a damn thing. But a few days in Jim's company, and he'd turned her back into the emotional young girl he'd seduced and destroyed all those years ago.

"Do you realize how humiliating it was?" she whispered. "To find out you were searching for her, so many years later? Searching for *her*, when you never gave *me* a second thought? And then to act like *I* did something wrong? You were using her, damn it! The same way you used me!" Her throat closed up, making it difficult to go on. "She was young and naive, just like I was. And you were fucking her to get to her father, just like you did to me."

Jim let out a breath. "I was on a government-sanctioned mission, Noelle. Dietrich was stealing military weapons and putting them in the hands of our enemies. Someone needed to take him down. Same way someone needed to take down your fa—"

"Don't you dare talk about him!" she roared.

She shot to her feet and advanced on him like a rabid animal. Her fists throbbed with the urge to pummel him, but she stopped herself from acting on the violent impulse. Instead she kept two feet of space between them as she glared at him in accusation.

"You are not allowed to talk about my father," she said viciously. "He was *nothing* like Dietrich!"

"And Ariana was nothing like you."

His quiet response was like a shotgun blast to the chest. She swayed on her feet, hot pellets of agony embedding into her flesh and burning her eyes.

"You don't have to remind me," she muttered.

"What I mean is—"

"I know what you fucking mean!"

She was beginning to come undone. God, it was hard to breathe. Her entire body was colder than a glacier. She was suddenly transported back to that rainy night in Berlin, when she'd looked across the crowded restaurant and spotted none other than James Morgan enjoying a candlelit dinner with a beautiful blonde.

It had been two years since he'd waltzed into her life and left it in shambles. She was about to turn twenty, and was working her very first solo mission. She'd changed after Jim's betrayal, adopted a cold and ruthless mentality that made her the perfect candidate for covert operations, and the French government had wasted no time in recruiting her for an elite intelligence unit, three days after she'd graduated high school.

Jim had been the last person she'd expected to see that night.

And then, to discover he was running the same con on another gullible girl? Noelle had been livid. Horrified. She'd jeopardized her own unrelated operation to conduct reconnaissance on Jim and Ariana, and when she'd witnessed how smitten the girl was with him, she'd been sick to her stomach.

She'd known right then and there that she couldn't let Jim get away with it again.

"She could have been killed that night." His tone was thick with disapproval. "In fact, your actions got three of my teammates killed, not to mention four members of Dietrich's household staff."

"Blame me all you want, but it never would have worked out with that girl, Jim. You were lying to her, same way you lied to me, and even if you reunite with her now, I get the pleasure of knowing you won't live to see a happily-ever-after with the little bitch. Her father will kill you long before that happens."

"Noelle . . ." A warning note crept into his voice.

"Now, I'm going to change out of this dress, get in the shower, and wash all traces of you off my body," she told him, finally feeling calm and centered again. "Please don't be here when I come back out." Noelle paused. "And just in case it's not clear enough? Our little cease-fire is officially over."

"What do you mean, he was in this house?" Dietrich was practically foaming at the mouth as he followed Nikolaus down the short flight of stairs toward the security room.

Nik's jaw was so tight he couldn't even unhinge it to answer, and his mind was only capable of formulating one thought.

James Morgan had been here tonight.

If he hadn't seen the man with his own eyes, he wouldn't have believed it. But Nik never forgot a face, and especially not the face of the man who'd stolen everything from him.

He couldn't even remember what he'd been talking to Henri about—all he remembered was stopping midsentence as a well-dressed couple appeared from nowhere and he'd come face-to-face with his old enemy. In that bone-chilling moment, he'd been too dumbfounded to act, but now that the shock had passed, he was finally able to think clearly again.

He and Dietrich marched into the large sunken room that housed the bank of security monitors that documented every inch of the property. Thierry, their head of security, glanced up from his seat, surprise filling his angular features. There was a half-eaten sandwich in front of him, next to a cup of coffee with steam rising from the rim.

"Monsieur Durand!" Thierry straightened up, quickly wiping the corner of his mouth with a paper napkin. "What can I do for you?"

Nik answered for his boss. "Bring up the exterior feed, Thierry. We need the front door camera. Play it back to approximately ten minutes ago."

The stocky man wasted no time following the command. His thick fingers flew across the keyboard with proficiency. A moment later, sped-up images whizzed by on one of the monitors as he attempted to access the correct time stamp.

Nik studied the screen. "Go back further ... Keep going ... Keep going—there! Freeze right there."

Thierry pressed a button and the monitor froze.

Both Nik and Dietrich leaned in for a better look. It was no mistake. Nik hadn't imagined it.

There he was, in perfect color, right there on the screen. James Morgan.

Dietrich's mouth twisted in a grimace. "Please give us a moment, Thierry," he said brusquely.

The man practically dove off his chair. "Of course, sir."

Once the door closed behind him, Dietrich shot Nik a cold look. "How is this possible? How did he get in?"

"I don't know." Grinding his teeth, he clicked his earpiece and addressed the man they'd entrusted with front door security. "Henri, please join me in the security booth."

Then he turned his attention back to Dietrich. "He must have finally tracked you down," Nik said flatly. "We know he's been searching for you. He came damn close in Pakistan last year."

Which was how they'd learned James Morgan's true

identity in the first place. They'd been negotiating a deal with the leader of an Al-Qaeda faction, but doing business with the Middle East was a delicate matter, so they were forced to meet the buyer in person. The deal had gone through, but afterward, a contact had informed Nik that a man had been asking around in Islamabad about Walther Dietrich.

His internal alarm system had immediately been triggered. Though it had taken many months and many dead ends, they'd followed the trail right to the nosy man who'd been asking too many questions.

Nik had been stunned to discover it was none other than James Morgan, aka James Hathaway, the name he'd used in Berlin all those years ago.

Morgan must have been keeping tabs on major arms deals throughout the world in order to track Nik and Dietrich, and once again, the bastard had decided to grace them with his presence.

Except this time, Nik would welcome him with open arms.

So he could kill him.

"And now he's in Paris, which means we're one step closer to eliminating him," Nik said. He could practically taste the victory on his lips.

Dietrich looked at the screen again and studied Morgan's companion. "Do you recognize the blonde?"

Nik studied her exquisite face, but he'd never seen her before. "No. Maybe she's his latest victim."

The fury that flashed in the older man's eyes matched the same burn in Nik's stomach. Neither one had a chance to voice their anger, because Henri chose that moment to obediently enter the room.

"Is everything all right?" he said timidly

Nik gestured to the screen. "Please come and look at this, Henri."

The big man approached the monitors, his wary gaze flicking to the screen Nik had pointed to.

"Did you let these people into the party tonight?"

After a beat, the man nodded. "I did." He paused, appearing defensive now. "The woman was on the list. Eloise Lambert."

"And the man?"

"He was her guest. Listed as her significant other, Monsieur Pariseau."

Nik nodded, then dismissed the man. "That will be all, Henri. Thank you."

Once they were alone again, Dietrich's nostrils flared. "That's not Éloise Lambert," he said curtly.

"He must have hired a woman to impersonate Lambert so he could gain access to the estate."

"To kill me?"

"I don't think so." Nik frowned. "I believe this was a reconnaissance mission. If he'd been certain about your identity, he wouldn't have put up a charade. I think he was fishing."

"Well, he must know the truth now," Dietrich snapped. "We need to kill the bastard before he comes after us. Before he comes after *her*."

Panic squeezed Nik's chest. No. *No*. James Morgan could not get anywhere near Ariana.

He'd die before he let that happen.

"You need to contact Girard," Nik told his boss. "The assassin he hired is taking too long."

"She still has two days to complete the job."

"Two days is plenty of time for Morgan to make his move. He needs to be terminated now."

Normally he wouldn't dream of questioning Dietrich's orders—he'd seen other men die for slights much less trivial than insolence—but for once, Walther didn't seem to mind being challenged. If anything, he looked more worried than offended.

Nik spoke again, his tone brooking no argument as he met Dietrich's dark eyes. "Tell Girard that the assassin no longer has exclusive claim to the target. The hit goes on the open market. Tonight."

Chapter 13

Seventeen years ago

They sat in the front seat of the unmarked black sedan, headlights off and car in park. The sun had set hours ago, and the moon was hidden behind a cluster of gray clouds, casting shadows on the residential street. They were in the wealthy neighborhood where the Dietrich estate was located—very risky, meeting so close to the target's home, but it was getting harder and harder for Morgan to sneak off. Ariana refused to let him out of her sight, which made checking in with his CO a difficult task.

In the driver's seat, Commander Jeremy Thomas didn't look thrilled by Morgan's report. "We need a goddamn name, Jim."

Frustration rose in his throat. "I know that, but Dietrich is a tough nut to crack. And he doesn't fully trust me yet. He won't reveal the mole's identity until I prove to him that I'm serious about joining his organization."

The other man frowned. "Even if you run some jobs for him, do you think he'll ever really give up the mole?"

Morgan paused to think it over. "I don't know," he admitted. "But we have enough dirt on him to make an arrest. If our guys at ATF bust him, maybe he can be persuaded to give up his military source in exchange for a reduced sentence."

"I doubt the bastard will talk, and arresting him now

would be a risk. We *need* that name. Whoever's helping him steal our country's weapons is as big a threat as Dietrich himself. The traitor needs to be located and eliminated." Jeremy pursed his lips. "Dietrich did say it was someone in Special Operations, high up on the food chain."

Morgan nodded.

"You sure the girl doesn't know anything?"

His chest clenched with discomfort. He hadn't told his CO about Ariana yet, and he'd spent the past two weeks working the various scenarios over in his head, the possible outcomes he'd face once he confessed everything. So far, he hadn't come up with a single one that would result in keeping Ariana in his life.

But he knew it was time to bring his CO into the loop. Things with Dietrich were heating up, and if he wanted to arrange protection for Ariana, it needed to be done now.

"Jeremy . . ." He cleared his throat. "It's time we talked about Ariana. I—"

The radio on Jeremy's belt crackled, cutting Morgan off.

"We've got movement at the house," a male voice reported. It was Sergeant Joe Rogers, one of the intelligence officers posted on the perimeter surrounding the Dietrich estate. "Looks like they're taking a trip."

Morgan's brows knitted together. What the hell was Rogers talking about? Morgan had been gone only twenty minutes, under the guise that he was going for a run. When he'd left the house, Ariana had been in bed and Walther was reading in his study; neither one of them had mentioned a trip.

"Staff is carrying suitcases out to the car," Rogers went on. "I just checked in with Kowalski—he says there's activity in Geronimo's private hangar at the airport."

Geronimo was the code name assigned to Dietrich, and the reports coming in brought a spark of worry to Morgan's gut.

"Sir, Kowalski here," a new voice blared out of the radio. "Geronimo's pilot just filed a flight plan—the jet's heading for Paris in an hour."

The worry transformed into full-blown panic. "Something's wrong," Morgan muttered. "Ariana would have told me if they were going somewhere."

"They're making a run for it," Jeremy said flatly.

"Why? What the hell happened to spook them?"

"Obviously your cover's been blown." His CO swiftly clicked the radio and brought it to his lips. "Rogers, you and the team need to move in—now. Your orders are to apprehend Geronimo—"

"Sir!" Morgan cut in as another jolt of panic shot through him. "We're not prepared for this. We can't—"

Rogers's brisk voice interrupted his protests. "Orders if the target engages?"

Jeremy didn't even hesitate. "You do what you need to do to protect yourself. But the goal is apprehension, not termination."

"Copy that."

"We're on our way." Jeremy was already starting the engine.

"No," Morgan blurted out, grabbing the gearshift before his CO could move it. "Call them off, sir. Let me take care of this." His breathing went shallow. "Let me get her out first."

"There's no time, Jim. If Dietrich gets in that car and makes it to the airport, we'll never see the bastard again." With a hard look, Jeremy yanked on the gearshift and slammed his foot on the gas.

The car lurched forward in a squeal of tires, the speedy pace matching the uncontrollable beating of Morgan's heart. He didn't know what had provoked Dietrich to flee, but nothing good could come of this.

Goddamn it, Ariana, why didn't you tell me?

The galloping of his pulse made it difficult to hear his own thoughts. As the car hurtled through the dark streets toward Dietrich's mansion, Morgan battled wave after wave of anxiety. He wanted to grab the radio and order Rogers and the team to stand down, but he knew they wouldn't listen to him if he did. Jeremy was in charge. Jeremy had ordered an ambush—and there was absolutely nothing Morgan could do to stop it.

They'd just reached the turn for Dietrich's street when he heard the gunshots.

His heart plummeted to the pit of his stomach, hand frantically reaching for the door handle. He flew out of the car before it even came to a stop, sliding his gun out of his waistband as he sprinted toward the massive iron gates blocking the mansion from the road.

A moment later, he encountered sheer and total chaos. Rapid gunfire echoed from the courtyard, and the air was thick with smoke. The team must have thrown smoke canisters to mask their approach, but Dietrich and his people hadn't been fooled.

Morgan's ears were ringing, his heart pounding, his hands shaking as he stealthily moved through the smoke. Something hot whizzed by his ear. A bullet. He flattened himself against the stone wall on one side of the gate, squinting at the thick gray haze obstructing his vision. He couldn't see a goddamn thing.

A small explosion several yards ahead of him suddenly shook the ground beneath his running shoes. Unconcerned with his own safety, Morgan continued forward. Half a dozen steps and he almost tripped over a crumpled body on the pavement. He flew to his knees, peering at the lifeless face, and cursed when he realized it was Jansen, one of his fellow soldiers.

Another round of gunfire deafened the air. Morgan kept moving, gripping his gun with two hands as he pushed forward. He didn't know where the rest of the team was, where Jeremy was, where *anyone* was. And he didn't care. All he cared about was finding Ariana.

Christ, he had to make sure she was safe.

Morgan took another step, then another—then flew through the air as a second explosion rocked the yard.

He landed on his back. Hard. As his head bounced off the asphalt, his vision became a sea of black and gray.

He must have passed out, because when his eyes opened again, he was no longer on the ground, but propped up against something solid. He blinked, realizing he was on the street and sitting against the property's outer wall. Blinked again, and noticed the flashing red-and-blue lights all around him. The various law enforcement and military vehicles. Black body bags being rolled toward the waiting coroner's van.

"Ariana!" Morgan shot to his feet, only to sway wildly as a rush of dizziness overtook him.

"Sit the fuck back down," came a sharp voice. "You've probably got a concussion."

As the dots in front of his eyes faded, the image of Jeremy's face came into focus. Morgan's CO looked livid as hell as he stalked toward him.

"Dietrich?" Morgan managed to croak.

"Gone." The CO's jaw hardened to stone. "No sign of him or the girl. Somehow they slipped through the perimeter."

Instantaneous relief flooded Morgan's chest at the knowledge that Ariana had survived. Followed by bone-crushing fear when he registered that she and Walther had gotten away.

He swallowed and met Jeremy's eyes. "Casualties?"

"Three of ours, four of theirs." The other man ran a hand through his dark buzz cut. "Heads are going to roll for this. My superiors are already demanding to know what the hell went down tonight."

"We weren't ready," Morgan mumbled.

"No shit," his CO snapped. "But we didn't have a choice. Dietrich was making a run for it."

"We don't know that for sure."

"Yes, we do. Confirmation came in when you were unconscious," Jeremy said grimly. "Dietrich made about a dozen wire transfers earlier today—most of his accounts have been drained. His jet was on standby, but he also booked several flights on various commercial airlines, probably to throw us off track. Since his plane is still at the hangar, we have to assume he and the girl have other means of transportation. Probably traveling under fake passports too."

The girl. Ariana.

Morgan suddenly felt sick. "We have to find her."

"She's not a priority. Our only objective is to apprehend Dietrich."

His CO's casual dismissal of Ariana brought a lump of bile to his throat. No, the US military didn't give a shit about Ariana. Neither did law enforcement. They would use all their resources to track Dietrich, but Ariana wouldn't even be a blip on their radar. She wasn't involved in the family business, nor was she privy to the details of it, which meant she was useless in the eyes of the intelligence community.

To Morgan, she was the *only* priority. Fuck Dietrich. Fuck the mole and the nukes and the whole goddamn mission.

He needed to find her.

"Commander!" One of the officers on the scene signaled for Jeremy to come over.

"Sit down, Jim," Jeremy ordered. "I'll send one of the paramedics to check you over."

Once he was alone, Morgan didn't do as instructed—rather than sit, he wandered farther away from the commotion, all the way to the stop sign at the end of the road. He needed to think, damn it. Needed to come up with a plan.

Walther and Ariana couldn't have gotten far. They were probably still in the city, making arrangements to skip town. If he could just tap a few contacts, maybe he'd be able to find them before they—

"Hello, Jim."

The female voice sliced through his chaotic thoughts.

His hand snapped for his gun just as a petite blonde emerged from the shadows of the driveway behind him. He spun around, weapon drawn, then staggered backward as if he'd been shot by a cannonball.

"Noelle?" His voice sounded weak and shaky to his ears.

"Long time," she said lightly.

Morgan stared at her. Shocked. Confused.

But not shocked and confused enough to stop the streak of joy that rippled through him.

Oh Lord, he'd waited so long for this. To see her again. To hear her voice. She'd be twenty now, he realized. And she was as beautiful as ever.

His gaze got lost in the sight of her. Big blue eyes and golden hair, perfect features and plump, red lips. He'd envisioned this reunion so many times before, practiced what he'd say when he saw her again, but now that it was finally happening, he couldn't do anything but stand there and stare.

It didn't take long for his awe to fade into wariness. Because now he was noticing other things. Like the hard line of her mouth. Her skintight black clothing. The smug satisfaction in her eyes.

"What are you doing here?" he said hoarsely.

Her lips curved in a smile. "Evening the score."

The cryptic response triggered another bout of confusion. He blinked rapidly, trying to ignore the pounding in his temples. Maybe he *did* have a concussion. Maybe he was hallucinating this entire encounter.

But no. This wasn't a hallucination. Noelle was actually here. The girl he'd desperately loved was right here in front of him.

Except . . . this wasn't Noelle, or at least not the one he remembered, and as her words registered in his head, suspicion snaked its way around his spine.

"What did you do?" he said slowly.

In a deliberate move, she cocked her head in the direction of the carnage he'd just left.

Horror slammed into him. "It was you?"

She simply arched a brow.

"Oh fuck. It was you," he mumbled. His head started spinning. "You tipped them off."

"She deserved to know what you were doing to her." Noelle's tone stayed calm and even, her expression without remorse.

Morgan felt like he'd been punched in the gut. His entire body trembled with anger, which only grew as the seconds ticked by. Ariana was gone. He might never see her again.

And it was all because of Noelle.

"You . . ." White-hot fury burned a path up his throat. "You don't know what you've done."

"Oh, I know *exactly* what I've done." Noelle smiled. "So. How does it feel, Jim? How does it feel to have the most important person in your life stolen away from you?"

His hands tingled wildly—every part of him wanted to wrap them around her throat and squeeze. His body was on fire, devoured by hot flames of rage until his vision became a mist of red.

"You have no goddamn idea what you've done," he hissed out. "I'm going to kill you for this."

"I'd like to see you try." She inched closer, and he flinched when she ran a cold hand over his stiff jaw. "I'm not the weak, naive girl you knew in Paris, honey. I can tear you apart now."

You already have.

His throat closed up to the point of pain. Hatred, stronger than anything he'd ever felt in his life, began to form in his gut. Fierce and volatile.

"Oh, and Jim?" Her evil smile widened. "Taking away the love of your life was the appetizer." She lightly stroked his bottom lip. "I'm just getting started, honey."

He was too enraged to move. To talk. To breathe.

In the blink of an eye, Noelle was gone. Vanished as if she hadn't even been there.

Morgan's gun dangled loosely in his hand, but he couldn't find the strength to raise it. To fire a shot in the direction she'd disappeared in.

Noelle had done this to him. She'd tipped off Dietrich and now he might never see Ariana again. He might never know if—nausea promptly seized his throat, cutting off the terrifying thoughts.

Morgan breathed through it. Ignored the sick feeling in his stomach and the throbbing of his temples and the agony shredding his heart to pieces. Instead he focused on the rage, the need to punish the person responsible for his torment.

He would make her pay for this.

Goddamn it, he would make her *pay*.

Chapter 14

Present day

Morgan paced the guest room as he waited for Sean Reilly to return his call. He'd put in an urgent request to the information dealer nearly two hours ago, and if the son of a bitch didn't get back to him soon, he was going to flip the fuck out. The longer he waited, the greater the chance that Noelle would storm in and kick him out of the town house by force.

Or maybe she'd put a bullet in his head. He supposed it depended on how furious she still was.

But Noelle would just have to suck it up and deal with his presence a little while longer, because he wasn't going anywhere until he got some answers to his questions.

The most pressing one being: Why the hell was Walther Dietrich in Paris?

He still couldn't wrap his brain around it. He'd been hunting Dietrich for almost two decades with zero results, and then, when he wasn't even looking, the man appeared in front of him like the fucking Ghost of Christmas Past.

Dietrich must have rebuilt his empire during his long absence from society. Clearly he was living under an assumed name these days—Maurice Durand, owner of a billion-dollar pharmaceutical company. But was the legitimate businessman thing a cover? It had to be. The Dietrich that Morgan had known was a ruthless criminal, an arms dealer who wasn't above selling guns to warlords or getting his hands dirty when he needed to. Morgan's elite intelligence unit had been assigned to the man after Dietrich had managed to plant a mole inside US Special Operations and stolen American warheads to arm rival governments.

There was no doubt in Morgan's mind that Dietrich was still dealing weapons, but he hadn't heard a peep about Maurice Durand in association with the arms game.

Fortunately, his phone rang before his brain imploded from all the questions and doubts running through it.

He picked up instantly, answering not with a hello, but with a brisk, "Well?"

"Hello to you too, Morgan," came Sean Reilly's Irish brogue. "You really are an ornery bastard, eh?"

"What did you find out about Durand?" he demanded.

"Not much. Which says a lot, actually."

Morgan settled on the edge of the bed and drummed his fingers against his thigh. "If you don't fucking elaborate in the next five seconds, I'm going to fly to Dublin and beat the shit out of you."

"Such violence! And to think, I actually wanted to come work for you, asshole."

Right. Morgan had forgotten about that. Trevor Callaghan had told him last week that Reilly had expressed interest in potentially coming on board, but he'd had other issues on his plate at the time. And although he knew he had to replace Holden eventually, he hadn't wanted to accept that one of his best soldiers—and his oldest friend—was gone for good.

But he didn't have time to think about any of that right now.

"Tell me about Durand," he said impatiently.

"Fine. This is what we know about the guy—he showed up in Paris ten years ago claiming to be the illegitimate son of Louis Durand, a reclusive millionaire from Lyon. Durand Senior rarely ever left his estate, he didn't have any family, but he was notorious for his affairs with the female members of his household staff, so nobody was surprised to hear he'd fathered a child. When the old man died, Durand Junior showed up with his birth certificate and a copy of a DNA test, proving he was the rightful heir. The lawyers didn't question it, those gullible oafs. But you and I both know bogus results could be bought if you just have enough money."

"So Dietrich inherited the old man's money?"

"Why are you so certain Durand and Dietrich are the same man?"

"They are," he said darkly. "Trust me."

"All righty, then. Well, yes, Durand Junior inherited a fortune, but he already had his own to bring to the table. Claimed he got it from investing wisely. Once he got to Paris, he bought out Beaumont Pharmaceuticals, renamed it, and has been growing his empire ever since."

"Anything else?"

"He's a recluse too. Hardly ever leaves his estate, except to pop into company headquarters once or twice a week. He doesn't go out socially, and when he does, he's always alone. Well, not alone—he travels with an army of bodyguards—but he doesn't show up anywhere with a guest."

Morgan swallowed. "No mention of a daughter?"

"None that's on record."

The news was disappointing, but Morgan knew it didn't mean anything. If Dietrich went to such great lengths to stay out of the limelight, then it stood to reason that he'd demand the same of Ariana. God knew that house was big enough to hide a hundred people inside it. Nobody but the staff would have to know she was on the premises, and even then, Dietrich could hide her existence from his employees if he really wanted to.

But why? Why not introduce Ariana as his child? Why keep her hidden?

Because he knows you're trying to find her.

Was that it? Was Dietrich protecting Ariana from the man who'd double-crossed her all those years ago?

It made sense—Walther had always been fiercely protective of his daughter. Ariana had led a sheltered life; she was a spoiled and entitled girl who couldn't survive a day in the world without her daddy.

"Anyway, I'll keep digging," Reilly told him. "I'm trying to get my hands on his birth certificate and find out what he did before he appeared on the scene. I put some calls in to a few contacts in French intelligence."

"Good." Morgan cleared his throat. "Hey, you still want to join the team?"

He got a long pause in response, then, "Why? Are you making me an offer?"

"You want the job, you've got it. But only if you get your ass to Paris ASAP. I need your help on recon."

He didn't typically make rash hiring decisions, but he could definitely use Reilly's help at the moment. He'd call Sullivan and Liam too. God knew they'd be over the frickin' moon—Sully had already left him half a dozen messages demanding to be brought in as backup.

"I'll be on the first flight out." Reilly's voice turned smug. "Boss."

After he'd disconnected the call, Morgan raked both hands through his hair and cursed softly. He'd come to Paris to find out who wanted him dead, but now all of a sudden, the objective had become even more critical.

Ariana was finally within his reach.

His throat tightened as the memory of her face suddenly came to him. Her bottomless dark eyes, always conveying that perpetual gleam of petulance. Lord, he could even hear her haughty voice echoing in his head. Every word she'd said had held that superior undertone. *Mine. Give me. I want it.* She'd decided that everyone in the world lived to serve *her*, and when she wanted something, well, God help anyone who tried to get in her way.

And she'd wanted Morgan from the moment she met him.

Letting out a breath, he rose from the bed and looked around, his gaze taking in the high thread-count sheets, the gleaming antique furniture, and the thick, navy blue drapes. The room gave off an elegant vibe, just like Noelle. But it was also slightly cold.

Just like Noelle.

He stripped off his tuxedo jacket and tossed it on the bed, then rolled up his sleeves and steeled his jaw. Time to get this over with.

When he walked into her bedroom, he found the terrace doors open, and the faint scent of tobacco floated toward him. Noelle was at the railing, her blond hair loose and undulating in the night breeze. She no longer wore her fancy dress, but a pair of black yoga pants and a cornflower blue shirt with billowy sleeves.

Morgan stepped outside, glimpsing the pack of cigarettes on the table next to the door. He swiped a smoke from the pack, lit it, and came up beside her, fixing his gaze on the twinkling cityscape beyond the railing.

"Listen, about Ariana—"

"I won't apologize for warning her," Noelle cut in angrily. "So if that's what you came out here for, you're going to be disappointed."

"I didn't expect an apology."

"Good. Because I'm not sorry." Noelle sounded embittered. "She deserved to know what you were up to. It's not my problem she told her father, and it's certainly not my problem that your team decided to ambush the house." She laughed harshly. "If anything, I'm glad Walther and Ariana made it out. I'm fucking *thrilled* they disappeared off the face of the earth. It means I got to watch you suffer for seventeen years."

Morgan raised his cigarette to his lips, then exhaled in a slow rush. "I never loved her," he said gruffly.

Noelle didn't answer, but he saw her shoulders go rigid.

He repeated himself. "I never loved her."

When she still didn't respond, he groaned in frustration. "That's just what I led you to believe, okay? I wanted to hurt you, so I let you think I loved Ariana. But I didn't." He inhaled a quick drag, then blew out a cloud of smoke. "I hated her. Goddamn it, I hated every second I spent with her."

Noelle finally acknowledged his presence by shooting him a skeptical look. "You hated her," she echoed.

He nodded miserably. "She was a spoiled, nasty woman, completely insufferable. I used to cringe when she walked into the room. I wanted nothing more than to run in the other direction whenever I saw her. I had to force myself to touch her. I forced myself to put on a smile and work the charm, and I hated myself for it. Fuck. I think I hated myself more than I hated her."

His fingers tightened on the railing, breaking his cigarette cleanly in half. The lit cherry fell over the balcony and disappeared on the street below, and he flicked the other half over the rail, feeling tired and glum.

"The first time I slept with her . . ." He swallowed. "It was the only time in my life I actually felt dirty. I felt like a fucking whore."

As he stood there staring at the city lights, the memories continued to haunt him. Kissing Ariana, escorting her to all those pretentious parties, going to her bed at night . . .

He'd pretended he was making love to Noelle.

Yep, he hadn't forgotten that part, either.

Probably the most despicable thing he could've ever done, but it was the only way to get his dick hard. The only way to get through the sex he hadn't wanted to have.

"I thought I could get close to her without taking her to bed," he said bitterly. "I never intended to. But she had other ideas. She wanted me, and she did everything she could to seduce me. It reached the point that if I said no, I'd blow the entire op."

"The things the mighty James Morgan does for his country." Noelle's voice oozed with venom.

Shame trickled down his spine like icy drops of water. "I'm not proud of it, all right? But Dietrich needed to be stopped. He was a threat to our country, and I was sent to Berlin to stop him."

"And what better way to do that than to use his daughter, right? That is your MO, right, Jim?"

"Yes, I used her. I used *you*. Is that what you want to hear?"

She didn't answer.

"Go ahead and criticize me for my tactics. I'm not proud of them either, okay? But I can't change what I did. All I can do is tell you why I did it—to stop Dietrich from putting US nukes in enemy hands. And I can also tell you that I didn't enjoy a second of the time I spent with that girl, Noelle." He repeated himself again, something he knew he'd have to do many, many more times. "I never loved her."

"You keep saying that, but your actions say otherwise. You've spent seventeen years looking for her and you expect me to believe you didn't love her? What do you take me for, an idiot?"

He sighed. "I'm telling you the truth."

"Yeah? Then why?" she challenged. "Why the fuck did you spend half your life searching for Ariana Dietrich if you didn't love her?"

His chest constricted as years of grief and agony came rushing back. The desperation that had pushed him to follow every trail no matter how cold it was. The brick walls he'd slammed into time and time again. The friendships he'd cultivated with soulless criminals in order to be kept informed of any and all developments in the arms trade.

It had been time-consuming and frustrating, but he'd forced himself to keep up the search.

"Why, Jim?" Noelle asked again. "Why did you keep looking?"

His stomach twisted into knots. "Because she was carrying my child."

Chapter 15

"Did you bring it?" Cate couldn't contain her excitement as her longtime friend walked into the room. She actually had to stop herself from rushing up to Gabriel and patting his pockets to see if he'd kept his word.

Gabriel gave an answering laugh in response, and as usual, the deep timbre of his voice startled her for a moment. She'd known him since she was seven years old, and she still remembered how confused she'd been when his voice had changed a few years ago. Suddenly it had become deep, cracking so often that she'd teased him mercilessly about it, but now it never cracked. Now, every time he opened his mouth, Cate was faced with the evidence that Gabriel wasn't a little boy anymore. He was eighteen years old. A *man*.

He'd also grown more than a foot in the past couple years. He towered over her, which meant she had to tip her head back to meet his brown eyes.

"Well?" she demanded.

He hesitated. "Yeah, I brought it."

Cate didn't even try to hide her delight. "Ha, I knew you would! Can I see it?"

With visible reluctance, he reached into his back pocket and extracted a small leather case.

Cate snatched it from his hand before he could argue, and quickly unzipped the case to peek at the rows of small tools strapped inside. A variety of rakes, hooks, tension wrenches—everything she'd been practicing with for the past few weeks.

"My father will kill me if he finds out I gave this to you," Gabriel warned her.

"I promise, nobody will ever know." Cate's finger traced the dimpled tip of a high reach hook, while her stomach continued to flutter with excitement.

As the son of a locksmith, Gabriel had access to all sorts of tools, which was super-convenient because Cate's grandfather would *never* allow her to own a lockpick set. Though in all fairness, most teenage girls didn't have much need for one, so it wasn't like her grandfather was denying her an important human necessity or anything.

Truth was, Cate had always gotten everything she'd ever wanted. The finest clothes, the best tutors, lavish vacations, constant love and attention. Nobody doted on her the way her grandfather did, and she knew with absolute certainty that Maurice Durand would protect her with his dying breath if it came down to it.

But as wonderful as he was, there was one thing he refused to give her—information about her father. He refused to discuss the subject, and after years of asking questions and receiving no answers, Cate had finally decided to take matters into her own hands.

"You're still going along with the plan, right?" She anxiously searched Gabriel's face.

He didn't look thrilled about it, but he nodded. "Yes. But if *Maman* finds out, I'm denying everything. She'll whip my ass if she knows I'm helping you snoop on Mr. Durand."

They were speaking in English, the way they always did when they were discussing something private. Most of the household staff spoke French and German, but very little English, which was a good thing because Cate couldn't risk being overheard, not about something this important.

She knew Gabriel was apprehensive, and she didn't blame him for being scared of his mother. Joséphine Traver ran the kitchen, and the woman terrified most of the people in the house, Cate included. She was a force to be reckoned with. Strict and mule-headed and insistent that her way was not just the right way, but the only way.

Yet despite her steely exterior, Joséphine was warm and

loving. When Cate was young, she and Gabriel used to play in the kitchen while Joséphine cooked, and Gabriel's mother had always been there to listen to Cate's problems or help with schoolwork.

As much as it pained her to admit it, Cate had always felt more comfortable with Gabriel's mother than her own.

"*Maman* can't find out, understand?" Gabriel repeated firmly.

She fought a rush of guilt at the thought of getting Gabriel in trouble, but it was too late to turn back now. "Don't worry. She won't. C'mon, Thierry is already downstairs. I went down there earlier to say hello to him."

"Why would you do that? Now he's going to be suspicious!"

"No, he won't. I say hello to him every morning."

It wasn't a lie—Cate was good friends with their longtime security guard. He had a great sense of humor and she liked talking to him, the same way she enjoyed interacting with the rest of the staff.

Her grandfather wasn't thrilled about the friendships she'd formed with the help, but what else was she supposed to do? She'd been homeschooled her entire life and wasn't allowed to leave the house without her bodyguards, which didn't give her many opportunities to socialize. Who else could she talk to if not the people who worked and lived with them?

Needless to say, her life was unbearably lonely at times. She understood why her grandfather was so overprotective, but although she was willing to follow his lead most of the time, there was one thing she refused to compromise on, and that was the issue of her father.

"You know what to do," she told Gabriel. "Just make sure Thierry doesn't see me on any of the monitors."

He sighed. "I'll do my best."

"I'll come downstairs in five minutes. Go do your thing."

"Yes, sir."

When a faint smile crossed his lips, Cate's heart skipped a beat. He was so handsome that sometimes it got hard to breathe when she was around him. She'd been feeling kind of edgy lately, hot and confused and . . . *Nope, not the time.*

Swallowing hard, Cate gave him a little shove. "Go," she repeated.

He rolled his eyes, then strode out of the room, leaving her to her nervous thoughts.

She had her own suite of rooms in the west wing of the house, complete with a living room, office, bedroom, private bath, and an entire room for a closet, which was full of beautiful clothes she'd never worn. Where would she even wear them? Should she put on a fancy Gucci dress just to go downstairs and have breakfast with her grandfather? Slip into a pair of Manolo Blahnik boots to walk around in the vast gardens surrounding the estate?

No, thank you. Besides, even if she did have a booming social life, fancy clothes weren't really her thing. She only felt comfortable in faded blue jeans and comfy tank tops, while her choice of footwear was either sneakers, or the scuffed-up black combat boots that her grandfather despised. He'd ordered her to throw them out on more than one occasion, but Cate always fought him tooth and nail. She was already living the most sheltered life on the planet—the least he could do was let her keep her darn boots.

Today she was wearing her trademark jeans and tank, but she'd added a flannel shirt to the mix. The shirttails hung down to her butt, effectively covering the lock pick case she'd tucked under her waistband.

She paced the thick carpet, checking her watch every other second. When her allotted five minutes were up, she hurried out the door.

This was it. Her one chance to get the answers she'd been seeking her entire life.

She forced herself to walk casually, praying that she didn't run into anyone. Her grandfather and Nikolaus had already left for the city, a rare occurrence because they didn't go to the office every day like normal people. Maurice Durand had managers and vice presidents to run his company for him, and he usually spent his days on the phone in his study or walking around in the gardens.

As Maurice's assistant, Nik was the only one who seemed to do any actual work, but Cate wasn't exactly sure what he did for her grandfather. He joked that he was a Nik-of-all-trades, taking care of anything that needed taking care of, and she'd never really questioned that.

Truth was, she really liked Nik, who'd been around for as

long as she could remember. He was the one who'd taught her how to ride a bike and sail a boat when they'd been living in Greece. He'd taken her hiking and mountain climbing on a trip to Peru, scuba diving when they'd gone to Australia. Unlike her grandfather, Nik genuinely seemed to appreciate her thirst for adventure.

When Cate reached the first-floor study, she tried not to feel guilty about going behind her grandfather's back. But what other choice did she have? He insisted that her father was dead, yet refused to say anything more on the subject, which was why she was so reluctant to believe it.

Because if her father truly was dead, what was the harm in giving her a few more details? How had he died? What had he done for a living? Maurice didn't want to offer even a sliver of information.

She wasn't sure what she expected to find today. Maybe her father *was* dead—she was fully prepared for that. But that didn't mean she wouldn't be happy with a few more facts. Just learning his name would be good enough for her.

Cate slid the leather kit out of her waistband and spared a nervous glance at the camera mounted in the corner of the ceiling, crossing her fingers that Gabriel was occupying Thierry like he'd promised.

Taking a breath, she removed a tension wrench and a shallow hook from the case. Gabriel had explained that this particular hook worked best on the high-security locks you usually found in Europe, which tended to have smaller, more restrictive keyways. The slender pick with its slack curvature would do the job when a standard short hook was too large for the hole.

She inserted the wrench into the lower part of the keyhole, then placed the hook in the upper part and began feeling for the little pins that kept the cylinder locked in place. She'd been practicing with Gabriel for weeks, but now that her new skill was being put to the test, it was harder than she'd thought.

Cate blew a strand of hair out of her eyes, wishing she'd tied her long hair in a ponytail. As she continued fiddling with the lock, she chewed on the inside of her cheek, willing the job to go faster. One by one, the pins in the lock were lifted by the hook and pushed out of the cylinder. When she thought she had the pins set, she held her breath, then turned the wrench.

Click.

Pride shot through her as the cylinder turned and the door was unlocked. She'd done it. She couldn't believe she'd gotten it on the first try, and she couldn't wait to tell Gabriel.

Without stopping a beat, she retrieved her tools, crept into the study, and quietly closed the door behind her. The room smelled like her grandfather, the familiar scent of leather and cologne filling her nostrils.

Floor-to-ceiling windows covered the back wall, and as Cate neared her grandfather's commanding desk, she caught sight of the garden hedge maze through the glass. Even after ten years of living on the estate, she still hadn't been able to finish that darn maze. Nik constantly tried enticing her to keep at it by hinting about the spectacular treasure she'd find in the center, but patience had never been Cate's strong suit. She usually wandered around blindly for ten minutes, fifteen tops, before she got bored and gave up.

Her grandfather told her that the maze was an exercise in focus and discipline, but she preferred doing things that got her adrenaline pumping.

Cate moved her gaze away from the windows and settled in the big leather chair behind the desk. She tried opening the top desk drawer. To her surprise, it was unlocked. Her grandfather probably didn't feel the need to lock anything inside the room since the locked door kept people out in the first place.

The first drawer contained nothing but office supplies, so she tried the next one and found a leather-bound ledger. She pulled it out, flipped through it, and saw nothing but appointments. The next drawer had a bunch of documents inside it, typed reports about prescription drugs with the most technical-sounding names. The information was so dense and boring that her eyes started to cross.

She shoved the papers back in the drawer, starting to get frustrated. There was no other furniture in the office except for the desk, the bookshelves, and the two armchairs in front of the stone fireplace, so if she didn't find anything in these drawers, she didn't know where else to look for information about her father. She had absolutely nothing to go on. Not even his name.

She reached for the handle of the bottom drawer, but it didn't budge.

Her suspicions were instantly roused. This drawer was locked. The others weren't. That had to mean something, right?

She hopped off the chair and kneeled down, pulling out the wrench and a smaller, more slender rake. It took much less time to pick this lock compared to the one on the door, and when the drawer sprang open, her gaze hungrily devoured the contents.

She pulled out several file folders. Opened the first one.

And stopped breathing.

It's him.

She didn't know where the certainty had come from, but as she stared at the picture in the folder she knew without a doubt that she was looking at her father.

Eagerly, she memorized every detail. Dark hair, so short it was nearly buzzed off. A handsome face with chiseled masculine features. Blue eyes.

Her throat clogged at the sight of his eyes. She'd seen that dark shade of blue in only one other pair of eyes in her life.

Hers.

She'd always figured she'd inherited her eyes from her father, because both her mother and grandfather had chocolate brown ones. And now her hunch was confirmed.

Her hand shook as she flipped to the next page. It contained lines and lines of information, like a celebrity's biography on the Internet. Age, height, weight, background.

But only one detail interested her at the moment. The line that read "name."

Her father's name was James Morgan.

Cate couldn't stop the tears that filled her eyes. After years and years of wondering, she finally had a name, a face, something tangible to hold on to.

The file didn't say whether he was dead, which was encouraging. It also omitted an address or phone number, though it did list some information about a security company that James Morgan apparently owned and operated.

Cate shot to her feet and dashed toward the multipurpose laser printer next to the fax machine. Her fingers trembled as she shoved the short stack of papers into the scan tray. She pressed the copy button, then waited anxiously for the copies to spit out. She'd already been in here way too long, and she knew Gabriel wouldn't be able to distract Thierry forever.

Once she had her copies, she returned the file to the drawer and slammed it shut. It automatically locked on its own, which was a great relief, because she had no idea how to lock a drawer with a wrench and a pick—she'd only practiced the opposite.

She rolled up the copies, tucked them and the lock pick case in her waistband, then dashed out the door, which also locked behind her. Thank God.

Cate held her breath and didn't release it until she was in the safety of her suite, where she collapsed on the edge of the bed and frantically studied the file again. She was still absorbed in it when Gabriel marched into the room, looking annoyed as he crossed his arms over his chest.

"Do you realize how crazy Thierry thinks I am? I spent the past ten minutes talking his ear off about the most ridiculous nonsense. We actually had an entire conversation about *whales*."

Cate didn't answer. She was too busy staring at the photograph of James Morgan.

His eyes. They were so intense.

"Cate? Are you even listening to me?"

She lifted her head, then held out the picture. "This is my father."

Without a word, Gabriel took the photo and studied it. "How can you be so sure?"

"The eyes. We have the same eyes."

He glanced at the picture again. "Similar," he admitted. "But . . . you shouldn't get your hopes up. It could also be a random stranger who happens to have dark blue eyes. It might not be your father."

"It is," she insisted.

As Gabriel joined her on the bed, she handed him the rest of the papers. They spent the next fifteen minutes leafing through them together, reading them several times, until Cate had every last detail memorized.

"So what are you going to do now?" Gabriel asked uneasily.

"I don't know." She bit her lip, torn. "I guess I should try to contact him."

"And say what?"

She opened her mouth to respond, but was cut off by the sound of footsteps in the hallway. Someone was coming toward her room.

"Catarina?" Nik's voice was followed by two soft raps on the door.

"Crap!" She hastily stacked up the papers and thrust them at Gabriel. "Put these in your pocket. Nik can't find them on me!"

Like the fantastic friend he was, Gabriel folded the papers and shoved them in the back pocket of his black jeans, two seconds before Nik entered the suite.

It irked her that Nik had just waltzed inside without permission, but she was too flustered to be indignant.

"Hi!" she blurted out, her voice coming out far too squeaky.

Great. Could she act any more suspiciously?

Nik clearly agreed, because his light blue eyes narrowed as he looked from her to Gabriel.

"Am I interrupting something?" he inquired in a clipped tone.

"Uh, no. Of course not. Gabriel and I were just . . . talking."

"Talking," Nik echoed.

Gabriel awkwardly got to his feet. "Yeah, but I was actually about to leave. My father gave me an extra hour for lunch so I could visit *Maman*, but he needs me back at work now."

Nik's expression only grew cloudier. "Yes, you should go now. I don't think Mr. Durand, or your mother, would approve of you being in Catarina's room. With the door closed," he said pointedly.

Cate's cheeks flamed when she realized that Nik thought she and Gabriel had been . . . Oh gosh, that was embarrassing.

But it also occurred to her that it was better to let him think he'd caught them fooling around than for him to discover what they'd *really* been doing.

Gabriel looked equally mortified as he scurried out the door, and the moment her friend was gone, Nik turned to her with a disapproving look.

"Catarina . . . Cate . . . I know you and Gabriel are close, but it's not appropriate for the two of you to be alone in your bedroom."

"You're right. I'm sorry. Next time I'll leave the door open."

Her easy agreement seemed to appease him, but clearly he wasn't done. "The boy's mother works for this household. Your grandfather disapproves of you spending so much time with our cook's son."

"He never minded before," she said testily.

Nik frowned. "Yes, but circumstances have changed. You and Gabriel are no longer children. You're young adults, and it's time the two of you started to behave like it."

She tried not to roll her eyes. "I'll do my best."

"Good." He cleared his throat. "Maurice sent me up here to tell you that he's going to visit your mother now, and he'd like for you to come. I'll give you a minute to change your clothes."

She scowled. "What's wrong with my clothes?"

"You know your mother doesn't like it when you wear stuff like that," Nik answered with a pained look. "Why don't you put on that lovely green summer dress you wore the other day? You know how much she likes that one."

She doesn't like anything! Cate almost shouted, but she gritted her teeth and held her tongue.

"Fine," she said. "I'll wear the dress."

"Wonderful. I'll see you downstairs in five minutes."

The second he was gone Cate closed her eyes and conjured up the image of James Morgan.

And wondered what the heck she was supposed to do next.

Chapter 16

Noelle walked into the dining room after a sleepless night that had left dark circles under her eyes. She wasn't surprised when she found Jim sitting at the table, looking as worn-out as she felt. He held a cup of coffee with both hands, wisps of steam curling upward into his handsome face. He hadn't shaved and the results were delicious. Dark stubble slashed his jaw, giving him a bad-boy look that probably would've turned her on if she weren't feeling so unhinged at the moment.

Ariana Dietrich had been pregnant.

Noelle still couldn't believe he'd dropped a bomb like that and walked away.

After he'd blurted out the confession last night, he'd left her on the terrace and retreated to his room as if he hadn't just knocked her entire world off-kilter. But she hadn't chased after him. The shock and confusion had been too much to sift through. Besides, she'd still been reeling from all the other little goodies he'd told her.

Like how he'd never loved Ariana.

Maybe it made her a total sucker, but she believed him. He might have fooled her once, but nowadays she could always tell when Jim was lying to her, and she didn't think he'd lied last night. And then, once she'd thought back to all the conversations they'd had after Ariana's disappearance, she'd realized that Jim had never actually said he'd loved Ariana. Noelle had accused him of it, railed into him for it, but not once had he used the L-word in connection to Ariana Dietrich.

Still, he hadn't corrected her either. For seventeen years he'd allowed her to believe he'd truly loved that girl.

Turned out he hadn't loved either one of them.

Maybe she and Ariana ought to form a club for gullible chicks who'd had their hearts broken by James Morgan.

Noelle swallowed her bitterness as she joined him at the table and reached for the coffee carafe.

There was a beat of silence before he lifted his head and looked at her.

"Let's just get it out of the way. Will you help me find her or not?"

She frowned at him. "You don't need my help."

"Yes, I do. You have contacts. You know the city."

His matter-of-fact tone raised her hackles. "And what do I get out of this?"

"Same thing as before. I'll owe you. Except it won't be just one favor this time. I'm offering you a lifetime carte blanche." His features grew pained. "Whatever you need, anytime you need it, I'll do it. No questions asked."

It was a very intriguing offer, and one she couldn't dismiss so easily.

Thoughtful, Noelle poured herself a cup of coffee and took a small sip. "How far along was she?"

The question caught him off guard. "What?"

"Ariana's pregnancy," she said irritably. "How far along?"

"Four months."

"I'm fascinated by your recklessness. You're usually very careful about birth control."

"She took the decision out of my hands." His jaw tightened. "She poked holes in the condoms."

Noelle's eyebrows shot up. "You're kidding me."

"Nope. She bragged about it the night she told me she was pregnant." Jim shook his head angrily. "Like I said, she wanted me, and she was willing to do anything to make me stick around. Even get herself knocked up."

Noelle spoke despite the lump in her throat. "Would you have married her?"

"Yes," he said with no hesitation.

She laughed harshly. "Even though you were supposed to take her father down?"

"I wasn't about to abort the mission, but I had every intention of being there for Ariana after I put Dietrich out of commission." He laughed too, just as harsh and humorless. "And I know she would've let me. She probably would've been resentful and pissed off at first, but I had no doubt she'd marry me. Ariana wasn't capable of taking care of herself—she needed a man to do it for her."

"You would have doomed yourself to a loveless marriage?"

"For my child? I would have done anything. I'd do anything." Desperation flashed in his eyes, and his knuckles turned white as he gripped his coffee cup. "I don't even know if she gave birth. Or if she even survived the ambush. There was so much gunfire that night. She could have gotten caught in the cross fire."

"I doubt it."

"Why's that?"

"Because if she'd died that night, Dietrich would have hunted you down and killed you a long time ago." Noelle pursed her lips. "I'm not sure why he waited until now to hire someone."

"Maybe it took him this long to find me."

"Maybe. But my gut tells me it's something else." She reached for the plate of croissants her housekeeper, Miles, must have brought out, and swiped one of the warm, freshly baked pastries. "Maybe he knew you were getting too close?"

"You think he got scared? Worried I was going to come after Ariana again?"

"I don't know." She bit into the croissant and chewed thoughtfully.

As Jim groaned in frustration, Noelle realized that she'd never seen him so upset.

"I need to know what happened to Ariana and the baby. Help me."

She kept chewing.

"Noelle. Please."

She swallowed and picked up her coffee mug.

"For fuck's sake, I'm begging you. I need you. Please."

The anguished crack in his voice shocked her. His warrior facade was crumbling right before her eyes, and Noelle had no idea how to respond to that.

She'd thought her heart was nothing but pure black steel, totally indestructible, but apparently her carefully constructed armor contained a few chinks she hadn't known about.

Because she opened her mouth and murmured, "All right."

Relief flooded his face. "Thank you."

She shifted in her chair, awkward as hell. "You're welcome."

Their gazes collided for a moment, and then he cleared his throat.

"Sean Reilly is flying in today, and I left a message for Sully and Liam to get their asses over here. I want twenty-four-hour recon on the Durand estate. If Ariana is there, we'll know it."

The emotional, wobbly-voiced Jim had vanished. He was all business now.

"Maybe we can try to plant some cameras inside the house," he added pensively.

Noelle answered in a grudging tone. "If we need to, I can ask Juliet to help with that."

He nodded in gratitude. "Thanks. Oh, and Sean's brother Oliver is taking over the intel thread. He'll keep digging, see if he can find out more about Durand and what he's been doing all these years."

"I have someone who can help with that too."

"Who?"

"An associate of mine. He operates out of Paris."

"Contract killer?" Jim said sharply.

"Yeah. I toss foreign jobs his way every now and then, but he likes to stay local. If you want to know anything about anyone in this city, Charron is your go-to guy."

"Call him."

"Will do." Noelle polished off her coffee, then set down the mug and scraped her chair back.

Jim's hoarse voice stopped her before she could reach the doorway.

"Thank you," he said again. "I really appreciate this."

She left the dining room without responding, and when

she stepped into the hall, she took a deep breath and fought the urge to kick herself in the shin.

What the hell was she doing, agreeing to help him?

He doesn't deserve to find his kid.

The angry indictment buzzed in her mind and made her heart clench in agony. Was she seriously going to help him track down his child? Give him the opportunity to be a father?

After he'd ripped *her* father right out of her life?

God, what was wrong with her? She needed to march back in there and tell him he could go do his own grunt work.

But instead, she continued down the hall to make some calls.

"Guess who's going to Paris," Sullivan announced as he burst into the kitchen. Looking positively smug, he tipped his head at Liam. "The boss just gave the word. He needs us for backup."

Liam instantly brightened when he heard himself included in the orders. He set down his coffee cup on the granite counter and held up his palm for a high five, which Sullivan merrily returned.

From his seat at the table, Ash cleared his throat loudly. "Um. Whose dick do I have to suck to get in on this?"

Sullivan snickered. "I'm guessing Morgan's, but he'd probably shoot you if you tried."

"He really didn't ask for me?" Ash was practically pouting.

"You know he likes to make sure there's always one of us here to guard the compound," Liam said tactfully, not wanting to add to Ash's visible disappointment.

"Fuck that," the rookie retorted. "Bill and Don are here. They're perfectly capable of manning the fort."

Ash raised a good point; the two men in charge of compound security were both former Delta. They could protect the place in their sleep.

"Aw, hell, let's bring him along," Liam said to Sully. "We both know Morgan will be pissed for all of two minutes before realizing he needs the extra manpower."

The rookie's face lit up. "I'll take full responsibility when he flips out." Ash suddenly grinned. "So, are French women as hot as everyone says?"

"Yup," Sullivan confirmed. "And there's none hotter than the one you're about to meet."

"Noelle." Ash looked more wary than excited now. "Should I be worried she'll try to kill me?"

Liam chuckled. "Nah. The boss is the only one she seems to want dead."

"Or naked," Sully added. "Trust me, kid, you're about to see some serious sparks."

"Yeah?"

"Oh yeah. Their chemistry is off the charts. Makes you horny just being around them."

"So they hate each other but they still want to jump each other's bones?" Ash said dubiously.

Liam shrugged. "Just the way it is. Some people are just hardwired to fuck each other." He grinned at the younger man. "Now go get our gear. We've got a plane to catch."

Ash scowled. "Why do *I* have to get everyone's gear?"

"Because you're the new guy, which means you have the honor of doing all the grunt work." The grin widened. "Consider it your hazing period."

"How long does this hazing period last?" Ash said suspiciously.

Sullivan beamed at him. "Forever."

"You guys are assholes." But even though he flashed them his middle finger, Ash still hurried out of the kitchen like an obedient little soldier.

"He's so easy to pick on," Sullivan said with a sigh.

Liam couldn't help but laugh. "I know, right?"

"I'm sure he'll stand up for himself one of these days." Sully headed for the door. "Gonna grab a quick shower before we go. I'll meet you out front in ten."

Liam was left staring at his teammate's retreating back. Unwittingly, his gaze traveled lower, snagging on the taut butt hugged by a pair of camo fatigues.

His cheeks instantly heated up. Fuckin' hell. What was the *matter* with him?

He tore his gaze away and went over to the counter, where he poured another cup of coffee and forced himself to concentrate on the upcoming mission.

And not his teammate's ass.

*   *   *

"I don't like being out in the open like this," Jim said darkly.

Noelle sighed. "Join the club. But Charron doesn't do business over the phone."

Her gaze did another sweep of the sidewalk in front of the corner café on the Rue de Douai, where her associate had arranged to meet them. Charron had chosen to hold this little rendezvous in Pigalle, one of the seediest areas of the city, and Noelle's least favorite place to conduct business. There were too many shady characters roaming the neighborhood, thanks to the plethora of strip clubs and sex shops.

"What about e-mail?" Jim grumbled. "Does he have something against that too?"

She glanced across the small patio table with a dry smile. "He's anti-technology. Claims that's how people wind up behind bars."

"Yet he had no trouble taking your information request via text. Why couldn't he just text you whatever he found? Why meet in person?"

Jim's shoulders had been stiffer than boards from the moment they'd arrived in Pigalle. They'd scoped out the area for more than an hour and found nothing to raise their alarms, but he still didn't look happy about being out in public.

Neither was she, but she'd chosen not to complain because she figured Jim was already tense enough for the both of them.

"That's just the way Charron is," she said. "He's been like that since I've known him."

"And how long is that again?"

"Ten years, give or take."

"And you trust him?"

"Of course not. I don't trust anybody." She rolled her eyes. "But Charron hasn't done anything to piss me off, and he hasn't betrayed me, so he's as trustworthy as it's gonna get." Her gaze once again focused on the street. "His text said he has a lot of dirt on Durand. I figured it was worth a meeting."

She caught sight of a guy in all black walking in their direction, and her hand instinctively hovered over the knife at her hip. Her long flowing top shielded the weapon from view, while her tight jeans hid the two pistols strapped to her ankles.

She relaxed when the kid got closer. Just a twenty-some-thing-year-old Goth wearing earbuds and bobbing his head to his music, no doubt some horrific thrash metal about skulls and death.

Noelle sipped her English breakfast tea and carefully catalogued the other patrons on the patio: two single women reading the newspaper at their respective tables; a trio of young male hipsters chatting animatedly over espressos; a lone young man talking on his smartphone; and a couple in their late teens who'd been arguing for the past five minutes, their voices slowly rising in decibels as the seconds ticked by.

"I *know* there's nothing going on between you!" the brunette was grumbling. "But she's still your ex-girlfriend and I don't want you hanging out with her!"

Noelle stifled a sigh. Ah, to be young again. In her life, she didn't lose sleep over whether the man in her bed remained friends with his exes—she was more concerned with putting bullets in people's heads.

"You don't get to decide who I'm friends with, Zoé!"

Tuning out the couple, Noelle turned back to Jim, who looked both preoccupied and alert.

"Charron's late," he said flatly.

She checked the time on her phone and saw that Jim was right. Charron was two minutes late. It wasn't an obscene amount of time, but it still troubled her. Her colleague was always on time, and he also happened to be as paranoid as she was, which meant he would've shown up early to recon the area, just like she and Jim had.

So where the hell was he?

"We wait one more minute and then we go," she replied, keeping her voice low.

He nodded in agreement.

"How would you like it if I was still friends with Louis?" the blustering Zoé demanded.

"That's different!" her boyfriend shot back.

As the couple beside them continued to bicker, Noelle didn't miss the annoyance in Jim's eyes.

"Did you talk to Juliet?" he said absently.

"Yeah. She can't help us out yet. Isabel just wrapped up her undercover job in South Africa—she was cozying up to Juliet's target—so Jules needs to go in and take care of it. She gave me an ETA of two days."

A flash of silver crossed Noelle's peripheral vision. She shifted her head and noticed that an older-model Mercedes had stopped at a red light in the intersection in front of the café.

"Two days is too long." Jim sounded frustrated.

"She's working. I can't just pull my operatives off a job to cater to your every—" Noelle halted abruptly. "Something's wrong."

Jim had stiffened at the same time she did. "Yup."

They were already sliding out of their chairs.

"Hurry," she murmured as he reached into his pocket for his wallet.

Her instincts hummed like a swarm of bees, the alarm bells in her head a clear indication that something was off about this entire situation.

There was a blur of movement in the corner of her eye, and she turned just in time to see the passenger's-side window of the Mercedes rolling down.

She automatically went for her knife, which was closer to her hand than the guns at her ankles.

"I don't *care* that you've known her since you were kids!" Zoé was shrieking. "You can't see her!"

Noelle glimpsed another flash. A hand at the window, the vague impression of a gun muzzle.

"That's it! I'm not having this conversation anymore!" Officially fed up with his girlfriend, the teenager at the next table bolted to his feet.

His sudden change of position placed him directly in the path of the Mercedes, effectively blocking Noelle and Morgan from view.

A nanosecond later, the kid's chest was riddled with bullets as gunshots exploded in the afternoon air.

Chapter 17

Morgan didn't have to time to think, only to react.

As a rapid wave of gunfire leveled the poor kid who'd been fighting with his girlfriend, Morgan flattened himself on the concrete floor and withdrew his Sig from his waistband.

"Take cover!" he shouted at Noelle.

He didn't have to bother—she was already on the ground, grabbing at the legs of their metal table so she could overturn it.

Pandemonium had hit the second the Mercedes driver had discharged his gun. Shrieks of terror echoed all around them and footsteps pounded on the pavement as screaming patrons and pedestrians fled the scene. Tables and chairs were knocked over as people ran for their lives, and the clay flower planters on either side of the café's front door exploded, sharp shards flying in every direction.

Morgan dove behind the cover that Noelle had provided them, then ducked out and opened fire. He half expected the Mercedes to be gone, but the car was still on the street, and its driver was still shooting at them.

The kid who'd chosen the most ill-timed moment to step away from his table lay on the ground five feet away. Flat on his back with his lifeless brown eyes staring up at the cloudless blue sky. Blood pooled all around him, crimson rivers that trickled toward the table Morgan and Noelle were hunched behind, like skinny red fingers trying to claw their way over.

"Xavier!" The petrified scream had come from the dead guy's girlfriend, who launched herself at him.

Earsplitting wails of horror ripped out of her throat as she touched her boyfriend's face, unconcerned about her own safety. Sobbing, she planted both hands on his torso and attempted to perform CPR on his bullet-ravaged chest.

"Get down!" Morgan yelled, but the girl was too focused on saving her boyfriend to listen to the warning.

And two seconds later, she wasn't alive to hear him.

The bullet struck her in the back of the head, an arc of blood spraying out as she collapsed on top of her boyfriend's body. Dead.

Morgan cursed and glanced at Noelle, whose expression was downright apoplectic.

Her associate had betrayed her. They both knew it, and he could see that she was practically foaming at the mouth over Charron's act of treachery.

Morgan fired two more shots, then took cover behind the metal table. But there was no return fire, no counterattack from the shooter. Only deafening silence.

For one blessed moment, he thought their assailant had driven off, but then he heard the slam of a car door, followed by the telltale click of someone sliding a magazine into place.

Shit. The shooter was out of the car, reloading his weapon.

Ballsy motherfucker.

A second later, they were under attack again. The sharp *rat-tat-tat* of a submachine gun blasted in the air. Bullets struck every corner of the patio, splintering the ceramic planters, bouncing off metal and concrete. The window behind them shattered into a million pieces, covering him and Noelle with a shower of glass.

When Morgan popped out to fire again, he caught a glimpse of a lanky man in black pants and a tight black muscle tee. The man staggered as Morgan's shot connected with his chest, but it didn't slow him down.

Fuck. The asshole was wearing body armor.

Screams continued to echo all around them, panicked footsteps, the squeal of car brakes as every vehicle on the road came to a screeching halt.

Through it all, the shooter kept advancing on their table like the goddamn Terminator.

Morgan turned to Noelle with urgency. "He's wearing body armor. Head shots only."

"Then shoot him in the fucking head." Her beautiful face was smudged with dirt, courtesy of one of the exploding flowerpots, but there wasn't an iota of fear in her eyes.

If anything, she seemed completely unfazed by the chaos around them.

"Hard to do when he's waving that fucking Uzi around," Morgan shouted over the din.

Another hail of bullets rocked the table, and he grimly noted that soon it would be nothing but a metal skeleton. At which point, they'd be royally screwed.

They had to make a move, and it needed to be now.

A soft curse of pain suddenly left Noelle's mouth, but when he glanced over, he didn't see any signs that she'd been hit. "You good?"

She nodded in response, gripping her pistol with ease. "I'm great. Now can we please take care of this bastard already?"

Adrenaline sizzled in his blood as his gaze met hers. He didn't have to say a word. Her imperceptible nod told him that she'd read his mind and was in total agreement about the unspoken plan that had formulated between them.

"One," he murmured.

Noelle let go of her gun and wrapped her fingers around the ox-bone handle of her knife.

"Two . . ."

She gave another brisk nod.

"Three."

They sprang to action in one simultaneous motion. Noelle's knife hissed through the air and lodged into the shooter's upper arm, causing him to falter and lower his gun, just for a split second. But a split second was all Morgan needed to finish it.

One bullet. Right between the eyes.

And the Terminator went down like a light.

In the ensuing silence, all Morgan could focus on was his even breathing, the steady beating of his heart, the lingering adrenaline coursing through his veins.

Then he drew a breath, stood up, and offered Noelle his hand.

After a beat of hesitation, she took it and allowed him to help her up.

As sirens howled in the distance, Morgan could feel dozens of shocked stares boring into his back. He looked around warily, unhappy about their audience. People were cowering behind trees and lampposts, hiding inside bus shelters and behind newspaper boxes. Every pair of eyes was glued to the grisly scene in front of the café.

Morgan approached the dead man on the pavement and studied his face, then glanced at the woman by his side.

"Charron?" he prompted.

"What the hell do you think?" She scowled, her incensed gaze fixed on her associate's corpse. "Come on. We have to go."

Morgan nodded. Yep, it was definitely time for them to get the fuck out of there. They couldn't afford to be around when the cops showed up and the entire area turned into a three-ring circus.

"We can't go back to my town house," she muttered. "It's been compromised now. I've got another safe house near the Right Bank."

"Good. Let's go."

He started to walk off, but Noelle didn't follow. To his surprise, she sank to her knees next to Charron's body and leaned forward so she could withdraw her blade from the dead man's arm.

"Are you kidding me?" Morgan couldn't stop a snort of amusement.

"It's my favorite one," she said defensively, sheathing the knife before gracefully rising to her feet.

He rolled his eyes at her, then concealed his own weapon by shoving it back in his waistband.

A moment later, the two of them hurried away from the scene of the crime, leaving dropped jaws and dumbfounded stares in their wake.

"That son of a bitch. Goddamn *traitor*."

Noelle stormed into the living room an hour later, still holding her cell phone in her hand. But it didn't stay there long—she was so livid she ended up hurling the phone at the cream-colored wall, putting a dent in the drywall and knocking an expensive framed print right off its hook. It came crashing to the hardwood right along with the phone, which slid under the end table and disappeared beneath the leather sectional sofa.

Noelle made no move to rescue the cell. Fuck, she'd probably shoot the damn thing if she ever saw it again.

"I take it you figured out why your friend decided to shoot at us?"

To her annoyance, Jim looked like he was fighting back laughter. He was standing near the window of the elegant penthouse, sipping on a bottle of Stella Artois he'd found in the fridge earlier.

He'd offered her one before she'd disappeared into the bedroom, but she'd declined. She was too riled up to drink, and after what she'd just discovered, she was even more pissed off.

"Apparently Gilles Girard decided to take away my exclusive claim to you," she said bitterly. "The contract on your head went wide last night."

"Shit."

"Yep, every contract killer in Europe will be coming after you now." She cursed under her breath. "Son of a bitch Charron. The second I asked him for intel about Durand, he must have known that I was in contact with you."

"Guess you weren't as close as you thought," he said dryly.

"We weren't close at all. But there's a little something called professional courtesy," she grumbled. "You don't go around poaching other people's hits or trying to kill another contractor. What happened to ethics?"

This time Jim didn't try to hide his amusement. The infuriating man started to laugh, for so long she almost marched over and slugged him.

To make matters worse, her arm was bleeding again, thanks to the piece of jagged metal that had sliced into it during the shoot-out. She'd just finished bandaging the wound, but evidently she'd misjudged its depth. Damn thing required stitches after all.

"Before we get into a ludicrous discussion about ethics,"

Jim said, "why do you think it was your questions about Durand that led Charron to connect you to me? I thought Girard went out of his way to keep his client anonymous."

"I already told you. Charron knows everyone in France. He probably knew something we didn't that connected Girard and Durand."

She crossed her arms and tried to apply pressure to her wound without alerting Jim, but his sharp gaze didn't miss a thing.

"You're hurt."

There was something hauntingly familiar about the way he phrased it, the flat tone he'd used. It took a few seconds, but it suddenly dawned on her that he'd spoken those same words, in that same tone, on the day they'd met.

And he wore the same fierce expression now as he had then.

She took a nonchalant step toward the door. "I'm fine. Some metal ricocheted off the table during the shoot-out and cut up my arm. I'm going to stitch it up now."

Before he could respond, she left the living room and strode down the corridor toward the rear of the penthouse, where the bedrooms were located. She rarely ever used this safe house; a few years ago she'd pretty much given it to Bailey, who stayed there between jobs.

Bailey had been out running errands when they'd arrived, and Noelle was genuinely eager for the woman to get back. It would be nice to finally have a buffer between her and Jim. He evoked so many conflicting emotions inside her, and when it was just the two of them, those emotions always managed to breach the surface. It was much easier to mask them when other people were around.

Noelle entered the guest bedroom she'd chosen to crash in. Even though she technically owned this place, it was more Bailey's than hers, and she wasn't about to commandeer the master bedroom from her operative.

And people said she didn't have a heart.

She stripped out of her long-sleeve shirt and carefully peeled the bandage off her arm, cursing when she saw the rapid flow of blood seeping out of the cut. With a sigh, she went into the bathroom to grab a first-aid kit, returning to the main room just as Jim appeared in the doorway.

"Give me the kit and sit on the bed," he ordered.

"I can stitch it up myself."

"Sit on the fucking bed."

Too tired to argue, she plopped down on the edge of the mattress and held out the first-aid kit.

He took it from her, then rummaged around until he'd retrieved a needle, antiseptic wipes, a pair of medical scissors, and transparent, dissolvable stitches.

"You want a painkiller or something?" he said gruffly.

"No." She winced as he used a disinfectant-soaked gauze pad to mop up the blood. "I don't like painkillers."

"Yeah, I remember."

"You do?"

He nodded. "You told me that when we first met. The doctor who splinted your fingers tried to prescribe you some painkillers, but you refused. I asked you about it later and you said you didn't like taking pills because you needed the pain to be fresh. You said you didn't want to forget it." She felt his blue eyes probing her face. "But you never told me why."

She hesitated at his unspoken question, then decided there was no reason not to answer it.

"Because of René," she said with a small shrug.

From the corner of her eye she saw him thread the needle. Then he gripped it between his deft fingers, poised over her flesh. "Ready?" he murmured.

"Do your worst."

She didn't even flinch when the needle pricked her arm. She was a master when it came to blocking out pain.

"So . . ." Jim cleared his throat as he skillfully maneuvered the needle through her skin. "What does René have to do with you taking pills?"

"At the beginning . . . when he first came to my bed . . ." She gritted her teeth as an acute pain gripped her flesh. "I didn't want to feel anything, so I stole some of my mom's painkillers. I figured if I popped enough of them, I'd get really drowsy, and then I wouldn't have to focus on what he was doing to me. I wanted to be so numb that I couldn't feel a damn thing."

His voice thickened. "Did it work?"

"Depended on how many pills I took. But after a while, I realized I didn't want to block it out."

"Why not?"

"Because I wanted to remember every second of his tor-ture, every disgusting, evil detail. Remembering helped me keep the hate alive, so that way I'd never forget to exact my revenge." Bitterness washed over her. "Not that it mattered. In the end, my revenge was stolen from me. I wanted to make him suffer, but the asshole got himself killed before I had the chance."

She figured Jim would press for details, but he didn't. A soft snip of the scissors, and then his warm hand left her arm.

"All done," he said briskly. "I'm not going to bandage it. You should probably let it breathe."

Noelle started to get up, but he stopped her by planting his palm on her thigh. The heat of his touch seared right through her jeans, and the rest of her body instantly re-sponded. Her nipples puckered and her clit throbbed in anticipation of the carnal fucking she expected to come.

She expected wrong. Because when she looked into Jim's eyes, she didn't see lust there. Only tenderness.

Discomfort rolled through her like tumbleweed. "Why are you looking at me like that?"

Rather than answer, he moved his other hand to her face and swept his thumb over her lower lip.

She jerked as if he'd struck her, and yet she didn't push his hand away.

"You said that if . . ." He trailed off, his expression hesi-tant and oddly defiant. "You said if I kissed you again with-out your permission, you'd slit my throat. Is that still the case?"

Surprise jolted through her, but somehow she managed to keep her voice steady. "Yes. It is."

He traced the line of her jaw with his fingertips. His touch was so gentle it ignited a spark of fear.

"Then I guess I'll ask permission." He paused. "Can I kiss you?"

The husky request sounded so earnest she couldn't help but search his gaze to see if he was playing games, mocking her again. But she found nothing to support that.

God. He was actually serious.

The scared feeling in her stomach turned into a rush of

fiery panic. A cold and ruthless Jim, she could handle. But not this tentative, vulnerable Jim. Whenever *he* lowered his guard, she was tempted to do the same, and she knew just how dangerous that could be.

If she let him in, she was one step closer to becoming that girl again. The girl who used to express her feelings openly, the girl who'd managed to hold on to her optimism in spite of the torment she endured on a daily basis.

The girl she'd been before Jim Morgan had blazed through her life and extinguished every ounce of joy from it.

"Can I kiss you?" he asked again.

"No," she burst out, shoving his hand away. "You can't."

Chapter 18

Noelle's rejection hit him like a slap in the face. He wanted to be angry with her, but he couldn't muster up a single drop of rage.

Truth was, Morgan didn't blame her for saying no. He had no business kissing this woman, especially when he felt so damn raw, like someone had turned him inside out and exposed his emotions for all to see.

Telling Noelle about Ariana had unleashed feelings that he didn't like to think about. Not the desperation and agony and helplessness—no, those emotions were constant; they'd been lingering beneath the surface for seventeen years, a gut-wrenching reminder that he might have a child out there somewhere. A child he'd never raise, a child he might never even meet.

No, admitting he hadn't loved Ariana had unearthed something even worse. Something that had occurred to him only once in all these years, and which he'd banished before the idea could take root in his brain.

But it had come back to him this morning, and now he couldn't get rid of it. It nagged at him like a stray dog, pawing at the door, whining to get his attention. Once upon a time he'd kicked that dog away. Today, he'd let it in.

All the years he'd spent hating Noelle . . . he'd really been hating himself.

It was a crushing realization. For years he'd condemned her for Ariana's disappearance, but what had she really done, aside from warning a girl who'd deserved to be warned? He'd used Ariana the same way he'd used Noelle, and he was a bastard for it.

And Noelle hadn't even known about the baby. She hadn't known that her interference would result in his child being stolen away from him, but he'd convinced himself that it was her fault. He'd needed someone to blame, someone to hold liable—otherwise he would've had to hold *himself* accountable, and that would mean having to admit he was a pure and total bastard.

A man who didn't *deserve* to know his own kid.

It was too much, too awful to accept, and so he chose to focus on the anger again. The burn of being rejected by a woman who had every right to reject him.

"So you'll fuck me, but you won't kiss me," he said coldly. "Is that it?"

"Yes."

"You have a strange sense of logic, baby."

Noelle shrugged. "Take it or leave it."

Her expression was a block of ice, with the merest hint of fire behind it. But there was never any real emotion there, nothing that resembled warmth or vulnerability. He doubted he'd ever see that in her eyes again, and that only made him angrier.

"So if you're not planning to fuck me," she went on, "I suggest you take your hand off my thigh and get the hell out."

He arched a brow. "Oh, I'm not going to fuck you."

"Then I repeat, get the hell out."

"No."

"For God's sake, Jim," she muttered in frustration. "Just go."

"No. I'm not leaving this room until I kiss you."

She scowled at him. "I said no."

"I don't care. I'm going to kiss you, Noelle." He reached for the button of her jeans and snapped it open. "One goddamn way or another, I'm going to kiss you."

Her blue eyes widened as he pulled her jeans off her legs, right along with her black bikini panties.

"You won't let me kiss your mouth? Fine. I'll just kiss you *here*," he rasped before latching his mouth on the inside of her thigh.

She jerked when he kissed her smooth, creamy flesh, but she didn't stop him. When he peered up at her, he was irritated to see the fascinated look on her face. He knew she could sense that his composure was unraveling, and he didn't like it one damn bit. He didn't want her to see . . . to see . . .

Christ, he didn't even know what he was trying to hide anymore.

He dropped hot kisses along the insides of her thighs, then spread her legs apart and gazed at her perfect pink folds. The moisture pooling there brought a surge of male satisfaction. She wanted this. No matter how much she might despise him, she would always desire him. Always welcome him into her body.

"And I'll kiss you here," he muttered, pressing his mouth to the top of her mound.

She shivered.

"And here." He planted a trail of kisses down her slit. "And here." He rubbed his lips over her clit before tonguing it gently.

Her throaty moan drove an iron spike of lust right to his cock. He was harder than ever, his balls tight and achy, but he wasn't going to fuck her. He wished he could say he was trying to punish her by depriving her of his cock, but deep down he knew he was punishing himself.

His mouth tingled as he kissed her glistening sex. He did it over and over again, sometimes using his tongue, other times just rubbing his lips over her clit in the softest of caresses. He made out with her pussy the way he wanted to make out with her mouth, teasing her until she cried out and fell back on her elbows as if she couldn't support her own weight anymore.

She tasted as sweet as he remembered, and he licked her up, drank her in, lost himself in her. She was a drug and he was an addict, hooked on her from the second he'd met her.

"Come for me," he whispered against her hot flesh.

He got a breathy sound in response, and he could feel her pulse pounding between her legs. Her excitement fueled his own. He was rock-hard and aching for relief, but he didn't reach down to stroke himself through his jeans. He needed his hands. One to grip her thighs in place in case she suddenly decided to resist or suppress her growing passion the way she always seemed to do around him. He needed the other hand to bring to her core, slipping two fingers inside her and working her until she was moaning in abandon.

He wanted her to come, wanted to feel her throbbing against his lips. Sex was the only time both of them dropped their guards, and he desperately needed her to be as vulnerable as he felt right now.

"Come. For. Me." It was no longer a gentle request, but a command.

"Make me," she said breathlessly.

His eyes narrowed into slits as he lifted his head to look at her. Her beautiful face was hazy with desire, her breasts heaving beneath her black tank top.

Keeping their gazes locked, he lazily slid his fingers in and out of her tight channel, then pushed them in deep and curled them so he could hit the one spot guaranteed to make her scream.

And she did, pleasure flooding her face as she thrust into his probing fingers.

With a satisfied smile, he dipped his head again and resumed feasting. He captured her clit between his lips, sucking rhythmically as he fingered her, and was rewarded by her cry of surrender.

"Jim."

His name echoed in the air as she convulsed in orgasm. She rocked her hips into his face, her hands coming down to grab at his hair. She trapped his head between her legs, but shouldn't have bothered—he wasn't going anywhere. When she finally grew still, he planted one last kiss on her swollen clit and raised his head.

"You're such a bastard," she sighed.

He chuckled. "Are you really insulting the man who just gave you an orgasm?"

"I sure am," she muttered, trying to catch her breath.

His fingers were still lodged inside her, coated with her juices. He slowly pulled them out and brought them to his lips, licking each one clean as Noelle watched with passion-glazed eyes.

She spread her legs wider. "I want you inside me. Now."

Morgan's gaze rested on the paradise between her thighs.

His cock twitched eagerly, and his hand moved to his zipper of its own volition.

And then a female voice piped up from the hallway.

"Boss? You in there?"

Noelle instantly straightened up. "Bailey," she told him, her expression growing uneasy. She raised her voice at the door. "I'll be right out."

Morgan experienced a rush of disappointment as she hopped to her feet and wasted no time getting dressed, but despite his cock's irritated protests, a part of him didn't even care that they weren't going to fuck.

He'd wanted to kiss her and he had. Well, kind of. But he was still more than satisfied.

"I'm just going to get cleaned up," Noelle said, heading for the bathroom. "Go introduce yourself to Bailey. I'll be out soon."

He frowned, wondering whether she was ashamed to be seen leaving the bedroom with him.

Nah, probably not. Noelle had never cared what other people thought of her, not even her own operatives.

When Morgan exited the bedroom, the hall was empty, but he could hear someone moving around in the kitchen. He followed the sounds to the large, modern kitchen, which boasted gleaming stainless steel appliances and dark brown granite counters.

A slender raven-haired woman was reaching inside one of the cherry-stained cabinets. She retrieved a bowl, then rummaged around in a drawer for a spoon before drifting over to the counter.

Morgan stood in the doorway and watched as she pried open a yogurt container and spooned the creamy substance into her bowl.

"So you're Jim Morgan."

She didn't turn around. Just kept preparing her afternoon snack, sprinkling granola on the yogurt, then walking over to the sink to rinse out a plastic container filled with blueberries.

"I've heard a lot about you," she added.

"And you're Bailey," he replied in amusement. "I'd like to say I've heard a lot about you too, but when I tried checking into your background, I came up with zilch."

"That's because I'm a ghost." Laughing, she finally turned around and provided him with a glimpse of her face.

She wasn't flawlessly beautiful like Noelle, but objectively attractive. Her slate gray eyes were framed by sooty black lashes, her skin was fair and smooth, and she had a wide mouth that lent her a sensual air.

"Let me guess," he said. "CIA?"

She smiled. Didn't confirm or deny it.

"Abby and Isabel tell me you're a good man," she said thoughtfully. "Are you?"

He had to think it over. "Most of the time. Other times, no."

"Isn't that how it always is?" Bailey dumped a handful of blueberries into her bowl, then leaned against the counter and stuck her spoon in her concoction. "Sometimes we're good. Other times we're not." She paused. "Now, Juliet is still on the fence about you."

"I'm still on the fence about her. She's distracting one of my best men."

"Ethan? Gosh, he's cute, isn't he?" Bailey chewed and smiled at the same time. "Jules is head over heels for him." There was a pause as she swallowed. "Should I be worried about him hurting her?"

Morgan grinned. "Nah. Ethan worships the ground that woman walks on. He'd never hurt her, not intentionally anyway."

"Good."

He tilted his head. "What would you do if he did? Kill him?"

"Maybe." Her expression turned impish. "I'm very protective of my friends, you know."

"Well, I'm very protective of my men."

"Fair enough." Shrugging, she took another bite.

Morgan continued to study her, realizing that she reminded him a lot of Isabel Roma, thanks to her easygoing nature. He had to wonder if she was as complicated beneath the surface as Isabel was, or if with Bailey, what you saw was what you got. Probably not. Noelle had a history of recruiting women with troubled pasts and dangerous secrets.

Women like her.

"So when do I get to meet the infamous team?" Bailey

asked curiously. "Is it safe to assume you called in your soldiers to help us out?"

"Us?"

"My boss says we're taking down the man who's trying to kill you. So yes, us."

Morgan headed for the counter and clicked on the coffeemaker. "A couple of the boys are showing up tonight. Reilly should be here sooner—any minute now, actually."

Suspicion clouded her tone. "Reilly? Last name or first?"

"Last. You probably know him—Sean Reilly. He and his brother Oliver are the information dealers Noelle uses."

Displeasure flickered in Bailey's gray eyes. "Yeah, I know them. Since when does Sean work for you?"

"Since yesterday."

"I see." She looked ready to say more, but Noelle chose that exact moment to finally grace them with her presence.

She glided into the kitchen wearing black leggings and a loose red sweater, slid onto one of the tall stools by the counter, and gestured to the coffeepot in Morgan's hand. "Pour me a cup?"

He prepared her a mug, and when she leaned across the counter to take it from him, her sweater slipped off one shoulder, revealing her smooth, tanned skin.

His mouth instantly went dry, tingling with the urge to kiss that bare expanse of skin, while his cock throbbed with the need to slide inside her.

You hate her. Don't forget that, a warning voice said.

Did he? It was getting hard to remember that these days.

"Bailey and Reilly have some history," Noelle informed him, giving away the fact that she'd overheard their conversation. "That's why she looks so incredibly *excited* at the prospect of working with him."

"I'd hardly call it history," Bailey said in a dry voice. "Will he be staying here with us?"

Morgan glanced over at her. "Will that be a problem?"

"Not on my part. But you should ask him when he gets here."

"He'll do what I tell him."

Bailey snickered. "Good luck with that. Sean doesn't like to follow orders. And he doesn't play well with others either. I'm actually kind of shocked he was interested in being part of a team."

Noelle swiftly changed the subject. "We need to figure out our next move."

He stifled a sigh. She was right. After Denis Charron's very public assassination attempt, Morgan now had to worry about getting his head blown off whenever he left the house.

"I'll get the boys to watch Durand's estate," he answered. "If Ariana is in there, we'll know."

Noelle tensed at the mention of Ariana. "What about our little contract killer problem?"

"I'll stay out of sight," he said with a shrug. "Once Durand is dead, the hit will be null and void. Is this place secure?"

She nodded. "But I don't want to stay here too long, just in case. If Charron told someone that I'm working with you, then I'm a target too. Anyone who digs deep enough will eventually be able to trace any safe house I own back to me, but it'll take time."

When his phone buzzed, he pulled it out of his pocket and studied the screen.

"Reilly's here." He gave Bailey a crooked grin. "Want to let him in?"

With an unenthused look, she took one last bite of yogurt before placing the bowl in the sink. "Fine. Might as well get it over with."

She left the kitchen, and a moment later, the muffled sound of voices drifted from the front entrance. Bailey and Reilly were clearly getting reacquainted, though their low tones and the absence of laughter hinted that their reunion wasn't quite sunshine and rainbows.

Morgan's phone buzzed again, this time indicating an incoming call from Kane.

"Mr. Popular," Noelle said sarcastically.

He ignored her and picked up without delay. "Hey. Everything cool down there?"

"All good, boss. No sign of any rebel activity."

"Good. What's up, then?"

Kane's tone became serious. "Have you checked your e-mail today?"

His brow furrowed. "No." He paused. "Why? Have *you* checked my e-mail today? Because hacking into other people's accounts is illegal, you know."

There was a snicker in his ear. "I didn't hack into shit. I'm talking about the company e-mail."

As usual, the word "company" threw him off, until he remembered that technically he *was* a company man. He was the owner and founder of a private security company specializing in military operations abroad, and although the work he and his men did sure as hell didn't feel like a business, they had no choice but to look clean on paper.

Still, that didn't mean he spent much time on the business side of things. He had a business manager, a financial advisor, and a damn good accountant to handle all that stuff. He spoke to them on the phone a few times a year and they took care of the paperwork—all Morgan had to do was scribble his John Hancock wherever the little yellow Post-its told him to.

The e-mail aspect, though, had been Holden McCall's job. Morgan had been making an effort to respond to all the messages in Holden's absence, but he realized now that he hadn't checked the company inbox for at least a week.

"I haven't even looked," he admitted. "When we get hired for a job, the contact usually calls me directly. Why? Is someone trying to contract us?"

"Not quite."

Kane's vague response was a cause for concern.

"What's going on?" Morgan demanded.

"Uh, yeah. Just go check your e-mail, Jim. And feel free to call me back after you do. In fact, I *insist* you call me back because I'm really fucking curio—"

Morgan had already hung up.

Never mind that Kane had called him "Jim," which the guy did only when something serious was up; Kane's refusal to relay the information over the phone was even more alarming.

"Everything okay?" Noelle asked from the counter.

"Not sure yet," he muttered, swiping his fingers over the touch screen of his phone.

Logging into the company inbox seemed to take forever, and then he had to wait a million more seconds for the new messages to load. He scanned each one, finding mostly memos from his accountant—shit, he really needed to start responding to the man's e-mail if he wanted to keep the IRS off his back—but it was the message near the top that caught his eye.

The sender's name read Cate4821, from a free account provider. Subject line: "Hi."

Okay. Cryptic enough.

Frowning, he opened the e-mail and read the first line.

And that was as far as he got, because his entire world had come to a grinding halt.

Mr. Morgan,
    I know this must sound crazy, but I think you might be my father.

Chapter 19

Morgan gawked at the screen, still stuck on the first line.

I know this must sound crazy, but I think you might be my father.

He'd stopped breathing, and his lungs burned from the lack of oxygen, but he was still too stunned to move, let alone breathe.

I know this must sound crazy, but I think you might be my father.

"Jim?"

He heard Noelle's voice, ringing with genuine concern. He vaguely saw her slide off her stool and walk toward him, but he couldn't focus on anything but the phone in his hand.

"Jim? What's wrong?"

I know this must sound crazy, but I think you might be my father.

It took everything he had to tear his gaze away from those words, but he wasn't worried about forgetting them. They were already burned into his mind like a cattle brand.

"I . . ." His throat was so dry he sounded like he was talking through a mouthful of sand. "I . . . I'll be right back. I just need to . . . read this."

He stumbled out of the kitchen.

Noelle called out after him, but he ignored her. In the living room, he bumped right into Sean Reilly, who opened his mouth to greet him, only to get ignored too as Morgan pushed past him without a word.

"Um . . . okay . . ." Sean's dry voice sounded from behind.

It was hard to walk in a straight line, but he managed to make it all the way to the guest room without falling over.

I know this must sound crazy, but I think you might be my father.

He lurched through the door and closed it behind him, and then his legs stopped working and he barely made it to the bed without collapsing. As his ass planted down on the mattress, he gripped his phone like it was a life preserver. He was scared that if he let it out of his sight, the e-mail would disappear.

He took pity on his lungs and drew in a breath, so deep he got a head rush from it. Black dots swam before his eyes, blurring the words on the phone display, and he blinked rapidly to clear his foggy vision.

Once he was able to see again, he peered at the screen and read the rest of the e-mail.

Mr. Morgan,

I know this must sound crazy, but I think you might be my father. My name is Catarina Durand, but my friends call me Cate.

My mother's name is Ariana Durand. She was born in Paris. So was I, but we moved around a lot and only came back to Paris about ten years ago. I think you met my mother when she lived in Berlin.

I don't want to get into too many details over e-mail, but I have reason to believe that I'm your daughter. If there's even the slightest possibility that you think it could be true, please get back to me so we can talk. Please text instead of calling.

—Cate

She'd left a phone number beneath her name.

He stared at it for a full minute.

Shit. He needed a smoke. He needed to think.

Morgan dove off the bed in search of the flannel shirt he'd worn earlier. His cigarettes were in the front pocket, and when he fished out the pack of Marlboros, his fingers shook so hard he could barely pull out a cigarette. He lit up with a silver Zippo lighter and inhaled a desperate drag, remembering at the last second that Noelle had told him not to smoke inside the apartment.

But he didn't give a shit. He was too wired. Too freaked-out. His mind was running a hundred miles a minute, and his hands continued to shake like flimsy branches in a brisk wind.

Christ, emotions were such an inconvenience. He always tried so hard not to experience them, but at the moment, he couldn't control the floodgates that had burst open in his chest.

His daughter.

Catarina. But her friends called her Cate.

Could be a trap . . .

He sucked on his cigarette, pacing the hardwood like a madman. Yes, it could be a trap. He had to consider that possibility. He had to consider *all* the possibilities before he acted.

Dietrich could be trying to lure him out. Maybe there was no child. Maybe Ariana had died during the ambush, but not before she'd told her father about the pregnancy. Maybe Dietrich was pretending Morgan's child had survived in the hope that Morgan would care enough about the kid to show his face.

So another assassin could shoot him dead.

Morgan walked over to the window and cranked it open, blowing cloud after cloud of smoke into the air. He was startled to notice that the sun was only now beginning to set. It felt like hours since Charron had attacked them, since Kane had called and ordered him to check his e-mail.

As he lit another smoke, he reread the message and slowly absorbed every last word. The details were wrong. Ariana had been born in Berlin, not Paris. She was German, not French.

Had the person who wrote the e-mail simply been reciting what she'd been told? Because if Cate truly was his daughter, there was no way Walther Dietrich would have told her the truth about her family's background. The girl probably believed every word she'd written.

The erroneous details also made sense if it had been Dietrich who'd sent the e-mail. If Dietrich wanted to make it look like Morgan's daughter was the sender, he'd certainly pose as a clueless teenager. He'd know that Morgan would never believe Dietrich had confided in a young girl about his criminal past.

So which was it? Had Dietrich written the e-mail, or had it been Cate?

His daughter.

He drew one last burst of nicotine into his lungs, then flicked the cigarette butt out the window and went over to the duffel that was sitting on the floor beside the bed. His breathing was unsteady as he unzipped the bag and pulled out the zippered case where he stashed his burner phones.

He grabbed one of the disposable cell phones and returned to the window, then lit a third cigarette and stared at the phone number Cate had provided him.

She'd asked him not to call, so he didn't. Instead, he brought up a new text message and . . . hesitated.

Shit, what the hell should he write? If it was a trap, he couldn't reveal too much. But if it was his daughter, he couldn't allow the first contact he had with her to come off as rude and unfeeling.

In the end, self-preservation prevailed. He had to treat it like a trap. There was no other choice.

He typed, "I got your e-mail. Now what?"

He half expected an answering message to pop up the very next second, but that was wishful thinking. The display didn't change, showing nothing but the message he'd just sent.

He started pacing again, his cigarette now hanging loosely from his fingers.

Jesus. What if this *was* his daughter?

That would mean . . . Well, it would mean he had a daughter. A frickin' daughter. He didn't even know how to begin wrapping his head around that.

You've had seventeen years to do it, idiot.

A hysterical laugh jammed in his throat. The taunting inner voice had a point. You'd think he'd be prepared for it, considering he'd spent years searching for Ariana. Ariana, who'd been pregnant when she disappeared.

He'd had a shit ton of time to accept the idea that he might have a kid out there, but it had always seemed like such an abstract concept.

Now it felt tangible. It felt *real*.

If it was real.

He stopped pacing, dragged one hand over his scalp. He heard the murmur of voices from somewhere in the apartment, but he couldn't bring himself to leave the room. Not until he composed himself. Not until he knew whether or not—

The phone beeped in his hand.

He lowered his gaze, and his heart jumped when he saw the response on the screen.

Is this James Morgan?

He leaned against the wall beside the window and sucked in some more nicotine. After a beat, he sent back a reply.

Yes. Is this Catarina?

The next reply was faster this time. Yes, but if you actually read my e-mail like you claim you did, you'd know I don't go by that name.

There was something defiant about the response, a hint of challenge that brought a faint smile to his lips.

Cate. You go by Cate.

Yes.

That was it. Just yes. Morgan's chest had just filled with disappointment when the burner phone beeped again.

So am I being crazy, or is there a chance this might actually be true?

He knew what she meant by "this." As in, him potentially being her father.

Gulping, he flicked the inch of ash atop his cigarette and typed out a response.

If the details you gave me were accurate, then
yeah . . . it might be true.

Then I guess the next step would be for us to
meet.

The girl didn't beat around the bush.

For a second, Morgan experienced a spark of excitement. Anticipation. The prospect of meeting this girl—his
daughter—was surreal and wonderful and slightly terrifying.

But then suspicion crept in to overshadow the joy, like
an oozing puddle of tar on a white floor, turning everything
in its path black.

If Dietrich was attempting to draw him out, then goddamn it, this was the way to do it.

Because no way in hell was Morgan saying no to this girl.
His daughter.

Or not, his internal alarm system warned him.

His fingers were poised to type another response, but a
follow-up message from Cate appeared on the screen before he could.

Just so you know, we'll have to meet on the
DL. Might be hard to meet privately because
I'm always being watched. But I can try to get
away tomorrow?

His brows knitted together. She was always being watched?
Why? What the fuck was that bitch Ariana doing to their
daughter?

He quickly inhaled a calming breath and responded
with: We meet on my terms.

Meaning what?

He could practically see the distrust dripping from each
word.

Meaning you follow my instructions to the last
letter. Only way we'll get out of this alive.

Two full minutes passed. He held his breath the entire time, releasing it only when he saw her reply.

Should I be scared?

He wrote, Should I?

That earned him an LOL, followed by, Well, I do have a black belt in jiu-jitsu, so yeah, maybe you should.

Morgan laughed despite himself. Was it possible to glean someone's personality based on text messages alone? Because he liked this kid a lot.

But maybe he was just being biased.

But it has to be in public. I don't trust you yet.

Her message stung, but the use of the word "yet" was promising. Besides, he thoroughly appreciated her caution. No kid of his would ever walk blindly into a situation like an oblivious fool.

I'll contact you in an hour with the details.
Message will come from a different number
so don't be alarmed. Delete this number now.
And our conversation.

She signed off with: Okay . . . TTYS.

TTYS . . . Talk to you soon . . .

Christ. He'd just had a conversation with his daughter.

Or not, his subconscious reminded him.

Morgan sank down on the bed again because his legs had gotten too weak to support his weight. He knew he needed to come up with a plan, but he was too shaken up to formulate one. He wasn't sure what to think, what to feel, what to do . . . He needed . . . needed to . . .

He promptly grew light-headed again, dropping his head between his knees just as the door opened and Noelle burst in.

"What the *hell* is going on?" she demanded.

He weakly lifted his head, and whatever Noelle saw in his eyes seemed to catch her off guard.

"Jim . . . are you okay?"

"Just peachy." He suddenly started to laugh, but he had no idea what was so funny.

Noelle approached him as if he were a rabid dog. "This might be a stupid question—but are you on drugs?"

Laughter continued to roll out of him. "Fuck, no."

"Then why are you acting like a crazy person?"

Out of nowhere, clarity sliced into him, and he rose to his feet feeling clearheaded and alert again.

"Come on," he told her. "We need to come up with a plan."

Her delicate blond eyebrows dipped in consternation. "What kind of plan?"

"I have a meeting tomorrow, and I need to make sure that a bunch of psycho contract killers don't pop up and try to kill me again." He paused. "And to make sure I'm not walking into a trap."

"A trap set by whom?"

"Dietrich."

She narrowed her eyes. "What the hell was in that e-mail, Jim?"

He let out a breath. "Everything."

"Jesus Christ, must you always be so cryptic? I'm not going out in public and risking my life for you unless you stop talking in code and give me a few more details. Who are you meeting? And I swear to God, if you say Ariana, I'm going to—"

"It's not Ariana," he interrupted.

She looked mollified. Slightly. "All right. Then who are you meeting that's so important you're willing to stick your neck out for them?"

He looked her square in the eye and said, "My daughter."

Almost an hour had passed, and Cate was still staring at her cell phone screen. James Morgan's messages were still there, undeniable proof that she'd actually had a conversation with the man. She'd read each message a dozen times, trying to get a sense of his personality based on his words, but it was hard. No smiley faces, no LOLs, but maybe that told her everything she needed to know. He was careful. Shrewd. Intelligent, judging by his coherent sentences.

That was a good start.

Meaning you follow my instructions to the last letter. Only way we'll get out of this alive.

She reread that part two more times, but it still made her apprehensive. Get out of this alive? As in, there was a chance they'd wind up *dead*?

She forced herself not to dwell on that, and skipped to the end of the conversation. He'd said he'd contact her in an hour. Well, the hour was almost up, and impatience was starting to build in her stomach.

She knew her grandfather would call her down for dinner soon, and she wanted to hear from Morgan before that. Otherwise she'd have to wait even longer before she got to read his response. She knew she'd be squirming in her seat the whole time if she had to sit through an entire meal without her phone.

Fortunately, she was spared any potential agony, because as if on cue, a text message suddenly flashed on her screen, exactly two minutes before the hour.

Morgan's message came from a different number just like he'd warned her, and as she carefully read the instructions he'd given her, she couldn't help but gape.

Wow. Talk about . . . what? Overkill? Overpreparedness?

But although it seemed a tad excessive, she refused to let it curb the excitement swirling inside her. All she needed now was an excuse for leaving the estate, a solid reason that her grandfather would never, ever question. Sure, James Morgan had just made the task a million times harder, but she was confident she'd be able to work around his crazy instructions.

With a little outside assistance, of course.

Sighing, she minimized the text window and pulled up her contacts list, which was pathetically meager seeing as she could literally count all of her friends using not one hand, but *half* a hand.

Gabriel picked up on the first ring, his deep voice tickling her ear. "Hey, Cate."

"Gabriel, hey . . . so listen . . . I need your help again."

Chapter 20

Jet lag fucked with a man's head. Or at least that was what Liam had decided to blame his confusion on. Jet lag. Because there was no way Morgan had just announced that tomorrow's mission involved meeting the guy's *daughter*.

As in, a child sired from the loins of one Jim Morgan.

"Dude . . ." Liam gaped at his boss. "That's not the kind of bomb you want to drop five seconds after someone walks through the door."

Next to him, Sullivan sounded equally bewildered. "For realsies. Can I at least take a piss first? Or maybe an anti-psychotic? Because clearly I hallucinated when I heard you tell us that you're meeting your daughter tomorrow."

Ash, who had just carted their gear into the penthouse, looked at his teammates, then the boss, then his teammates again. "Wait—why didn't I know that the boss has a daughter?"

"Because he bloody doesn't!" Sullivan burst out.

"At least not one we were aware of," Liam said dryly.

"Our boss likes to keep his secrets, lads. Haven't you figured that out by now?"

When he heard the Irish brogue, Liam turned around to find a familiar face. Sean Reilly leaned against the living room doorway, his green eyes dancing with amusement.

"Irish!" Sully said with genuine delight. "Whatcha doing in Paris?"

"And what do you mean, *our boss*?" Liam demanded.

"He didn't fill you in? See, I told you he likes secrets."

Sean strode toward them, his long legs encased in green fatigues, while a faded gray T-shirt stretched across his lean, muscular chest. His blond hair had grown out since they'd last seen him, no longer a buzz cut, but shaggy and mussed up.

Morgan, who hadn't said a word during the exchange, turned to his men with a sigh. "Reilly's part of the team now. Guess that makes him the new rookie."

Ash's expression brightened. "Fuck yeah! I've been promoted."

"You wish," Sullivan said. "Reilly's run missions with us before, so technically, he's an old pro. You, on the other hand"—he jabbed a finger at Ash—"still the rookie."

Liam glanced back at Morgan. "Are you being serious here? Do you really have a kid you didn't tell us about?"

"I didn't know about her either until tonight." Morgan's voice was gruff, a tad embarrassed even. He sighed again. "C'mon. I need a drink."

With that, the boss stalked off.

Liam had to admire the spacious penthouse as he trailed after Morgan. It was a nice place, a lot bigger than he'd expected. The low-rise building hadn't looked like much from the outside, but it was pretty damn elegant inside.

They walked into a living room with a cathedral ceiling and an entire wall of windows. Liam immediately noticed the pretty, dark-haired woman sitting on a stool in front of the bar. She was facing out toward them, her elbows resting backward on the granite bar top.

"Why, hello there," Sullivan said, his ladies' man instincts kicking in, as usual. "And who might you be?"

The woman rolled her eyes. They were dark gray, Liam noticed. Big and doelike, but he got the feeling there was nothing fragile about her.

"I might be Bailey." She didn't get up to greet them. "And you guys must be Morgan's A-Team."

"Damn straight," Sully answered, wasting no time striding toward her.

Liam didn't miss the way his teammate's biceps bulged as he leaned in and shook Bailey's hand. Dude had great arms. And he wore way too many tight T-shirts for Liam's comfort.

Wrenching his gaze off Sullivan's arms, he went over to greet Noelle's latest chameleon. And damn, he really liked what he saw. She wore faded blue jeans that hugged a pair of long legs and a V-neck tank top that outlined her perky tits.

"Where's your boss?" Liam asked.

"Right here."

Noelle appeared behind them without warning, and Liam hid a grin when he saw Ash's eyes glaze over a little.

Yup, that was usually the response Noelle elicited from men. While her operative looked casual from head to toe, Noelle exuded pure carnal sex, from her ass-hugging leggings to the black halter top that emphasized her full breasts. Her long golden hair streamed down her back, and her red-painted fingernails tapped the side of the wineglass she held. She was drinking red wine, of course. Dark as blood and probably expensive as shit.

Noelle glanced at Bailey. "I see you've met the Hardy Boys." She smirked at Sully and Liam, and then her pale blue eyes shifted to Ash. "But this one is new." She tossed a look in Morgan's direction. "You didn't tell me you had a new recruit."

Morgan looked annoyed as he made the introductions. "Ash, Noelle. Noelle, Ash."

Ash suddenly blinked as if he'd been snapped back to reality, but his green eyes remained glued on Noelle. "Nice to meet you," he said in his faint drawl.

"A southern boy, huh?" She looked him up and down, and must have liked what she saw, because her eyes gleamed seductively. "What do you say you leave Jim's band of merry men and come work for me?"

Ash's tongue was all but hanging out, which was probably the proper reaction to have when a woman as gorgeous as this one was devouring you with her eyes.

"Ash isn't going anywhere," Morgan said coldly, before turning to address his men. "Put away your gear. I'll debrief you in five."

At the bar, Bailey hopped off her stool and gestured to their duffels. "Come on, I'll show you to your rooms. Only two are available, so you boys will have to double up."

"I'll bunk with Reilly," Sullivan offered. "We've got a lot of catching up to do."

Sean grinned at him. "Hell yeah. Slumber party."

Liam knew the two men had hit it off when Sean had helped the team out in Monte Carlo a while back, but for some reason, the easy camaraderie between them made his jaw tense. He forced himself not to overthink the unwelcome response as he followed the others toward the back corridor.

After they'd deposited their gear in their rooms, everyone took a few minutes to wash up and regroup after the long flight, and then they reconvened in the living room, where Morgan and Bailey were huddled together on the couch.

The two of them were studying Morgan's cell phone, while Noelle stood at the bar, sipping her wine.

"I can work with this," Bailey was saying. "How tall is she again?"

"Five-seven. Three inches taller than you," Morgan said grimly.

"Don't worry. The shoes I've got can give me at least two more inches."

After the men wandered into the living room, Liam noted with interest that Reilly had made a beeline for the couch and plopped down right next to Bailey. There was no mistaking the way she stiffened, or the dark look she flashed Sean before refocusing her attention on Morgan.

Ash and Sullivan settled on the other couch, but Liam headed for the bar, leaning against it as he looked at his boss. "So. How about you tell us about this kid of yours."

Morgan's eyes stayed glued to his phone. "I don't know much more than you do."

"Are those pictures of her?" Liam asked, gesturing to the cell.

The boss nodded absently.

Liam would've given his left nut to sneak a peek at the photos, but the boss didn't seem inclined to share. His dark blue eyes didn't leave the screen, his expression holding a tinge of wonder, as if he couldn't believe the person in the photographs was real.

"So are you ever going to tell us about her or are we just going to sit here in silence?" Reilly said sarcastically.

Morgan finally glanced up. "Look, I wasn't kidding. I just found out about her. Well, that's not entirely accurate. I always knew there was a chance she existed, but it wasn't confirmed until earlier today."

"So who's the baby mama?" Sully piped up.

Every person's gaze, including Liam's, traveled to Noelle. Who balked.

"Hey, don't look at me," she muttered.

"Her mother's name is Ariana Dietrich," Morgan said gruffly. "I hooked up with her seventeen years ago in Berlin."

Noelle snorted. "Gee, that's a nice way of rewriting history."

Liam glanced from his boss to the blonde. As usual, the ever-present sexual tension between them was setting the air on fire.

Morgan's jaw was so rigid it was a miracle he could even speak. "I hooked up with her during an op," he amended. "I was sent in to get close to her father." He glanced at Liam. "During your stint in the DEA, did you ever hear about Walther Dietrich? He didn't run drugs, but he was a major player in the arms game."

Liam's eyes narrowed. "Yeah, I've heard of him. German kingpin, had the reputation for slicing the throat of anyone who crossed him. Didn't he die during an arrest attempt by the ATF?"

"ATF and military Special Forces. It was a joint task force." Morgan paused. "But he didn't die during the ambush. He got away, and so did his daughter—Ariana."

Sullivan shot their boss a knowing look. "Ah, I see. You set a honey trap. Screw the daughter to get to the father."

Morgan nodded, his features pained.

"But she got pregnant."

Another nod. "And then she disappeared. Both of them did. I spent years trying to track them down, but Dietrich was richer than Midas—he had enough money to completely take himself off the grid. I've been keeping tabs on every major arms deal that's gone down over the past two decades, had PIs investigating every arms dealer operating on the globe. But I couldn't find squat."

Morgan sighed. "I thought I got close last year. Remember when I went AWOL after the compound was attacked?

I was in Pakistan chasing down a lead. Dietrich's name had come up in regards to a big weapons deal, but it was a dead end. If they were talking about him, he was long gone before I got there. I know that a deal did go through, but I couldn't get any intel about the seller."

When he went quiet, Noelle picked up where he'd left off. "Dietrich is going by the name Maurice Durand now. He owns a pharmaceutical company on paper, but what he does off the books is still a mystery. I'm guessing he's back to his old tricks, though."

"So Dietrich is the one who hired you to kill Morgan?" Liam asked Noelle.

"That's what we think."

"Where does the daughter—Ariana—fit in?" Ash spoke up.

"She gave birth to my baby," Morgan said roughly. "Or at least someone is claiming she did. Catarina Durand." His gaze softened as it lowered back to his phone. "She e-mailed me today saying she thinks I might be her father. She wants to meet me."

"Trap," Sullivan and Reilly said in unison, then glanced at each other and grinned.

"Trust me, I've considered that," the boss muttered. "But in the event that she's for real, I can't ignore this."

"Okay, so what's the plan?" Sully asked.

"We've arranged to meet at the Eiffel Tower."

Liam let out an incredulous groan. "Are you serious? The place is crawling with tourists. It'll be impossible to vet everyone in the area."

"I had another site in mind, but she insisted on a public place, and she said it had to be a 'believable' one, whatever that means," Morgan said wearily. "The Eiffel Tower was her idea, which means we have to play the hand we've been dealt." He gestured to the map stretched out on the glass coffee table. "Here's what I'm thinking."

Liam moved away from the bar and sat down in the armchair across from the sectional, leaning in for a better look.

Morgan's finger pointed out various locations on the map. "I want snipers positioned here, here, here, and here. All four corners need to be covered. That means Boston, Ash, Reilly, and Noelle."

Noelle wandered over to the couch. "I'm on sniper duty?"

Morgan gave her a brisk nod. "I want you out of sight in case Cate's guards recognize you from the party at the Durand estate."

"Cate?" Liam echoed.

"Guards?" Sully chimed in.

"Catarina. She goes by Cate. She travels with bodyguards, according to her text." He tapped the map again. "Sully, I want you on the ground. Blend in with the crowd, keep an eye on anyone going in and out of the tower."

"Where are you meeting her?" Sullivan asked. "Inside?"

"Top floor."

"Might be a better idea to stay outside where it's more crowded. It'll be easier to lose the guards if you have to."

"Don't worry. The guards won't be looking at us. They'll be focused on our decoy." Morgan gestured to Bailey.

"Bloody hell!"

Sean Reilly's outburst came out of nowhere and had everyone glancing over in surprise.

The Irishman's green eyes glittered with disapproval as he focused them on Bailey. "You're the decoy?"

She looked annoyed. "Of course. Who else?"

"This is too risky," Reilly muttered, his accent becoming more pronounced in his anger. "How many guards does Catarina travel with?"

"She said usually no more than two," Morgan answered.

"Two. That means two pairs of eyes on you," Reilly told Bailey. "If those assholes get a close enough look and realize you're not their charge, they'll shoot you down."

Morgan spoke up confidently. "They won't get close. Cate is going to make sure of it."

Reilly's gaze never left Bailey. "You're willing to put your life in the hands of a teenager?"

"I've done riskier things," she said coldly. "And you're not running this op, nor do you run my life, so how about you chill the fuck out, Sean?"

Liam raised his eyebrows. Well. Clearly those two had a history.

If he had to choose sides, he'd probably go with Bailey on this one, though. The woman worked for Noelle—of course she was capable of getting the job done.

"Bailey will be outside." Morgan's sharp voice invited no argument. "She'll keep the guards' attention on her while I meet with Cate."

"For how long?" Reilly demanded.

"Hopefully no more than thirty minutes. Barring any unforeseen hitches, we should be able to fool the bodyguards and leave without them ever knowing I met with Cate."

"And if there is no meeting?" Noelle countered. "If this is Dietrich launching an ambush?"

"He's not going to shoot up the Eiffel Tower," Morgan said assertively. "If anything, he'll try to apprehend me, or maybe he'll have a sniper waiting. But we'll stake out the entire area before we go in. If we sense anything fishy, we abort. But I don't think it's a trap. I think this is real."

"You think it is, or you want it to be?"

Noelle had voiced what they were all thinking, but Morgan didn't answer. He just stood up and dismissed them all by walking away, while Noelle marched after him in irritation.

With that, the briefing was over.

Liam lingered in the living room, unhappy about the plan that had been outlined. It contained too many unknowns. Too many variables. They could stake out the area, sure, but it was a large enough perimeter that a sniper could easily slip through.

Shit. He really hoped the boss knew what he was doing.

The other men stood up, Ash heading for the doorway.

"I'm turning in," the rookie announced. "I'm way too tired right now to think about what a clusterfuck tomorrow is gonna be."

After Ash had disappeared in the corridor, Liam noticed Bailey trying to make a discreet exit herself, moving in a slow glide toward the front hall.

"Where are you going?" Sean demanded.

Her back stiffened. "I'm going to the bar down the street to grab a drink."

Sean pointed to the bar. "There're drinks right over there."

"Noelle doesn't keep tequila in the house."

"Bloody hell, Bailey, it's one in the morning."

"And I want a drink." Her tone went razor sharp. "I didn't realize I needed to ask your permission."

Sean took a step forward. "Fine. I'll go with you."

"No, thank you. I don't want your company."

"Tough shit."

They stood there glaring at each other for so long that Liam felt compelled to step in. The look in Bailey's eyes made it clear she didn't want to spend a single additional second with Reilly, but Liam knew an alpha male when he saw one, and there was no way in hell Sean was letting the woman roam the streets alone at one o'clock in the morning.

"How about if I join you instead?" he suggested, seeking out Bailey's annoyed gaze. "I could totally go for a shot of tequila before bed."

Bailey hesitated, then nodded. "Fine, you can come." She pointed a finger at Sean. "You, on the other hand, cannot."

And then she marched out the door.

When Reilly tried to follow her, Sully quickly clapped a hand on his arm. "I think you might need to let the lady win this one, mate. Boston will make sure she stays safe. Right, Liam?"

He nodded briskly. "Right."

Unhappiness colored Sean's eyes.

"Unless you'd rather *I* go with her?" Sully said, raising one eyebrow.

A grin sprang to Sean's lips. "No fucking way, Aussie. I don't want your man-whore hands anywhere near her."

Sully grinned back. "Good call." He gave Sean a good-natured punch on the arm. "C'mon, I haven't seen you in ages. Let's have a drink and catch up."

After a beat, Sean capitulated. "Fine, you guys win. I'll back off. Tonight," he added meaningfully.

Liam caught up to Bailey just as she was stepping into the elevator. Her eyes continued to glitter with irritation as she pressed the button for the lobby.

"So what's the deal with you and Reilly?" he asked with a grin.

Bailey sighed. "We slept together once, and now he thinks I belong to him."

She didn't elaborate, and he didn't want to pry, so he ended up changing the subject to tomorrow's mission. They discussed the logistics of it on the way to the bar, and five minutes later, they were seated side by side at the counter, ordering tequila shots.

Liam was surprised by how empty the place was. Most bars were jam-packed on Friday nights, but here, nearly every stool, chair, and booth was unoccupied.

Bailey followed his gaze and offered an explanation. "This new pub opened around the corner. The drinks are dirt cheap, so all the tourists go there now. You won't find me complaining, though. I love this place, and back in the day, it used to have a line all the way down the block."

He liked it too. It was definitely a bar aimed for men, with its wood-paneled walls, large booths, and pictures of European soccer players plastered on the walls. They had the entire counter to themselves, except for the lone male patron sitting at the far end of it nursing a glass of vodka. He wore the weathered look of someone who'd run into hard times, staring vacantly at the neon sign above the shelves of liquor bottles.

After the bartender had slid two shots in front of them, they tapped their glasses in a toast, tipped them back in unison, and ordered another round.

"Reilly's a decent guy, you know," Liam had to say out of loyalty to his friend. "He helped us out in Monte Carlo last year."

Bailey stared at him. And then she said, "He pretended to be his twin brother the night we slept together."

Liam's mouth fell open. "Oh. Shit."

"I think 'oh shit' just about sums it up," she said flatly.

He had a million more questions, but she didn't give him the chance to voice a single one.

"What about you?" she asked. "Do you have a girlfriend?"

"Nope," he answered.

"Any hobbies?"

"You mean, other than kicking ass and taking names?"

She rolled her eyes. "Yes, other than that."

Liam had to think it over. "Honestly, I've never had much free time. I joined the DEA right after college and was pretty much married to my job. Then I quit and signed up with Morgan's crew." He shrugged. "I don't do much during my downtime. Hang around at the compound, shoot pool with the boys, play poker. Not very exciting, huh?"

"Do you ever take vacations?"

The question summoned the memory of the last trip he'd taken. He and Sullivan had spent two months traveling the Mediterranean on Sully's sailboat the previous summer, docking at every port and hooking up with an obscene number of beautiful women. In fact, it had been the first time they'd ever had a threesome.

After that, threesomes became a staple in their friendship—and Liam had enjoyed the hell out of every single one. His Irish Catholic background had never meshed well with the wild, sexual streak running through him. He'd spent years ignoring his dirty fantasies, the wicked thoughts that probably would've sent his local priest into cardiac arrest. Then he'd met Sullivan, a man who didn't give a flying fuck what other people thought. A man who acted on impulse, grabbed life by the balls, and did whatever the hell got him off without worrying about the consequences.

It had all been fun and games until . . . Christ, until last month, when he and Sully had picked up a cute tour guide from the bar in San José. That night, Liam had been balls-deep in the lovely redhead, drilling her hard while she sucked Sullivan off, and in that moment, his thoughts had turned from wicked to downright filthy. He'd been looking at Sullivan, at that broad chest carved out of stone, the tight six-pack, the thick cock filling the redhead's eager mouth, and he'd come so violently he'd almost passed out.

And now, every time he climaxed, it was to the thought of the person he shouldn't be thinking about rather than the one he was fucking.

"What's that look for?"

Bailey's inquisitive voice drew him back to the present.

He shifted on his stool. "What look?"

"I don't know . . . You got real agitated all of a sudden. What's on your mind?"

"Trust me—you don't want to know."

The bartender delivered their next round of shots, and this time Liam didn't wait to toast. He just gulped down the tequila and hoped the alcohol burned away all thoughts of Sullivan Port.

"I totally want to know," Bailey insisted. When he hesitated, her eyes gleamed. "Girl trouble, huh?"

"God, I fucking wish."

She laughed. "Fine, don't tell me. But for future purposes, you should know I'm really good at keeping secrets."

He didn't doubt it—she worked for Noelle, after all—but he also wasn't ready to spill his guts to a woman he'd just met.

With another sigh, he stole her shot glass right out of her hand and slugged it back.

Her jaw dropped. "Totally uncool. Just for that, big boy, I'm forcing you to tell me what's bothering you."

Liam couldn't help but grin. He really liked her. She was so easygoing, and she had a great laugh. A great rack too—the way she was leaning forward gave him an eyeful of cleavage, and he sure as hell wasn't complaining about the view.

"Stop leering at my tits and get talking."

He let out a breath. "Fine. Okay. So . . . it's my teammate . . . Sullivan."

"The hot Aussie?"

"Yup."

"What about him?"

Liam swallowed, hesitation tightening his chest. He didn't normally confide in strangers, but this stuff with Sully had been eating at him for weeks now. Maybe if he said it out loud, if he *heard* himself say it, then he'd snap out of this insanity and things could finally go back to the way they were.

He drew a deep breath and met Bailey's curious eyes. "I can't stop thinking about screwing him."

She blinked.

Then grinned.

Then held up her hand and signaled the waiter. "Barkeep, we're gonna need a couple more of these."

Chapter 21

The next morning, Cate joined her grandfather for breakfast in the dining room he insisted on using even when they didn't have guests. The gleaming walnut table seated eighteen, but most of the time it accommodated only three — Cate, her grandfather, and Nikolaus, who hadn't come downstairs yet. She'd always thought it was weird that her grandfather's employee lived with them, but Nik had been around for as long as she could remember.

Truth was, he was probably the closest thing she had to a father. When she was little, she'd asked him all the time if he was her daddy, and he'd always sounded so incredibly regretful each time he told her he wasn't.

As she'd gotten older, she'd begun to suspect that although Nik wasn't her dad, he *wished* he was. Which made a lot of sense in conjunction with her other longtime suspicion — that Nik was in love with her mother.

But she'd never had the courage to ask him about *that*, mostly because it made her super-uncomfortable.

"Good morning, sweetheart." Her grandfather greeted her in German, as he always did.

Although he'd insisted that Cate be fluent in several languages, Maurice had made it clear that he preferred they speak German at home. He claimed to like the way it rolled off his tongue, which Cate found odd, because in her opinion, German was brusque, even aggressive at times. She thought French and English flowed way more smoothly, with Italian coming in as a close third.

Once she'd settled in her chair, their maid, Audrey, immediately appeared to pour her a glass of orange juice. Cate took a quick sip, then swiped a hot, buttery croissant from the plate on the table.

In the chair opposite hers, her grandfather raised his coffee cup to his lips and took a delicate sip. She was always startled by how youthful he looked. He was in his sixties, but he appeared decades younger, and he was healthy as a horse, which was pretty darn impressive.

"Grandpa . . ." she started awkwardly. "I wanted to ask you something."

"What is it, Catarina?"

She nibbled on her croissant, then set it down on her plate. "Gabriel and I were talking the other day when he came by to see his mother, and somehow we got into a conversation about the Eiffel Tower. He was so horrified when he found out I've never been."

Maurice chuckled. "I don't know why anyone would want to visit that tourist trap."

Cate stifled a groan. Okay. Not the response she'd been hoping for.

"Well . . . um . . ." She felt her cheeks heat up. "I wouldn't mind seeing it. I mean, I have seen it, in pictures, and a few times when we drove by it, but I'd really like to see the view from the top."

Her grandfather put down his cup, his dark eyes studying her intently.

"Gabriel offered to take me this morning," she said with a hopeful look. "Would it be all right if I went?"

Now he looked displeased.

"Please?" she pleaded. "I think it would be really fun, and we wouldn't be going for too long, just an hour or two. I already finished all the homework Monsieur Paschal assigned, so I have nothing else to do."

Her last remark got his attention. "Perhaps you can visit your mother, then."

Cate's composure wavered. "Oh. I . . . I thought she went to the spa on Saturdays."

"She does, but I'm sure she'd rather see you if she had

the chance." He must have glimpsed her reluctance, because he softened his tone. "You're her daughter, Catarina, and she loves you. I know she misses you. I can see it in her eyes whenever we talk about you."

An unhappy sigh lodged in Cate's chest. She couldn't see a way out of this hole she'd dug herself into, but damn it, she wasn't giving up yet.

"Maybe Gabriel can drop me off at *Maman*'s after we visit the tower?" she suggested.

Her compromise brought a satisfied smile to Maurice's lips. "I believe you have yourself a deal, young lady."

It was ridiculously hard to stop the excited grin from stretching across her face, but she knew she couldn't appear too eager. Besides, she wasn't done asking for favors.

"One more thing," she hedged. "Do you think you could ask Bruno and Christian to stay away today?"

Her grandfather was quick to shoot her down. "Out of the question. You will not leave this house unprotected."

"No, that's not what I meant," she said hastily. "Obviously they'll come with us, but I was just hoping they could give us some . . . distance, I guess. Every time I go somewhere, they're always hovering over me. I just want to be a normal teenage girl today and walk around with my friend without my bodyguards breathing over my shoulder."

"But you're not a normal teenage girl. You're the granddaughter of a powerful man, and powerful men have enemies. I can't ever lose you, Catarina. I love you too much."

"You won't lose me, and I love you too." She sighed. "But just this once, can you settle for being protective, and not *over*protective? I understand why I need bodyguards, but can't they watch me from afar today? Give us just enough space that I feel normal for a change?"

Her grandfather went quiet. She could practically see his shrewd brain mulling over all the implications. The longer his silence dragged on, the less hopeful she became. Crap. He was going to say no. She could see it in his eyes.

But the moment he opened his mouth, an unexpected savior strode into the room.

"I couldn't help but overhear, Maurice, and truth be told, I think our Catarina has a point." With an indulgent smile, Nikolaus sat in the chair next to Cate's before addressing her grandfather again. "There's no harm in agreeing to her request. Let her have one day where she doesn't feel like she's being fussed over."

Still smiling, Nik poured himself some coffee, then withdrew a silver flask from the inner pocket of his navy blazer. He uncapped it and added a splash of whiskey to his cup.

Cate tried not to gape at him, but her shock hadn't come from seeing him add alcohol to his cup—he always drank his coffee that way. No, what surprised her was that he was actually taking her side. The other day he'd all but forbidden her to spend time with Gabriel, and now he was encouraging it?

Probably because we'll be in public, where we can't have sex, she thought wryly.

"What's the harm?" Nik said again. "Bruno and Christian can drink their cappuccinos and keep an eye on the kids from a distance."

After another beat of silence, her grandfather capitulated. "All right. I suppose I'm worrying for nothing. And it will only be a couple of hours, right?"

She nodded eagerly. "Maybe even less. Gabriel has chores to do around the house, so he can't be gone for too long."

Trying to appear casual, she finished her croissant and polished off the rest of her juice, then scraped back her chair. "I should go upstairs and get ready before Gabriel arrives."

Maurice narrowed his eyes. "I suppose he'll be picking you up on that motorcycle of his?"

"It's a Vespa. And he's a very good driver."

"He has a helmet for you?"

Cate had to laugh. "You know he does—you're the one who bought it and insisted he keep it on him at all times."

"That's right. I did." Her grandfather reached for his coffee. "All right. Have fun today, Catarina. And tell Gabriel he can drop you off here when you're done. We'll leave for your mother's house the moment you get back."

With a nod, Cate hurried off, still amazed that she'd gotten him not only to agree to let her go, but also to ease up on her security detail.

But Nik backing her up? What the heck was *that* about?

On the other hand, who was she to look a gift horse in the mouth?

As butterflies of excitement fluttered in her belly, she dashed upstairs and made a beeline for her bedroom. The second she was alone, her excitement transformed into a serious case of nerves, and she found that her palms were damp as she closed the door.

She leaned against it and took a deep breath, her mind beginning to race.

What if she was wrong and James Morgan wasn't her father?

What if he *was* her father and he turned out to be a total dick?

Or worst of all—what if he turned out to be amazing? What if he was everything she'd ever dreamed of?

A part of her almost hoped he wouldn't be, because even though she'd reached out and made contact, she had the sinking feeling that this would be the only opportunity she'd ever get to see him, at least if her grandfather had anything to say about it.

Which meant she had to make every second count.

Noelle was smoking a cigarette on the balcony when Bailey stepped through the French doors wearing blue jeans and a faded green tank top.

At first glance, Bailey could be considered average looking. At second glance, maybe even pretty. But Noelle knew firsthand that the woman was stunning when she wanted to be. Bailey's face was like an empty canvas. One stroke here, another one there, and she was able to transform into an exquisite beauty. She was a master of disguise, just like Isabel Roma, except Bailey was even more exceptional at altering her appearance.

"We have to go," Bailey informed her.

"I know."

When Noelle didn't budge, Bailey leaned against the doorframe with a thoughtful tilt to her head. "So . . . what's going on with you and Morgan?"

She shrugged. "Absolutely nothing."

"Then you're *not* sleeping with him?"

"I didn't say that."

The other woman seemed to be fighting back laughter. "Interesting. So you're screwing the guy, but there's nothing between you."

"Yep."

"Okay, then. Ready to go?"

Noelle hid a smile as she put out her cigarette in the glass ashtray on the railing. One of her favorite things about Bailey? The woman didn't pry. Unlike Isabel, who poked at people until they caved, or Juliet, who taunted the details out of them. But Bailey and Abby, well, they knew when to leave certain matters alone, probably because they lived with so many secrets of their own.

As she walked inside, she had to wonder why she was even still here. She should be long gone by now. Sunbathing on her private island in the Maldives, meeting some old friends in Tokyo, lying around in her Sicilian villa. She could be doing any damn thing she wanted, and yet she was here. At Jim's side.

Helping him meet his daughter.

Ever since she'd found out about the girl, Noelle had been trying valiantly not to think of her, or how under drastically different circumstances, Catarina Durand could have been hers.

Hers and Jim's.

There was a time when she would have happily given birth to the man's child. Not just happily, but *eagerly*. She'd wanted nothing more than to spend the rest of her life with him and be a mother to his children, but then he'd betrayed her, officially squashing any notions of happily-ever-after. Not to mention motherhood.

She supposed it wasn't too late, though. She was only in her midthirties—women were popping out rugrats well into their fifties these days.

But who was she kidding? She would never have a child. She was a killer, and killers weren't allowed to have kids. Any social service worker worth their salt would snatch her kid away if they discovered what she did for a living.

"Boss?"

Her head jerked up at the sound of Bailey's voice. "Did you say something?"

"I said I'm going to take the Ducati and meet you guys there. I'm popping out here."

"Sounds good," she said as the other woman headed for the front door.

After Bailey was gone, Noelle continued toward the elevator, where she found Jim waiting for her. His men had left a short while ago, but for some reason, he'd decided to ride with her.

To keep an eye on her, maybe? It wouldn't surprise her. She'd made no attempt to hide her displeasure about today's plans, and she got the feeling Jim didn't trust her to back him up.

"Ready?" he said roughly.

"Always."

She didn't meet his eyes—she was too busy looking at the cell phone in his hand. The same phone that contained the photographs Catarina had e-mailed him yesterday.

Noelle suspected he'd stayed up all night staring at those photos, because he hadn't joined her in bed, and when she'd walked into the living room this morning, he'd been sprawled on the couch, clutching that damn phone against his chest.

She hadn't asked to see the pictures. She couldn't stomach the thought of seeing a mini Ariana looking back at her.

The elevator doors opened. Jim stepped through them first, and Noelle eyed his getup as she followed him into the car.

He was lightly armed, which was all he could get away with in his cargo pants, T-shirt, and thin blue long-sleeve. In the summer heat, he'd stand out like a sore thumb if he wore a jacket or bulkier shirt; even his button-down seemed excessive, considering the day's sweltering temperatures. But the shirt was there to shield the handgun in his waistband, and it was doing its job—the bulge of the weapon was only visible if you peered closely, as she did now in order to check out his ass.

Lord, she couldn't deny that he had a great ass. Deliciously taut, with just enough meat on it for a woman to grab onto.

She still wanted him. As disheartening as it was, there was no denying that either.

She was nowhere close to getting her fill of the man, though she imagined that after today, there'd be no more sex. No, his attention would be elsewhere from this point on.

His attention would be on his daughter.

His and Ariana's daughter.

Bitterness rose in Noelle's throat as she once again allowed the thought to sink in. It didn't matter what Jim might or might not have felt for Ariana Dietrich—the woman had still given birth to his child, which meant that depending on how today's meeting went, Ariana was about to be part of Jim's life again.

Forever, this time.

Well, Noelle didn't plan on sticking around for the family reunion. She might not have fucked Jim out of her system yet, but she was willing to sacrifice her libido and leave the city unfulfilled as long as it meant not having to see him get his happily-ever-after.

Her throat burned from the irony of it. Jim had snatched away *her* storybook ending, and now here he was, getting his. Christ, he didn't deserve it.

Then take it from him. Kill him.

Noelle swallowed a sigh, not even bothering to pretend the threat held any weight. She'd already proven that she couldn't kill Jim. Whenever he got close enough, she ended up sleeping with him instead.

God. Her lack of willpower was pathetic.

But not anymore. Nope, after today she refused to give him any more power over her. Sexually, emotionally, mentally—Jim Morgan wouldn't be able to touch her anymore.

Because after today, he would never see her again.

"Are you nervous?" Warmth and tenderness clung to Gabriel's tone as he pulled the key out of the Vespa's ignition.

Cate's heartbeat was erratic as she ran her hand over her scalp to smooth out her helmet hair. "A little."

His brown eyes twinkled knowingly. "A little?"

She bit her lip. "Okay, a lot."

With a gentle smile, Gabriel reached out and stroked her

cheek. Cate's heart did a wild flip because it was the first time he'd ever touched her like that.

"It's okay to be nervous," he said softly. "I mean, this is a big deal."

"I know."

He brushed his thumb over her cheek in a soothing motion, and she found herself leaning into his touch. Gosh, it felt good. It felt really, really good.

Swallowing, she swept her gaze over his face. He was so good-looking, so masculine, and she wasn't comfortable with these new and terrifying feelings he evoked in her. She'd known this boy her entire life, but the hot, achy way he made her feel was a recent development.

Face it, you're in crush with him.

Oh God. It was true. She was totally crushing on Gabriel Traver.

Unfortunately, now was definitely not the time to think about that.

"You know, you don't have to do this," he told her.

She swallowed again. "Yes, I do."

As if on cue, her cell phone buzzed, and she reached into the front pocket of her jeans to get it. The message on the screen only triggered a fresh burst of nervousness.

"He says it's a go," she murmured. "The decoy is waiting."

Gabriel looked unhappy. "I don't like this, Cate. What if Christian and Bruno figure out I'm not with you?"

"They won't." She spoke with confidence she certainly didn't feel, but she figured only one of them was allowed to worry, and Gabriel was already filling that role.

She, on the other hand, was determined to have faith in James Morgan.

Clearly the guy was some kind of supersoldier, judging by the ridiculously detailed instructions he'd given her. Last night she'd sent him nearly a dozen photos, shots of her from various angles, pictures of the clothes she planned on wearing, her shoes, accessories, the whole nine yards.

And the orders hadn't stopped after he'd received the pictures. He'd asked her to wear her hair down, to bring sunglasses even if the day ended up being overcast, to give her cell phone to Gabriel before she entered the tower.

It seemed like a huge amount of trouble for one little meeting, and yet Cate trusted him in spite of all of his insane requests. Did that make her equally insane, though? To readily trust a man she didn't even know?

As she and Gabriel hopped off the Vespa, she glanced over at the shiny black Audi that had followed them into the pay parking lot just southeast of the tower. Her bodyguards were sitting inside the car, waiting for her and Gabriel to embark on their day trip.

The two men had assured her they would keep their distance today; Bruno had even winked at her when Gabriel picked her up at the estate earlier. Evidently her bodyguards had figured out what she herself had only realized today, and they seemed more than happy to give Cate and her "date" some much-needed privacy.

"Ready?" Gabriel held out his hand.

She placed her palm in his, and her pulse sped up when he laced their fingers together. It was the first time she'd ever held hands with a guy before.

She kinda liked it.

"Cate?"

She moved her gaze off their interlocked fingers and noticed his questioning expression.

"Ready?" he said again.

She managed a nervous nod.

"All right, then. Let's go meet your father."

Jim Morgan didn't get scared. He was a hardened mercenary, for fuck's sake. He'd been shot. Knifed. Nearly blown up by grenades. He'd tangled with criminals, warlords, enemy soldiers. He'd almost died more times than he could count.

And not once, not one measly time, had he ever been scared.

Until today.

No, that wasn't true. The fear had actually taken root yesterday, the moment he'd laid eyes on those photographs of Catarina Durand.

He'd spent hours staring at the pictures, hadn't slept a wink because he was too fascinated with the face peering at him from his phone. Now he was about to see her in person, and his palms were clammy as hell, his heart pounding incessantly and his throat tight with apprehension.

"She's here."

Liam's Boston accent came over the comm, a reminder that Morgan wasn't just here to visit one of the world's most famous landmarks. His team was positioned around the perimeter, ready to swoop in and save his ass if things went south.

"Just pulled into the lot we told them to park in," Liam reported. "We've got two bodyguards in a black Audi, but they're keeping their distance."

"Could still be a trap." Sean Reilly's voice filled the line.

It's not a trap, Morgan almost blurted out, but he held his tongue.

"All clear from where I'm standing," Ash checked in.

"Everything down here looks secure," Sullivan piped up.

When Noelle didn't check in, Morgan scratched his cheek, the motion of his hand triggering the nearly invisible mic tucked in his ear. The earpiece was motion-activated, which meant that the speaker's voice would only be transmitted over the comm when he wanted it to, leaving the feed free of constant chatter.

"Noelle?" he murmured without moving his lips.

There was a beat, and then, "All clear. No sign of trouble."

He relaxed the instant he heard her voice. A part of him wished Noelle was on the observation deck with him, and that told him he was even more nervous than he'd thought. The woman had never caused him anything but extreme agitation, and now he wanted her by his side?

He couldn't even begin to decode that fucked-up logic.

Pushing away the troubling notion, he fixed his gaze on the elevator across the platform. Bailey hadn't checked in either, but he knew she had a lot on her plate at the moment. She and Cate were scheduled to rendezvous in the bathroom of a small café near the tower, where Bailey would not only have to transform, but do it well enough to fool Cate's bodyguards.

Morgan found himself holding his breath as he waited for Bailey's report. He curled his fingers over the railing and shifted his gaze, taking in the spectacular view in front of him. He focused on the Arc de Triomphe in the distance, slowly releasing his breath as he stared at the majestic monument.

"She's on her way up." Bailey's soft voice finally echoed in his ear.

"Everything go okay?" he demanded.

"Easy as pie," Noelle's chameleon said cheerfully. "You'll see."

The feed went quiet after that. Morgan once again glanced at the elevator, once again holding his breath.

An eternity seemed to pass as he waited for Catarina Durand to appear. The elevator doors opened on two different occasions, a fresh rush of tourists pouring out each time. And each time, his chest squeezed with disappointment because Cate wasn't among them.

Eventually the disappointment became impatience, then concern. She should have been there by now. Something was wrong.

He went to trigger his mic, but suddenly the doors opened again and he saw her.

Holy mother of God.

She was beautiful. His daughter was beautiful.

The long, dark blond hair from her photos was gone, replaced by a black wig with sweeping bangs, but it wasn't her hair that ensnared his gaze, nor was it the pretty yellow dress clinging to her willowy body. It was her face, heart-stoppingly beautiful, pure and total perfection.

She hesitated in front of the elevator, looking around nervously, and then she spotted him, and her eyes widened slightly.

From across the room, he gave an imperceptible nod.

A second later, she began making her way to him.

His gaze stayed glued on hers, while his pulse drummed in his ears in a fast, deafening tempo. By the time she reached him, his entire mouth had gone dry. He couldn't believe she was actually there, standing two feet away from him. He quickly memorized every detail of her face—the slight pout of her lips, her rosy complexion, the tiny beauty mark high on her left cheek. But it was her cobalt blue eyes that transfixed him, making it impossible to look away.

Morgan gulped hard, trying to bring moisture to his

cotton-stuffed mouth. "You . . ." He swallowed again, his voice coming out hoarse. "You have my eyes."

Cate looked startled for a moment. And then she nodded.

"I know."

Chapter 22

Morgan had no idea what to say next. He was too busy staring at Cate, too overwhelmed by the entire situation. He saw her resemblance to Ariana, but there was something more refined about Cate's features. And her expression conveyed a gleam of intelligence that Ariana had never possessed.

"Did everything go okay down there?" he asked awkwardly.

"Oh, you mean when I walked into the bathroom and a strange woman ordered me to change clothes with her? Sure, it went great. Super fun."

His lips twitched. "I'm sorry for all the theatrics, but I like to take certain precautions."

"Really? I never would have guessed." She offered a dry grin, but it faded fast, as another wave of discomfort hung over them.

"I . . ." He cleared his throat. "I don't know where to start."

Cate fiddled with the strap of her brown leather purse, which Bailey must have given her because the photos she'd sent him of her outfit had shown a green canvas messenger bag. "Me neither," she admitted. "I didn't think it would be this awkward."

As she went quiet again, Morgan forced himself to quit staring at the girl and act like a soldier. They might have eluded Cate's guards for the moment, but that didn't mean he was allowed to relax. For all he knew, he could still be walking into an ambush.

"So..." He paused. "You're turning seventeen soon, huh?"

"In a couple of weeks, actually."

"Do you, uh, go to school?"

"I'm homeschooled." She rested both hands on the railing, peered out at the cityscape for a moment, then glanced back at him. "I'm graduating early, though. Just finishing up my last two senior courses now."

He knitted his brows. "In the summer?"

"Education doesn't take a vacation." A blush rose in her cheeks. "Sorry. That's what Grandpa always says."

Morgan froze.

Grandpa.

Out of nowhere, a bolt of fury struck him down, making his hands tremble.

Walther Dietrich had played a part in Cate's upbringing.

Morgan hadn't allowed himself to dwell on that horrifying truth, but he couldn't ignore it now. Christ. A ruthless arms dealer had raised his daughter.

And yet... she seemed normal. She seemed... good.

He didn't sense an ounce of pretension in her, and certainly not the nasty streak that had been running inside of Ariana. Walther had raised Ariana too, and she'd been a spoiled brat who'd treated the people around her like trash.

A part of him had expected Catarina Durand to be the same, but the young girl in front of him looked and acted like a smart, well-adjusted kid.

"Uh..." He searched for something to say. "Do you have any questions for me?"

He'd expected her to hesitate, but there was absolutely no delay in her response. "Why did you leave my mother?" she said bluntly.

Morgan blinked. "Oh. You don't pull any punches, huh?" He paused again. "How much has your grandfather told you?"

Frustration clouded her face. "Nothing. He told me nothing."

"He never said anything about me?" Morgan said with a frown. "Nothing about my relationship with your mother?"

"He told me that you never loved her, and that you left her when she got pregnant. He tried to track you down after I was born, but apparently you were already dead."

Morgan's jaw went rigid. "He was lying to you."

She rolled her eyes. "No kidding, seeing as you're standing right here in front of me." Her amused expression dissolved into anger. "But he knew the truth the whole time. He knew you weren't dead. I found a file about you in his office—that's how I got your contact information."

"You snooped around in his office?"

The look she shot him was downright defiant. "I picked the lock and broke in."

He choked down a laugh. "You picked the lock," he echoed.

A faint grin tugged on her lips, and she didn't appear at all remorseful. "My friend is the son of a locksmith. He taught me how to do it."

"Your friend . . . the one you came here with today?"

She nodded. "Gabriel. We pretty much grew up together."

Morgan narrowed his eyes. "Is he your boyfriend?"

His tone came out sharper than intended, and was laced with disapproval neither of them had expected, which swiftly brought the gleam of defiance back to her eyes.

"And if he is? What are you going to do about it? Forbid me to see him?"

He drew in a frustrated breath, but at the same time, he couldn't fight a spark of pride. Man, this girl wasn't afraid to speak her mind. He liked that. It told him she had a backbone. She had *fire*. It was a healthy fire, the kind that gave a person drive and confidence.

"I guess I don't have any right to do that, do I?" With a rueful shake of his head, he met her eyes and added, "You should know that some of the things your grandfather told you were true. I didn't love your mother."

"I see."

It didn't surprise him that she took his confession in stride. He got the feeling nothing fazed this girl.

"But that doesn't mean I didn't care about you." He swallowed again, wishing he was better at articulating himself. Wishing he wasn't a gruff motherfucker who didn't know the first thing about talking about his feelings. "I searched for you. I've been searching for you since the day I found out your mother was pregnant."

Her mouth puckered in a frown. "Haven't you ever heard of a phone book?"

"It's more complicated than that. There are so many things you don't know."

"Duh. How about you tell me?"

Her sarcasm made him smile. Lord, how was it possible for her to be so much like him when they'd never met before today?

There was so much he wanted to say to her. So much he wanted to *know* about her. But he had to tread carefully. He couldn't bombard her with questions, and he certainly couldn't give her too many answers. Not until he was certain that her motives for coming here were pure. And besides, no matter how he felt about Walther and Ariana, they were a major part of Cate's life, and he knew he couldn't drag their names through the mud in front of her.

"I will tell you," he answered. "I'll tell you whatever you want to know, Cate. Only it can't be today. We don't have a lot of time."

"I know." She sounded genuinely regretful.

He reached into his pocket for the burner phone he'd brought, his fingers trembling as he handed it to her. "Take this. From now on if you need to contact me, use this phone. It can't be traced back to either one of us."

Nodding, she tucked the phone into her purse. "'Kay. Thanks."

"I want to see you again," he said hoarsely. "How can we make that happen?"

"I don't know." She nibbled on her bottom lip. "My grandfather wouldn't be happy if he found out I saw you. I mean, he told me you were *dead*. I'm pretty sure that means he doesn't want me to have any contact with you. And my mother . . ." She stopped talking, looking even more distressed than before.

Morgan bit the inside of his cheek, then forced himself to ask, "How . . . how is your mother?"

A groove of hesitation dug into Cate's forehead. "It's complicated."

As frustrating as her response was, it brought another flicker of pride. Everyone he knew always accused him of being a cryptic motherfucker, and it turned out his kid was just the same.

"Is she well?" he pressed. "Was she good to you when you were growing up?"

He didn't miss the sorrow that floated through her eyes. "More or less." She shrugged. "My grandfather is my guardian. *Maman* has no say in my life."

The confession roused curiosity as well as suspicion. What had Ariana done in order to be replaced as Cate's guardian? He was dying to ask, but he got the feeling Cate wouldn't tell him, so he didn't push her.

"Walther takes care of you, then."

Her face donned a blank look. "Walther?"

He quickly corrected himself. "Maurice. I meant Maurice."

"I think you said exactly what you meant." Her mouth tightened, but again she proved just how alike they were, because she also didn't push. "I guess there *is* a lot I don't know."

Morgan moistened his dry lips. He suddenly found himself yearning to hold her. Just throw his arms around her and envelop her in a warm hug, but he was terrified that if he did, she'd recoil in horror.

"So what now?" he said softly.

Cate sighed. "I'm going to tell Grandpa I know the truth. That you're alive, and I saw you."

"I don't know if that's a good idea."

"It might be the only way I'll get to see you again. I don't have a lot of opportunities to sneak around. I'm watched all the time."

"Why?" he asked sharply. "Why do you need bodyguards, Cate?"

"Grandpa is very rich, which means he has a lot of enemies. I used to think he was overprotective, but as I got older I understood where he was coming from. There was this . . . incident . . . a while ago, and it made him even more paranoid—"

"What kind of incident?" Morgan cut in.

"That's not important. But it means I'm not free to see

you whenever I want. If I want you in my life, he's going to have to agree to it."

Morgan's heart clenched. "Do you? Want me in your life, I mean?"

She was quiet for so long he thought she wouldn't answer, but finally she nodded. "Yeah, I think I do."

He hesitated. "Your grandfather will never agree."

"How can you be so sure?"

Because he hired someone to kill me.

Morgan reined in the words before they came rushing out. He didn't want to frighten her, first and foremost, but considering she'd spoken about her grandfather without malice or contempt, he doubted she'd believe him anyway.

But he knew without a shred of doubt that Walther Dietrich would never allow him to have contact with Cate. Morgan had made an enemy out of Dietrich the moment his deception had come to light, and the only way this war between them would end was when one of them was no longer alive to fight it.

"Why don't you come with me?" The question popped out before he could stop it.

Cate looked startled. "What?"

"Instead of going back to Wal—Maurice. You can just leave here with me. Today. Right now."

"And go where?" she asked with a frown.

"My house. You could come and live with me."

Christ, what was he doing? Every word that left his mouth sounded like pure and total insanity, even to him. And even more insane were the thoughts running through his head. He was actually contemplating how to take her with him if she refused, the orders he'd give his team if he needed their help in subduing her.

Jesus. He was seriously considering abducting his own kid.

Cate spoke again, sounding as panicked as he felt. "I can't do that. I already have a home. And friends. And my grandfather . . ." Anxiety flooded her blue eyes. "I love my grandfather. He's a good person, no matter what he might have done in the past, and he loves me. I can't just leave him."

Morgan's pulse kicked up a notch. "But he's not a good

person, Cate. There's so much you don't know, but that's the one thing I *can* tell you. Your grandfather is a very dangerous man. He's not who you—"

"I don't believe you," she interrupted angrily.

When several people turned to stare at them, Cate took a deep breath and quickly lowered her voice.

"I'm not going anywhere with you. I don't even know if you're my father, for Pete's sake. Yeah, we have the same eyes, but that doesn't mean anything. Shouldn't we do a DNA test or something? To prove it?"

"We can if you want. You can give Bailey a hair sample when you meet with her again, and I'll take care of it."

"Then do it. But until I know for sure, I'm not going to see you again."

His heart stopped. "Cate—"

"I have to go. I'm sorry, but I can't . . . I can't be here anymore." Her eyes conveyed nothing but panic again. "I'm glad we met, I really am, but this is too much to absorb right now. I have to go."

"Cate—"

"Tell Bailey I'm coming downstairs. I'll meet her in the café in five minutes."

And then she was walking away.

No, *running* away. She practically sprinted to the elevator, keeping her back to him as she waited for the car.

He could have gone after her, but he didn't want to draw any attention to them, and he certainly didn't want to pressure her, so he stayed put.

When she disappeared into the elevator a moment later, a wave of despair washed over him, so powerful his entire body felt weak and wobbly. He felt devastated. Destroyed.

She was gone.

He'd met his daughter, but she was gone now.

And he got the heart-wrenching feeling that he would never see her again.

He was probably being paranoid.

Nik was fully aware of that as he made his way down the narrow hallway toward Gabriel's bedroom. He wasn't worried about surprising Joséphine and Tristan Traver; both were at the Durand estate at the moment, the former bustling around in the kitchen while the latter changed all the locks in the servants' wing. Nik had made sure to occupy the boy's parents in order to break into their home undetected.

And yes, it was most likely paranoia driving this little fishing expedition of his, but at the same time, he wasn't comfortable with all the time young Gabriel was spending with Ariana.

You mean Cate.

Nik froze in the middle of the corridor, suddenly disoriented. Right. Cate. Of course he'd meant Cate.

But sometimes . . . sometimes he confused the two. Maybe if the girl didn't look so much like her mother, he wouldn't mix them up in his mind as often as he did. They had the same dark blond hair, the same heart-shaped face. Even their voices were identical. Lord, when Cate spoke . . . it was like hearing Ariana talk to him.

And now that Catarina was getting older, now that her body had taken a womanly form . . .

Nik took a deep breath, forcing the inappropriate thoughts out of his head. No. Catarina was a child. Ariana was the woman he loved, and Cate was her daughter. If circumstances had been different, Cate would have been his daughter too, and he'd vowed a long time ago to love and protect her as if she was.

That was what he was doing now—protecting her. Gabriel Traver was a nice boy, but he was poor and unrefined. Not to mention reckless, speeding around on that scooter of his.

The boy wasn't good enough for Cate. His parents were pleasant, but Nik had never entirely trusted their son. He'd convinced Walther to allow Cate and Gabriel their outing today in order to give him time to investigate, though he still wasn't sure what he expected to find.

The Traver house contained only two small bedrooms; it was easy to guess which one was Gabriel's. With posters of sports cars pasted on the plain white walls and piles of dirty clothing littering the floor, it was clear that a teenage boy resided there.

Nik wrinkled his nose in distaste. He'd grown up in a strict German household with dozens of servants to pick up after him, but he'd been tidy and organized even without the maids. Cleanliness was next to godliness, after all.

He began his search at the small wooden desk beneath the window against the back wall, but all he found were completed homework assignments and a stack of university applications in the process of being filled out. The boy was interested in higher education. Nik found that surprising.

Moving away from the desk, he swept his gaze around the room and wondered where to look next. Wondered what he was even looking for.

Maybe he was being ridiculous. Maybe the misgiving he'd been harboring ever since he'd caught Catarina and Gabriel alone in her bedroom was completely unwarranted.

But Nik's instincts had never failed him before, and they didn't fail him now—the second he spotted the papers peeking from the pocket of a discarded pair of black jeans, alarm bells went off inside him.

Narrowing his eyes, he snatched the papers and unfolded the thin stack, then smoothed out the first page.

When he saw what was on it, fiery rage consumed his body.

He stared at James Morgan's face, those piercing blue eyes that had haunted him for years.

He'd been in the same room as Morgan only a handful of times, usually watching from afar as the bastard worked his charm on Ariana, who'd been too sweet and innocent to know she was being played.

But Nik had known. He'd always known. He'd tried warning Walther about the man, but Ariana had her father wrapped around her little finger, and she'd insisted that James Morgan was the one she wanted.

And Nik, the man she was *supposed* to be with, the man who'd been promised her hand in marriage, had been left out in the cold.

Ariana had been his, damn it. Their families had arranged the union before Ariana was even old enough to walk.

He fought another burst of anger. That son of a bitch had stolen his wife. And now he was going to steal the daughter who should have been Nik's.

How had Gabriel Traver gotten his hands on this file?

But the real question was—had he shown it to Catarina?

Ice hardened Nik's veins as he pondered the implications of that, and he quickly reached in his pocket for his cell phone. He dialed Dietrich without delay, his jaw tense as he awaited a reply.

"We have a problem," he said after Walther picked up. "Are you with Catarina?"

"Yes, the Traver boy just dropped her off. We're about to leave for Ariana's house."

"Tell Cate to wait in the car. I don't want her to overhear this."

After a few seconds of silence, Dietrich returned with a brisk, "What is it, Nikolaus?"

In a terse voice, he told the older man what he'd discovered—and what it could mean for them. When he'd finished, Dietrich sounded thoroughly disgruntled.

"Do you think my granddaughter has seen the file?"

"I'm leaning toward no. You know Catarina—she doesn't shy away from confrontation. She would have come to you immediately and demanded answers."

"I'm inclined to agree with that." Dietrich paused ominously. "The boy is on his way home. I assume you're capable of handling this?"

"Yes," Nik said grimly.

"Good."

A click sounded in his ear.

Still gripping the papers, Nik went back to the desk and pulled out the rickety wooden chair. He stiffly lowered his body into it, leaned back, and waited.

Chapter 23

"Is everything okay?" Cate asked when her grandfather rejoined her in the backseat. He'd just stepped out to answer a phone call, and now there was a deep line digging into his forehead.

"Of course," he answered. "Just a business call."

As the car started moving, leaving the mansion in the rearview mirror, Cate stifled a weary sigh and hoped her grandfather didn't pick up on her current state of agitation.

She couldn't stop thinking about James Morgan. Maybe she'd been too hasty, running away from him like that. She still had so many unanswered questions, so many things she wanted to say to him, but when he'd asked her to come home with him, right out of the blue like that, she'd panicked.

Your grandfather is a very dangerous man.

Those ominous words continued to float around in her head, but she couldn't bring herself to believe them. Morgan was wrong. There was nothing dangerous about her grandfather. He was overprotective, sure, but that didn't make him *dangerous*.

And truth was, Cate couldn't deny that her grandfather had every reason to worry about her. He'd already lost so much, and she didn't blame him for going out of his way to keep her safe. Her grandfather loved her, damn it.

How could she abandon him for a man she didn't even know?

A man who might not even be your father.

Cate dismissed the thought the second it entered her head. She might have demanded a DNA test, but she knew without a shred of doubt that James Morgan was her dad. And in the brief time they'd spent together, she'd felt a real connection to the man. He exuded a sense of strength and honor that fascinated her, and an intensity that Cate recognized in herself.

"Catarina?"

She looked up guiltily. "What?"

Maurice frowned. "I asked if you enjoyed your visit to the Eiffel Tower today."

"Oh. Yes. Yes, I did. It was a lot of fun."

"You should have bought a souvenir for your mother. You know she loves those little souvenir shop knickknacks."

"Does she?"

The frown deepened. "Yes. And you might have known that if you spent more time with her."

A frustrated breath got stuck in Cate's throat. God, she was so tired of his guilt trips. She saw her mother as often as she could, but it was never enough for him.

"I'll tell her all about my visit to the tower when I see her," she said meekly. "I'm sure she'll love hearing about it."

That got her a pleased nod, and then her grandfather focused his attention on his smartphone, his wrinkled fingers moving over the touch screen.

She was grateful for the reprieve, but her stomach was still in knots, and it only got worse when they arrived at her mother's house. Her palms became damp and sweaty as their driver punched a code into the panel at the wrought-iron gate.

She hated these visits. It probably made her the worst daughter on the planet, but sometimes she desperately wished she never had to see her mother again.

Once the car came to a stop, Cate reluctantly stepped outside. Her gaze rested on the beautiful Tuscan-inspired house with its terra-cotta roof tiles and limestone-sheathed walls. The entry courtyard consisted of a lovely stone wall and ivy-draped trellises, and as she walked up the driveway, a citrus-tinged scent wafted toward her from the direction of the grove directly behind the house. Her grandfather had shipped most of the fruit trees in from the UK; a team of landscapers worked around the clock to tend to the delicate trees, which didn't always thrive in the French climate.

Cate and her grandfather were greeted at the door by her mother's butler. "Herr Durand, Catarina," the man said in German. "Ariana has been waiting for you."

A burst of annoyance exploded in Cate's stomach. She knew Maurice had instructed the staff to say stuff like that, but she was so sick of hearing it.

"Go on ahead," her grandfather urged, his dark eyes fixated on his phone. "I have a few more calls to make."

With a nod, she crossed the grand parlor toward the twin staircases that curved upward. She climbed the steps on heavy legs, then made her way across the expensive Aubusson rug toward the master suite at the end of the wide hallway.

A moment later, she walked into the elegant sitting area she'd visited a thousand times before.

"Catarina!" Mimi, the dark-haired maid with gentle brown eyes, greeted Cate with a warm smile. "Perfect timing—your mother's masseuse just left."

Like the butler, Mimi addressed her in German, the same way she spoke to Cate's mother. Maurice insisted that Ariana preferred it.

As Cate headed for the bedroom, Mimi took a discreet step to the door. "I'll give you some privacy."

Cate hesitated in front of her mother's room, then took a deep breath and pushed open the French doors.

"Hi, Mama," she said softly.

As usual, the woman on the bed didn't respond.

When Cate was a little girl, she used to pretend not to notice her surroundings. She would look at the bed and see her mother's petite form tucked under the thick, gold-hued duvet. She'd see long blond hair fanned on a crisp white pillow, beautiful chocolate eyes peering up at her with love and adoration. She'd even hear her mother's voice, melodic laughter that tickled her ear and warmed her heart.

But she wasn't a little girl anymore, and she no longer pretended she was seeing anything other than sad, grisly reality.

Ariana lay motionless on a bed flanked by machines on either side. Her dark eyes were open and unblinking. There were tubes everywhere—the feeding tube that gave her nourishment, the ventilator that kept her breathing, the IV drips dangling from metal poles and sticking into her arms. A kidney dialysis machine tended to her failing organs, while her heart monitor released a steady series of beeps that sounded deafening to Cate's ears.

She collapsed in the comfortable wingback chair next to the bed, but didn't reach for her mother's hand—Ariana's skin was always cold, bringing chills to Cate's body.

She swept her gaze over the vast amount of equipment keeping her mother alive, then focused on Ariana's face, which held a fake rosy hue courtesy of the makeup Maurice insisted that the staff apply daily. It was just another one of the macabre details that made Cate extremely uneasy, but she'd come to accept her grandfather's delusions.

No matter what the doctors told him, no matter how many times they threw around words like "brain-dead" or "unresponsive," Maurice refused to admit his daughter was gone, and that she'd been gone since before Cate was even born. Several years ago, one of the nurses had confessed to Cate that Maurice had ordered Ariana's doctors to keep her alive so she could carry the pregnancy to term, but after her baby was born via cesarean section, Maurice had continued to keep Ariana on life support.

For seventeen years she'd lain there with no brain activity, no chance of survival, dead from the bullet that had entered her right temple all those years ago. And for seventeen years, Maurice Durand had lived in denial, unable to accept that his daughter was never waking up. He demanded that everyone treat Ariana as if she were alive and functioning, and Cate was no exception to his rules.

"You look well," she told her mother, the lie burning her throat before it left her lips.

Ariana didn't answer. The soft whoosh of the ventilator echoed in the air.

Cate swallowed hard, wringing her hands together in her lap. She spared a quick glance at the door, then lowered her voice.

"I saw my father today."

No response. The heart monitor beeped in a constant rhythm.

"He wanted me to go home with him, but I said no." Tears stung her eyes as she pictured the devastation on James Morgan's face. "He was upset. I think I hurt him."

No response. The IV lines continued to drip.

"I know I have to tell Grandpa about it, but I'm nervous. He's going to be so mad." Cate gazed at her mother imploringly. "Why did he tell me my father was dead? What happened between the two of you?"

Ariana's vacant gaze stared back, triggering a spurt of anger. God, she couldn't do this anymore. Couldn't look into those lifeless eyes and hold those ice-cold hands, talking to a woman who couldn't hear her. A woman she felt no connection to.

She'd been battling the guilt her whole life, wishing she could feel something for the woman on that bed, but she didn't. Ariana Durand was a stranger to her.

No. Ariana Durand was a *corpse*.

The tears spilled over and streamed down Cate's cheeks. She hated herself for even thinking such a terrible thought, but it was the truth. Her mother was dead. She'd died a long time ago.

When she heard footsteps behind her, Cate whirled around to find her grandfather in the doorway.

A deep frown puckered his mouth when he glimpsed her tears. "Catarina," he said sternly. "You know how much tears upset your mother."

He strode into the bedroom and swiftly reached for Ariana's limp hand. "Don't mind her, darling," he clucked softly. "Catarina is just crying because she's so happy to see you. Isn't that right, Cate?"

"Y-yes," she stammered. "That's why."

Maurice smiled broadly as he stroked his daughter's hand. "See, your daughter is just happy to see you."

Cate wiped her eyes with the back of her hand and mustered a smile.

"Now," her grandfather said briskly, "why don't we tell your mother all about the lovely day you had?"

Chapter 24

Nineteen years ago

They met in the same park that Jim had taken her to last month, where they'd danced in the fountain before getting chased by a security guard, and Noelle couldn't help but smile as she looked around. What a wonderful night that had been. Then again, every moment she spent with Jim was wonderful.

She wished he were here right now. She'd wanted so badly for him to meet her father, but Douglas Phillips had been adamant that she come alone. He'd sounded so agitated on the phone that Noelle had experienced a pang of worry, but she'd told herself it was no big deal. Her father had always been overly paranoid, and considering the covert nature of his job, she didn't really blame him.

But tonight he was acting even more paranoid than usual. He hadn't stopped checking his watch since he'd emerged from the shadows and joined her on the bench, and she got the feeling he was eager to go.

"Are you all right?" she asked in concern.

His blue eyes softened. He was still as handsome as ever, looking so much younger than his forty-two years. His blond hair gleamed beneath the glow of the lampposts, and he was as muscular as she remembered, his black wool coat stretching across a pair of broad shoulders.

"I'm fine," he assured her. "I'm sorry. I know I'm acting

a little strange tonight, sweetheart, but these last few months have been stressful." He smiled at her, but his mouth seemed strained. "I missed you."

"I missed you too."

She brought her gloved hands to her collar and wound her wool scarf around her neck a second time, hoping to ward off the chill. It was cold out, and both of them were bundled up in their winter coats, drinking hot tea from the thermos she'd brought. She wished they could just go to a café, or a restaurant, or anywhere warm, really, but her father had shot down the suggestion when she'd raised it.

"Listen . . . Noelle . . ." She detected the trepidation in his voice. "There's something I need to tell you."

"What is it?"

"I have to go away for a while."

Her forehead creased. "How long is a while?"

"Might be a long time," he admitted. "Months . . . years, maybe."

Alarm shot through her. "Years? Where are you going?"

"I'm not sure yet."

"Is it for work?"

He nodded.

Noelle's lips tightened in an unhappy line. "Will I be able to visit you?"

"I don't know."

Those three frank words were like a dull knife to the heart. Her father was leaving for months, possibly *years*, and she couldn't see him at all during that time?

Suspicion crawled up her throat as she searched his gaze, but it was veiled as always. It was impossible to read Douglas Phillips, especially when he didn't want you to.

"I don't like this either," he said sadly, "but I don't have much of a choice." He hesitated. "And I want to tell you something else."

"More bad news?" she muttered.

Douglas sighed. "Sweetheart. Look at me."

She lifted her head, not bothering to mask her misery.

"You're a warrior, Noelle."

She blinked in surprise.

"A survivor," he went on. His tone rang with both pride

and regret. "When I look at you, I see my greatest achievement."

"Dad ..." she started warily, but he didn't let her continue.

"Even though it might be a while before we see each other again, I'm not going to worry about you, sweetheart. I raised you to take care of yourself. I raised you to be strong and fearless."

Her confusion intensified, bringing a queasy feeling to her stomach.

"You're going to have to be strong and fearless for me now," he said softly. "You might hear some things about me—"

"What things?"

"—but I know you're strong enough to handle it. I know you won't believe what they tell you."

"Who's they?" she blurted out in bewilderment. "What are you talking about?"

He opened his mouth to answer, but then his jaw slammed shut. He glanced around before turning to her with narrowed eyes.

"Who did you tell?"

Noelle had never been more flustered in her life. "What?"

"You told someone you were coming to meet me. Who was it?"

His outraged voice startled her. And it brought a rush of guilt to her chest, because she couldn't even deny the accusation.

"I told you not to say anything," Douglas hissed out. "Who did you tell, Noelle? Was it your mother? René?"

Her heart started pounding, and her hands shook so wildly she almost dropped the thermos. The fury in her father's eyes was the most terrifying thing she'd ever seen. And the betrayal burning there ...

She'd told Jim about the meeting.

Just Jim.

But only because she'd been so excited about seeing her father again and she'd needed to tell someone.

And because she'd trusted Jim to keep it a secret like she'd asked him to.

How had her father known? And why was his gaze darting around like that? It was as if he sensed a threat, as if he expected someone to pop out of the bushes any second, but that was insane because they were the only ones there. They were the only two people in this stupid park. Just him and her, just the two of them.

When a booming voice broke through the silence, Noelle realized just how wrong she was.

Chapter 25

Present day

"I'm going to check on Morgan," Liam announced.

As he started to rise from the couch, Noelle stopped him by raising her hand. "For fuck's sake, Macgregor. He's not a child who needs to be 'checked on.'"

"He's been holed up in that room for more than an hour," Sullivan protested, also starting to get up.

She stifled a sigh. "Sit down, both of you. If you're so worried, I'll go, all right?"

She didn't wait for a response, just marched to the corridor and headed for the bedrooms, growing more and more annoyed with each step she took. She was supposed to be on her jet, damn it. Curled up in a plush cabin chair, sipping cappuccino, getting serviced by the delectable Joachim. Her pilot had been on standby since before they'd left for the Eiffel Tower, but instead of going straight to the private airport, she'd come back to the penthouse with the others.

As she stalked down the hall, she tried to convince herself that she'd stayed in the city to make sure there was no fallout from Jim's meeting with Catarina Durand, that she was simply looking out for herself. And checking on Jim right now? Well, she told herself she was only doing that because his men were worried about him.

But she wasn't worried in the slightest. She didn't care that he was hurting right now. Didn't care that he hadn't said a single word during the ride back, or that the second they'd entered the penthouse, he'd disappeared into the guest room and hadn't emerged since.

Nope, she didn't care at all. The only reason she was checking in on him was because his men had asked her to.

They didn't ask . . . You offered.

"Same fucking difference," she muttered to herself.

With a sigh, she paused in front of the guest room and tried the handle without knocking. It was unlocked, so she strode into the room, and found it dark and empty. She shifted her gaze to the bathroom. Light pooled beneath the door, and she heard the muffled sound of the shower running.

Well. He was alive, at least.

Comforted by the fact that he hadn't put a bullet in his head, she cautiously approached the bathroom. This time she considered knocking, but with the shower on, she figured she wasn't about to catch Jim on the john, so she walked in without bothering to alert him.

The air was damp and steamy, causing beads of sweat to pop out on her forehead. Frowning, she spotted Jim behind the foggy glass doors. He had one arm braced against the tiled wall, his forehead resting on it, shielding his face from view. Water coursed down his naked body, sliding over the defined muscles of his back, clinging to his firm ass, pooling at his feet. For a second she thought he was jerking off, but a glance south revealed his free arm hanging loosely at his side.

That was when she noticed the shaking. His long, muscular body shuddered violently as he stood under the shower spray, face buried in his arm, shoulders hunched over.

Shock torpedoed into her when she realized what was happening.

He was crying.

And seeing him like that evoked the most startling response inside her. Something happened to her chest. It got hot and tight and achy, and the strange emotion circling her heart felt way too much like . . . compassion.

It was so incredibly rare to see a man as powerful as Jim look so vulnerable, and all she could do was stand frozen in the doorway, watching in wonder as silent sobs racked his body.

She should have walked away. He hadn't spotted her yet. She could simply duck out. Pretend she'd never been there.

Instead, she found herself undressing.

Her hands trembled as wildly as Jim's broad shoulders. Her heart stayed lodged in her throat, perilously close to breaking for him.

When she opened the shower door, Jim's head snapped up and his harsh intake of breath echoed in the air.

His red-rimmed eyes met hers, and she inhaled just as sharply as he did. He looked . . . broken.

Noelle didn't say a word. Locking her gaze with his, she stepped into the stall and moved in close, until their naked bodies were inches apart. Whatever torment he was feeling, his cock clearly didn't share, because it thickened right before her eyes, until an impressive erection jutted out and brushed her stomach.

Drops from the faucet sprinkled her naked flesh, bringing a flurry of goose bumps. She swept her gaze over his magnificent body, watching the water snake down the carved muscles of his chest, his trim hips, his muscular legs.

Without a word, she reached out and encircled his erection with her fingers.

He instantly thrust into her hand, his blue eyes still fixed on hers. The emotion she saw swimming there floored her. Sorrow, anger, and agony, with a flicker of pleasure soon joining the fold when she gave his cock a slow stroke. He leaned into her, his chin dropping against her shoulder, as if he needed to draw strength from her. The notion sent ripples of self-loathing through her, because she hated herself for bringing him comfort.

But the steam from the shower must have clouded her mind and stolen her judgment, because suddenly she was sinking to her knees in front of him.

She opened her mouth and took him in, and his answering groan mingled with the steady rush of the water. He filled her mouth and her body loved it. Her nipples puckered into tight buds. Her thighs quivered. Her clit swelled with need.

She ignored her rising desire and cupped his heavy sac with both hands, continuing to move her mouth along his shaft.

"More. Take it all in." His hoarse voice bounced off the tiles and vibrated against her lips.

She licked her lips, then sucked him deep, all the way to the base. She didn't slow the pace, not even when his tip nudged the back of her throat; she'd performed oral sex on enough men that she knew what she was doing, knew she could take every inch of him without gagging.

But Jim wasn't other men. When she was sucking Jim . . . God, it was different from all the other times, all the other men. She loved every second of it. Craved more every time. All she had to do was peer up and see his features go taut with pleasure, and her heart pounded so hard it was a miracle her ribs didn't crack.

"Fuck. Yes," he mumbled.

His hands tangled in her hair, but he didn't guide her head. He just stroked the wet strands, rocking his hips into her mouth as she worked his cock.

Noelle was so turned on she could hardly breathe. She squeezed and fondled his sac as her mouth kept a tight suction on his cock, as her tongue danced around his blunt head on each upstroke.

"Faster. Use your hand, baby."

Her lips released him with a soft *pop*, and she replaced them with her fist, giving him a few lazy strokes before bringing her mouth back into play.

He hissed softly. "Oh yeah. Just like that."

She increased the tempo, sucking and pumping until he was moaning with abandon. He cupped the back of her head and fucked her mouth, the salty, masculine taste of him coating her tongue and fueling her excitement. He was harder than steel, but his shaft was soft as velvet. Her fist glided over it, her tongue stealing delicious licks whenever it could.

When his hips started to move faster, she knew he was close, and suddenly it became her life's mission to make him come.

Moaning against his throbbing cock, she increased the suction, squeezed his balls, and listened to her name fly out of his mouth.

"*Noelle.*"

He came with a husky cry, and she greedily drank up his

release, refusing to let him withdraw. But he wasn't going anywhere—he kept thrusting, kept moaning, giving her everything she wanted.

It was seconds, hours, before he finally grew still. With a groan, he gently reclaimed his cock from her mouth, then grasped her upper arm and yanked her to her feet.

He didn't reach for her, didn't try to pull her closer. He simply looked at her, his heavy-lidded gaze resting on her mouth before seeking out her eyes again.

"Can I kiss you?" he said gruffly.

She swallowed the nervous saliva that had pooled in her mouth.

And then she slowly shook her head.

Morgan staggered out of the bathroom after Noelle, who'd jumped out of the shower stall so fast that for a second he actually wondered if he'd hallucinated that unbelievable blow job.

He didn't bother with a towel, just strode into the bedroom naked and wet, dripping water all over the hardwood. He didn't give a shit about the floor, though. He felt raw and battered and he wanted to lash out. Hit something, throw something, kick something.

No, what he really wanted was Noelle. The orgasm she'd just given him wasn't nearly enough. He wanted to bury himself inside her, but the way she hurriedly gathered up her clothes told him she wasn't in the mood to fuck him.

And damned if that didn't piss him off even more.

"I don't want to play games anymore," he burst out.

Her expression revealed nothing. "I'm not playing games."

He curled his hands into fists, which she immediately noticed, because she raised her eyebrows and said, "Seriously? You're this angry about a stupid kiss?"

"It's not about the kiss. It's ... it's ..." He couldn't even finish the thought. The turbulent emotions he'd been battling all day had finally caught up to him.

When he felt his legs giving out from under him, he stumbled forward and collapsed on the bed, bare ass planting on the mattress.

Son of a bitch, he refused to burst into tears like a fucking sissy again. It was bad enough that Noelle had found him in such a sorry state. He couldn't break down again. He couldn't.

"Jim . . ." It was her turn to trail off, as if she had no idea what to say to him.

Anguish clogged his throat, and he had to avert his eyes so she wouldn't glimpse his pain. "I let her walk away."

He heard her sigh. Heard the bedspread rustle as she sat down beside him, a good foot away. His peripheral vision caught nothing but golden hair and bare skin. She hadn't gotten dressed yet.

"I just let her go," he muttered. "I gave her back to a man who sells guns and kills people. What kind of father does that?"

"You couldn't force her to come with you," she said quietly. "You had no choice."

"I did have a choice! I could have taken her! Tied her up, drugged her if I had to. Anything to keep her away from Dietrich." His breaths turned into shallow pants. "But instead, I let her go. *I let her go*."

Noelle didn't answer, and her silence almost felt like a reprimand.

"You should have seen her," he mumbled, choking on the lump obstructing his throat. "She's so beautiful. And smart. She's so fucking smart." His hands shook as he raked them through his damp hair. "I wasn't there for her. I missed out on her entire life."

As Cate's face flashed in his mind, it killed him to realize just how much time he'd lost with her. He hadn't seen her take her first step, hadn't been there to hear her first word. He hadn't held her hand on her first day of school. Hadn't helped her with her homework or given her advice about school or friends or boys.

And he could never get any of those moments back.

"Dietrich watched her grow up. That son of a bitch took my kid and disappeared off the face of the earth for seventeen years. He and Ariana—they got to raise her. And me . . . her father . . . I missed it all."

Resentment burned in his blood like jet fuel. The urge to slam his fist into something returned, more violent than before.

"Cate needed a father," he burst out. "Kids need their fathers, damn it!"

As he tried to breathe through the pain, he became aware of the increasing tension thickening the air. Inhaling slowly, he turned his head—and was startled by the malevolence blazing in Noelle's eyes.

"I can't believe you," she spat out.

Wariness trickled through him. "What did I do now?"

"You seriously have the nerve to talk to me about fatherhood? About kids needing their fathers?" She shot off the bed, her expression sizzling with unbridled rage. "You have the *fucking nerve* to talk to *me* about fathers? After you *killed* mine?"

Chapter 26

•

And there it was.

Truth was, he'd been expecting it. Whenever the two of them crossed paths, Morgan held his breath and waited for the inevitable explosion. She was like a volcano that had lain dormant for years, wisps of ash and spikes in temperature hinting at impending catastrophe, but you never knew when it would erupt, when that hot lava would destroy everything in its path.

Well, it was happening now. Almost two decades since the last eruption, and now here it was again, hitting him when he was at his most raw, his most susceptible.

"I didn't kill your father, Noelle." His voice was low and even, but not without regret.

"No, you didn't do the actual deed," she agreed bitterly. "You didn't put those bullets in his chest. That's awfully convenient, right, Jim? Because the truth is, you're the reason it happened. You're the reason he died, and guess what. To me, that's the same fucking thing as being the one who held the damn gun."

He rose from the bed with a degree of calm he certainly didn't feel. "I'm going to tell you the same thing I told you all those years ago—your father was selling highly classified secrets to foreign governments. He jeopardized the lives of hundreds of intelligence agents operating around the globe by selling their locations to our enemies. He was a traitor to his country, Noelle."

She looked at him as if he'd raised a hand to her. Her bare breasts heaved as she struggled for air, but she seemed completely oblivious to her nudity, too consumed by fury to care or notice.

"He sold out his country," Morgan said in a monotone voice, like he was reciting passages from a history textbook. "I was assigned to find him and bring him in. He was taken for interrogation. He was not being tortured, he was simply being questioned, and he was the one who decided to disarm the interrogating officer. He was the one who shot and killed two other military servicemen before he was finally brought down by six bullets to the chest."

Noelle's face became ashen. "Whatever he may have done, he didn't deserve to be killed."

Frustration crashed into him like a tidal wave. "He got *himself* killed! And he murdered two people beforehand!"

"Because you put him in that position!"

Morgan inhaled deeply. Christ, he couldn't do this again. They'd had this same argument the day after her father's arrest. Noelle had been released into the custody of her stepfather—there'd been no evidence to connect her to her father's crimes—and she'd come directly to Morgan's hotel room, just as he'd known she would. He'd been dreading the confrontation, and it had been as gut-wrenching as he'd known it would be.

"You took him away from me," she said fiercely. "He was my father. He was a *good* father. All he ever did was try to protect me."

"Protect you?" Morgan cut in, an edge to his voice. "The way he protected you from Laurent?"

Shock filled her eyes, and she faltered for a moment before responding. "He didn't know about René. I kept it a secret from him."

"For fuck's sake, Noelle, Douglas Phillips was a *spy*. You truly think he didn't know what was going on in that house?"

"He. Didn't. Know." Pure venom dripped from her voice.

"He knew," Morgan said flatly. "He just didn't do a damn thing about it."

Noelle was glaring daggers at him now, but it was too late to stop the course he'd set them on. And fuck, maybe it was time she knew the truth.

"He knew," Morgan repeated. "He told me so himself, Noelle. He *knew* his daughter was getting raped every fucking night, and he stood by and let it happen. He was a selfish, greedy motherfucker who didn't give a shit about anyone but himsel—"

Her fist connected with his left temple before he could react.

The force of it snapped his head back and made his ears ring, and as pain shot through his temple, all he could do was gape at her.

"You don't know a goddamn thing about him," Noelle hissed out. "You never did."

Morgan met her eyes. "He knew exactly what was happening to you, Noelle."

This time he was expecting the attack, but he didn't back away from it. He stood there and let that lethal right hook smash into the side of his mouth. Blood soaked his lips and filled his mouth with its coppery flavor.

"You done?" he said tersely.

"Not by a long shot."

Her fists shot up like a boxer's, like she was anticipating having to block his retaliation, but when she realized he wasn't going to fight back, she struck out again, coming at him so fast he almost fell on his ass.

For a moment he'd forgotten that this woman was trained in every martial art known to man, and it took everything he had to deflect her deadly blows—quick jabs to the face followed by a kick to his ribs that made him gasp. An uppercut that brought stars to his eyes, followed by two sharp hooks, left and right, the latter of which split his eyebrow open.

Blood streamed down his face, but he had no time to wipe it away. He was focusing all his energy on blocking a series of lightning-fast karate moves that would have seriously injured him if he hadn't been vigilant.

"Hit me back!" Desperation lined her voice, and her eyes glittered with frustration.

When he didn't take the bait, she stumbled backward and grabbed the drinking glass on the end table, then hurled it at him. He batted the glass out of the way and it crashed to the floor, breaking into a hundred little pieces.

With a growl, Noelle came at him swinging again.

He grabbed her forearm before she could land another punch. Twisted it hard. "Stop. I'm not going to hit you, damn it!"

Christ, he'd never seen her so enraged. She shrugged out of his armlock with astonishingly little effort and struck again, blindsiding him with a low kick that sent him toppling right off his feet.

He landed on the floor with a heavy thud, flat on his ass, the wind completely knocked out of him. Shards of broken glass dug into his back, bringing little stings of pain. Stunned, he managed to regain his senses just as Noelle launched herself at him, and then there was a bone-jarring crunch as her fist smashed into his jaw.

Hot waves of pain rippled through him, blood continuing to drip down his face, but he planted both palms on the hardwood and forced himself not to strike back. She needed this. Fuck, maybe he needed it too. Maybe he deserved this after what he'd done to her.

As he lay there at her mercy, he suddenly became aware of her tears. Clinging to her thick eyelashes, sliding down her cheeks, soaking his bare chest. She was still straddling him, but no longer moving. She'd hung her head in defeat, as if she'd finally accepted he wasn't going to fight her.

And seeing her surrender absolutely killed him.

"I'm sorry," he whispered.

Those two words seemed to drain away whatever energy she'd had left. She collapsed on top of his chest, her wet face sticking to his neck and her long hair fanning over his pecs like a silk sheet.

His arms came around her and he held her tight, stroking her bare back. He wanted to say something, anything, but he was only capable of formulating those two bleak words.

She lifted her head slightly, and when he saw the devastation in her eyes, he wanted so badly to kiss her. But he didn't dare, afraid she'd just start hitting him again.

So he rolled them both over instead, covering her body with his and burying his face in her neck. He felt her trying to wiggle out from underneath him, but he didn't let her. He cupped her cheeks with his hands and forced her to look at him. "I'm sorry," he said firmly.

"Don't say that to me."

"I'm sorry."

"Stop it, Jim."

"I'm so sorry for what I did to you."

"Stop saying that!"

He wasn't sure which one of them guided his cock between her legs, whether it was his hand or hers, but suddenly their bodies were joined, and he was slowly moving inside her.

Noelle gasped beneath him, but she didn't push him away. If anything, she deepened the contact by arching her hips and wrapping her legs around his waist.

"Fuck me hard," she choked out.

"No." He gritted his teeth when she tried to quicken the pace by thrusting her pelvis upward. "It's going to be slow and sweet and you can't do a goddamn thing about it."

Anger flared in her eyes, but he refused to give her what she wanted. His cock slid into her in excruciatingly gentle strokes. The light rocking of their bodies seemed almost absurd in juxtaposition to the brutal chaos of before. His face was still bleeding, drops of crimson staining Noelle's golden hair. Pieces of glass were embedded in his skin, and probably hers. Her knuckles were bloody and torn; his body was aching from her assault.

And yet he fucked her with infinite tenderness, his gaze never once leaving hers.

Their quiet breathing filled the air. Glass shards crunched against the hardwood as he filled her thoroughly, sweetly, gliding his cock in and out of her wet sheath until she was clinging to his shoulders and moaning in ecstasy.

He waited until she cried out in release before he let himself go, and then he was squeezing his eyes shut and spilling his seed inside her as waves of pleasure pulsed through his body.

When his eyelids fluttered open, he found Noelle staring up at him. She looked sated and sad. Aroused but defeated.

"Again?" she murmured.

With a curt nod, he scooped her into his arms, stood up, and carried her to the bed.

* * *

Liam jerked when another loud crash sounded from the vicinity of the bedrooms. Lord, what were those two doing in there? Smashing everything in sight? Fucking all the furniture to pieces?

He stifled a sigh and tried to focus on the television screen, but it was impossible to concentrate on a soccer game when a sexual hurricane was ripping through the penthouse. Morgan and Noelle had been locked in their bedroom for hours, and it didn't take a genius to figure out what they were doing.

Considering they were broadcasting it to the whole damn neighborhood.

Liam had been sporting a semi all day, and he knew he wasn't the only one suffering from a serious case of *turned on*. Sully, Sean, and Ash kept rearranging their pants and weren't bothering to be discreet about it anymore, and even Bailey seemed affected by the sounds of hard-core fucking reverberating in the apartment.

Thump.

Thump.

Thump-thump-thump.

A groan lodged in his throat as the rhythmic banging of a headboard smacking the wall echoed through the penthouse.

On the other side of the sectional, Sullivan didn't even bother stifling his groan. It slipped out, low and husky and tinged with arousal.

The tortured noise sent a spike of lust right to Liam's groin. He forced himself to breathe, trying not to think of all the other times he'd heard Sully make that sound, usually when a pretty girl was about to strip off her clothes for them.

"I'm going for a walk." Bailey abruptly shot up from the couch, her face taking on a frazzled look. "There are way too many hard-ons in this room."

Liam almost offered to go with her, but closed his mouth when he saw Sean glaring at him. Crap. He'd been hoping Reilly hadn't noticed all the time he'd been spending with Bailey, but judging by that deep scowl, he totally had.

In Liam's defense, there was absolutely nothing romantic between him and the dark-haired operative; Bailey was simply helping him work through his messed-up issues. Weirdly enough, he'd felt a lot more at ease ever since he'd confided in her. Rather than tease him or recoil in disgust, Bailey hadn't been fazed when he'd confessed to fantasizing about his best friend. Whenever they could get a moment alone, she used that laid-back, no-nonsense attitude of hers to try to help him make sense of his jumbled thoughts, which he totally appreciated.

He just wished the making-sense part would come soon, because right now, he still had no clue how to deal with his . . . crush?

Was *that* what it was? A *crush*?

God help him.

As Bailey strode out of the room, Sean heaved out a breath and headed for the terrace doors. "I need a smoke," he announced.

Ash was on his feet next. "Fuck. Me too."

"You don't smoke," Liam said dryly.

"I do now," the rookie muttered before following their new teammate outside.

Liam turned to grin at Sully—and found him about to leave the room.

"You're abandoning me too?" he cracked.

Sullivan looked over with a sardonic expression. "What, suddenly you're talking to me again?"

Before Liam could answer, his friend was gone.

"Sully. Wait."

He hopped off the couch and hurried after him, but the other man kept walking. Effectively dismissing him.

Liam caught up just as Sully reached the guest room. Frowning, he clapped a hand on his teammate's arm. "Sullivan," he said firmly.

Without a word, Sully shrugged out of his grip and strode through the door.

Liam walked right in after him, shutting the door behind them. "What the hell did you mean by that?" The demand was accompanied by a pang of guilt, because damn it, he knew *exactly* what his friend had meant.

Sullivan grumbled in annoyance. "It means I'm not stupid, and I'm not blind. I don't know what the hell is going on with you, and if you don't want to tell me, fine. But don't act like you haven't been avoiding me, mate. You haven't said a word to me since you went for drinks with Bailey, and every time I turn around, the two of you are whispering together in the corner."

His jaw tensed. "So you're jealous that I'm spending time with a beautiful woman?"

An incredulous laugh burst out of Sullivan's mouth. "I'm not jealous, and I don't give a bloody hoot who you spend time with. If you want Sean to murder you, that's your prerogative. Just don't pretend that things are cool between us. You're ignoring me. I've noticed it. This shit is real."

A wave of hesitation washed over him. Sully was right. Things *weren't* cool. They hadn't been ever since that last goddamn threesome.

Bailey had urged him to talk to his friend and be honest about why he was acting so distant, but for the life of him, he couldn't seem to say the words out loud.

So he lied.

"I'm not ignoring you," Liam muttered. "You're imagining things."

"Bullshit."

"Sully—"

"Just go." Those gray eyes darkened with anger. "I'm serious, Liam. Unless you're in the mood to watch me jerk off, I suggest you give me some bloody privacy."

Despite his better judgment, he glanced at the other man's crotch, which sported a very visible bulge.

He suddenly found it difficult to breathe.

"No joke, mate. I'm two seconds from pulling out my dick."

Sully was mocking him now. His lips had curved in the sensual smirk Liam had seen many times before, usually right before the guy fucked a woman senseless. Tension gathered in the air, hanging over them like a canopy.

Liam's mouth went drier than a sack of flour. He continued to hold Sullivan's gaze, and was taken aback when he glimpsed a gleam of challenge.

His pulse promptly sped up. Shit. He got the feeling his teammate was goading him, but . . . into what? What the hell was Sullivan trying to accomplish right now? Liam was used to the guy's impulsive nature, his act-first-and-think-later mentality, but right now, in this moment, he had no clue what Sully's endgame was.

Or hell, maybe there *wasn't* an endgame. Maybe Sullivan really just needed to beat one out and Liam was simply getting in his way. They'd been listening to two people have ferocious sex all day long—any red-blooded man with a healthy libido would need some relief after that.

Sullivan lowered his hand to his zipper. "Last chance, Boston."

His breath hitched, and his friend must have heard it, because Sullivan froze. For a moment, he looked stunned.

Then he started to laugh as understanding dawned on his rugged face. "Oh, man. Is *that* what this is about?"

Liam swallowed. "I don't know what you're talking about."

With an amused expression, Sullivan slanted his head. "So then you *don't* want to fuck me?"

Simultaneous bursts of heat and panic went off in Liam's body. He wanted to voice a denial, but his vocal cords had seized up. He could barely even breathe, thanks to his tightening throat.

His heart beat louder and faster when his friend took a dangerous step toward him. "I can tell when someone wants me, Boston. You don't have to look so freaked-out about it, either. I'm totally down for . . . whatever you have in mind."

Gulping, Liam took a step back. "You're wrong."

Sullivan furrowed his brow. "Am I?"

"Yes."

"You sure about that?"

His teammate moved closer.

Liam moved back.

"I should . . . go," he mumbled.

"Then go."

Their gazes locked for one heart-stopping moment.

And then something happened. Something Liam didn't expect, and didn't have the willpower to stop.

His best friend slid toward him, grasped his chin with one powerful hand, and brought their mouths together.

A hot rush of lust instantly swept through him, sizzling right down to his cock and turning it into a slab of marble.

Sweet Jesus.

Sully's lips were hot and firm, and the feel of his stubble scraping the edge of Liam's jaw was the most surreal sensation on the planet. The kiss lasted only a few seconds. The locking of their mouths, the sensual sweep of Sullivan's tongue, and then those wicked lips were gone, and Liam was left gasping for air, stunned into speechlessness.

The shock didn't last long. It swiftly transformed into bone-deep panic that had him stumbling backward. "Fuck," he choked out.

He thought he glimpsed a flicker of remorse in Sullivan's eyes, but he was too stricken to be sure.

"Liam—" his friend started.

He threw a hand up between them. "Don't." A ragged breath flew out. "Just . . . don't."

Without another word, he stalked out the door and slammed it behind him.

Chapter 27

The next morning, Morgan entered the living room and spotted his men having breakfast out on the terrace. He heard Sean Reilly, from his perch near the French doors, entertaining everyone with what sounded like a disastrous experience with a Dublin prostitute, while the other men exploded in laughter.

The visible camaraderie between Reilly and the men was an encouraging sign. Reilly was undeniably intelligent, shrewd and resourceful, and a damn skilled soldier, but he'd been working solo for so long Morgan wasn't sure how Sean would fare as part of a team.

He was still hoping he wouldn't live to regret his decision to take the Irishman on, but he couldn't second-guess himself now. As of this morning, he wanted every available man watching the Durand estate, and that included Reilly. Not only was he desperate to keep an eye on Cate, but it was also time to find out what Ariana's role was in all this.

It troubled him that nobody could offer a single detail about Ariana Dietrich, but he intended to change that. He *had* to find a way to see Ariana. Maybe if he talked to her, he could ... what? Convince her to let Cate come live with him?

Wishful thinking, made all the more unlikely when he remembered that Ariana wasn't even Cate's guardian. Walther was. And Morgan wasn't naive enough to think that

Walther Dietrich would ever relinquish his granddaughter into the custody of a man he loathed.

Tamping down his frustration, Morgan stalked outside to address his team, only to find every single man gaping at him.

Oh, right. He'd forgotten about his appearance.

"Fun night?" Reilly asked with a smirk.

Morgan stifled a sigh. He knew exactly what they were seeing, because he'd just seen it himself in the bathroom mirror. His face was beat to shit—swollen lip, blood-caked eyebrow, a bluish bruise on his right cheekbone. And that was just the visible damage. Beneath his white T-shirt and olive fatigues were even more bruises, and he wouldn't have been surprised to learn that Noelle had fractured at least one of his ribs.

He looked like he'd fought a battle and lost. On the other hand, he'd also fucked her more times than he could count, so didn't that make him more winner than loser?

And as usual, after the explosive sex had come to an end and he'd passed out naked beside her, the answer to the inevitable question remained *no*. No, she wasn't out of his system. No, he didn't want to stop.

"You have glass in your hair."

Morgan ignored Liam's dry observation.

And Reilly's widening grin.

And Sullivan's twitching lips.

And Ash's extremely impressed face.

"I need you guys on surveillance," he said gruffly. "All eyes on the Durand estate—I want to know who goes in and who comes out. I want an assessment of the security system, and the locations of every single camera, motion detector, and guard on the property."

"You should ask Juliet to help," Reilly suggested. "In case you want some covert B and E."

"We won't be breaking in. Just watching for now."

"And how long are we gonna be doing that?"

Until I convince my daughter to come home.

He didn't voice the thought. He was aching to swoop on the estate and take Cate by force if he had to, but he couldn't risk his daughter getting caught in any cross fire. And it didn't feel right *forcing* her to be with him. He wanted her to make that choice on her own.

"As long as we need to," he muttered, before glancing at Sullivan. "You're team leader on this one. Break down the assignments as you see fit."

The blond Australian beamed at him. "Well, hot damn. I never get to be CO."

Morgan turned for the door. "I'll meet you guys there in an hour or two. I need to tap a few of Noelle's sources first." He turned to Sean. "Did your brother check in?"

Reilly nodded. "About an hour ago, but I didn't want to wake you up." A hint of a smirk lingered. "I figured you might need your beauty rest."

"What did he say?" Morgan asked with a frown.

"He still hasn't found anything about Ariana Dietrich, at least nothing after you left Berlin. It's like she doesn't exist anymore."

"Well, I know for a fact she does. Tell Oliver to dig deeper."

"Got it, boss."

Morgan left the boys to their own devices and headed toward the kitchen. He was craving a cup of coffee. Or maybe ten. His temples were pounding, though he wasn't sure whether it was due to lack of sleep, a need for caffeine, or Noelle's fists.

Bailey was at the counter when he entered the room, her hair loose and falling over one shoulder as she leaned forward to read the newspaper lying on the black granite.

"Morning," she greeted him.

"Morning," he murmured, making a beeline for the fancy-pants coffeemaker. "Is Noelle back yet?"

"No, she's still meeting with her lawyer friend."

He nodded. Noelle had gone to do some more digging about Gilles Girard, Dietrich's assassin-hiring lawyer, in the hope that she might be able to uncover Ariana's whereabouts.

"Hopefully he has some information for us," Morgan said.

He felt Bailey's dark gray eyes on him as he poured himself some coffee. He still wasn't entirely comfortable with the woman, though he couldn't deny that she'd done a damn good job yesterday. Although he hadn't seen her in action, she'd fooled Cate's bodyguards with her disguise, and thanks to her, he'd been able to meet his daughter without a single snag.

"How was your night?" Amusement rang in Bailey's voice.

Irritated, he turned to face her. "Christ, can everyone quit looking at me like that? I got laid. Big deal."

"Normally I don't care about other people's sex lives, but this time it's hard not to. My boss doesn't usually hop into bed with men she despises." Bailey paused thoughtfully. "Then again, I suppose there's a thin line between love and hate, huh?"

His back went ramrod straight. "Your boss doesn't love me."

Newspaper forgotten, Bailey rested her elbows on the counter and studied his face. "But you love her."

Discomfort coiled around his spine. "I did once."

She slanted her head. "Yeah?"

He brought his mug to his lips and slugged back some caffeine, wishing Bailey would stop staring at him like that. He opened his mouth intending to change the subject, but the words that slipped out startled the hell out of him.

"She thinks I was pretending, but she's wrong. I *did* love her." His voice thickened. "I never loved anyone before I met her, and there's been nobody since."

Bailey looked equally stunned. "Oh. Um. Okay." Her expression grew wary. "Why are you telling me this?"

He sighed. "Because I have nobody else to tell it to." A faint smile tickled his lips. "And I get the feeling you're good at keeping other people's secrets."

Her laughter echoed in the kitchen. "You're right about that." She hesitated. "So what did you do to make her hate you?"

Morgan leaned against the counter and wrapped both hands around his mug. "I used her to draw her father out of hiding. And then I arrested him, and he died three days later during an escape attempt."

"Well," Bailey remarked, her tone tactful, "I can see why she feels the way she does about you."

His chest clenched. "She idolized that man, but goddamn

it, he didn't deserve her devotion. He abandoned her, left her in the clutches of a sadistic bastard. And he was a traitor to his country—good people lost their lives because of him."

Bailey frowned. "Does Noelle know that?"

He shook his head in frustration. "Doesn't matter how many times I try to tell her—she's never going to believe that her father was anything less than a national hero."

"Right there is your problem. Telling her won't make a lick of difference. You need to show her."

"Show her?"

"You know Noelle as well as I do, maybe even better. She doesn't trust people, and she operates under the assumption that every word a person says is a lie. She won't believe an accusation like that without proof, tangible evidence to back it up." Bailey arched one eyebrow. "I don't suppose you have proof?"

That gave him pause. "Proof."

"Yeah. Can you prove that her father is everything you say he was?"

"No," Morgan said slowly. "But I might know someone who can."

An idea took root in his mind, but he wasn't sure it was even possible.

Doesn't hurt to try, a little voice pointed out.

Hell, what did he have to lose? He might not have a clue about what was going on between him and Noelle, what he felt for her outside the realm of sexual desire, but whatever they had, whatever they *could* have . . . It would never work unless he redeemed himself in her eyes.

"You're buzzing."

Bailey's voice drew him back to the present, and he realized his phone was vibrating in his back pocket.

He quickly set his mug on the counter and took out his phone, his breath catching when he glimpsed the number flashing on the screen. It was the same number he'd called yesterday, when he'd informed the private lab tech that Ash was on his way to drop off some DNA samples.

"It's the lab," he told Bailey.

"I see," was all she said.

Swallowing hard, Morgan answered the call with a brusque hello, then said, "Do you have the results?"

"Yes, sir, I do," came the reply on the other end.

His heartbeat accelerated as he listened to the technician's long, scientific report, but he tuned out halfway through, eventually cutting the guy off. "That's all I needed to know. I appreciate the rush job—my associate will transfer the rest of your money shortly."

He disconnected the call, his pulse hammering and his palms damp.

"Well?" Bailey said.

A lump rose in his throat. "Cate is my daughter."

Bailey gave a brisk nod. "So what now?"

The lump got bigger, making it difficult to get a word out, but somehow he managed an entire sentence.

"Now we figure out how to get her out of that house."

Cate left her bedroom that morning without an ounce of enthusiasm, but she forced herself to stick to her usual routine. Sunday-morning breakfast was usually followed by a visit to her mother, but she desperately hoped her grandfather wouldn't insist on it today. Yesterday's visit had been hard enough. The last thing she wanted was a follow-up.

Maurice and Nikolaus were already in the dining room when she walked in. Their noses were buried in their respective newspapers, but both men glanced up to greet her with warm smiles.

"Good morning, sweetheart," Maurice said.

"Good morning," she murmured back.

She mustered up a smile, all the while wishing she could crawl back under the duvet and shut out the world.

She'd spent the entire night tossing and turning in bed, her brain refusing to shut down as she'd replayed the encounter with James Morgan over and over again in her head. And her visit with Ariana. And thrown into the mix were her strangely terrifying feelings for Gabriel, whom she hadn't heard from since he'd dropped her off at home yesterday. He wasn't answering his phone, and she couldn't even pop into the kitchen to ask his mom if he was avoiding her, because Joséphine had Sundays off.

"Did you sleep well?" her grandfather asked pleasantly.

"Like a rock," she lied.

"I'm glad to hear it." He poured himself some coffee from the stainless steel carafe, then reached for the cream dispenser. "Your mother was very happy to see you yesterday."

No, she wasn't! She can't feel anything!

Cate worked hard not to show her frustration. "It was good to see her too," she said meekly.

Her grandfather's eyes narrowed, as if he knew she wasn't being genuine, so she pasted on another smile, hoping this one looked more sincere.

God, keeping up the charade was unbearable sometimes. He acted like Ariana was alive, when every doctor who'd ever treated her insisted that she was gone. The machines kept her body functioning, but her mind and her soul and everything that had once made her a living, breathing human—that had been extinguished like a candle the moment she'd been shot.

Without technology, Ariana would have slipped away a long time ago, and sometimes Cate wished her grandfather would let it happen. At least then her mother could finally be at peace.

It seemed cruel to allow her to live that way.

Your grandfather is a very dangerous man.

Once again, Morgan's warning crept into her mind. And once again, Cate rejected it.

Fine, so maybe her grandpa wasn't in his right mind when it came to her mother, but that didn't make him dangerous. He was simply a father who refused to grieve, and Cate suspected he blamed himself for Ariana's attack. After all, it had been one of *his* business rivals who'd tried to kill him, only the attempt had gone horribly wrong and Cate's mother had been hit instead.

"You need to see her more often." Maurice's cluck of disapproval jolted Cate out of her thoughts. "You know, when Ariana's mother was alive, the two of them spent every waking moment together."

"Are we going to visit her today?" She held her breath, praying with all her might that he'd say no.

"Of course we are." He seemed surprised that she would even ask. "Ariana will be disappointed if we don't."

Fortunately, two of their maids entered the dining room before he could glimpse the frustration in Cate's eyes. She hadn't been able to mask it fast enough, and she knew her grandfather would be angry if he realized just how badly she wanted to avoid her mother.

The maids served breakfast in an efficient manner, setting down plates of steaming crepes, ceramic bowls piled with blueberries, little dishes of warm, melting butter. When Audrey, the younger of the women, placed a small bowl of strawberries in front of Cate, she smiled at the woman, a genuine smile this time. Audrey knew that strawberries were Cate's favorite, and she always made sure to bring some out for her.

"Thanks, Audrey," she told the brunette.

Audrey averted her gaze, and that was when Cate noticed her red-rimmed eyes. Had Audrey been crying?

Before she could ask whether Audrey was all right, the woman darted out of the room, with their other maid, Priscilla, at her heels. Cate could have sworn she heard the two females whispering on their way back to the kitchen, but neither her grandfather nor Nikolaus seemed to notice.

"Is everything okay with Audrey?" she asked.

Maurice glanced up from his newspaper. "I don't see why not. Why do you ask?"

"She was acting strange just now ..." Cate ended up shrugging. "Never mind. I was probably just imagining it."

In the chair across from hers, Nik delicately cut into his food with his knife and fork. He took a bite of his crepe, which was piled with ham and melted Swiss cheese, then swallowed before focusing his blue eyes on Cate. "Did you have fun at the Eiffel Tower yesterday?"

"Uh-huh." She popped a strawberry in her mouth, keeping her tone casual. "It was fun."

"I didn't get to talk to you when you got back from Ariana's. You had already gone up to your room, and you didn't join us for dinner."

"I was trying to get a head start on the paper Monsieur Paschal asked me to write, so I asked Audrey to bring my dinner upstairs. And then I went to bed early."

She was becoming an exceptionally good liar. Probably not something to be proud of, but she knew the truth wouldn't go over well. Not only had she stayed awake all night, but she'd done it while clutching the disposable phone James Morgan had slipped into her hand at the tower yesterday.

She'd lain in bed riddled with indecision, wanting so badly to text him but not knowing what to say. She knew she couldn't see him again until she spoke to her grandfather, but at the same time, she wasn't sure she even *wanted* to see him again.

"Cate?"

She found Nik eyeing her expectantly. "Sorry. What did you say?"

"I asked how your paper is going. Is this the one about the French Revolution?"

She nodded. "It's going really well so far. Pretty much writing itself."

"Well, let me know if you need any help."

"I will."

Audrey reentered the room at that moment with a glass pitcher of freshly squeezed orange juice. She ducked her head as she poured Cate a glass, as if trying to shield her face from view.

"I'm also getting help from Gabriel," Cate added absently, watching as Audrey rounded the table to refill Nik's coffee cup. "He's really into all that history stuff. I should ask him to come over today to edit what I wrote."

A soft wail broke the air.

Cate sharply glanced over in time to see Audrey covering up the anguished sound with a cough.

"I apologize," the maid murmured. "I didn't mean to interrupt." She hurried off again, and this time Cate knew she hadn't imagined a thing.

"Something's wrong," she said grimly. "May I be excused so I can go and talk to her?"

Nik abruptly scraped back his chair. "I'll do it." He glanced at Maurice, who appeared irritated by the disturbance. "Catarina is right—something is going on with the staff."

A moment later, his footsteps echoed in the hall as he stalked toward the kitchen. Cate strained her ears, but she couldn't make out any voices.

Frowning, she turned back to her grandfather. "What do you think happened?" Her breath hitched. "Oh gosh, do you think something happened to Audrey's son?"

It was the only plausible explanation she could think of for Audrey's visible distress. Cate had met Audrey's young son earlier in the summer when she'd brought him to the estate so he could try to solve the hedge maze, and little Etienne was the sweetest kid Cate had ever met. She knew Audrey didn't have a husband or any immediate family in the area, so Etienne was her entire life.

"I hope not," her grandfather said, sounding worried now.

Cate couldn't eat a bite as she waited for Nik to come back. When he finally did, she took one look at his face and knew that something terrible had happened.

"What's wrong?" she demanded. "What did Audrey say?"

"Catarina . . ." Nik hesitated, and rather than return to his seat, he knelt down in front of her chair.

Her pulse kicked off in a gallop. "What's going on, Nik? Why is Audrey so upset?"

Deep regret flickered in his eyes. "I'm afraid I have some bad news. Gabriel was in an accident."

Cate's heart lurched, then stopped beating altogether. "*What?* Oh my God! Is he okay?"

Nik's long pause was even more terrifying than the nervous look on his face.

"Is he okay?" she repeated.

"I'm afraid not, sweetheart. He was riding his motorcycle yesterday and—"

"Vespa," she choked out.

"—he was hit by a car. He wasn't wearing a helmet, Cate. His neck snapped when he hit the ground . . . He died on impact."

Horror slammed into her. "That's not possible. He *always* wears a helmet!"

"I'm sorry, sweetheart."

She struggled for air, feeling like she'd just been struck in the chest with a sledgehammer. "I don't believe it. You're wrong."

Nik and her grandfather exchanged a somber look, but she refused to acknowledge the sorrow hanging in the air.

Panicked, she flew off her chair and glared at Nik. "You must have got the details wrong. I'm going to talk to Audrey myself. I'm sure Gabriel is fine. He's *fine*."

Nik swiftly blocked her path. "He's not fine, sweetheart. I know you don't want to accept it, but I'm telling you the truth." He met her eyes with a heavy sigh. "Gabriel is dead."

Chapter 28

Gabriel was dead.

Dead.

Dead.

Cate's brain kept getting stuck on that one word, unable to process the meaning behind it. Because Gabriel couldn't really be *dead*, right? Nik was wrong. Audrey was wrong. They were all wrong.

But even as she repeated the mantra in her head—wrong, wrong, *wrong*—her aching heart told her to stop living in denial. She'd spoken to Audrey, who'd been in tears when she explained how Gabriel's mother had phoned the estate to share the news with the staff. Cate had called Joséphine herself, who'd confirmed the tragic news.

Gabriel was gone. He was actually gone, and all Cate could do now was lie in bed and stare up at the ceiling. Numb.

Images of Gabriel flashed in her mind. His dark eyes shining with amusement as he teased her about not being able to finish that damn hedge maze. The dimple in his chin that popped out when he smiled. God, that lopsided smile. She would never get to see it again.

She suddenly realized how fleeting it all was. You always thought you had all the time in the world. You took it for granted that the people you cared about were always going to be there. But that wasn't true, because Gabriel was gone, and now all she had left were the things she'd never get to do with him.

Hear him laugh. Hold him. *Kiss* him.

Her throat closed up, and somehow her thoughts shifted from Gabriel to Morgan, the man she'd run away from in the Eiffel Tower.

What if something happened to him too? James Morgan had been alive when she'd left him, but what if that changed? He ran a security company that specialized in military operations, a job that had danger written all over it. What if her father died protecting someone who'd hired him for security?

What if he was erased from her life the same way Gabriel was?

A rush of panic filled her chest, propelling her into action. She stumbled off the bed and dove into her walk-in closet, where she'd hidden the secret cell phone Morgan had given her. She had to contact him, tell him she needed to see him again.

To her surprise, after she turned on the phone and the screen came to life, she found a message already waiting for her.

Results are in. You're my daughter.

The DNA test. Their samples must have been a match.

James Morgan was really her father.

Cate's heart did the impossible—it soared and plummeted at the same time, as joy and unhappiness warred inside her. She realized that she couldn't text him back, at least not until she spoke to her grandfather. She refused to sneak around for the rest of her life, which meant that if she wanted to have any sort of relationship with her father, her grandfather had to agree to it first.

Cate left the closet with determined strides. Now probably wasn't the time to confront her grandfather, but she knew she couldn't delay it any longer.

Gabriel's death had left her ravaged and grief-stricken, but James Morgan was still very much alive, and she wasn't about to lose a single additional second with him.

And who knew? Maybe her grandfather would react well to the news. Maybe he'd even allow her to see her father tonight. Morgan could stop by the house, talk to Maurice. They could face their past, come up with some kind of agreement, and plan out a visitation schedule of sorts.

She knew she'd find her grandfather in his study—he always went in there for a drink after dinner—but as she hurried down the spiral staircase, it occurred to her that he might have gone out to eat. Surely her grandpa wouldn't have asked the staff to cook for him in the midst of a tragedy, right?

Turned out she was wrong, because when she walked past the dining room, she spotted Audrey collecting dishes from the perfectly set table.

Cate battled a burst of anger. He'd actually made the staff serve him dinner? When they were all grieving for Gabriel?

As she neared the study, she forced herself to swallow her resentment. She couldn't be angry when she spoke to him. No, the only way to get him on her side was to state her case calmly and maturely, and hope that he understood how much she needed this.

Her bare feet didn't make a sound on the marble floor as she approached the door. She heard voices behind it—Nik's silky baritone, Maurice's deep timbre. She raised her fist to knock, but froze when she caught the tail end of her grandfather's remark.

". . . did a good job taking care of the boy."

Something about his tone made her blood run cold.

She slid closer and pressed her ear to the door, trying to make out Nik's response.

"It was a difficult task. He wasn't a bad kid. Just misguided."

Wariness trickled down her spine, bringing a queasy feeling to the pit of her stomach. Were they talking about Gabriel?

"And you took care of the Morgan file you found in his custody?"

Cate sucked in a breath. The Morgan file? Oh God. Did they mean the same file she'd found and photocopied in her grandfather's office?

The file she'd asked Gabriel to hide the night Nik walked in on them.

Panic darted inside her like a skittish animal, dampening

her palms. She'd forgotten to ask Gabriel for the papers, which meant he'd probably had them on him when . . . when what? Had Nik and her grandfather somehow managed to find the photocopies?

". . . swore he never showed them to her." Nik again, firm and confident.

". . . believe him?"

She strained to hear better, but they were speaking too quietly now.

". . . very convincing." Footsteps sounded from behind the door, and then Nik's voice grew more audible. ". . . said the door was unlocked and he wandered past it on the way to see his mother. He found the file on the desk."

"He's lying. It was in a locked drawer. The little bastard must have picked the lock."

"The question is . . ." Nik's words became muffled again. ". . . his own curiosity? Or did Cate ask him to?"

Her pulse raced as the question hung in the air. They knew about the file. And for some reason, Gabriel had lied to them when they'd confronted him about it.

But it was only a matter of time before they figured out she was behind everything.

Except . . . that wasn't even the terrifying part, she realized.

If she'd heard them right, then that meant . . .

Oh God.

Nik had killed Gabriel.

He'd *taken care of the boy*, as her grandfather had so casually referred to it.

A frightened yelp flew out of Cate's throat.

Instantly, she slapped a hand over her mouth to cover up the sound, but it was too late. The voices in the study had gone quiet. Soft footsteps came toward the door.

She spun around, about to take off in a run, but she wasn't fast enough.

The door swung open.

"Catarina?" Nik's eyes widened when he spotted her, and then his expression grew wary. "How long have you been out there?"

She couldn't breathe, couldn't move. All she was capable of doing was staring at him accusingly. Hatred gathered inside her and crawled up her body, bringing bile to her throat.

"Answer the question, Cate."

She finally found her voice. "Long enough."

"What exactly did you hear?"

"Everything," she whispered. "I heard everything."

Nik took a step forward. His mouth opened to say something, but the last thread of Cate's control suddenly snapped, and she found herself lunging forward, pounding at his chest with her fists.

"You killed him!" she burst out. "You *killed* Gabriel!"

He grabbed at her hands, trying to still her frantic blows. "Catarina, stop it."

"You killed him!"

She swung at him again, only to find her wrist locked between his strong fingers. A shadow appeared in her peripheral vision, and she swiveled her head to see her grandfather in the doorway.

"You're mistaken, Catarina." His voice remained calm, rippling with authority. "You misunderstood our discussion."

"I didn't misunderstand a goddamn thing!"

Maurice's dark eyes flashed. "Watch your language."

She ignored him, her breath coming out fast and erratic. "You found the file I gave him, and you tried to shut him up because you thought he hadn't told me about it yet!" She directed a vicious glare at Nik. "You. Killed. Him."

Maurice looked taken aback. "The file you *gave* him?"

A tornado of emotion spiraled through her as she met her grandfather's eyes. Horror, triumph, agony, disbelief—she was too overwhelmed to concentrate on any one emotion. All she could focus on were the two men standing before her.

The two men who'd killed her best friend.

"I'm the one who snuck into your study. I'm the one who broke into that locked drawer and copied the file." She was so enraged, so horrified, she could barely go on. "You lied to me. My father isn't dead. You fucking lied."

"But he is dead," Maurice said stiffly. "The man in that file isn't your father. He's simply a business associate I had some dealings with in the—"

"Stop lying to me!" she roared. "He *is* my father! We did a DNA test to prove it!"

Silence crashed over them.

"That's impossible," her grandfather finally spat out, his expression revealing barely restrained fury.

"No, it's not. I gave him a sample of my hair and saliva, and he took it to a lab, where they compared it to his DNA."

Maurice and Nik exchanged an indecipherable look, and then the former addressed her as if she were a small child.

"You don't know what you're saying, Catarina."

A hysterical laugh popped out of her mouth. "I don't know what I'm saying? I *met* him! Yesterday, at the Eiffel Tower."

Nik's eyes clouded over. "How is that possible?"

"I lied to you," she retorted, her tone defiant, satisfied. "When Bruno and Christian were following us? It wasn't me walking around with Gabriel—it was a decoy. Morgan arranged it!"

Her grandfather glowered. "Are you saying you had contact with that man?"

"My father," she corrected. "Not *that man*, my *father*. And yes, I did. We didn't talk about much because there wasn't a lot of time, but I did glean one thing from the meeting, which is that *he's not dead*. You lied to me. You've been lying to me my whole life." She gasped for air as the horror returned. "And you killed Gabriel. Oh God. Oh my God. Morgan was right—you *are* dangerous. You . . ."

She stumbled backward. Swaying, shaking, unable to think clearly anymore. She stared at the two men who'd raised her, the two men she'd trusted most in the world, and she didn't recognize them anymore. They'd transformed into strangers right before her eyes, and the mere sight of them made her feel like throwing up.

"I don't know who you are," she mumbled. "I don't know either one of you."

Nik took a step toward her, slow and cautious, as if he were approaching a feral animal. "Cate . . ."

Her hand flew up, palm out. "Don't come any closer."

He kept inching forward.

"No! Don't come near me, Nik!"

Gabriel's face flashed in her mind. Morgan's face. Ariana's face.

Ariana. God, had her mother really been shot during an assassination attempt gone wrong, or was that another lie they'd told her?

Nothing made sense anymore. Nothing was real.

"Catarina, get back here!"

She hadn't even realized she was running away. But she was. Running so fast her lungs burned, so fast that her surroundings were nothing but a blur, a whiz of doors and windows and expensive art, all disappearing in the blink of an eye.

She tore down the hall with no idea where she was running. She heard footsteps pounding behind her. Nik called out her name, but she didn't stop, didn't turn around. She kept going, bare feet slapping the marble floor until finally she lurched into the sunroom and had to halt for a moment to catch her breath.

"Cate! Stop! Just listen to me!"

When Nik appeared in the doorway, her panic returned in full force, squeezing her chest like a vise.

"I don't want to hear anything you have to say," she choked out, and then she dove through the French doors and hurried across the stone terrace, making a beeline for the stairs.

The sun had set, but the cobblestone pathways winding through the gardens were lit up, illuminating her way. Her gaze landed on the entrance of the hedge maze, several yards away and shrouded in darkness.

"Goddamn it, Cate! Come back here!"

Without looking back, she ran toward the maze as if her life depended on it.

Adrenaline surged through Nik's blood as he raced after Catarina. He hadn't experienced fear this strong since he'd cradled Ariana's body in his arms the night the Dietrich estate had been attacked. He still remembered the chaos—gunshots exploding through the house, the air thick and gray, thanks to the smoke bombs. Carrying the woman he loved to the tunnels beneath the house, fleeing the scene of the ambush with Walther at the wheel.

Now that same paralyzing terror had seized his bones. He caught a glimpse of Cate's retreating back as she disappeared into a sea of green, and he had to draw a much-needed breath in order to regain his composure.

He needed to talk to her.

He needed to make her understand.

He hurried through the two massive hedges marking the maze's entrance, then took a moment to orient himself. He'd completed the maze more than a dozen times, knew its layout like the back of his hand. He also knew that Cate had never had the patience for it, and she always took the same path when she was inside.

He immediately dove to the left, his brown leather loafers thudding on the hard-packed ground. Hedges loomed on either side of him, nearly ten meters tall and emanating an odor that was a mixture of earthy evergreen and a hint of cat urine. He welcomed the distinct scent of the boxwood leaves; it served as a reminder of where he was, where he had to go. Some people found mazes claustrophobic, but Nik could solve this one in his sleep.

He picked up his pace, and it wasn't long before he heard her footsteps several feet ahead of him. He was gaining on her.

"Cate!" he shouted.

Her muffled response reached his ears. "Leave me alone!"

He could smell the sweet fragrance of her shampoo now. She was close.

He ran faster, turned right, then left, then raced down the narrow path, all the way to the end. He spotted her the moment he rounded the corner, her blue cotton pajama pants and loose white tank top reflecting the shards of silvery light from the sky above them.

A moment later, he'd grabbed hold of her arm and was yanking her backward.

"Listen to me!"

"No!" she spat out, trying to shrug out of his grip. "Get away from me!"

He planted both hands on her shoulders and shook her hard. "Goddamn it! Let me explain!"

"Explain what?" Venom dripped from her words. "Explain how you killed Gabriel? You know what? Fine! Go ahead and *explain*! Tell me how you did it, Nik. Tell me how you mowed him down with your car!"

His chest constricted when he glimpsed the tears in her eyes.

"Did he die when you hit him?" she panted. "Or did you snap his neck afterward? Come on, *tell me*!"

The guilt that poured into him was so powerful it blurred his vision. She would never know how difficult it had been for him to kill that boy, but he'd had no other choice. He'd left the boy with a warning and gotten into his car, all the while knowing that Gabriel would hop on his scooter and go to Cate.

And then he'd gone after him, eliminating the threat with a heavy heart.

He hadn't derived any pleasure from the task. Lord, how could he? He wasn't a killer. He oversaw smuggling routes, for Christ's sake. But someone had needed to silence the Traver boy, and unfortunately, that someone had been him.

He had to make her understand. He had to make her see that he'd only done it to protect her. That was all he'd ever wanted—to protect Ariana.

"Please," he pleaded. "Please, sweetheart, don't look at me like that."

He tried to touch her face, but she batted his hand away. When he noticed the flicker of fear in her eyes, something inside him split apart.

"Don't look at me like that!" he howled.

Her eyes widened as he backed her into the prickly wall of the maze and slammed his thigh between her legs.

"Stop looking at me like I'm going to hurt you! I would *never* hurt you!"

"Wh-what are you doing?"

He grabbed her chin with both hands. "I love you! Don't you understand? All I've ever done is try to protect you!"

"Let go of me," she whispered.

"Damn it, Ariana! I *love* you! Don't you see it?"

His mouth crashed down on hers before she could respond. He registered her horrified gasp, but it sounded like it had come from far away, and he ignored it, because the pleasure that flooded his body was too overwhelming. He kissed her with everything he had, years of pent-up passion exploding inside him.

He groaned into her mouth, vaguely aware of the sensation of something hitting his chest. But he ignored that too, because the kiss was too incredible, too beautiful.

He'd ached for this moment. He'd missed her so much.

His hand trembled as it slid down to cup one firm breast. Another groan ripped out of his throat. Lord. So sweet, so beautiful.

"Ariana," he moaned.

A jolt of pain slammed into his nose.

"Don't ever touch me again!"

Nik blinked, his vision rapidly coming into focus to find a pair of blue eyes blazing fiercely at him.

Blue eyes. Not chocolate brown.

"Catarina," he choked out.

Her voice was low and deadly. "Don't come near me."

"Cate . . . I didn't mean to . . . I didn't mean . . . I . . ."

He couldn't hear himself over the loud pounding of his heart. He'd kissed her. He'd *fondled* her. Bile coated his throat as the full weight of his actions sank in. He'd disgraced himself in front of Ariana's daughter.

"I'm so sorry," he stammered. "I'm so sorry."

When he took a step toward her, her fists snapped up in a defensive stance.

"Don't you fucking come near me, Nik."

Tears stung his eyes. "I didn't mean to do that, Cate. I . . . got confused." He blinked rapidly, then cleared his throat. "It's time for us to go back inside."

"I'm not going anywhere with you."

As the broken pieces of his composure fused back together, he looked at her with genuine regret. "You don't have a choice, sweetheart. You know it as well as I do."

Cate's panicked gaze darted around them as she considered her options, but they both knew she had nowhere to run.

"I'm sorry," he said quietly. "I really am, but you're coming back inside with me. Your grandfather will be wanting to speak with you."

Her bottom lip trembled.

"I'm not leaving this maze without you." His voice

cracked. "So either you walk out with me on your own two feet, or I'm afraid I'll have to carry you."

"No! You're never touching me again!" she blurted out.

Shame spiraled through him. He wanted to apologize again for his indiscretion, promise that it would never happen again, but he knew it wouldn't make a difference.

After a few long moments, her face collapsed in defeat.

"Let's go," she mumbled.

He kept three feet of distance between them as he guided her out of the maze, and when they emerged into the garden, she froze in place, her expression clouding over as she gazed at the house.

"I don't want to be here," she whispered.

Nik swallowed a lump of pain and met her helpless eyes. "This is where you belong," he said simply.

Chapter 29

Noelle didn't get back to the penthouse until later in the evening, after spending an exasperating day talking to various contacts, all of whom had zero intel for her. With that bastard Charron turning on her, she'd had to take even greater precautions before and after every meeting, and she was tired and annoyed as she stalked into the living room.

Jim's newest recruit was sprawled on the couch, his green eyes popping open at her entrance.

"Where's Jim?" she said in lieu of greeting.

Ash hooked his thumb at the corridor. "Bedroom."

She rolled her eyes. "Sulking again?"

"Not sure. He's been holed up there for a couple hours with a bottle of tequila."

Fucking hell.

Noelle scowled at the dark-haired rookie. "And you're—what?—just catching a little nap while he drinks himself stupid?"

"I drew the graveyard shift tonight. Gotta get some sleep before I go." His voice contained a southern drawl that was no doubt a big hit with the ladies. "And if the boss wants to drink himself stupid, there ain't much I can do about it, darlin'."

She raised her eyebrows. Not many men had the balls to use sugary endearments in her presence. Clearly this kid was fearless.

"Go back to sleep, *darlin'*," she said mockingly. "A growing boy needs his rest."

She heard him snickering as she headed for the bedroom, and she fought a smile. How did Jim always manage to find the most charming guys to work for him? She wondered whether it was a requirement for joining his team of scoundrels.

She wasn't sure what she was expecting when she strode into the bedroom, but it certainly wasn't the sight of Jim sprawled on the bed, bare-chested and barefoot, with his eyes wide-open and a bottle of tequila tucked at his side.

"Hey, baby," he rasped. "Took your sweet-ass time getting home, didn't cha?"

Noelle sighed. "You're drunk."

His sensual mouth formed a smirk. "Just a li'l bit."

"Wow. You're a real bastard—you know that? Lying here shit-faced while everyone else carries out *your* mission." Jaw tight, she gestured to the bottle. "Where'd you get that?"

"I sent Ash to the liquor store." Disbelief entered his voice. "Did you know you don't have any tequila in the house?"

Of course she knew. She purposely didn't stock her bar with it because the blasted drink reminded her too much of *this* asshole.

Even in his drunken state, Jim proved that he was still more than capable of reading her mind. "Shit," he blurted out. "You don't keep it around 'cause it makes you think of me, eh?"

Noelle went to the foot of the bed and crossed her arms. "Get off your ass, Jim. You need to sober up and take control of yourself."

He ignored the command. "Why do you have to pretend you don't think about me? We both know you do. You remember everything."

She shot him a cool look. "Remembering and thinking isn't the same thing."

"Yeah, guess you're right." He raised the bottle to his lips and took a hearty swig. "Case you were wondering, I think about you."

She masked her surprise. "Yeah?"

"Uh-huh. I think about you whenever someone passes me a saltshaker."

Noelle couldn't stop the laugh that popped out of her mouth. "And why is that?"

"'Cause you always oversalt your food." He narrowed his eyes. "Do you still do that?"

"I like salt," she said defensively.

He threw his head back and laughed, and the deep rumble made her heart skip a beat.

Goddamn it. A sober, surly Jim she could handle, but an intoxicated, scarily candid one? She wasn't equipped to deal with it, and she feared this encounter was veering into very dangerous territory.

"Oh, and I think about you when I jerk off."

Her breath caught. "Really."

His blue eyes smoldered. "It's the fastest way for me to come."

She didn't know whether to be insulted or flattered. Or maybe a bit of both. What she did know was that Jim was positively plastered. The alcohol had brought a flush to his cheeks and a slur to his words, and she knew that when he sobered up, he'd probably regret every word he was saying to her.

"Admit it," he taunted. "It's the same for you. No man has ever fucked you the way I do."

Noelle briefly closed her eyes, trying to tamp down her rising desire. "Why are you in here drinking?" she said quietly.

He barked out a laugh. "What else am I s'posed to do? Watch Dietrich's house like a pathetic fool hoping to catch a glimpse of my kid? What's the point? My daughter doesn't want to see me. She'd rather live with a criminal than be with me."

"What did you expect? Dietrich is the only parent she's ever known."

Bitterness hardened his tone. "Shoulda been me."

Noelle arched a brow. "I take it you're about to blame me again?"

"Nah. Not your fault. My fault," he mumbled.

This time she couldn't hide her surprise. "Since when?"

"Since always."

He struggled to shift into an upright position, the muscles of his chest bulging and flexing. With a grumble of annoyance, he finally slid up against the headboard and tried to place the tequila bottle on the nightstand.

He wasn't successful—the bottle wobbled, bobbled, and toppled right off the table. Amber-colored liquid spilled all over the floor, forming a puddle next to the bed.

"Shit," he muttered. "Sorry."

She stifled a groan. Wonderful. First a fistfight that had left the bedroom a glass-covered mess, and now tequila soaking into the hardwood—she and Jim were well on their way to destroying her home.

"Anyway . . . not gonna blame you," he went on, rubbing his eyes with his fist. "I used you, remember? I used you, and you got your revenge by warning Ariana about me." His powerful chest rose as he drew a breath. "She needed to be warned. I was using her too, y'know."

Noelle took an irritated step away from the bed. "I'm not in the mood to attend your pity party, Jim. Come find me when you're sober."

His husky voice stopped her before she reached the door.

"Don't go."

When she turned to face him, she saw that his hand had moved to his waistband, uncoordinated fingers fumbling with his zipper.

She sighed again. "You're in no condition for that."

"Says who?"

And then he pulled out his cock, leaving no question as to whether or not he was up for it.

His erection, long and hard, jutted out enticingly. Noelle glimpsed the drop of moisture pooling at his tip, and her body responded accordingly, growing wet and achy and unbearably hot.

"C'mere and ride me," he commanded.

She ignored the desire tingling between her legs. "That's probably not a good idea right now."

"Sure it is." He yanked off his pants and boxers, and threw them aside. "C'mon, baby, I need the distraction."

She supposed she could have said no, but how often did

an opportunity this delicious come along? There was nothing sexier than the sight of Jim stretched out on the bed, gloriously naked and hers for the taking. The tight ripples of his abdominal muscles, his sculpted pecs, the dusting of dark hair that arrowed down to his groin—everything about him radiated potent masculinity.

She craved him on a whole other level, the kind of craving that made her heart pound and her mouth go dry. The kind of craving that erased all common sense and turned her into a hot, needy mess.

The kind of craving that only this man could satisfy.

As she watched him stroke his own cock, she could no longer fight the demoralizing truth. Jim Morgan would *never* be out of her system. She would never stop wanting him, no matter how hard she tried.

"Take off your clothes, Noelle."

Her hands involuntarily reached for her waistband. She shoved the leggings down her hips and kicked them away. Her tight black tee came off next, then her bra, her red boyshort panties, and then she was as naked as Jim was, standing there on display.

His blue eyes burned with approval. "Christ, you're beautiful. Have I ever told you that?"

The intensity of his tone startled her. "Not in a long time."

"Well, you are. You're the most beautiful woman I've ever known."

Her breath got caught in her throat. "Thank you."

"I wanna touch you, but you're too far away."

"Is that your way of asking me to come closer?"

"Uh-uh. I want you to stay right where you are." He gave his erection a slow pump, then absently stroked the tip with his thumb. "Touch yourself for me."

"Or I can come and ride you like you wanted."

"Not yet," he said with a stubborn shake of the head. "I want you to touch yourself, and pretend it's me doing it."

She decided to humor him. "Where would you like me to touch?"

"Your breasts. Cup them."

Keeping her gaze on his face, she lowered both hands to

her chest and cupped the heavy weight of her breasts. Her nipples stiffened, the sensitive buds straining against her palms.

"Squeeze," he ordered.

She squeezed. Pleasure danced through her body and settled in her core, forming a knot of anticipation.

"Play with your nipples." His hand moved over his erection in lazy strokes, while his blue eyes stayed glued to her breasts.

Noelle rubbed the pads of her thumbs over the puckered buds, enjoying the flurry of shivers that skipped along her skin.

"Feels good?" Jim murmured.

She nodded.

"Take one hand and put it between your legs."

She did as he asked, her palm covering her slick folds and gliding over her clit.

He inhaled sharply. "Slide a finger inside."

Swallowing, Noelle used her index finger to toy with her opening, then pushed it into her aching sex.

"Are you wet?"

Her breathing grew labored as she fingered herself, slow and steady. "Very."

Jim let out a groan. "God. C'mere."

Shooting him a seductive smile, she climbed onto the bed and sat astride him, her knees on either side of his muscular thighs. He wasted no time moving his hand south and slipping one long finger inside her.

"Fuck. You *are* wet."

Disappointment rippled through her when he withdrew that wicked finger, but she didn't have time to voice it, because suddenly he was reaching for her breasts.

"Gimme," he ordered. "I wanna taste."

Noelle slowly eased forward and brought a breast to his mouth, moaning when his tongue came out to flick one rigid nipple. He wrapped his lips around it and sucked gently, and the warmth of his mouth set her hypersensitized skin on fire. When he shifted his attention to the other breast, teasing and sucking her other nipple, another moan slipped out and she sagged into his gentle assault.

"Love this. I fucking love this." His deep voice vibrated against her breasts.

Her head lolled to the side as his mouth enclosed her nipple again. He kissed it with unexpected tenderness, then sucked using that same gentle approach. Each soft pull sent a shiver up her spine and a rush of sweet agony to her core. God, this man was liable to kill her. She squirmed on his lap, so turned on she could barely breathe, surrendering completely to his delicate ministrations.

When she felt his finger probing her entrance, she squirmed even more, desperate to feel him inside her.

"Fucking hell," he ground out once his finger was lodged deep. "So goddamn wet. Is it all for me?"

She managed a nod.

"You want me."

"Yes," she whispered, her eyelids fluttering closed as she rocked into his talented finger.

"You missed me."

Her eyes flew open. "No."

Rather than argue, Jim just nodded. "I guess I deserve that."

The air of defeat emanating from his powerful body was disconcerting. She didn't like this subdued, beaten version of him, with his slumped shoulders and tired eyes and discouraged attitude. Jim Morgan was a warrior, damn it, and as much as she hated his alpha asshole-ness at times, his strength and intensity were what had drawn her to him in the first place.

Gritting her teeth, she reached out and slapped him.

"What the fuck, Noelle!" Blinking wildly, he rubbed his cheek. "Didn't you get your fill the other day? What the hell was that for?"

"For being a pathetic loser. You're not this man, okay? You're not the guy who drowns his sorrows in cheap corner-store tequila and laments about his past mistakes. You're James fucking Morgan! You don't hide and whine when things don't go your way. You go out and make shit happen."

He seemed utterly fascinated by her words, which only pissed her off all the more.

"Stop being a whiny baby," she snapped. "You want to

win over your kid? Then come up with a fucking plan and do it."

She felt like a coach addressing his losing team at half-time, but the cheesy speech had flown out before she could stop it.

Except now Jim was staring at her with unbelievable lust in his eyes. And his erection looked impossibly thicker.

Noelle sighed. "Seriously? That silly pep talk actually turned you on—"

She was on her back before she could finish that sentence. Jim's heavy body crushed hers, his blue eyes gleaming down at her as he guided his blunt head to her opening and plunged inside, summoning a desperate noise from her throat.

She gasped when he started to move. She was so wet from arousal that his cock slid in and out of her body with ease, and each time he drove in again, he hit a sweet spot deep inside and unleashed a new flurry of shivers. Her sex stretched around his cock, her inner walls quivering, clasping him tight.

"Feels so good," he mumbled. "Always feels so damn good."

His fingers dug into her hips as he quickened his strokes, but then he abruptly went still and voiced a question that threw her for a loop. "Have you fucked a lot of men since . . . since me . . . ?"

She paused. "You know the answer to that."

"Yeah, I figured. I've been with other women. A lot of women. But it wasn't like this with them. Never like this."

His hips shot forward in a hard thrust that stole her breath.

"Not enough," he rasped. "It's never enough."

She knew exactly what he meant. The sexual need between them was unbearable. She didn't just feel desire for the man—it *consumed* her. It was the most powerful thing she'd ever experienced in her life.

As their bodies frantically moved together, he slid his hands beneath her back and wrapped his arms around her, holding her like he was drowning at sea and she was his life preserver. His strong grip heightened her excitement, and the pressure between her legs intensified, a ball of tension that grew and grew and grew until finally it burst apart and a mind-blowing orgasm swept through her.

Jim cried out a moment later, burying his face in her neck as he shuddered in release.

Afterward, he collapsed on top of her in a blissful heap, his heart hammering against her breasts, matching the erratic beating of hers. Then he rolled over and pulled her close, his fingers tangling in her hair, stroking the long strands.

She wasn't sure how long they lay there, but she eventually became aware of his even breathing, his closed eyelids. He'd fallen asleep, and she'd never seen a sexier sight as she propped herself up to watch him. His features softened in slumber, making him look younger, less cold and savage.

Her gaze rested on his mouth, those firm, sensual lips that she had yet to kiss. By choice, anyway. The last two times they'd kissed didn't count because she hadn't asked for it. But now . . . now she couldn't stop thinking about it. She was longing to press her mouth to his, but she knew that the moment she did, everything would change.

She suddenly registered the wetness on her cheeks, and was horrified to discover she was crying. Goddamn it. What was wrong with her?

She wiped the tears with the back of her hand, still staring intently at his mouth. Maybe she ought to do it. Just kiss him. Now, when he was sleeping and unaware. She could succumb to the craving without him ever knowing she'd surrendered to him.

Swallowing hard, Noelle swept her fingertips over his bottom lip in a timid caress. As indecision floated through her, she slowly brought her mouth close to his, hesitating when their lips were millimeters apart.

Just as she was about to bridge that infinitesimal gap, a cell phone vibrated.

Her head snapped up guiltily, but Jim didn't stir. He was still sound asleep, oblivious to the buzzing sounds coming from the nightstand.

Collecting herself, Noelle took a deep breath before leaning toward the end table to grab Jim's phone. She'd thought a call was coming through, but when she checked the screen she realized it was a text message.

Unconcerned with pesky issues like privacy, she clicked on the message and quickly scanned its contents.

Then, with a heavy sigh, she placed a hand on Jim's bare chest and gave it a nudge. "Wake up," she said grimly. "You need to see this."

Chapter 30

Twenty minutes later, Morgan hung up the phone and turned to Noelle and Ash with a grave look. "Liam says something went down at the house tonight."

"Care to elaborate?" Noelle prompted.

She stood in the open doorway of the terrace with a cigarette dangling from her hand, and the smell of smoke only made Morgan's temples throb harder. He'd chugged a gallon of water and two coffees in an attempt to sober up fast, but it still felt like someone was operating a jackhammer in his head.

"Would you put that thing out?" he grumbled.

"Yes, sir." Rolling her eyes, she ducked out to extinguish the cigarette, then stepped back inside. "Now tell us what happened."

"Cate came running out of the house and disappeared into the maze. Apparently she was being chased by a blond man who was screaming her name." As Morgan repeated what Liam had reported, his chest clenched with worry. "Liam and Bailey couldn't see what was going on in the maze — the thing is too damn tall — but after about five minutes, Cate and the man walked out. Liam says she looked upset, but she wasn't fighting the guy. They went back inside, and there's been no activity since."

His head continued to pound, but now his heart had joined in, so loudly it felt like a damn drum circle had possessed his body. He wanted to hijack Noelle's Town Car and speed over to the Durand estate, but Liam had assured him that Cate hadn't looked injured as she'd walked into the house.

But how long would it stay that way?

Rage bubbled inside him as he thought about the mysterious man Liam had mentioned. Christ, if that bastard hurt so much as a hair on Cate's head, Morgan was going to go postal on him.

"Did Macgregor recognize the blond?" Noelle asked with a frown.

"He said it wasn't Durand, that much we know."

She went quiet. He could see the wheels in her head turning.

"What is it?" he said sharply.

"The night of the party . . ." She trailed off for a moment, her frown deepening. "When we were leaving, I spotted a blond guy on the front steps. Did you happen to get a look at him?"

Morgan searched his brain and came up empty-handed. Not much of a surprise—the shock of seeing Walther Dietrich that night had sent him reeling. He'd been too distracted to pay attention to anyone else, and if he were being honest, the only reason they'd made it out of the party undetected was thanks to Noelle's quick thinking.

"No, I don't remember seeing anyone," he admitted. "Did you recognize him?"

"He looked familiar but I couldn't place him at the time."

"What do you remember about him?"

She licked her lips in thought. "He was tall. In good shape, but more lanky than muscular. Light blond hair, blue eyes, clean-shaven face. I remember his eyebrows being darker than the hair on his head, dark enough that someone might think he dyed his hair."

Morgan froze.

Noelle, as usual, was attuned to his every nuance. "Do you know him?"

"Maybe." He raked a hand through his hair. "Do you by any chance remember a man named Nikolaus Bauer?"

She paused for a second, then sucked in her breath. "Son of a bitch. You might be right. The man at the party definitely could've been Bauer."

From his seat on the couch, Ash tentatively joined the conversation. "Who's Nikolaus Bauer?"

"Ariana's fiancé," Morgan said flatly. "Or at least he was supposed to be. They grew up together, and their families were tight. It was pretty much a given that they would get married someday and unite the family fortunes."

"So what happened to him?" Ash asked.

"I happened. I came into Ariana's life, she decided she wanted me, and she tossed Bauer aside like a piece of garbage."

"Charming girl," Noelle muttered.

"I told you, she wasn't a very nice person," he muttered back. "Anyway, after Walther and Ariana disappeared, I kept tabs on Bauer for a year. He was just going about his same old routine in Berlin. He worked at his father's shipping company, which was a front for a drug-smuggling operation. Far as I could tell, he had no contact with Walther, so eventually I stopped monitoring him."

"Well, they must have made contact at some point," Noelle said. "Because the more I think about it, the more I'm certain it was Bauer I saw that night."

Morgan gave a harsh chuckle. "I guess he ended up with Ariana, after all." Something else occurred to him. "Bauer must be the guy my informant told me about last year."

Noelle wrinkled her brow. "What are you talking about?"

"The arms deal I was tracking in Pakistan," he clarified. "You know, when you headed up the op in Monte Carlo after our compound was attacked? I heard some rumblings about a major deal, and I thought Dietrich might be involved, but when I flashed his picture around, nobody recognized him. One of my contacts said that the seller involved in the transaction did resemble the man in the photo, only he was much younger and had light eyes instead of dark. I think he was talking about Bauer."

"So he's active in the arms trade too," Ash commented.

"Like I said, the two families were tight. Bauer's father focused primarily on drugs, but his smuggling operation overlapped with Dietrich's gun routes. I think Bauer Sr. often helped Dietrich with his shipping needs, and Bauer Jr. took over the business when his father died, so I'm guessing Nikolaus was always heavily involved in both operations."

As he finished talking, his gaze strayed to the phone he'd left on the glass coffee table, and a flood of anger filled his gut.

"Bauer grabbed my daughter."

Noelle took a step toward him. "Jim . . ."

"He laid a hand on her, Noelle. Liam saw him grab her."

"Don't jump to any conclusions just yet. You don't know the circumstances that led to it."

"We don't know anything!" As he stalked to the table and grabbed his phone, another gust of worry blasted through him. "All we have is Liam's report, and this text message Cate sent twenty minutes ago. That's all we fucking know."

He clutched the phone in his hand, but didn't bother pulling up the message again. It had been sent from the burner phone he'd given Cate at the Eiffel Tower, and he'd already memorized every damn word.

You need to come get me. I'll text you the time and place tomorrow.

That was it. Two sentences. Zero details.

He'd texted her back, but he'd yet to receive a response. He suspected she'd turned off the phone, but that was just another cause for concern. He had no clue what had happened tonight, but he knew his daughter was scared. Noelle had insisted it was impossible to discern fear from a text message, but she was wrong. Cate was terrified—he *felt* it, damn it.

"We could go in tonight," he said in a low voice.

Noelle wasted no time shooting down the idea. "No way. We have no idea what the security inside the house is like. We could be walking into an ambush."

"It's a chance I'm willing to take."

"And risk your kid's life in the process?" she challenged.

Fuck. Noelle was right. They couldn't go in blind and risk Cate getting hurt.

"You have to trust her," Noelle said, her voice surprisingly gentle. "She said she'll contact you tomorrow, and I have no doubt that she will. Once we know more, we can extract her."

Hesitation rippled through him.

"Jim." She marched up to him and grasped his chin with one hand. "Look at me."

He slowly met her eyes, not bothering to mask his despair.

"We'll get her out of there," Noelle said firmly. "But we have to be smart about it. Okay?"

He swallowed, his gaze dropping to the phone in his hand.

"Jim. Hey. Look at me, babe. You good?"

From the corner of his eye, he glimpsed the fascination on Ash's face, but it was impossible to focus on anything but Noelle. Her blue eyes, shining with intensity. Her voice, ringing with confidence.

He took a shaky breath and managed a nod. "Yeah. I'm good."

Chapter 31

Cate approached her grandfather's study on stiff legs, working hard to control the ferocious eddy of hatred rolling around in her stomach.

Was it possible to love someone one day and loathe them the next? Because in less than twenty-four hours, everything she'd ever felt for her grandfather had vanished like a puff of smoke. The love. The respect. It was all gone, replaced by white-hot hostility that continued to wreak havoc on her body.

The events of last night had made it even more imperative that she get out of this house. She couldn't stay there for one more second, couldn't share the same space or breathe the same air as the two murderers who'd been lying to her since the day she was born.

But escaping wouldn't be easy. She'd discovered that the hard way yesterday, and each time she thought about what had happened in the maze . . .

A wave of nausea swept over her, making her gag. She still remembered the wet warmth of Nik's mouth. The way his fingers had quivered when he'd touched her breast.

Cate halted in front of the study door, breathing through the nausea. She couldn't think about Nik right now. And she certainly couldn't think about Gabriel—that was guaranteed to make her fall apart again, and right now, she needed to stay strong.

She had a plan to carry out, a plan that wouldn't work unless she managed to keep her cool.

Taking a breath, she rapped her knuckles on the door and waited.

When it opened, she was startled to find Nik in the doorway.

"Cate," he said softly.

Every muscle in her body coiled tight. "Where's my grandfather?" she demanded instead of offering a proper greeting.

"He's attending the quarterly board meeting at company headquarters. He mentioned it at breakfast yesterday. Don't you remember?"

She blinked in disbelief. "Gee, Nikolaus, I apologize for not remembering. I guess I was too busy thinking about my best friend being dead. You know, the boy you murdered?"

His eyes flickered with regret. "Cate . . ."

"Don't worry," she spat out. "I won't threaten to call the police again. I heard Maurice loud and clear."

In fact, her grandfather's speech had been buzzing around in her head all morning, kindling the fire of anger still burning inside her. Maurice had been waiting for her when Nik escorted her back into the house last night, but the long reprimand she'd expected, the excuses and lies . . . They hadn't come. He'd simply spent a total of four minutes spelling things out to her.

Gabriel had been killed for his "interference."

Calling the police would not help her because Maurice owned the police department.

She was never to see James Morgan again.

And she was never to step foot outside the house without supervision.

Short and sweet, a cold, emphatic speech that left no question in Cate's mind about her new position in the household. She was a prisoner now, and there wasn't a solitary thing she could do about it.

But she'd be damned if she meekly rolled over and allowed her grandfather to get away with what he'd done.

"Cate," Nik said again, gesturing to the doorway. "Come in so we can discuss what happened last night. Please."

"I don't want to *discuss* anything," she said coldly. "I want to see my mother."

He looked startled. "You do?"

"Yes." Determination hardened her jaw. "I can't stomach another second of being in this house. I want to go to my mother's."

"I don't think that's a good idea, sweetheart."

"I don't give a damn what you think. She's my mother and I want to see her. Send a hundred guards to accompany me if you want, but don't bother arguing with me about it. I'm going."

Hesitation creased his forehead. She could see him mulling it over, weighing the implications, but then he released a breath.

"Give me a moment to discuss it with your grandfather."

Nik strode back into the study, but Cate stayed rooted in place. She refused to step foot in that room, breathe in the familiar scent of leather and aftershave, look at all her grandfather's expensive paintings. Any reminder of Maurice Durand was liable to make her throw up.

She waited in the hall and listened to Nik's quiet voice as he spoke to her grandfather on the phone, and when he walked out a minute later, she knew she'd won this round.

"Your grandfather has agreed to let you go," he said woodenly. "Bruno and Christian will take you there shortly. I'll be joining you as well."

"No." She shot him an icy look. "I don't want you to come."

The guilt in his eyes was unmistakable. "Cate . . . I know I scared you last night, but . . . I wasn't in my right mind. I thought . . ."

"You thought I was my mother?" she supplied tersely. "Yeah, Nik, I got that. But forgive me if I don't want to be around the man who tried to rape me."

His jaw fell open. "I . . . I would never . . . That's not what happened, Catarina, and you know it."

"Maybe. But my grandfather doesn't know that, does he?" She offered a sugary sweet smile. "So here's the deal, Nik—you're going to walk back into the study and close the door behind you. I, on the other hand, am going out to the car so Bertrand can take me to my mother's house. If you try to come with me, I'm going to call Maurice myself and tell him all about what you tried to do to me in the maze last night."

His eyes flashed. "Are you blackmailing me, Catarina?"

"Call it whatever the hell you want. But I don't want you anywhere near me ever again."

They stared at each other. Seconds ticked by in silence, until finally, Nik's shoulders drooped in defeat.

"You win, Cate." He sounded sad and ashamed as he turned to the door. "Enjoy your visit with Ariana. Please tell her I said hello."

Feeling vindicated, Cate marched off before he could change his mind.

Thirty minutes later, she walked into her mother's suite flanked by her bulky bodyguards, who refused to give her even an inch of personal space.

When the two men followed her right into Ariana's bedroom, Cate had finally had enough. Whirling around, she crossed her arms over her chest and scowled at both men.

"Could I please have some privacy?" she snapped. "I want to be alone with *Maman*."

Her guards exchanged an uneasy look.

She didn't bother hiding her aggravation. "I get it, guys. Nik told you not to leave my side. But what exactly do you think is going to happen?"

She gestured to her motionless mother, then swept her hand over the various machines surrounding the bed.

"I'm not going anywhere," Cate muttered. "I'm going to sit in that chair, the one right over there, take my mother's hand, and spend the next hour talking to her. Maybe I'll tell her about Gabriel." She shot them a pointed a look. "You remember my best friend, Gabriel, don't you?"

Christian softened his expression first, and it didn't take long for Bruno, the more stoic of the two, to follow suit.

The sadness on their faces threw Cate for a loop. She'd figured that everyone on her grandfather's security staff must know that Nikolaus had killed Gabriel, but her guards looked genuinely grief-stricken.

"Gabriel was a good boy," Christian said quietly.

"Good boy," Bruno agreed, his tone gentle. "My heart goes out to his family."

Christian spoke again. "I'm very sorry for your loss, Catarina."

She fought a rush of suspicion as she listened to their condolences, but whether or not they were being sincere didn't matter at the moment. She needed to send them away, and by mentioning Gabriel, she'd succeeded in doing just that.

"We'll wait for you outside the suite," Christian told her. "Take your time."

"Thank you," she murmured.

Once they were gone, she let out a breath of relief, then checked her watch. It was nine thirty. She'd texted Morgan earlier and arranged for him to come at ten o'clock. That gave her a half hour to figure out how the heck she was going to slip away without alerting her guards or any of the household staff.

But first, she had to say good-bye to her mother.

She was feeling surprisingly emotional as she approached the bed. Ariana's cheeks revealed a rosy blush, her eyelids held a hint of cream-colored shadow, and her hair was perfectly brushed, which told Cate that the stylist had already paid her mother a visit.

"I wish I got to know you when you were . . . alive, I guess." Her voice cracked. "I bet you were even more beautiful."

Sadness washed over her. God, it wasn't fair. Ariana hadn't deserved this fate.

"I'm going to be with my father for a little while," she whispered. "I hope you're not upset that I'm leaving you. Actually, I know you aren't. I know you can't hear a word I'm saying right now."

Her grandfather might believe otherwise, but Cate knew better. She'd read about coma patients waking up and claiming to have heard their loved ones talking to them, but her mother wasn't in a coma. Her mother was brain-dead. She had no sense of cognition. She was simply . . . there.

"I think he's a good man. Grandpa says he isn't, but I don't believe much of what he says these days. He did something terrible, Mama. Something I can never forgive him for."

As her throat closed up, she forced herself to banish Gabriel from her mind. She would grieve for him later. Once she was actually free to do it.

"I have to believe that James Morgan is good. You must have seen something good in him, right? The two of you conceived me, after all."

Cate trailed off, having a tough time picturing her mother with Morgan. Growing up, she'd pored over the family photo albums her grandfather kept in his study, and from what she'd been able to glean, her mother had been a lively, outgoing person. The pictures of her revealed the devilish twinkle in her eyes, the confidence in her posture. She'd seemed like a girl who liked to go out and have fun.

But James Morgan didn't strike Cate as a fun-loving guy. He was more serious, and incredibly difficult to read.

Ironically, she'd felt more of a connection to him in the twenty minutes they'd spoken than in all her visits with Ariana combined. She was never able to get a clear sense of her mother. Maurice revered her, but who was Ariana Durand, really? Who had she once been?

Cate had no answer for that, and no time to think about it, because her watch revealed she had only fifteen minutes left.

She needed to find a way out.

Squaring her shoulders, Cate left her mother's room and headed for the door of the suite. When she opened it, she found her guards lurking in the hallway, much to her dismay.

She cleared her throat. "I was just going to run down to the kitchen and grab a cup of tea. It's kind of cold in there."

Bruno immediately straightened up. "I can do that. Go back inside and sit with your mother, and I'll bring it in for you."

Frustration seized her spine. "Okay. Great. Thanks, Bruno."

"No problem." He hurried off, leaving Cate alone with Christian.

She searched her mind, but for the life of her, she couldn't think of a way to get rid of him, so she simply wandered back to the suite and returned to her mother's bedside.

She found herself reaching for Ariana's hand, something she rarely did, but she was too distracted at the moment to notice the ice-cold flesh beneath her fingers. As anxiety rose inside her, she absently stroked her mother's knuckles and struggled to come up with a plan.

When Bruno strolled into the room five minutes later, she was no closer to finding a solution.

He handed her a cup of tea on a delicate saucer. "Here you go."

"Thank you," she murmured, then waited until he was gone before releasing a frustrated groan.

She checked her watch for a third time. Damn it. Only ten minutes to make her way outside.

But how?

How could she escape without alerting Bruno and Christian? She certainly couldn't outrun them—they were both former soldiers with endurance to spare. And they carried guns. What if they shot her?

She contemplated going out the window, but it was a two-story jump down to the ground. She was afraid she'd break her leg, which would officially squash any hope of making it to Morgan's car. Heck, even an ankle sprain would slow her down.

Her head lifted when she heard a female voice out in the hall. Her mother's nurse. But Mimi didn't come into the suite. She stayed outside the door, chatting with Cate's guards.

Cate turned back to her mother, but not before her gaze rested on the power bar in the wall beside the bed. Dozens of cords were plugged into it, belonging to the machines that kept her mother's various organs working.

That was when something unthinkable occurred to her.

So unthinkable, in fact, that it brought a rush of sickness to her throat.

Cate jumped off the chair, barely making it to the private bathroom before the nausea spilled over. She collapsed in front of the toilet and heaved, emptying the contents of her stomach as horror spiraled through her.

Oh God. How could she have even considered such a thing?

Is it so preposterous?

She promptly threw up again.

And when there was nothing left to throw up, she remained huddled over the porcelain bowl, dry heaving. It took every ounce of strength she had to raise her head and check her watch again.

Nine minutes.

Her legs were shaking as she left the bathroom and returned to her mother. She stood at the foot of the bed, staring at the electrical outlet before focusing her attention on the ventilator, which slowly expanded as it released even bursts of oxygen into her mother's lungs.

Ariana's vacant eyes stared back at her. Normally Cate closed her mother's eyelids when she came to visit. She hated seeing those unresponsive pupils, the unblinking expression. She'd left them open today so she could feel like her mother was actually looking at her when she said good-bye.

But seeing them staring so vacantly made her realize that they'd said good-bye a long time ago. They'd said good-bye when Cate was just a fetus in her mother's stomach. Ariana had died with her baby inside her, and only the miracle of technology had allowed for Cate to be born.

This wasn't her mother lying there. It was a slab of meat her grandfather insisted on keeping fresh.

Cate gagged again, unable to control the revulsion gripping her stomach.

"You don't deserve this," she whispered to her mother.

The earsplitting drumming of her heart drowned out her thoughts. She walked to the side of the bed. Stood there. Stared at the tubes taped to her mother's mouth and nose.

She felt like she was having an out-of-body experience. She was watching herself do the unthinkable. Seeing her own hand gently peel the tape off her mother's face. Seeing her shaky fingers struggle to unhook the plastic pieces.

She felt sick again. Faint.

Breathing hard, she popped the tube out, and recoiled when a loud wheeze echoed in the air, like a balloon that had just been deflated.

Ariana didn't move. Her chocolate brown eyes stayed blank.

Cate could barely see through the sheen of tears. Very slowly, she leaned down and kissed her mother's forehead.

"You can rest now, Mama. I love you."

Then she looked at the heart monitor.

And waited.

*   *   *

"Still no sign of her." Ash's green eyes were focused on the house, his fingers drumming the steering wheel of the SUV.

They'd been waiting for almost five minutes, parked in the narrow driveway at the side of the house, which Cate had explained was used primarily by the staff. The driveway had its own gate separate from the one at the main entrance; Cate had given them the code for it and said she'd be outside at exactly ten o'clock.

But it was 10:05, and she was nowhere in sight.

Morgan couldn't control his growing worry. He suspected they were at Ariana's house, but he hadn't caught a single glimpse of the woman he'd seduced all those years ago. The only car in the main driveway was the one Cate told them she'd be arriving in, but he supposed Ariana could have a vehicle or two stashed in the three-car garage.

Christ, he hated feeling so powerless. He wanted to run into the house and get Cate, but he forced himself to heed Noelle's advice.

You have to trust her, she'd said firmly.

At the moment, Noelle was out front with Sean Reilly. They'd reported seeing an armored sedan drive through the gates. Cate had gotten out of the backseat and entered the house sandwiched by two beefy bodyguards, the same ones who'd been at the Eiffel Tower with her.

It concerned him that neither Dietrich nor Bauer had accompanied her today. Dietrich was attending a board meeting in the city, which had been confirmed by Bailey, who was staking out the headquarters of Durand Enterprises.

Sully and Liam had remained at the Durand property, and they'd checked in to report that Bauer had walked Cate out to the car but hadn't joined her. Liam had managed to snap a photo and send it to Morgan, who'd grimly confirmed the identity of one Nikolaus Bauer.

Fuck, he had no idea what was going on. Why was Cate so desperate to escape? What had happened in that maze?

And where the hell *was* she?

"There," Ash said suddenly, his hand moving to start the engine. "She's coming out."

Morgan instantly hopped out of the passenger seat and saw her walking toward the car.

Her dirty blond hair was arranged in a long braid, and she wore jeans, a white tank top, and a blue gingham shirt tied around her waist. It didn't escape him how similarly they were dressed—he had jeans and a white T-shirt on, and a flannel shirt he'd tossed in the backseat because it was too damn hot today.

But he didn't have time to dwell on their clothing, because he took one look at Cate's face and knew that something was wrong. Her expression was eerily vacant, and she was moving like a zombie, her arms hanging limply at her sides.

"Are you okay?" he demanded when she reached him.

She offered a weak nod. "We have to go. Now."

He wasn't about to argue. He opened the back door for her and she quickly slid inside. Rather than return to the passenger seat, Morgan got in next to Cate, then slammed the door and rapped the back of Ash's seat.

"Go," he ordered.

Ash was already reversing toward the gate.

Morgan clicked his earpiece and addressed Noelle. "We've got her. Meet us at the rendezvous."

"Yes, sir." A mocking note in her voice.

He cut off the feed and immediately refocused his attention on Cate. "Tell me what's going on."

When she turned to face him, he was stunned to find unshed tears clinging to her eyelashes.

Alarm flared in his chest. "Cate. What happened?"

"I . . ." She made an anguished sound. "I killed her."

Chapter 32

As shock slammed into him, Morgan met Ash's eyes in the rearview mirror. For a second he thought he'd misheard, but the severe look on Ash's face confirmed that he'd heard her loud and clear.

"You killed who?" he said softly.

She repeated herself, her face devoid of emotion. "I killed her."

"Your ... mother?" he hedged.

"But she was already dead," Cate whispered. "I didn't really kill her because she was already dead, right?"

Morgan couldn't make sense of it. He reached out for her, but she backed away from him, until her side was pressed against the car door. The rejection hurt, but he ignored his own pain because Cate's suffering was clearly a million times worse. She was going through something, something he still didn't understand.

"I can't answer that, sweetheart," he said gruffly. "Not until you make me understand."

"Brain-dead," she choked out. "*Maman* has been brain-dead for seventeen years."

Morgan froze. "How is that possible?"

"She was shot in the head during an assassination attempt on my grandfather. One of his rivals tried to kill him."

The revelation brought a frown to his lips. He knew that was what Cate must have been told, but it sounded like a load of bull to him. Businessmen didn't customarily go around solving problems with bullets.

And she'd said seventeen years. There'd been only one attempt on Dietrich's life seventeen years ago. The ambush in Berlin.

Son of a bitch.

Ariana had been shot during the ambush.

Morgan drew in a breath. "Was she pregnant with you when she got shot?"

Cate nodded numbly. "There was no brain activity, but her body could still function with the help of machines. The doctors monitored her carefully throughout the pregnancy and delivered me through a C-section. And then afterward, they kept her alive. But she wasn't really alive. She wasn't."

Despair swam in her eyes. "She lived with us at the beginning, back in Greece. But it was too hard to see her like that, day in and day out. My tutors convinced Grandpa that she belonged in a private clinic, but he didn't want her to be in a hospital. So he bought a house, just for her and the nurses, and then when we moved to France he bought her another one. This place. He made me visit her every week."

Morgan's heart ached for the girl beside him. Christ, being forced to see her mother like that . . . It must have been torture for her.

A loud honk suddenly captured his attention. He glanced out the window in time to see a red BMW cutting off the car in front of them. Nobody was tailing them, thank God.

He watched the scenery flash by, relieved to realize that the airport wasn't much farther. It was the one he always used when he was in Paris, conveniently located closer to Dietrich's countryside estate than the city itself.

He turned back to Cate, whose expression was lined with despair. "I dreaded the visits," she mumbled. "Does that make me a bad person? Because I didn't want to see my own mother?"

"You're not a bad person, sweetheart." His throat was so tight it hurt to speak.

Her face collapsed. "I pulled out her breathing tube. I was going to take out the feeding tube but it would have taken too long for . . . for the heart monitor to stop. You can survive for days without a feeding tube. Did you know that?"

He gulped.

"They all rushed in . . . the nurses . . . Bruno and Christian . . . They didn't notice when I slipped away. But her heart had already stopped. They won't be able to resuscitate her. They shouldn't even try." Anger hung from her voice now. "She didn't deserve to live like that."

This time when he pulled her close, she didn't protest. She buried her face against his shoulder and sank into his embrace, whispering against his chest.

"You can't kill someone who's already dead . . ."

His heart officially cracked in two. He wanted to reassure her, to tell her everything would be all right, but he didn't know how. He'd never been good at sharing his feelings, or comforting other people when they were hurting.

God, how was he ever going to be a father to this girl?

He tried to quell his rising panic. He'd figure out the whole fatherhood thing later. Maybe he'd be shitty at it. Maybe he'd be great.

Right now, the only thing that mattered was bringing his daughter home.

Cate was groggy as hell when she opened her eyes. For a moment, she had no idea where she was, and it took several seconds to orient herself. She heard quiet voices from somewhere behind her, the soft hum of an engine. She blinked, and noticed the plush white armrests of her seat, the off-white and dark wood interior of a spacious cabin.

The jet. They were on the small jet they'd boarded back in France.

It all came rushing back to her. Arriving at the private airport, her father's strong arm around her as they crossed a cavernous hangar toward a sleek white plane. He'd held her hand as they'd climbed a set of metal stairs, and then he'd settled her in a comfortable chair before going to talk to a beautiful woman with golden hair. Two men had joined the hushed discussion, one with scruffy blond hair and stubble on his face, and a dark-haired one with a southern accent.

Cate had been too numb to pay much attention, but she

remembered the queasy feeling in her stomach when the plane had taken off, and her father asking her if she wanted something to help her sleep. She'd nodded, eager to shut out the world, and then she remembered swallowing two pills—and that was all.

She sat up and rubbed her eyes. The cabin consisted of two aisles with four seats on either side, each pair facing the other. Nobody was beside her, but the brown-haired guy who'd been talking to her father sat in the seat opposite hers, his green eyes focused on her face.

"How'd you sleep?" he asked.

"Terribly," she admitted, before looking around in search of her father.

He was across the aisle, his eyes swimming with concern as their gazes locked. "Hey," he said gruffly.

"Hey." She shifted in her seat, then stood up on shaky legs. "I need to use the washroom."

Morgan was instantly at her side. "C'mon, I'll take you."

She didn't protest as he took her hand and led her to the back of the plane. He opened a door for her and she walked through it, finding herself in a bathroom that was as elegant and spacious as the rest of the jet. After she'd done her business, she splashed cold water on her face, then examined her reflection in the mirror and saw nothing but an impassive face looking back at her.

Her heart clenched as she remembered what she'd done.

She'd pulled the plug on her own mother.

God, it sounded like a plot straight out of a cheesy television movie—only it wasn't. It was real. She'd actually done it.

She wasn't sure she'd ever be able to forgive herself, but at the same time, she refused to let herself regret her decision. She'd had no choice; she needed to create a distraction in order to slip away from Bruno and Christian. But more than that, she'd wanted to set her mother free, once and for all.

She'd wanted Ariana to finally be at peace.

Cate tore her gaze off her reflection and stepped out of the lavatory.

Morgan waited outside the door. "Want something to drink?"

"Some water would be great."

"Sure thing. I'll be right back."

As he disappeared behind a blue curtain to their left, Cate wandered back to her seat. The dark-haired guy was still there, and now that she was more alert, she realized he was actually really good-looking. And young. He was at least five years older than her, but far younger than everyone else on board.

"We weren't properly introduced," he said with a smile. "I'm Ash."

"Cate," she murmured back, then felt like an idiot because obviously he already knew her name.

He gestured to the other side of the plane. "That's Sean Reilly. And the woman next to him is Noelle."

"You doing all right, luv?" Reilly had an accent too, an Irish one, and he sounded genuinely concerned as he looked over at her.

"Yeah, I guess," she said before focusing on the woman who'd been introduced as Noelle.

The blonde gazed back with shuttered blue eyes, offering a brisk nod.

That was it. No *hello*, no *how are ya?* Noelle just sipped her coffee, continuing to watch Cate over the rim of her cup.

"Are we the only ones here?" she asked Ash.

"Yep. Just us. Oh, and Giovanni. Our pilot," he clarified after seeing her puzzled look. "There's no crew on board. Morgan doesn't like to travel with attendants."

She opened her mouth to ask why, but Morgan chose that exact moment to appear with a bottle of water in his hands.

"Here," he said, handing it to her.

"Thanks." Cate untwisted the cap and took a quick sip. "How long was I sleeping?"

He didn't sit down, just hovered over her, and it suddenly registered how big he was. Definitely taller than six feet, with a broad, muscular body you saw only in action movies, not real life. But then she glanced at Ash and Reilly, and realized they were just as ripped.

"Eleven hours," Morgan told her.

Her eyebrows shot up. "Seriously? Wow. Those are some powerful sedatives you gave me."

He shrugged. "You needed them."

Cate shifted her gaze out the window, which revealed nothing but a thick carpet of fluffy white clouds. "I never even asked where we were going."

The realization was a tad unnerving. How was it possible that her trust in this man ran so deep that she'd willingly gone to a strange airport with him and boarded a plane without knowing where it was headed?

"Costa Rica," he answered. "Our compound is near San José."

"Hey, boss," Sean Reilly called. "Sully's on the sat phone."

"I'll be right back," Morgan muttered.

After he'd stalked off to take the white satellite phone Sean was holding out, Cate turned to Ash in confusion. "Do you guys all live together?"

"Most of the team does. A few guys live off-site."

"The team," she echoed. A pang of embarrassment tugged at her. "I just realized I don't even know what you guys do. Security or something?"

"Or something," he said with a grin. "Ever heard the term 'soldier of fortune'?"

"You mean, like mercenaries? You kill people for money?"

"Nah, that's contract killers."

He grinned again, and this time a set of dimples appeared, bringing a stab of pain to Cate's heart. Gabriel had had dimples too.

Gabriel was dead.

She reached up to rub her temples, forcing herself not to dwell on that right now. It still wasn't time to grieve.

"We focus mainly on extractions," Ash explained. "Rescuing people."

"Like who?"

"Whoever needs rescuing. You'd be surprised by how many dumb-asses get themselves captured nowadays."

She found herself smiling for the first time all day. She wanted to ask him a million more questions, but they were interrupted by a male voice.

"We're starting our descent," their pilot called through the open cockpit door. "Buckle your seat belts. We'll be landing in San José in the next twenty minutes or so."

Cate snapped her seat belt into place. When she lifted her head, she found Ash's sympathetic green eyes on her.

"I'm sorry about your mother," he said quietly.

She swallowed. "Thanks."

"It's rough . . . what you had to do . . ." He shrugged awkwardly. "I know it must hurt pretty bad right now, but for what it's worth, I think you did the right thing."

She looked up in surprise. "You do?"

Ash nodded. "Nobody should have to live like that. It's not fair to them, or the people they left behind."

His words succeeded in easing some of the pressure in her chest. She nodded in gratitude, then glanced across the aisle again. Her father was still on the phone. Sean Reilly was next to him, flipping through a magazine, and Noelle was still drinking her coffee, her blue eyes fixed on Morgan.

Cate had never seen a more beautiful woman. Or a more aloof one.

Lowering her voice, she turned back to Ash. "Is that Morgan's girlfriend?"

"I honestly don't know."

"She's not part of your team, though."

"No. She's . . . Well, it's complicated."

Cate opened her mouth to ask another question, but all of a sudden a loud *bang* boomed from behind them and the plane lurched so hard that if she hadn't been wearing a seat belt, she would have been thrown out of her seat.

"What was that?" she blurted out.

Ash frowned. "I don't—" He stopped midsentence.

Because all hell had broken loose.

A deafening blast rocked the plane, and the lights flickered wildly before shutting off completely. A rush of air blew through the cabin, and for a second Cate thought the door had been blown off, but when she frantically twisted her head to look, she saw that the door was still intact.

Her heart raced as a cacophony of noise blared all around them. The shriek of the wind that had somehow penetrated the cabin, the shrill ringing noises from the cockpit, the metallic grinding, and a rattle that vibrated beneath her feet. And then there was a popping sound and the oxygen mask over her head released from its compartment and dangled in front of her face.

As terror shuddered through her, she clutched her armrests in a death grip, scared she was going to be sucked out of the plane, but clearly she was the only one worrying about that because everyone else was on their feet, rushing past her as they shouted things she couldn't make out over the uproar.

She experienced a wave of dizziness and hastily reached out for the oxygen mask. She brought it to her face and inhaled deep gulps, trying not to let the panic take control of her.

"Cate, get up!" someone shouted.

It was Ash. He appeared in front of her, bending over to unbuckle her seat belt for her. She wanted to bat his hands away, to stop him from taking away the one thing guaranteed to protect her, but he tugged her onto her feet and pulled her from the safety of her seat.

Her eyes widened when another grinding noise screeched in the air. She desperately searched the dark cabin for her father, finally spotting him in front of the cockpit door, his shoulders tense as he spoke to their pilot. She couldn't make out their words, but the high-pitched alarms coming from the cockpit didn't sound good. At all.

Cate stumbled toward her father. Her heart dropped when she peered past his shoulders and noticed that the jet's dashboard was lit up like a Christmas tree. Lights flashing, needles on the instruments spinning, and then in the blink of an eye, everything went silent.

"Engine failure," a female voice muttered. Cate looked over in time to see Noelle rushing toward the tail of the plane.

Cate's heart thumped faster, and everything around her seemed to be swaying. It took a moment to realize that *she* was the one swaying. In spite of the damage the plane must have sustained, it was retaining its speed, gliding along harmlessly as if oblivious to the pandemonium inside it.

"What the fuck is going on?" Reilly shouted when Morgan finally marched out of the cockpit.

Even in the darkness, Cate could see the grave look in her father's eyes.

"We're going down," he announced.

Chapter 33

"What do you mean we're going down?" his daughter yelled over the deafening noise.

Morgan sprang into action, hurrying across the shadowy cabin to the far wall where Noelle was digging through a compartment stocked with the plane's emergency gear. Cate was hot on his heels, her eyes wide with panic as she grabbed his arm.

"Tell me what's happening, damn it!"

"The engines were taken out," he said tersely. "Most likely by a pressure bomb that was armed the moment we went down in altitude."

He reached Noelle just as she slammed her hand against the wall and let out an angry expletive. "No chutes," she informed him.

His body went colder than a block of ice. "What the fuck are you talking about?"

"There's nothing here, Jim. Someone cleaned out the emergency gear."

"Sergio," he muttered, referring to the owner of the private airport.

Son of a bitch.

"Son of a bitch!" Noelle snapped, voicing his thoughts. "I thought you said you trusted the guy."

"I never had reason not to trust him before," he snapped back. "I've used his services dozens of times."

"Well, the bastard sold you out!"

For the first time since he'd known her, Noelle actually looked worried. Her blue eyes darted around the cabin, then focused on the open door of the cockpit, where their pilot was struggling to keep the plane in the air.

"Air pressure keeps dropping," Giovanni yelled out to them. "Commencing rapid emergency descent!"

Morgan took a breath, tried to assess the situation with the meager facts he had. All right. He knew that a small explosion near the tail had crippled both engines. The jet was gliding now and would continue to do so, and the oxygen masks in the cabin were functional and would ensure that everyone stayed conscious if the pressure continued to drop.

At the moment, they were safe, and they might be able to stay that way if Giovanni executed a successful emergency landing.

But there was no guarantee of that. And no guarantee that the fire in the tail wouldn't find its way to the wings, where the jet's fuel was stored.

If that happened, they'd all die in a giant fireball before they even hit the ground.

With a grim look, he turned to Noelle and voiced his concerns, and she immediately vetoed the idea of sticking it out.

"I'm not dying in a goddamn plane explosion," she announced. "I'd rather jump out without a parachute."

"No need. I've got some chutes right here."

The smug announcement had come from Ash, who strode up to them with his duffel bag hanging off his shoulder.

Relief blasted into Morgan's chest. "Are you serious?"

Ash grinned. "As a heart attack. Never fear, the rookie's here." Without time to waste, he dropped the bag and bent down to unzip it.

"You carry extra chutes in your go bag?" Reilly demanded from his perch near the door, his green eyes sparkling with amusement despite his ashen complexion.

"I was a Boy Scout," Ash called out. "Always be prepared and all that shit."

The rookie tossed a backpack to Reilly, then held up the remaining two and glanced at Morgan. "That's all I've got."

He cursed out loud. "You only brought three? So much for being prepared."

"One for me, the other two for Liam and Sully, because the three of us left Costa Rica together."

Morgan took a second to go over the logistics. "We'll jump tandem. Noelle's with me. Ash, you take Cate. Reilly, you're with Giovanni."

He turned to his daughter, and noticed that even though her face was whiter than snow, she looked surprisingly calm. "You okay, sweetheart?"

"Yeah, I'm good." She took a breath. "Are we really jumping out of this plane?"

"It's either that, or we go the crash-landing route and hope the fuel tanks don't blow up before that."

"I still don't understand," she burst out. "What the hell is a pressure bomb?"

Ash fielded the question as he strapped his backpack on. "You ever seen the movie *Speed*?"

Cate nodded.

"You know how the bus was rigged to explode if the speedometer dipped below fifty? Well, it's the same thing with this plane, only it's altitude instead of speed." Ash rubbed his hands together, then reached into his bag for a coil of rope. "And fuck what everyone else says—Keanu Reeves rocked in that film. Dude's a legend."

"Save that bullshit for your film criticism seminar," Morgan muttered as he shrugged into his chute pack.

He left Cate in Ash's capable hands and raced back to the cockpit, where Giovanni was fighting with the throttle.

"Giovanni, we're bailing. Can't risk the explosion reaching the fuel line."

The pilot glanced over his shoulder. "I can land this bird."

"Sorry, man. We can't risk it." Morgan snapped his harness into place and tightened the straps. "Come on, Gio, we've gotta go."

"I can land this thing," Giovanni insisted as he wiped the sweat off his brow. Beads of it clung to his thick mustache and dripped down his tanned face, but the determination in his eyes didn't waver. "Go on without me. I'll get this bird on the ground."

"You sure?"

The pilot gave a firm nod. "Go. I'll see you on the ground."

Reluctance seized Morgan's chest, but he didn't have time to argue with the man. If Giovanni wanted to go down with his plane, then that was his choice. Morgan had to focus on saving his daughter, and Noelle, and his men, not a crazy maverick who seemed to almost be enjoying himself as he prepared for an emergency landing.

Spinning around, Morgan ran back to the cabin in time to catch the rope Ash threw at him. Christ, he didn't like this. Tandem jumping without a secondary harness was dangerous as hell.

Noelle didn't look too thrilled about it either, but she hurried over when Morgan gestured for her to come. He looped the rope around his waist, then knitted his brows in concentration as he pondered the best way to secure Noelle to him.

"If you let me go, I'll kill you," she said fiercely.

It amazed him that even in a life-and-death situation, she was able to bring a grin to his lips. "What's your poison, babe? You want it face-to-face, or ass to groin?"

"What the hell do you think?" She stepped toward him face-first, her breasts crushed against his chest as he used the rope to tie her to him.

Near the door, Reilly was already harnessed up and ready to go. "Where's Gio?" he yelled at Morgan.

"Being a hero," he yelled back. "He's gonna try and land this thing."

He tested the rope, praying it would do the trick and keep Noelle tucked against him, and then he checked on Ash's progress and saw that the rookie had used the same method to secure Cate to his body. Her blond head was pressed against Ash's broad chest, and she looked so damn delicate in the younger man's arms that it brought a lump to Morgan's throat.

He met Ash's eyes and gave the kid a stern look. "Take care of her."

"Will do, boss."

Swallowing, he peered down at Noelle, floored by the sheer calm reflecting back at him. "You okay, babe?"

She rolled her eyes. "Of course. What do you think I am, a pansy-ass damsel who weeps at the first sign of trouble?"

He choked out a laugh and edged them toward the cabin door, where Reilly waited with an expectant expression, completely unfazed by what they were about to do.

"Ready?" the Irishman said cheerfully.

Morgan nodded.

A second later, Reilly opened the door and they were hit with a gust of frigid wind that chilled Morgan to the bone.

"Later, guys." With a hearty laugh, Sean Reilly hopped out of the plane feetfirst and was instantly whisked out of sight.

Morgan turned his head and noticed Ash whispering something to Cate. He couldn't hear what it was, but it seemed to relax her. She gazed up at Ash with trust in her eyes, and a second later they were gone, carried away by the same wind hissing in Morgan's ears.

He hesitated at the door, then lowered his head so his lips brushed Noelle's ear. "Can I kiss you?"

Her petite body vibrated with laughter. "Nope."

Morgan sighed. "Figured it was worth a shot."

And then he held her tight and jumped out of the plane.

Nik sat in the armchair next to the stone fireplace, staring at the bookshelf in front of him without really seeing it. A full glass of bourbon rested in his hand, but he didn't raise it to his lips. He'd already consumed too much alcohol today and he felt sick to his stomach.

And sick in his heart.

Cate was gone.

Ariana was gone.

The pain was still so visceral, leaving him cold and deadened and unable to concentrate on anything around him. He vaguely heard Walther barking orders into his phone, and every now and then the older man crossed his peripheral vision as he paced the red-and-gold Aubusson rug spanning the study's floor.

Normally it was Nik who stepped up to the plate and took care of whatever needed to be done, but not tonight.

He couldn't stop thinking about the deafening silence that had greeted him when he'd walked into Ariana's bedroom. The nurses had shut off all the monitors around the bed, and the silence had been eerie and unexpected. It had made it impossible to deny the truth. Ariana was truly gone. He'd lost her.

Except a part of him knew he'd lost her a long time ago. When she'd chosen James Morgan over him.

So many years he'd spent blaming Morgan for that, but deep down he knew it wasn't entirely the man's fault. Ariana had made the decision all on her own. She'd been seduced but not coerced, and that was just another slap in the face.

But Ariana hadn't deserved to die for the choice she'd made. She hadn't deserved to take a bullet for it.

And the blame for *that*, well, it fell squarely on James Morgan's shoulders.

Nik's throat squeezed with anger as he realized that Morgan had done it again. Ariana had died once, thanks to the bastard, and today, he'd killed her all over again.

He'd killed her, and then stolen her daughter, right from under their noses.

The tumbler in his hand began to shake, and Nik had to place it on the table before he spilled bourbon all over Dietrich's expensive rug.

A curse from the desk snapped him back to the present. He turned to see Dietrich's dark eyes blazing.

"Nobody can locate them," the older man announced. "I've got everyone in Paris on the alert, but there's no sign of them."

Nik stood up wearily. "It's been hours. He could have taken her anywhere by now."

With a roar of fury, Dietrich swiped his arm over the desktop, sending papers and supplies flying. The keyboard clattered to the ground, and the computer mouse dangled over the edge of the mahogany desk, swinging back and forth like a pendulum.

"He killed my daughter!" Dietrich raged. "He kidnapped my granddaughter! I want that son of a bitch! I want to slit his throat!"

A ringing phone interrupted the man's tirade, and it took a second for Nik to realize that it was his. When he checked the screen, he saw Gilles Girard's number and suppressed a sigh.

"It's Girard," he told Walther.

The older man looked annoyed. "Answer it. He might have information for us."

Nik reluctantly took the call, immediately greeted by Girard's tense voice.

"It's done."

He wrinkled his brow. "What are you talking about?"

"I just received confirmation from one of the contractors I hired. James Morgan is dead."

Nik's entire body went cold. "What do you mean, Morgan is dead?"

That got Dietrich's attention. He swiftly rounded the desk, kicked a metal container of ballpoint pens out of his path, and marched up to Nik. "Speakerphone," he ordered.

Nik's fingers trembled as he fumbled with the icons on the touch screen. "Maurice is here with me," he told the lawyer. "Tell us what happened."

"I just got off the phone with the contractor. He was monitoring all the private airfields outside the city, and bribed the owners to contact him if someone matching Morgan's description chartered a flight. Earlier this morning, he got a call from one of his informants."

Dietrich frowned. "And?"

"And he planted a bomb on the plane Morgan chartered. The bomb was designed to go off upon descent. He didn't want it exploding over France, said there'd be too many questions that might lead back to him or us. Ten minutes ago he got word that the plane exploded outside of San José."

Nik almost dropped the phone.

Oh dear God.

"Anyway, he wants us to wire the money to a numbered account in—"

"Money?" Dietrich screamed. "He wants *money*? My granddaughter was on that plane!"

There was a long silence.

"I'm sorry ... I don't understand," Girard finally sputtered.

"James Morgan abducted my granddaughter! She was on the plane, you stupid fool!"

Nik felt sick to his stomach. When he pictured Cate's beautiful face, he grew even sicker, dangerously close to vomiting.

Ariana. Cate.

Both of them. Dead.

How was that possible?

Dietrich was foaming at the mouth as he snatched the phone from Nik's numb fingers. "You tell that son of a bitch he's not getting a goddamn dime! In fact, tell him I'm giving him an hour's head start before I hunt him down and skin him alive!"

With that, Dietrich disconnected the call and whipped the phone across the room. It smashed against the bookshelf before crashing to the floor.

Nik couldn't breathe; the shock was too paralyzing. Catarina couldn't be dead. Girard was wrong. There was no plane. No explosion.

She couldn't be dead.

Dietrich had started panting like a rabid dog, his fair face stained crimson. "Call every contact we have in South America!"

Nik swallowed. "What for?"

"There could have been survivors," Dietrich snapped. "Do you really think a man like Morgan wouldn't have a few extra parachutes on board? She might still be alive!"

Nik blinked in confusion.

"Are you listening to me, Nikolaus?"

He tried to breathe again but his lungs had seized up.

"Goddamn it, Nikolaus! Pick up the phone! Do you understand me? Call every goddamn contact we have! *She might still be alive!*"

Chapter 34

By the time two o'clock in the morning rolled around, Cate had given up on trying to sleep. She never slept well in unfamiliar beds, and besides, she'd pretty much been comatose for eleven hours today. Not to mention the adrenaline kick that came from being forced to jump out of a plane. She was too wired to sleep, and found herself wandering the dark halls of James Morgan's house with no idea where she was even going.

The house was enormous, but surprisingly cozy. Pretty landscape paintings lined the cream-colored walls, and all the furniture had a rustic feel to it, reminding her of a homey ski chalet. Morgan had told her they were still getting settled there. Apparently he and his team used to live in Mexico, but they'd had to relocate after their compound had been attacked. Morgan hadn't offered any more details, and when she'd asked Ash about it later, he'd shrugged and said he hadn't been around for it.

Cate tried to walk quietly as she made her way downstairs. Thanks to the tour Morgan had given her, she remembered that the kitchen opened onto a huge patio that overlooked the backyard, and she suddenly felt like getting some air. Maybe the humidity would lull her into a sleepy state.

When she stepped outside, the night air was indeed humid. Within seconds, she was sweating in her cotton shorts and tank top. Morgan had deposited the clothes on her bed earlier, but she hadn't asked whom they belonged to. Probably Noelle.

At the thought of Noelle, Cate realized she hadn't seen her since they'd arrived at the compound. No doubt the woman was in one of the many rooms in this big house, sound asleep after the chaotic events of the day.

"Couldn't sleep?"

She jumped, startled by the deep voice that came out of nowhere. Spinning around, she found Morgan sitting at the wrought-iron table, smoking a cigarette.

A frown reached her lips as he took a deep drag. She hadn't known he smoked.

Then again, there were hundreds of other things she didn't know about him.

"I'm too wound up," she admitted. "I think the adrenaline is still running through my veins."

He gestured to the seat across from him. "C'mon, sit down."

She joined him at the table, toying with the end of her braid as she watched him take another pull of his cigarette.

"So how did you enjoy your first foray into skydiving?" He looked like he was fighting a smile.

"It was terrifying. And thrilling."

In fact, she was still having trouble adjusting to the feel of the ground beneath her feet after experiencing that incredible free fall. She knew she'd never forget it—being thousands of feet up in the air, her heart in her throat, clinging to Ash as if her life depended on it. They'd plummeted so fast she'd been certain they would crash into the ground and die on impact. But then Ash had pulled the rip cord and suddenly they'd been floating, and a strange sense of peace had washed over her. She'd wrenched her head off Ash's chest and peered around his shoulder, finally working up the nerve to look down.

She remembered seeing a sea of blue, a carpet of green—the ocean and jungle, so vast and beautiful beneath them. Once they got lower, she'd glimpsed the tops of houses, cars that looked like tiny ants, little roads winding through the landscape.

They'd landed on a deserted beach, like a scene right out of a movie, and then they'd hiked for two hours before they'd reached civilization, where they waited for a "pickup," as Morgan had referred to it.

A man with sandy hair and light green eyes had come to get them in a beat-up black Jeep. Kane something or other—she still couldn't match all the names to their corresponding faces. She'd met so many people today, more people than she'd ever interacted with in her entire life.

But she knew Morgan's face. Every last inch of it.

"What happened to the plane?" She hadn't thought to ask before, but now it occurred to her that she had no clue whether their pilot was even okay.

Morgan's expression was bleak as he leaned forward to put out his cigarette. "It exploded in a clearing about a hundred miles east of San José." Sorrow flickered in his eyes. "Giovanni didn't manage to land his bird, after all."

Her heart squeezed. "I'm sorry. Was he a good friend of yours?"

"Not really. He'd only flown us a couple times." His features hardened. "But Sergio . . . I thought *he* was a friend."

"The man who owns the airport?"

Her father nodded. "He sold us out. I don't know to whom, but clearly he told someone I would be on board. The bastard removed the emergency gear and let someone plant a bomb in the tail."

"Betrayal sucks, huh?"

His gaze softened. "Does that mean you're finally going to tell me what got you so spooked that you decided to run away from your grandfather?"

Cate's fingers tightened around her braid. "He killed Gabriel."

"Your friend . . . ?" Morgan hesitated. "The one who drove you to the Eiffel Tower?"

She nodded. "It was my fault. I gave Gabriel the file on you so Nik and Grandpa wouldn't find it on me, and they killed him for it. They thought he hadn't told me about it yet." She bit her lip. "They didn't realize I was the one who gave it to him."

"I'm sorry, sweetheart."

Her throat tightened. "Gabriel was a good friend. He was a really good friend."

Neither of them spoke for a moment, but that didn't

mean there was silence. Cate was surprised by the amount of noise coming from the jungle. Screeching and squawking, a monkey's high-pitched howl, the flapping of wings and the drone of insects.

"Is it always so loud here?" she asked.

"Yeah, but you get used to it."

She hesitated. "There are so many people living in this house. I wasn't expecting it."

"You'll get used to that too. But don't worry. It's not always so packed. Kane just wrapped up a job in Ecuador. He flew back this morning." He paused. "Did you meet Abby?"

"The redhead, right?"

"Yeah. She's married to Kane." Another pause. "They're good people." His voice went gruff. "You'll like it here."

"And if I don't?" she felt compelled to ask.

"Then we'll go somewhere else," he said simply. "We'll go wherever you want, Cate."

Warmth infused her heart, but it was accompanied by a trickle of uneasiness. "How is this . . . any of this . . . going to work? I mean, you're my father, but . . . I don't know you."

His dark blue eyes took on a gleam of intensity. "You'll get to know me."

"Will I? Because you don't seem like much of a talker."

Now he chuckled. "I'm not. But for you, I'll make an exception."

"Fine. Then I'll call your bluff. Tell me how you met my mother."

Morgan's face grew pained. "That's not a very pretty story, I'm afraid."

"I don't care."

"You might hate me after you hear it," he warned her.

Cate set her jaw and said, "Try me."

Morgan felt utterly drained when he returned to his bedroom just before dawn. He'd spent hours on the terrace with Cate, doing more talking than he'd ever done in his life. He'd told her about the botched mission in Berlin, about Walther's criminal activities, Ariana's seduction. He hadn't even held back the details regarding Cate's conception, and although she'd frowned when he confessed how Ariana had sabotaged their contraceptives, she hadn't commented on her mother's deceitful behavior.

Once he'd finished talking, it had been Cate's turn. She'd told him about her life, how sheltered she'd been, the restrictions Dietrich had placed on her.

Morgan had been startled to learn that Nikolaus Bauer had been a constant presence since the day Cate was born. Bauer had never married, and he'd come to live with them in Athens about a year after Morgan stopped keeping tabs on him. When he'd discovered that, he'd cursed himself for calling off his surveillance on Bauer. If he hadn't, he might have found Cate sooner.

But she was here now, and he couldn't deny he was downright smitten with the girl. She was smart, funny, and so damn strong it made his chest swell with pride. He'd watched her jump out of a plane today without an ounce of fear, and she'd orchestrated her own escape from Dietrich and Bauer without batting an eye. He'd honestly never felt prouder of anyone in his entire life.

It had been such an astonishing, cathartic night, but even as he basked in the joy of bonding with his daughter, he had to wonder, how long would this wonderful reunion last?

When he'd checked in with Sullivan this morning, his soldier had informed him that both Dietrich and Bauer were still at the country estate. Sullivan and Liam were sticking around to monitor the situation, but so far there were no signs of trouble. No movement whatsoever. Which was troubling, because Cate's grandfather must have figured out she was gone by now.

So why wasn't he making a move to come after her?

A knock on the door interrupted Morgan's train of thought, and he answered with a brisk, "Yeah?"

Abby poked her head into his room. "Got a sec?"

He furrowed his brow, surprised that she was up so early. "You realize it's five in the morning, right?"

The redhead shrugged as she entered the suite. "I'm an early riser. I saw the light under your door, so I figured this would be a good time to discuss that message you left for me."

Morgan tensed. Shit, he'd forgotten about that. He'd left Abby the message days ago, after his conversation with Bai-

ley back in Paris, but so much had happened since then that
it had totally slipped his mind.

He held his breath. "Did you look into what I asked?"

She nodded.

"And?"

He could tell from her expression that she wasn't going
to tell him what he wanted to hear.

Sighing, she shook her head and said, "There was nothing in any of Jeremy's safe-deposit boxes. My lawyer found
about three dozen flash drives full of data, but nothing re-
lated to what you were asking about. Sorry, Jim."

Aside from Noelle, Abby was one of the only people who
called him that, probably because her foster father had done
the same. Morgan remembered being shocked when he'd
learned that his commanding officer had adopted a teenage
girl with a troubled past, but Jeremy Thomas had always
been full of surprises. And once Morgan met Abby, he'd realized why Jeremy had been so ardent about rescuing her.

Abby Sinclair was tough as nails, a shrewd, resourceful
woman who could survive anything life threw at her. She
reminded him a lot of Noelle, except he'd never felt the
same burning desire for Abby as he did Noelle.

At the thought of her, he suddenly realized he hadn't
seen Noelle since they'd gotten here. For all he knew, she
was already on her way back to Paris.

"She's in the blue room," Abby said, as if reading his
mind. "But she's planning on leaving today."

He swallowed. Yeah, he'd figured she'd cut and run the
second they wrapped up the job. Noelle didn't like to linger.

"I like your kid, by the way. I just ran into her in the
kitchen. Told her I'd teach her how to shoot later."

He narrowed his eyes. "Why?"

"Because she said she wanted to learn." Abby grinned,
which was a damn rare occurrence. "Oh shit, are you gonna
go all Papa Bear on us? Because word to the wise: overprotective parents breed rebellious children."

"You never rebelled against Jeremy," he pointed out.

"Jeremy wasn't my father. He was just the prickly black-
ops soldier who decided to adopt a fucked-up kid like me."
Her voice softened. "He was my hero."

"Mine too," Morgan admitted, his thoughts once again

drifting to his former commanding officer. "He was a good man."

Abby hesitated.

"What?" he said roughly.

"So are you, you know. I mean, you're a total bastard at times, but you are a good man, Jim."

He shifted in discomfort.

"Okay, I can see you getting all squeamish about this heart-to-heart. Don't worry. I am too."

He had to chuckle. "Yeah?"

"Definitely. You know I'm not into all that emotion crap." She gently ran a hand over the small bump at her belly, the gesture effectively contradicting what she'd just said. Then, with another grin, she headed for the door. "Come to the range in an hour and watch your daughter shoot. I bet you she'll be a natural."

Yeah, he'd make that bet too. And he couldn't wait to see Cate shoot. Hell, he'd be happy to just sit there and watch her read a frickin' book for ten hours, as long as it meant spending time with her.

But first, he had something else to take care of.

Noelle was on the balcony when she sensed Jim's presence behind her. She always knew when he was close by—her body hummed every time, like an early alarm system for impending tension.

She kept her gaze on the gorgeous sunrise beyond the railing, admiring the incredible view. She hadn't watched a sunrise in years, and she was surprised that she was still able to find beauty in something. Brilliant pinks, yellows, and oranges filled the sky as the sun soared upward, casting a halo over the jagged mountain peaks dotting the horizon.

"You were up all night," she remarked without turning around.

Jim came up beside her and swiped her coffee cup right out of her hands. "I was with Cate," he admitted after he'd taken a quick sip.

"I figured."

He handed the cup back and rested both hands on the rail, his blue eyes somber as he focused them on the horizon.

"So serious," she murmured. "What's going on?"

"Abby says you're leaving today."

"Yep. You know I don't like to overstay my welcome."

He let go of the railing and shoved his hands in his pockets, shifting his feet awkwardly. She could feel his gaze on her now, but he didn't say a word. He just watched her, his expression flickering with hesitation.

"What's on your mind, Jim?" she said with a sigh.

"I want to talk to you about your father."

When Noelle stiffened, he quickly held up his palm. "Wait. Before you go into street-fighter mode, just hear me out, okay?"

She shot him a terse look. "Fine. Say your piece."

"I called Abby the other day. I, uh, asked her to check Jeremy Thomas's safe-deposit boxes. It was just a shot in the dark—I mean, I didn't expect to find anything, but I know that Jeremy used to keep backups of certain mission files for his personal records. He also made copies of interrogation tapes."

Noelle froze.

"I was hoping he might have a copy of your father's, but Abby didn't find anything. If there was ever a record of Douglas's interrogation, Jeremy didn't have a copy of it. Or maybe it was destroyed when the unit was disbanded. I don't know." His deep voice cracked. "I'm trying to give you proof that Douglas sold out his country. But I can't. I don't have a tape to show you, or a file for you to read. All I have is my word."

"I don't need your word, Jim." She exhaled slowly. "I have the tape."

Surprise filled his eyes. "What?"

Her voice cracked too, just as badly as Jim's had. "I'm not as naive as you think I am. The night he was arrested . . . he was acting so strange. I didn't want to admit it at the time, but I knew there was something off about his behavior. An innocent man wouldn't have acted like that." She sighed. "I paid your CO a visit a couple years after you and I parted ways. You weren't off base just now—Thomas *did* keep a copy of the interrogation. It's in my safe at the Paris penthouse."

Jim's jaw went tighter than a drum. "So all these years . . . this whole time you knew I was telling the truth?"

She answered with a harsh laugh. "Do you really think that made a difference to me? So what if you had good reason to arrest him? You still *used* me. You fucked me, literally and figuratively, just so you could carry out your mission. And there's nothing you could have said then, or say now, that will excuse what you did to me."

He shook his head in frustration. "The other night when you went postal on me for bringing up your father ... What's *your* excuse, Noelle? Why fly into a rage if you already knew the truth?"

A spike of agony drove straight into her heart. For a moment it got hard to breathe, but she managed to draw another shaky breath into her lungs.

"That's not what set me off, and you know it," she said hoarsely. "What you said ... that was something I *didn't* know. Whether or not my father was a traitor didn't matter to me. It didn't affect me. But René ..." She swallowed. "Did my father really admit to you that he knew what René was doing to me?"

Jim responded with a slow nod that brought another slice of pain to her heart.

"I didn't know. I kept it a secret from him because I was certain that if he ever found out, he would kill René, and I was scared he might end up in jail for it. I was trying to protect my dad." She bit the inside of her cheek. "And then to find out that he knew what was happening to me ... and didn't do anything to stop it ..."

"He was a bastard, Noelle. He never deserved your loyalty."

She pressed her lip together, afraid that if she opened her mouth, a sob might fly out of it. Her silence dragged on for so long that Jim finally slid his hands out of his pockets and took a step back.

"Anyway ..." He cleared his throat. "That's all I wanted to say."

She trailed after him through the French doors and they stepped into the guest room she'd stayed in last night.

He halted near the bed and turned to look at her. "You know ..." He shrugged. "You're welcome to stay for as long as you like."

His expression was so reluctant she almost laughed. Obviously he didn't want her to stick around but felt obligated to make the offer, and knowing he didn't care whether she left or not made her heart ache.

But what had she really been expecting? For him to get on his knees and beg her to stay?

Why would he? They weren't a couple. They weren't in love. They could fuck each other for the rest of their lives, and it still wouldn't make their relationship any less complicated.

And "relationship" wasn't even the right word to describe what they had. She and Jim, they simply . . . collided. They burst into each other's lives every so often and then they went their separate ways.

Except this latest collision had been . . . different. First and foremost, there was the sex. But there had also been something more, something . . . different.

Way to articulate yourself there.

She stifled a groan, wishing she could put her doubts and confusion into words, but she couldn't for the life of her make sense of what she was feeling at the moment.

She suddenly became aware of Jim's soft breathing, and realized that he was still there, still standing in front of her, making no move to go.

"Is there anything else?" Noelle cocked her head expectantly.

Her breath hitched when he bridged the distance between them.

"Can I kiss you?" he murmured, dragging his callused fingertips over her cheek.

After a long moment of silence, she shook her head.

Disappointment flickered in his blue eyes. "You're never going to trust me again, are you?"

When she didn't answer, he released a heavy sigh, dropped his hand from her face, and headed for the door.

"What, not even a good-bye lay?" she called after him.

He spun around, the heat in his eyes telling her that he wasn't the least bit insulted by the suggestion. "Is that what you really want?" he said roughly.

She responded by taking off her shirt.

With a soft chuckle, Jim locked the door and made his

way back to her. "You know, you're the most aggravating woman I've ever known."

Yet despite his visible irritation, he wasn't denying her, and she found that incredibly intriguing.

When she cupped the bulge in his pants, his head lolled to the side and a groan slipped out of his mouth. "Fuck. I love it when you touch me."

The hoarse admission sent shivers of desire skimming up her spine. She stroked him over his pants for a moment, before dragging his zipper down and coaxing his erection into her hand. She gave it a squeeze, then wrapped her fingers around the shaft and pumped him slowly, rubbing her thumb on his tip with each upstroke, enjoying the husky sounds that left his throat.

When she quickened the pace, he groaned louder and stilled her hand. "I'm gonna come if you keep doing that."

She smiled impishly. "I thought you were a master of endurance."

"Not when the sexiest woman on the planet is jerking me off," he grumbled, swatting her hand away and taking a step back.

He tugged his shirt over his head, providing her with an eyeful of his bare chest. God, that spectacular chest.

Noelle moved closer and pressed her mouth directly between his pecs, and his breath promptly hitched in surprise.

It wasn't quite the same as kissing his lips, but this she was willing to do. As her pulse raced, she kissed every inch of his chest. When her tongue came out to tease a flat brown nipple, he shuddered, and she couldn't help but reach down to grasp his erection again. She stood there in front him, her lips devouring his hot male flesh while her hand pumped his cock in a languid rhythm.

Eventually his hands embarked on their own exploration. He reached behind her and deftly unhooked her bra, then tossed it aside and cupped her breasts.

Noelle sighed in pleasure. She released his cock and grabbed the back of his head, pushing it down to her aching breasts. He immediately captured a nipple between his lips and sucked, sending a lightning bolt of pleasure straight to her core.

Before she could blink, he scooped her into his arms and carried her to the bed, laying her down on the mattress as his body covered hers. He moved his hand between her legs and lightly stroked her mound over the booty shorts she'd worn to bed.

"These shorts are so sexy," he choked out. "You look fantastic in them."

She grinned up at him. "They'd look better off me."

"Oh, I don't doubt it, baby."

With that, he peeled the shorts off and threw them aside, and then his hungry mouth roamed her body. He kissed and suckled her breasts until she was writhing with need, and when he crawled between her legs and touched her clit with his tongue, shock waves rocked through her.

"You taste so fucking good," he muttered as he licked his way down her slit and circled her opening with his tongue. "Like heaven."

When he speared her core with that wicked tongue, she came hard and fast, the unexpected orgasm curling her toes and sending a rush of intense pleasure through her body. She lay there stunned, too startled to move, unable to believe what had happened.

Jim seemed more amused than shocked as he lifted his head, his mouth glistening. "Seriously? Are you trying to break a Guinness record for fastest climax?"

"Couldn't help it. I was really wound up," she said defensively. "I mean, we did jump out of a plane yesterday."

Laughing softly, he climbed up her body, his cock thick and heavy against her belly.

"Yeah, I don't think I'll last long either," he said ruefully. "I need this too much."

"Then take it," she murmured.

Heat flared in his eyes. He shifted so that the tip of his erection nudged her opening, and when he slid inside her, they released simultaneous moans.

"Oh yeah, I won't last at all," he ground out.

He gripped her hips and rose up on his knees, while she lay sprawled beneath him, his for the taking.

Noelle shivered, then lifted one leg in the air so he could rest it on his shoulder. The position allowed for a deeper angle, his cock filling her so completely that her sex tingled again, the tension building once more.

He plunged into her, his roped arms flexing as he gripped her leg, but he didn't go fast. He filled her with deep, lazy strokes, absently shifting his head so he could plant a tender kiss on her calf.

"God, that feels good," she whispered. "Keep going slow like that."

The only sounds in the room were their soft breathing, the wet glide of his cock sliding in and out. His gaze stayed locked with hers as he slowly rocked into her, and she peered up at him, enthralled by what she saw. Handsome features stretched taut, blue eyes glittering with passion. His powerful chest heaved with each breath he took, and his cock seemed to thicken inside her, pulsing in her core.

"Gonna come soon," he mumbled.

"Not far behind you," she mumbled back.

She brought her hand between her legs to speed up the process, rubbing her swollen bud in a circular motion guaranteed to push her over the edge.

Jim growled at the sight of her fingers working her clit. "Fuck, that's so hot, baby. I can't hold back anymore." His tempo increased as his hips started to piston, his cock driving in deep.

Noelle stroked herself faster, getting closer and closer to the brink.

They came at the same time, and she moaned when she felt the warmth of his release fill her throbbing channel. He collapsed on top of her, his soft hair tickling her ear as they lay there gasping, recovering from their respective orgasms. Eventually they both went quiet, their bodies still joined together, their hearts vibrating against each other as their chests remained locked.

But the moment of contentment was interrupted by the buzz of a cell phone.

"I hate phones," he grumbled into her neck. "Seriously. I wanna go back in time and murder Alexander Graham Bell." He sat up with a groan. "Or was it Edison who invented the phone? I can never remember."

She had to laugh. "I'm pretty sure it was Bell."

With extreme reluctance, Jim climbed off the bed in search of his pants. He swiped them off the floor and drew out his phone, his expression going serious when he checked the screen.

"It's Sully." He quickly answered the call. "What's up, Aussie?" He listened for a moment, then barked out, "Stay there. I'll call you back."

"What's going on?" Noelle asked after he'd hung up.

"Dietrich and Bauer just boarded a private jet at Charles de Gaulle." He grimaced. "How much do you want to bet they're on their way here?"

Noelle was already hopping off the bed. "I assume you have a solid exit protocol in place?"

"Yes, but we won't be using it."

Her surprised gaze flew to his. "You're going to risk another attack on your compound?"

"Dietrich won't attack. Not with Ariana's daughter on the premises."

His confidence wasn't at all reassuring. "So what's the plan, then?" she asked suspiciously.

"We let it play out. Let them come."

"No offense, but that's fucking crazy. We shouldn't be here when they show up, Jim."

"You can go if you want." He shrugged. "But I'm staying."

"Jim—"

"I'm staying," he repeated firmly. "If Dietrich wants to come after me, great. I'll be right here waiting for him." His mouth set in a tight line. "It's time to end this, once and for all."

Chapter 35

Morgan decided not to tell Cate about their impending visitors. Instead, he spent the entire day with his daughter and enjoyed every last second of it.

Abby hadn't been wrong—Cate was a natural with a rifle. Pride had filled Morgan's heart as he'd watched his daughter hit every target, including the moving ones he'd decided to toss her way when it became obvious that the static targets were too easy. Each time she'd knocked one of the empty bottles out of the sky, she'd laughed in delight, and the impressive display had eventually attracted an audience.

By the time Cate fired her last shot, all of Morgan's men, along with Abby and Noelle, had congregated at the fence near the edge of the outdoor range to watch Cate shoot. Ash and Reilly had applauded her several times, and Kane had high-fived her when she finally strode back to the fence.

Despite the lighthearted atmosphere, everyone but Cate remained on the alert. Morgan had warned his team that Dietrich was on his way, and they were all on guard, ready to flee if necessary.

But he didn't intend on running from a fight. He'd already lost one compound to an unexpected attack—he wasn't about to lose another. His first priority was keeping Cate safe, but he wasn't cutting and running unless he absolutely had to.

He was surprised that Noelle had stayed, though. She'd helped him bring his daughter home just like she'd promised, which meant she had no reason to stick around. Morgan kept expecting her to leave at any second, but a part of him hoped she wouldn't.

But why? What exactly was he expecting to happen between them? What did he *want* to happen? He hadn't let himself think beyond the sex, but now that he was, his thoughts had turned into a jumbled mess, plagued with so many questions his mind was spinning.

Could they ever really have a future together? There was so much bad blood between them, so much baggage, but he no longer felt the burn of hatred he used to feel in her presence. Their time together had chipped away at it, made him realize that he'd been blaming the wrong person all these years.

It was *his* fault Ariana had gotten away. Noelle might have been the catalyst for Ariana's disappearance, but he was the one who'd set it all in motion when he'd betrayed the woman he'd loved.

As the group headed back to the house, he felt Noelle's eyes on him, but when he glanced over, he couldn't read her expression.

"You staying for dinner?" he asked casually.

She tossed her blond hair over her shoulder, pursing her lips for a moment. "I guess I could. My pilot is on standby at the airfield, but I suppose he can wait awhile longer."

It didn't escape him that she hadn't provided a specific time of departure.

And he didn't mind in the slightest.

Cate sidled up to them, looking happy for the first time since they'd left France. He knew she was still upset about her friend's death, not to mention what she'd had to do at her mother's house in order to evade her guards. He knew the guilt must be eating her up inside, but he was hesitant to raise the subject.

He still couldn't believe Walther had kept Ariana alive for all those years. It was . . . sad. That was the only adjective he could think of, and yet when it came down to it, he knew he shouldn't be surprised. Walther Dietrich had worshiped his daughter—it made sense that he would refuse to let her go.

Morgan unwittingly glanced at Cate, realizing that he

and Dietrich had at least one thing in common. They both refused to give up their daughters.

He didn't miss the way Noelle had quickened her pace when Cate had joined them, and she was already walking ahead of them, as if she was eager to get away from the teenager. It might have grated, if not for the fact that Noelle was like that around *everybody*. The woman always went out of her way to make sure nobody ever got too close.

Though he supposed he was to blame for that.

"Your girlfriend doesn't like me." Cate's low remark confirmed that she'd noticed Noelle's hasty retreat.

He sighed. "She's not my girlfriend."

"No? Because it sure seems like it." Cate reached up to play with the bottom of her braid, which he'd noticed was a nervous habit of hers. "I can't decide if I like her."

Morgan had to chuckle. "Yeah, most people have that problem. She's a difficult woman."

"No kidding. She's beautiful, though. Like crazy beautiful."

Another sigh slipped out. "That she is."

"What exactly does she do for a living? Nobody will tell me."

He thought about it for a moment, then said, "It's complicated."

His daughter snorted. "That's your go-to answer, huh?"

"Pretty much." He flashed her a grin before turning the tables on her. "What about you? What do you want to do for a living? Do you have any plans for after you graduate?"

"Honestly? I have no clue. I like to write, but I don't think I could cut it as a novelist. But I think I'd be good at writing scathing editorials, so maybe journalism is the way to go. Or photography. I'm obsessed with taking pictures."

"I'll buy you a camera," he said immediately.

She blushed. "Oh. You don't have to do that."

"I want to." He shot her a sheepish look. "But I should probably buy you some clothes first, huh? That way you don't have to keep wearing Abby's."

Speaking of Abby, Morgan discovered that she was the center of attention when he and Cate joined the rest of the group on the terrace. Everyone had already settled around the large wrought-iron table, and the three dogs that lived on the compound were circling Abby's chair, whining with excitement as they shoved their wet noses in her direction in a plea for attention.

"Jesus Christ, leave my wife alone," Kane grumbled. His green eyes flickered with disbelief as he looked over at Cate. "You know I have to kick them out of our bed every night? They refuse to leave her side."

From the other side of the table, Reilly wiggled his eyebrows. "Clearly the pups have good taste. Your wife is hot, mate. Deal with it."

Morgan sat down at the head of the table and reached for the bottle of Bud that Inna had placed next to his plate. Their Russian housekeeper had gone all out for tonight's dinner. She'd set the table with their finest dishes and silverware, arranged a row of pretty tea-light candles down the center of the table, and even prepared an elaborate centerpiece consisting of fragrant purple wildflowers, flowing white ribbons, and what looked like pieces of bark from one of the trees beyond the swimming pool.

It seemed like a lot of effort for a run-of-the-mill dinner, but Morgan had come to expect that from Inna. Times like these, though, he really missed Lloyd, their previous housekeeper, who had been killed during the attack on the Tijuana compound. Lloyd had been a former Mafia enforcer, a giant man with simple tastes and an efficient, no-nonsense way of running a household, and he would never dream of picking flowers and peeling the bark off a tree and sticking them in the middle of the table.

But despite her girly tendencies, Morgan couldn't deny that Inna was growing on him.

"Boss, you listening to me?" The question came from Kane, who was looking at him with an amused expression.

Morgan shifted his gaze off the fancy-pants centerpiece. "Sorry—what?"

"I was saying that Ethan and D checked in about an hour ago. They finished debriefing the officials in Quito. They're heading home tomorrow."

"What about Trevor and Luke?"

"Wrapped up the security gig and are making their way home to their women as we speak."

Morgan nodded absently, mentally debating whether he should reroute Trev and Luke to the compound instead. They might need the manpower, depending on what Dietrich had in store for them.

Just as the thought entered his head, one of the compound's security guards appeared in the doorway that separated the terrace from the kitchen.

Morgan's shoulders tensed as he met the other man's eyes. "Everything okay, Bill?"

The dark-haired man shook his head, a grim look on his face. "We've got visitors."

Chapter 36

"The perimeter is secure, sir." The report had come from the leader of the mercenary team, who awaited Nik's orders with expectant eyes.

Nik turned away from the massive electric fence closing off James Morgan's property from the clearing.

"Thank you, Ivan. Maintain your positions. We move on my signal."

The bulky Serb nodded before disappearing into the trees. Ten mercenaries were already stationed at various points of the perimeter, but Nik, Dietrich, and the ten remaining men had congregated in the hills bordering one edge of the vast property. The hillside overlooked the eastern face of the Spanish-style home, offering a perfect bird's-eye view, and close enough to the compound that a strategically placed shot from an RPG would blow a hole in the side of the house.

But they weren't planning on doing that. Not yet, anyway. Not until Cate had been removed from Morgan's clutches.

Nik had been overcome with relief when he'd learned that Cate had survived the plane crash. Or at least that was what the evidence had led them to believe. Nik's source confirmed that only one body had been found at the site of the crash—a male in his forties. Burned to a crisp, which made identification difficult, to say the least.

But Nik wasn't naive enough to believe that the corpse

had belonged to James Morgan. According to the man who'd arranged the charter, there had been six people aboard the Gulfstream. Four males, including the pilot, and two females. One man was now dead, which meant that the others had survived the crash. Since no footprints or tracks had been discovered at the crash site, it stood to reason that the five passengers on board had parachuted out. The owner of the airport in France claimed that he'd rid the jet of all its emergency gear, but James Morgan was a pro—surely he would carry parachutes in his gear.

So Morgan probably wasn't dead yet, but he would be soon.

Oh yes, that bastard was going to die for what he'd done to Ariana; Nik would make sure of it. But right now, his first priority was getting Catarina back.

"Has Girard gotten us a phone number yet?" Dietrich came up beside him, his features creased with impatience.

"He's still working on it," Nik replied.

As he gazed at the compound again, he hoped that the mercenaries they'd hired were up to the task. Nik had run into several snags when hiring the soldiers; ironically, most of his contacts had referred him to the same private military company—owned by one James Morgan. It had enraged Dietrich to no end that one of the most skilled mercenary teams currently operating in the world happened to be the one whose compound they were targeting.

They'd had to settle for the Serbian team Nik had secured through a middleman in Russia, though the Serbs had a good reputation for getting the job done, according to his contacts.

As his own impatience grew, Nik pulled out his phone. "I'll call Girard again and see what the holdup is."

The moment he went to dial, the cell phone rang in his hand.

"Who is it?" Dietrich said sharply.

"Private number."

With a frown, Nik decided to answer the call. "Who's this?" he barked.

"Is that you, Nikolaus? Cate gave me your number. I hope you don't mind."

The familiar male voice made his blood run cold.

"Morgan," he spat out.

"Are you with Walther, by any chance? Put me on speakerphone if you are."

As anger sizzled in his veins, Nik pressed the speaker icon and held up the phone in front of Dietrich, who immediately leaned in and spoke in a tone cold enough to freeze an ocean.

"Where is my granddaughter?"

"Hello to you too, Walther."

Dietrich's cheeks hollowed, his jaw working hard, as if he were trying to grind his molars into dust. "Where. Is. She."

"Don't worry. She's here with me, safe and sound. No thanks to you," Morgan said bitterly. "You planted a bomb on my plane, you son of a bitch. She could have been hurt."

"You have the nerve to lecture *me* about hurting people?" Dietrich boomed. "After what you did to my daughter yesterday?"

There was a pause, and then, "How about we don't talk about Ariana? Cate is the one we need to worry ourselves with at the moment."

"I want her back, Morgan," Dietrich hissed out. "Catarina belongs with me."

"I guess we can agree to disagree on that." Another pause. "Cate's not going anywhere. She's staying right here with her father."

Dietrich let out a stream of violent curses that caught Nik off guard. He'd never seen the man this shaken up before, and he quickly intervened before Dietrich said or did something that jeopardized Cate's life.

"Let me tell you how it's going to be, Morgan," Nik snapped into the phone. "There are twenty mercenaries surrounding your compound at the moment. They're armed with powerful assault weapons and RPGs, and if you don't return Cate to us in exactly one hour, these very skilled men will blow your compound to hell."

"No, they won't." Morgan's confidence rippled over the line. "Do you honestly expect me to believe you'll launch a military attack on the house that Cate is in? When Ariana was a victim of a similar attack? No, you won't risk Cate's life. And just so you know, she doesn't want to leave. She's happy right where she is."

Nik wished Morgan were standing in front of him so he could strangle the life out of him. But the bastard was right. They would never endanger Cate's life.

Or at least that was what he thought before Dietrich spoke up again.

"You think I'm bluffing," he said coldly, "but I assure you, I am not. Yes, I want my granddaughter back, but if Catarina chooses to stay with you, then I'm afraid she will have to suffer the consequences. I'd rather see her dead than with you, Morgan. Do you understand me?"

Nik sucked in a shocked breath. He swiveled his head toward Dietrich, but the man was too busy spouting threats.

"You will pay for killing my daughter. I'm going to make sure of it. And if I have to sacrifice Catarina in order to make that happen, I won't hesitate to do it."

Nik opened his mouth to interject, but Dietrich cut him off. "One hour," he spat into the phone. "If my granddaughter doesn't walk out the front gate in one hour, I'm ordering my men to attack."

The older man disconnected the call, as Nik stared at him in disbelief.

"You don't mean that," he stammered.

Dietrich's features went harder than granite. "Yes, Nikolaus. I do."

Noelle could tell from Jim's expression that the phone call with Dietrich hadn't gone the way he'd expected. His blue eyes had darkened with concern, and his face lost some of its color, which was not at all encouraging.

"What did he say?"

Kane was the first one to voice the question they were all thinking. The small group had gathered in what Jim had referred to as the war room, an enormous space below-ground consisting of a conference area with a long table, and an entire wall of computer monitors. Ash and Reilly had stayed upstairs, sniper rifles locked and loaded as they kept an eye on the mercenaries surrounding the property, and the two security guards who manned the compound were monitoring every camera for the slightest hint of movement.

Abby was already gone. She'd left the compound through

the underground tunnels, after being banished by Kane, who refused to take any risks when it came to his pregnant wife. Abby had checked in twenty minutes ago to report she'd made it to the team's chopper and was waiting for them to join her.

Noelle stood next to Jim, whose expression was dead serious. Across the room, Jim's daughter lingered in the doorway, wearing a pair of yoga pants and a loose tank top. Her dark blond braid hung over one shoulder, and she was toying with the end of it, her gaze fixed on her father.

"Why aren't you answering the question?" she demanded.

Noelle couldn't help but be impressed by how calm Cate sounded, and she found herself experiencing grudging respect for the girl. Sure, the kid's expression revealed that she was scared to death, but she was still able to keep her cool, and Noelle appreciated that.

"He says he's blowing up the house if you don't come out within the hour," Jim finally revealed.

Cate's eyes widened.

"So what are you thinking?" Kane asked, his tone grim.

Jim sighed. "We've got twenty mercenaries out there gunning for us. Meanwhile, most of our people are scattered all over the globe. We're outnumbered."

"Then we go," Kane said briskly. "The tunnels are secure, and we can make our way out before those mercs even realize we're gone."

"Yeah, I don't see any other choice," Jim answered, though he didn't look thrilled about admitting it. "We can't risk being here when they attack." He glanced at his daughter. "And there's no way in hell I'm letting them get their hands on you."

"So we run," Cate said bleakly.

"You run," he corrected.

Noelle's spine stiffened. The moment she saw the hard glint in his eyes, she knew exactly what he was planning to do.

So did Kane, who'd worked with Jim long enough to know how the man's mind worked. "No fucking way, boss. You're not going all Rambo on us."

"What is he talking about?" Cate blurted out.

Noelle suppressed a sigh. "Your idiot father is about to

take on twenty mercs all by his lonesome, while the rest of us whisk you away to safety."

Horror flooded the girl's face. "No." She spun around to glare at Jim. "No way. You're not doing that."

He released a hasty breath. "I'm not taking on twenty men. Only two."

Noelle couldn't fight the wave of annoyance that rose in her body. "Do you really think you can get close enough to Dietrich and Bauer to take them out? Without getting your head blown off by all those men with guns pointed at you? Come on, Jim."

"I'll have the element of surprise on my side. I'll leave the compound through the tunnel and backtrack from the jungle. They won't see me coming."

"I won't let you do this," Kane said curtly.

"Well, then I guess it's a good thing you're not calling the shots." Jim clapped his hands together, his tone brooking no argument. "Gather the necessary supplies. I want everyone in the tunnel in five minutes." He turned to address Noelle. "Can you stick around and make sure Cate gets to the chopper okay?"

"Dietrich could be watching the airfields," she pointed out.

"You won't be going to an airfield. The chopper's stashed in a clearing about two miles from here. We'll drive the Humvees out of the tunnel, ditch them in the jungle, and hike to the bird."

"While you hike back here." She scowled deeply at him.

"For fuck's sake, not you too. Seriously, babe, don't fucking argue with me about this."

She arched a brow and didn't say another word. Instead, she stayed at her spot near the table, watching as Jim and Kane stalked to the door.

Jim paused in the doorway to touch his daughter's cheek. "Don't worry, sweetheart. We'll be outta here before they even realize we're gone. I'll come back and take care of things, and then we'll see each other again in no time."

Cate was too stricken to answer. Her blue eyes shone with worry as she stared at her father's retreating back.

Noelle turned away from the door and focused on the wall of monitors behind her. She found herself looking at the backup feed for every security camera on the property, immediately pinpointing the one that featured the most activity. Two military Jeeps had taken position on the eastern hillside, and she glimpsed several shadowy figures lingering near the tall electric fence.

"You don't like this plan."

Cate's blunt voice had her spinning around in surprise. The girl hadn't gone after Jim like she'd thought—she remained in the doorway, carefully watching Noelle.

"Doesn't matter if I do. Jim calls the shots around here," Noelle said with a shrug.

"But you don't agree with what he's doing."

"No, but like I said, it's not my call."

"He's going to get himself killed, isn't he?"

Noelle ignored the burst of pain that went off inside her. "Probably."

"And you don't care?" Cate marched over and rounded the table so that she was standing directly in front of her. She crossed her arms tightly over her chest. "Why didn't you try to stop him, damn it? Convince him to run with us?"

"Because he'd never do it." Noelle sighed. "And he knows as well as I do that running is a temporary solution. If you run now, you'll always be running. Your grandfather will never stop looking for you, Cate. He'll never stop hunting Jim."

"You're right," the teenager whispered.

"Of course I'm right."

"So you're just going to let him get killed?"

"Have you ever tried arguing with that man? It's like talking to a brick wall."

Cate's throat dipped in a swallow. "Okay . . . what would *you* do, then? I saw your face when you were looking at those screens. You have an idea, don't you?"

She shrugged.

"Then why didn't you suggest it?" Cate demanded.

"Because I knew Jim would never go for it."

"Why not?"

"Because it involves you." Breaking the eye contact, Noelle strode toward the door. "Don't worry your pretty little head about it, honey. Come on, let's go."

The girl stayed rooted in place. "No. I want you to tell me your plan."

Aggravation clamped around Noelle's throat. She stared at Jim's daughter, startled by the fortitude hardening those blue eyes. God, the girl looked so much like Jim right now. But she also reminded Noelle of herself—Cate had the same combination of innocence and grit that Noelle had once possessed. Before she'd become a coldhearted bitch.

"Tell me," Cate insisted.

Noelle battled a rush of indecision, then let out a weary breath.

And told the girl what she wanted to know.

Nik stiffened when his phone chimed in his pocket. He'd been watching the house through his binoculars, standing in the shadows as he monitored the situation. Although the hillside was bathed in darkness, lights continued to gleam from inside the compound, and the exterior floodlights affixed to the fence lit up the entire property and offered a perfect view of the front gate.

Cate had yet to walk through that gate, and Nik was growing more and more frightened as each minute ticked by. The look in Dietrich's eyes had been unmistakable—the man was seriously willing to sacrifice Catarina's life if she chose to remain with Morgan.

Swallowing his fear, he checked his phone and saw the same words as before flashing on the screen. Private number.

"It's him." He gestured to Dietrich, who approached with brisk strides.

"Let's hope the son of a bitch has decided to see reason," Dietrich muttered. "Put it on speakerphone."

As Nik touched the screen, Dietrich promptly leaned closer and said, "Have you reconsidered your stance about my granddaughter's living arrangements?"

There was a beat, before a familiar female voice wafted out of the speaker.

"Grandpa?"

Dietrich's shoulders tightened. "Catarina?"

"Yeah, it's me."

"Are you all right?" her grandfather demanded. "Are they treating you well?"

"Of course. I'm not a prisoner here." An edge had crept

into her tone, but it quickly softened. "It was my choice to come here." There was a pause. "And it's my choice to leave."

Nik sucked in a breath.

Beside him, Dietrich gave a pleased nod. "I knew you'd see the error of your ways."

Another wobbly breath shuddered over the line. "But before I do that, I need you to promise me something."

Dietrich narrowed his dark eyes. "What is it?"

"You have to send those mercenaries away. I mean it, Grandpa. Please don't attack this house. Promise me you won't harm anyone in it."

He looked annoyed. "I'm afraid I can't do that."

"Fine. Then go ahead and blow us all up. I'd rather die with Morgan and his team than have their deaths on my conscience."

Nik didn't miss the flicker of hesitation that crossed Dietrich's expression. He held his breath, praying that the other man reconsidered, that he wouldn't sacrifice his granddaughter as he'd threatened to do.

"Please, Grandpa," Cate pleaded, sounding so much like Ariana that it broke Nik's heart. "Send those men away. I'll come out and get in the car, and we'll drive to the airport and go home. Morgan has promised not to come after me."

"He spent years looking for you. Do you honestly expect me to believe he'll willingly let you go?"

"He doesn't have a choice," she said firmly. "He might be my father, but I don't know him. We don't have a relationship, or a history, or even all that much in common. I'm choosing to go home with you, Grandpa, but I wouldn't be able to live with myself knowing that my decision to run away got other people killed."

Dietrich sounded skeptical. "Morgan really agreed to let you go without a fight?"

"He'd rather see me alive than dead, even if it means me going back to you." When her grandfather hesitated again, Cate stubbornly went on. "I won't come out until Morgan's security guard confirms that the soldiers you hired are gone. Once that happens, I'll walk out on my own two feet and come home."

Dietrich's answering silence seemed endless.

Nik's pulse raced as he waited for the other man to make

a decision, but the longer he remained quiet, the more discouraged Nik felt.

And then, to his surprise, Dietrich clucked in agreement. "Fine, we'll do it your way, Catarina. I'll call off the men."

Her relief was unmistakable. "Thank you. I'll call you back in five minutes to make sure it's done."

After she'd disconnected, Dietrich swiftly reached for the radio tucked into the waistband of his black trousers. He clicked it on, and, as Nik stared in amazement, ordered the Serbs to retreat.

"What are you doing?" Nik demanded.

Dietrich held up a finger to silence him as he continued to address the leader of the mercenary team. "But don't go too far, Ivan," he finished. "I want you and your men out of sight, far enough that none of the cameras pick you up. The moment I give you the signal, you're to move in on the compound."

He shut off the radio with an evil smile.

"You promised Cate you weren't going to attack," Nik said slowly.

"Nikolaus, please. Do you truly think I'm about to take orders from a seventeen-year-old girl?" His lips curled in a sneer. "James Morgan is going to die tonight. I'm getting Ariana's daughter back, and then I'm killing the man who ruined my daughter's life."

Despite the guilt he felt about lying to Cate, Nik didn't challenge his boss. He might not have been on board with the original strategy, the one that could have resulted in Cate's death, but he wholly supported this latest plan.

James Morgan deserved to die for what he'd done to their family.

It was an agonizing five-minute wait before the phone rang again, and when it did, Nik wasted no time answering. This time he didn't bother with speakerphone; he just brought it to his ear and eagerly welcomed the sound of Cate's voice.

"Is it done?" she asked.

He had to smile. "You mean you're not checking the security monitors as we speak?"

She paused. "You got me, Nik. I can see that the men are gone."

"Good. So you know we've held up our end of the bargain. Can you see us on the monitor as well?"

"Yes."

"Good," he said again. "We're driving down to the front gate. You're going to walk out slowly, and if you're not there in ten minutes, your grandfather will have no choice but to call the men back. And you'll walk out alone, Cate. If we see Morgan or any of his soldiers anywhere near you, we'll be forced to open fire." He swallowed. "Please don't make us open fire."

"I'll be alone," she said tersely.

The phone clicked in his ear. She'd hung up on him.

A moment later, Nik got behind the wheel of the covered Jeep, Dietrich slid in beside him, and they were pulling away from the fence.

The four-by-four vehicle easily maneuvered through the hillside, wheels bouncing when they reached the bumpy dirt road that wound around the compound. They followed the narrow road all the way to its end, where it turned into a gravel-littered path that stopped in front of the commanding wrought-iron gate. The first of three gates, in fact, but Nik didn't attempt to drive any farther. Each gate seemed to require a code, and Cate hadn't provided it for them.

He put the car in park and hopped out, hurrying toward the front of the gate as he raised his binoculars to his eyes to study the house up ahead.

His heart jumped when he saw the front door open.

A second later Cate stepped onto the porch.

She was three hundred yards away. The binoculars didn't zoom in that far, but he was still able to get a vague look at her. Her hair was braided, and she wore jeans and a light blue sweatshirt. Her hands were in her pockets, her shoulders slumped as she descended the wide porch steps. He could see the discouragement in her body language.

She didn't want to do this, and a part of him didn't even blame her, especially when he thought of all those men hiding in the jungle, waiting to strike the moment Cate was safely in her grandfather's arms.

"She'll be punished for leaving us," Dietrich murmured.

Nik swung his head in surprise. "Punished how?"

"I don't know yet." The older man rolled his eyes when

he saw Nik's stricken face. "Relax, Nikolaus. I would never hurt her. But I will find a way to make it clear that she's never to disobey me again."

Gulping, Nik turned his attention back to Cate. It was too dark to make out her expression, and it didn't help that her head was down so he couldn't see her eyes. Her pace was reluctant but brisk, and Nik had to wonder whether this was a trap. Would James Morgan truly allow this to happen?

But at the same time, Morgan had to have heard the grim confidence in Dietrich's tone. The man would not have hesitated to kill Cate right along with everyone else in the house, and Morgan must have known that.

Perhaps he was a better man than Nik had thought, if he was willing to give up his daughter in order to keep her safe.

Anger jolted through him when he realized he was actually empathizing with James Morgan of all people. No, the man didn't deserve an ounce of empathy. He was losing Cate because she didn't want to be with him. Because she'd chosen to leave him and come back to Nik.

He was her true father, the only father she would ever need.

As he watched through the binoculars, Cate stopped at the first gate and punched a code in the key panel. When the gate slid open with a loud grinding noise, she walked through it and continued toward the second one. She halted again, input another code, and again began to walk.

The closer she got, the more anxious Nik felt. He couldn't help but remember what he'd done to her in the maze, and he didn't know how to even begin gaining her forgiveness.

But she was willing to come home. That was a start, at least.

"Good girl," Dietrich murmured as Cate approached the third gate.

Her head was still down, her blond braid shining in the moonlight. She entered another code into the electronic keypad, and the final gate creaked open.

She strode past it, stopping when she was ten feet from the two men.

When she looked up, Nik recoiled in horror.

Because it wasn't Cate.

An exquisitely beautiful face peered back at him. The

blonde from the party, he realized. The woman who'd accompanied Morgan to the estate.

A faint smile crossed her lips as her hand slid out of her pocket.

And that was when he saw the gun.

"Where's Noelle?" Jim glanced around the underground garage at the end of the tunnel and took in the scene before him.

Two Humvees, stocked with gear and supplies.

Kane opening the back door so the three Labrador retrievers could jump into the backseat.

Ash checking the clips of his weapons.

No Reilly, but he'd already gone ahead in the third Humvee with Inna, driving her to safety.

Cate was wringing her hands together, the fluorescent lighting in the tunnel emphasizing the groove of worry in her forehead.

But Noelle was nowhere to be found.

Kane slammed the Humvee door and straightened up, his eyes narrowing as he looked around. "I don't know." Frowning, he turned to Cate. "She was with you in the war room. She didn't come down with you?"

Cate shook her head. She quickly averted her eyes, but not before Morgan glimpsed a telltale flicker of guilt.

He was at her side in a heartbeat. "Where is she?" he demanded.

Cate met his eyes, but didn't say a word.

A curse flew out of his mouth as realization dawned on him. "Goddamn it! Fucking *hell*. What has she done?"

But he already knew. She'd gone out there herself. Taken it upon herself to eliminate Dietrich and Bauer before he could.

As a gust of panic blasted into his chest, he grabbed Cate's chin, harder than he meant to. "She went after them, didn't she?"

After a beat, his daughter nodded.

"You knew?" Uncharacteristic fear pounded inside him, making him sway on his feet. "And you didn't say anything?"

He was gone before she could reply, sprinting off in the

other direction. Every muscle in his body had seized with anger, but somehow his stiff legs managed to propel him forward. He heard footsteps behind him, felt Kane at his side, and spun around to fix the other man with an incensed glare.

"No," he snapped. "Stick to the plan! I want you to get Cate out of here. Now, goddamn it!"

Morgan took off running again, coming to a screeching halt in front of the hatch that led upstairs. He climbed the metal ladder two rungs at a time, emerging into the large walk-in pantry and heaving himself onto the tiled floor. Someone hopped out after him, and annoyance rippled through him as he turned, expecting to find Kane.

But it was Cate, gasping for air as she jumped to her feet.

"Get back downstairs," he ordered.

"No! I'm not letting you go out there! Noelle said she would take care of it!"

"The damned woman is going to get herself killed!" he roared.

Cate faltered. "What are you talking about it? You were planning on doing the same thing yourself!"

He gritted his teeth. "From the jungle, with the element of surprise on my side. I wasn't going to walk out the front door, damn it! I know this jungle like the back of my hand. They wouldn't have seen me coming."

"She has the element of surprise too," his daughter argued. "They won't be expecting her."

His spine stiffened. "Why do you say that?"

"Because they think she's me."

He didn't have time to question that infuriating response. Evidently his daughter and Noelle had conspired together, but now was not the time to reprimand her. He needed her back in the tunnel, damn it. He couldn't risk her getting hurt or slowing him down.

Fortunately, another arrival swooped in to save the day, as Ash lifted himself out of the hatch.

"Take Cate back to the tunnel," Morgan commanded, snapping the magazine of his submachine gun into place.

The rookie nodded, already reaching for Cate's arm. "Yes, sir."

Morgan whirled around without another word, hearing

Cate's squeaky protest echo behind him as he ran toward the front of the house. He bumped into Bill in the hallway, nearly knocking the security man off his feet.

"I was just coming to find you!" Bill exclaimed. "We've got activity at the main gate."

The two of them took off toward the entrance, while Bill continued to spit out words. "Blond female came out of the house, started walking toward the gate. We've got a vehicle parked out there, two men standing in front of it, both armed. I think it's your daugh—"

"It's not Cate," he cut in. "It's Noelle."

When they reached the door, Morgan glanced at Bill. "Get Don and go down to the tunnel. I can take it from here."

Unlike Cate, Bill didn't argue—he dashed off immediately, leaving Morgan alone in the parlor.

Taking a deep breath, Morgan burst out the door and flew onto the front porch, unsure of what he would find. But the courtyard was empty save for the collection of vehicles parked on the gravel.

With his MP5 in hand, he raced across the yard toward the first gate at the fence, and as he hurriedly disarmed it, he cursed himself for the overly cautious approach he'd taken with this new compound. Stopping at each gate only slowed him down, and a part of him worried that a sniper would take his head off any second. But no shots came. No movement from beyond the fence. All he could hear was the thump of his Timberlands on the gravel, the steady hiss of his own breathing.

Goddamn woman. She never listened to a word he said, never followed a single fucking order. What had she been thinking, going out there alone?

Christ, he was going to throttle her when he saw her.

But first, he had to save her ass.

He'd just reached the last gate when a gunshot cracked through the air.

The terrifying sound didn't slow him down. He kept going, ignoring the fear squeezing his heart, the adrenaline coursing through his blood.

Through the iron bars of the gate, he caught a glimpse of blond hair. His gaze registered a male body toppling to the pavement, another man raising a handgun. A slender arm whipped up in the direction of the armed man, but not fast enough.

A second shot rang out, and this time Morgan couldn't ignore the paralyzing terror as he watched Noelle go down.

Chapter 37

Morgan's heart stopped, then pounded with rage when his gaze collided with the triumphant look on Nikolaus Bauer's face. The man's head swiveled in Morgan's direction. When their eyes locked, the same horror and fury that he was feeling reflected back at him.

From the corner of his eye he saw Noelle lying on the gravel. He wanted to go to her, but he didn't get the chance because Bauer's weapon was now trained on him. But the man had no time to pull the trigger, because Morgan had hurled himself forward and proceeded to tackle Bauer to the ground.

The gun slipped from Bauer's hand, sliding underneath the Jeep behind them. Morgan lost his own weapon, watching it fall from his grip and skitter across the pavement.

It didn't matter. His fists were all the weapons he needed. He straddled Bauer's body and pummeled the man's face with everything he had. The caged rage inside him had been set free, and his pulse drummed in his ears as he pounded his fists into Bauer's face, the satisfying sound of flesh slapping flesh ringing in the air.

But Bauer wasn't an old man like Dietrich. He was a strong, fit male in his midthirties, and he wasted no time fighting back. His hand sliced up to jam into Morgan's throat, making him gag as his head was thrown back.

And clearly he'd underestimated the extent of Bauer's anger—suddenly the man was flipping him over in a feat of superhuman strength. Breathing hard, Morgan deflected the blows that came at his face, and managed to roll them over again. They slammed into the side of the Jeep, where Bauer yet again gained the upper hand, straddling Morgan's chest as he went on the attack.

A fist crashed into his jaw, reopening the cut Noelle had inflicted on his lip not too long ago. He spit out the blood that filled his mouth, then clocked Bauer right in the eye.

The man reeled back, growling in pain, and giving Morgan just enough time to roll out from under him and get the other man in a headlock. He squeezed hard, ignoring the arms that were swinging at him as Bauer tried to land another punch. Satisfaction sizzled in his blood when he tightened the hold and felt the other man begin to go slack.

But a pained groan suddenly captured his attention, distracting him for a second. He glanced over and saw Noelle stirring, and the split second of distraction was all it took for Bauer to wiggle out of the submission hold.

Morgan found himself on his back with the wind knocked right out of him, Bauer's heavy body yet again crushing his chest. He struck out, but not fast enough. A pair of strong hands wrapped around his neck, spittle splashing his face as Bauer hissed in triumph.

"You don't know how long I've been dreaming of this moment." The man's eyes were wild, his cheeks flushed with pleasure. "I've dreamed of it since the day you walked into my life."

Morgan curled his fingers around the guy's forearms and tried to pry him off, but Bauer's grip was too strong. Stars danced in front of his eyes as his windpipe started to ache, protesting against the lack of air.

"You stole the woman I loved," Bauer muttered. "Not once, but twice. You took her away from me seventeen years ago, and then you did it again when you pulled that plug."

Black dots flashed across his vision now. Fuck, he couldn't breathe. He felt himself starting to lose consciousness and he fought the darkness that was trying to envelop him.

"You're going to rot in hell for what you've done, James Morgan."

"He didn't do it."

Another voice penetrated the fog, a female one, but it sounded so far away. It sounded like Cate. But that couldn't be right. He'd told Ash to keep her safe. Hadn't he? He couldn't remember anymore.

The claws around his throat loosened. Just slightly. But not enough. He still couldn't draw in a single burst of air. His eyes started to water, wetness sliding down his face. Bauer's head was a shadowy blur over him.

"Catarina!" the man shouted.

He hadn't imagined it. She was actually here. But no, she couldn't be. She had to go. She had to be safe.

Morgan's arms felt like lead pipes as he tried to hit Bauer again, but he didn't have an ounce of strength left. Christ, he was perilously close to passing out.

"He didn't unplug *Maman*'s breathing tube," he heard her say. "I did it."

"You . . . you . . ."

The blackness continued to devour him, and then, in the blink of an eye, a crack boomed in the air. Thunder? No, that wasn't right.

But something had happened. And there was water on his face. A lot of it. Was it raining?

Suddenly the hands squeezing his throat were gone.

Gasping for air, Morgan tried to sit up, but he was too dizzy and his limbs refused to cooperate. He couldn't seem to make them function. And a heavy weight was still crushing his chest. Bauer's body, he realized. The man was lying on top of him.

Morgan sucked in gulps of air. His throat burned, and when he tried to talk, he couldn't make a single sound. He managed to let out a groan, hoarse and pained, as he tried to move Bauer's deadweight off him.

And then the load seemed to lift on its own, and he saw two shadowy faces peering down at him.

"You okay, boss?" Ash's voice.

Morgan blinked rapidly, his vision coming into focus. "Fine," he wheezed out. "Cate . . . ?"

"I'm right here," came her soft voice.

"I'm sorry, boss. She kneed me in the balls and took off."

Ash sounded furious. "Are you a fucking track star or something? I've never seen anyone run that fast."

"They needed help!"

"I ordered you to stay put!"

"I won't apologize for saving my dad's life!"

Morgan sat up with another groan, trying to clear the fog from his head. "Noelle," he choked out. "Where's Noelle?"

Ash disappeared from his view. A moment later, Morgan heard a soft curse cut through the air.

"Let me see your throat."

Warm hands touched his sore flesh, and he realized Cate had knelt down beside him. His neck throbbed with pain, and he knew it was probably redder than a fire engine, but he didn't care about himself at the moment. Where was Noelle?

His eyes strayed to Bauer's body, focusing on the puddle of blood pooling around the man's head.

Cate's breath hitched as she followed his gaze. "I shot him," she said flatly.

"I know." Morgan slowly got to his feet, swaying like a tree in a windstorm the moment his body went vertical.

"You shouldn't be walking!" Cate protested. "Sit down!"

He ignored her and stumbled toward the gate. Ash was kneeling on the ground, leaning over Noelle's body. A metallic hiss rang out. The rookie was unzipping Noelle's sweatshirt, Morgan realized. And he could hear soft gasps now. Was Ash panting?

No, the sounds were coming from Noelle.

As alarm rippled through him, Morgan dropped down beside them, just as Ash touched his earpiece.

"Kane, we need you ASAP. Bring the field med kit."

"What's going on?" Morgan wheezed, his vocal cords still too tender to function properly.

His gaze lowered to Noelle, registered the black Kevlar strapped to her chest, and overwhelming relief crashed into him. She'd donned a vest. Thank God.

So why did Ash look so worried?

It took a second for it to dawn on him. Noelle's pale face, her unfocused blue eyes. The breathless sounds shuddering out of her throat. Gasping like she couldn't get any air.

"Fluke shot," Ash muttered, looking over at Morgan. "Got her right under the arm through the side of the vest. Hit her lung."

Morgan ignored the rush of terror that filled his chest, forcing himself to focus on Noelle.

She was coughing now, her eyes beginning to glaze over.

"Don't pass out on me," he mumbled. "You hear me, babe? Stay with me."

The wheezing seemed to get worse. "Can't . . . breathe."

He and Ash quickly removed her vest, undoing the Velcro snaps to find a dark red bloodstain on her white tank top, right beneath her arm. Morgan lifted her up slightly so he could search for an exit wound, and his heart jumped in relief when he spotted the puckered hole. The bullet wasn't lodged inside her.

But it had still done its intended damage, and her shortness of breath had become so severe that he and Ash exchanged a worried look.

"Is she going to be okay?" Cate blurted out.

"Her pleural cavity is filling with fluid," Morgan muttered, his voice starting to come back to him. "We need to drain it or she'll drown in her own blood."

"Pleural cavity?"

"The space around the lungs," Ash explained, then clicked his earpiece again as his sharp gaze moved beyond the gate and focused on the house. "Damn it, Kane, move your ass."

Morgan cupped Noelle's cheeks and studied her face, but he saw no fear in her eyes. Just sheer calm, intermingled with flashes of pain.

"You're going to be just fine," he said firmly.

She continued to release fast, shallow breaths, but he knew that no air was getting in, and her pale face worried him.

Luckily, Kane chose that moment to dive through the gate. "What the hell happ—" He stopped midsentence when his gaze registered the scene before him.

"We need to drain the lung cavity or she won't make it," Ash told the new arrival.

Kane was already unzipping the bulky canvas medical kit and rummaging around inside. When his hand emerged with a massive syringe, Cate gasped.

"What are you going to do?" she said uneasily.

"You heard the rookie," Kane replied, his tone ringing with self-assurance. "We're draining the blood. Get out of the way, Jim. Unless you want to do the honors?"

Since his hand was shaking way too hard to hold a syringe, Morgan reluctantly moved aside and allowed Kane to take his place.

"You sure you know what you're doing?" Ash asked warily.

"Easy peasy. Just like Nicaragua. Remember? When Castle took two to the chest?"

Morgan felt sick as he watched Kane lean over Noelle's body. A second later, the needle disappeared in her flesh, and the syringe immediately began to fill up with a pinkish fluid.

"I think I'm gonna be sick," Cate mumbled.

From the corner of his eye he glimpsed his daughter stumble off, but he didn't tear his gaze off Noelle's face. "It'll be okay, baby. Kane is going to help you breathe, and then we'll take you to the hospital to get you patched you up."

As her gasps grew more violent, her expression got hazier and hazier.

"Stay with me," he pleaded with her.

But she'd already lost consciousness.

Chapter 38

"Morgan? You want anything from the cafeteria?"

Morgan lifted his head to find Cate in the doorway. He met her eyes, then glanced back at the beautiful blonde lying in the hospital bed next to his chair.

"Nah, I'm good. But thanks, sweetheart." Christ, it still hurt like a bitch to talk, but the doctors had assured him there would be no permanent damage to his windpipe.

She ignored his response. "I'll bring you back a sandwich."

Once she was gone, he couldn't stop the smile that tugged on his mouth. Truth was, the only reason he'd eaten a bite these last few days was because his daughter had practically force-fed him. Cate had flipped out when she'd shown up the morning after Noelle's surgery to discover he hadn't eaten a thing all day, and she'd been fussing over him ever since.

He had to admit he kind of liked it. He'd thought he'd be the one taking care of her, considering everything she'd been through—losing her mother, her best friend, her grandfather, killing Bauer. But Cate was the most resilient girl he'd ever met. Ash kept calling to report that she was fitting right in at the compound. Enjoying target practice, diligently doing her schoolwork despite the fact that nobody was forcing her to. She was disciplined as hell. Just like he'd been when he was younger.

Morgan hadn't been home since the night all hell broke loose, but Kane had also been calling in with reports. After

Dietrich and Bauer were killed, the Serbian mercenaries staked out in the jungle had simply gotten up and left; with their bosses dead, they had no beef with the compound. And courtesy of Morgan's friends in the CIA, a cleanup crew had been happy to take care of Dietrich's and Bauer's bodies. Dietrich had been a wanted man for more than four decades, and the US government was thrilled that he was finally out of commission.

With Dietrich out of the picture, Cate was officially safe, much to Morgan's relief.

Noelle was another story. She'd been unconscious for three days, but the doctors didn't seem worried about it. The surgery had gone well, and thanks to Kane's and Ash's quick work in the field, she'd suffer no permanent damage either.

But she still refused to wake up, and Morgan refused to go anywhere until she opened her damn eyes.

"Oh brother. Are you seriously sitting vigil at my bedside?"

Her husky voice startled the shit out of him. When he saw those incredible blue eyes peering up at him, the joy that exploded in his chest was so strong he almost fell out of his chair.

"You're awake." He dove out of the chair and went to sit at the edge of the bed, gently touching her cheek. Her skin was cold, but the color was slowly returning to her face.

"How are you feeling?" he said hoarsely.

"Like I got shot." Groaning, she tried to sit up.

He quickly moved in to help her, and once he'd gotten her settled, he tucked a strand of blond hair behind her ears.

"You okay? Do you want some ice chips?"

She harrumphed. "No. I want whiskey."

A crooked grin lifted the corner of his mouth. "You're going to be one of those difficult patients, aren't you?"

"Patient? Yeah right. I've already discharged myself in my head. I'll be out of here before the nurses even know I woke up."

He couldn't help but frown at her. "What the hell were you thinking, facing off with Dietrich and Bauer by yourself?"

She scowled. "I was thinking I couldn't let your dumb ass do it."

Surprise washed over him. "You were trying to protect me?"

"Hardly," she scoffed. "I was trying to protect your daughter, you moron. You're the one who gave me that whole speech about kids needing their fathers, and yet you were willing to abandon your kid all over again by going after Dietrich?"

His chest tightened with emotion. "You went out there so Cate could have me around?"

Noelle sounded defensive now. "Don't look at me like that."

"Like what?"

"Like I did something heroic." She shifted in discomfort. "I just wanted to give the girl a fighting chance, okay? So she wouldn't end up like me."

Tenderness softened his gaze. "Wouldn't be the worst thing if she did."

She laughed weakly, and he realized she thought he was kidding. Then she shifted again, trying to slide up higher, and a wince creased her face.

"Quit moving around," he grumbled. "You're recovering from surgery."

Sighing, she leaned her head back against the plastic edge of the bed. "What happened to Bauer?"

"Dead."

"Dietrich?"

"Dead. Nice shot, by the way. You got him right between the eyes."

She looked pleased. "Thanks. I would've gotten Bauer too, but the asshole got a lucky shot off. Total fluke that his bullet missed the vest. Just my luck, huh?"

To his amusement, she yanked the IV right out of her wrist without so much as flinching. "There, that's better," she said with a happy purr.

"You're unbelievable."

"Your sarcasm isn't appreciated right now, Jim."

"I wasn't being sarcastic. You really are unbelievable. You're incredible."

She must have picked up on the emotion thickening his throat, because an awkward glint entered her eyes. "Jim . . ."

His voice went croaky again. "I have to ask you something."

Her expression became downright wary. "What is it?"

"I was seeing someone in Costa Rica. It's over now—well, it never really began, if I'm being honest. But anyway, she asked me about the woman I lost, and . . ." His voice cracked. "I told her about you. Not a lot, just a few things. She asked if you were dead . . . And I said yes."

"Gee, thanks."

"That's what I used to believe," he admitted. "I believed that you were dead—not literally, I mean. But figuratively. I couldn't imagine that the girl I'd loved in Paris was still alive. But now I know she is."

Noelle shook her head. "Sorry to disappoint you, but that girl doesn't exist anymore."

"Bullshit." Swallowing, he reached out and placed his palm right above her left breast. "I *know* she's in there somewhere. You just have to open your heart to me again and let me see her."

"God, Jim." She looked flustered. "Why are you acting like a sappy fool?"

"Because . . ." His throat ached again, and not because he'd nearly been choked to death. "Because I don't want you to go. I want you to stay. With me."

"Why?" Now she seemed even more agitated.

"Because I love you, damn it."

He held his breath, waiting for her to say something, anything, but her expression had become veiled, and not a single word escaped her mouth.

"Noelle?" he murmured.

"You should find the nurse. Tell her I'm awake."

The dismissal sliced into his heart like a hot blade.

"No," he burst out. "You don't get to fucking ignore this. You're going to sit there and listen to every word I have to say."

"Jim—"

"I fell in love with you the moment I met you at that café in Paris. I know you think I faked it, but damn it, I didn't." Frustration jammed inside him. "And there's been a gaping hole in my heart ever since. Goddamn it, I'm *empty* without you. I tried to fill that void—believe me, I tried. I fucked other women, saved lives, took lives. But nothing worked. Nothing fucking worked."

He was embarrassed to feel the sting of tears in his eyes. "I know we can never have it back. We can't be what we once were. But even though we've changed, one thing hasn't. You're the only woman for me. The only woman I've ever wanted."

She opened her mouth, but he wasn't done. He wasn't even close to done.

"I've missed you every day for the last nineteen years. There was never any hope of getting you out of my system— because you're part of me, baby. There's nobody for me but you. Only you." He blinked through the tears swimming in his vision. "I can't lose you again. I need you ... God, I just need you to forgive me."

She still didn't speak, and he fought a jolt of desperation.

"I used you," he choked out. "I used you and I lied to you. But I never lied about the way I felt. I loved you then, and I love you now."

There was no response. Nothing but silence. He felt like he was talking to the damn air.

"Please," he begged. "Just fucking say something."

He waited. Implored her with his eyes.

And then she finally spoke.

"Can you go find the surgeon who operated on me? I want him to talk me through the surgery."

The agony was so great, it felt like his chest had been ripped open with a pair of rusty pliers. "That's it? Nothing else?"

Her blue eyes met his. "That's it."

Somehow he managed to stand up.

Somehow he managed to make it all the way to the door.

Once he got there, he halted. Swallowed the lump in his throat and turned to look at her again. "Think about it," he mumbled. "Maybe you'll have something different to say when I get back."

Ten minutes later, after he'd tracked down her surgeon and returned to her room, he discovered that she still had nothing to say.

Because she wasn't there.

Noelle was gone.

Chapter 39

Two days later

Cate poked her head into her father's office, clutching a white envelope in her hands. "Do you have any stamps?" she asked. "I need to mail a letter."

Although he nodded absently, his blue eyes never left the computer screen. Cate suspected he hadn't heard a word she'd said.

They'd been spending a lot of time together since he'd gotten back from the hospital in San José, but the distracted cloud that surrounded him refused to disperse. She knew he was thinking about Noelle, but he hadn't mentioned the woman since she'd pulled a disappearing act at the hospital. An orderly claimed that he'd seen her getting into a taxi wearing bright green scrubs, but Noelle hadn't gone back to the compound, not even to get her purse.

Cate had no idea how the woman had managed to leave the country, but her father had received confirmation yesterday that Noelle was back in Paris.

"Morgan? Did you hear me?"

He tore his gaze off the monitor and glanced over at her, and as usual, she experienced a burst of relief that he was here with her, safe, alive. Every time she looked at him she remembered how he'd almost died last week, and no part of her regretted the decision to pull the trigger and shoot Nikolaus. In that moment, she'd chosen to save her father's life instead of the man who'd raised her, and she refused to feel badly about it.

"Sorry, sweetheart. What did you say?"

"I asked if you had stamps. I need to send a letter."

Cate's throat clogged up as she stared at the address she'd scrawled on the envelope. She knew Gabriel's mother would be happy to get the letter. They'd spoken on the phone a few times since Cate had left Paris, and Joséphine had been overjoyed to learn that Cate was all right. Word of Maurice Durand's death had spread like wildfire through the city, and now his household staff was scrambling to find other jobs. Cate would have loved to send Gabriel's parents some of her own money, but her grandfather's funds had been frozen, thanks to his criminal activities, and she probably wouldn't inherit a dime from him.

But Morgan had been happy to write her a check to send to the Traver family; it was currently tucked inside the envelope she held in her hand.

"Leave it here with me," he said, sounding distracted again. "I'll make sure it gets sent."

His gaze returned to the computer, and then he clicked the mouse and the printer on the table behind him hummed to life.

With hesitant steps, Cate came forward and perched herself on the edge of his desk. "So . . . has she contacted you?"

Morgan shook his head, and Cate's heart ached when she saw the flicker of pain in his eyes.

The other day, he'd finally told her all about his history with Noelle. He'd admitted just how much he loved the woman, and it made Cate sad that Noelle had left him. But Morgan insisted that he'd deserved it, that Noelle was too scared to trust him again and he had nobody to blame but himself.

"Well, aren't you going to do something about it?" Cate asked in irritation.

"Of course I am."

He looked surprised that she'd even asked, which in turn surprised her. "Really?"

Morgan rolled his eyes. "Cate, there's one thing you need to know about your old man, which is that he doesn't give up. Ever. When he wants something, he damn well gets it."

She found herself laughing. "Good to know. So then what's the plan?"

"Well, my heartfelt speech went nowhere, so it's time to bust out the sweeping romantic gesture."

To punctuate that, he pointed to the sheet of paper that had just popped out of the printer.

Curious, Cate wandered over and lifted the paper out of the tray.

She blanched the second she looked at it, then spun around to gape at her father. "Are you frickin' kidding me?"

He wrinkled his brow. "What?"

"*This* is your idea of a romantic gesture?"

Morgan gave her a faint smile. "Trust me, Noelle will get it."

"This is going to backfire horribly," she grumbled.

His grin faded, but the determination in his eyes burned strong. "I guess we'll find out."

"Okay, this is getting annoying." Bailey cornered Liam outside his room at the Paris penthouse, folding her arms over her chest as she fixed him with a stern look. As usual, the woman didn't beat around the bush. "Things aren't going to change if you two dumb-asses keep acting like nothing happened."

Liam ran a hand through his sleep-mussed hair. "It's too early in the morning to have this convo, B."

"Tough shit, *L*." She rolled her eyes. "I've done my damnedest to try and help you these past few days, and all you've done in return is be a stubborn ass."

She was right. Ever since that terrifying, unexpected kiss in the guest room, the tension levels between Liam and his teammate had skyrocketed. To make matters worse, Morgan had ordered them to stay in Paris to monitor any fallout from the mission, which meant Liam couldn't flee the city like he desperately wanted to. Luckily, the boss had finally given them the green light to come home, putting an end to the excruciating discomfort Liam had been plagued with for days.

He and Sully still hadn't exchanged a single word about the kiss, though Bailey had been going out of her way to fix that. The woman had dragged them to a hundred places—tourist romps, restaurants, more than a few bars. Her endless energy and laid-back personality had succeeded in easing some of the tension between them, but it hadn't resulted in any sort of discussion regarding the fact that Liam's best friend had *kissed him.*

And he'd *liked* it.

Lord. His stomach churned each time he thought about it, unleashing panic and apprehension he'd never experienced before in his life.

That queasy feeling arose now as he met Bailey's eyes. "I'm . . ." He swallowed. Lowered his voice to a barely audible pitch. "I'm not gay."

She sighed, her expression softening. "Is that what all this avoidance is about?"

He nodded weakly.

"C'mere." She tugged him into the bedroom and shut the door, then cupped his cheeks with her hands. "I get it, okay? You want to do your buddy and it's freaking you out—I don't blame you one bit. But being attracted to him doesn't mean you have to make any monumental life changes." Her lips twitched. "Look, I think we can agree that there are hundreds of women who can vouch for your heterosexuality."

Liam grinned. "Damn right."

"So yeah, maybe you're straight. Maybe you're bi, or gay, or maybe this attraction you're feeling toward Sullivan is just plain old curiosity. Either way, you'll never know for sure unless you *talk* to him about it."

The grin faded fast. "What do I even say?"

Bailey shrugged. "Tell him you liked the kiss. Tell him you want to do it again." Another shrug. "Or tell him the opposite. Doesn't really matter—just tell him *something.* You two can't keep going around treating each other like strangers. You're BFFs, for fuck's sake."

A heavy breath slid out of his chest. "You're right."

Approval shone in her eyes. "Of course I am. Now, get out there and talk to him." To punctuate that, she gave his butt a little slap and nudged him toward the door.

Despite the excessive pounding of his heart, Liam managed to drop a quick kiss on the top of her head. "You're one in a million, B." Then, before he could change his mind, he marched out of the room.

He found Sullivan on the living room couch, eyes glued to some French reality show flashing on the TV screen. In his cargo pants and wifebeater, the other man looked casual as hell, but there was nothing casual in his expression when he lifted his head.

"Hey," Sullivan said gruffly.

"Hey." Clearing his throat, Liam headed for the sofa. He settled on the opposite end and met his friend's gaze. "So . . . listen . . . I wanted to apologize for—"

"No," Sully cut in.

He blinked in surprise. "What?"

"You have no reason to apologize, mate." Embarrassment reddened Sullivan's cheeks. "I'm the one who needs to say sorry. I . . . um . . . Oh bloody hell, I'm sorry for doing what I did, okay? I was all wound up from the boss's sex fest, and pissed off about being ignored, and I wasn't thinking clearly."

Liam opened his mouth to interject, but his friend wasn't done.

"I know you're not into blokes, and I'm an asshole for doing what I did," Sullivan hurried on, sounding sheepish as hell. "Sometimes I forget that not everyone is on board for all the kinky shit I'm into. I shouldn't have kissed you, and I'm sorry."

Liam's throat turned to dust. There were so many things he wanted to say.

It's all right. I wanted it too.

I've been thinking about it for weeks.

I don't know what the hell is going on with me.

But the words refused to exit his mouth. All he seemed capable of doing was sitting there in silence.

"So . . ." Sullivan searched his face. "Are we cool?"

Liam drew an unsteady breath, difficult to do when his chest felt so damn tight. He thought about Bailey's advice, *knew* he should follow it, but . . . goddamn it, he wasn't ready for this. He wasn't fucking ready.

So instead, he took the out that Sullivan had dangled in front of him.

He nodded, met his friend's eyes, and said, "Yeah. We're cool."

*   *   *

Noelle zipped up her suitcase and rolled it toward the door, then did a quick scan of the guest room to make sure she had everything. She was eager to leave, but since she wasn't planning on coming back anytime soon, she couldn't afford to leave anything behind.

And God, "eager" didn't even begin to describe her need to flee. She was a loner, and she didn't fare well with others crowding her personal space, especially when they were two men who reminded her of Jim.

For some irritating reason, Sullivan Port and Liam Macgregor were still at the penthouse, despite the numerous not so subtle hints Noelle had dropped about them not being welcome. Bailey, however, seemed to want them around, and the trio had been spending a lot of time together, seeing the sights, enjoying the Paris nightlife. Which was equally perplexing, because Bailey was a loner too.

Just like her.

Yep, they were both loners. Destined to be alone forever. *Oh, stop the pity party. You're better than that.*

She was, wasn't she? And besides, hadn't she just had an opportunity to change her loner status? Hadn't Jim all but poured his heart out to her?

And like the coldhearted bitch she was, she'd walked away from him.

Still, as guilty as she felt about deserting the man after he'd opened his heart to her, she found his naïveté so damn infuriating. How could he possibly believe they were capable of having a real future? They'd hurt each other too many times over the years. She'd hated Jim for so long she didn't remember how to love him.

And even if she did believe, for one second, that he'd loved her all those years ago, they couldn't go back. She wasn't the young girl he'd fallen in love with. She'd changed, and definitely not for the better.

No, they weren't destined for happily-ever-after. But at least she'd ensured that Jim could have a happily-ever-after with his kid.

Jim had Cate now, and Noelle couldn't deny she liked the girl. Cate was strong and smart and fearless, and although Noelle got the feeling that the girl would be a handful, she figured Jim deserved a little gray hair.

A knock on the door made her sigh. "What do you want?" she called out to the intruder.

"Why so rude?" Sullivan popped through the door, his eyes gleaming with amusement. "I thought we were buds now."

"We are not, nor will we ever be, 'buds.'" She shot him a cool look. "What do you want, Port?"

He held up a manila envelope. "This was just FedEx'd for you."

Frowning, Noelle accepted the envelope, studied the return address, and handed it right back. "Not interested."

She gripped the handle of her suitcase and headed for the door.

Sullivan swiftly intercepted her path with his six-foot-three frame. "Bloody hell. Why is every woman on the planet so bloody stubborn? Would it kill you to open it?"

"Would it kill you to get out of my way?"

"Yes."

Noelle gritted her teeth. "Get out of the way."

He crossed his arms over his broad chest and said, "Nope."

"Oh for fuck's sake, am I going to have to pull out my knife?"

"You can if you want, but you're still about to get some advice, whether or not I get stabbed."

She blew out a breath. "Spit it out, then. I have a plane to catch."

"You're making a mistake," he began.

"Sorry you feel that way. See you later."

She tried to brush past him, but he sidestepped her. "Look, Liam has this theory—he thinks some people are hardwired to fuck one another."

Noelle couldn't help but snort.

"It's chemistry," Sullivan went on. "Bodies needing to screw. But I think the same thing applies to love." He offered a sheepish look. "You can't help who you fall for, love. And sometimes, the person you think is all wrong for you, well, they're actually the right one."

"Thank you, Ann Landers. Will you get out of my way now?"

"Fine, be stubborn. You're the one who'll wind up alone."

"Story of my life, honey."

"Whatevs." With great annoyance, he dropped the envelope on top of her suitcase. "Just open the damn thing, would ya?" With that, he marched off, leaving her to stare at the envelope.

The familiar address, the scratchy male handwriting.

Goddamn him.

Couldn't he leave well enough alone? They weren't destined to be together. They'd fallen in love when they were kids. She, a foolish young girl who'd believed she'd found her knight. He, a soldier following orders.

Maybe he'd loved her. Maybe he hadn't. It didn't change everything that happened afterward, or erase all the years they'd spent plotting each other's deaths.

They couldn't come back from that, damn it. She knew it, and yet her curiosity only heightened as she gazed at the envelope.

Despite the warning bells going off in her head, Noelle picked up the envelope. She dug a fingernail under the flap and ripped it open, then extracted the single sheet of paper inside of it. God. Had he written her a love letter?

No, the paper was too glossy for that, she realized. It was a photograph, then, but she couldn't bring herself to turn it over and take a look.

She should just throw it away. Toss it in the wastebasket, get on her jet, and spend the next two months on her private island, forgetting all about Jim Morgan. Learning to hate him again.

But the curiosity refused to ebb, and eventually, she took a deep breath and flipped the photo over.

Chapter 40

Noelle found him on the terrace. His strong forearms rested on the railing as he gazed out at the property, and although he didn't turn around, the tensing of his shoulders told her that he knew she was there.

After a moment of hesitation, she nervously raked a hand through her hair and walked up beside him.

"It was you," she said quietly.

Jim turned, his blue eyes somber, his voice gruff. "It was me," he confirmed.

She swallowed. "When?"

"A year and a half after I left Paris. But you knew that."

"How'd you do it?"

"You know that too." He shrugged. "Snapped his neck and shoved him down the stairs. I knew the coroner would blame the broken neck on the fall."

Her tone turned incredulous. "And then you hung around and snapped a picture of it?"

He nodded.

"Why? Why take a picture? Why kill him at all?"

"I took the picture because I was planning on sending it to you, so you would know it wasn't an accident. So you'd know that you got your revenge, after all." He sighed. "And then all that stuff with Ariana happened, and in my anger, I decided not to give you that closure. I'm a real shit, huh?"

"Damn right you are." She shook her head as the truth of what he'd done sank in. All these years she'd cursed fate, cursed the drunken stumble that had stolen her vengeance from her, but René hadn't fallen down the stairs like she'd thought. Jim had killed him.

For *her*.

Noelle stared at him with wide eyes. "I can't believe you did that." She bit her lip. "You still haven't told me *why*."

"I think we both know the answer to that one too." He shot her a meaningful look. "Don't we?"

Her throat closed up to the point of suffocation. "You killed René because you loved me."

"Yes."

"You kept tabs on me after you left."

"Yes."

"And then you went back and killed my stepfather for me."

"Yes."

"Because you really did love me."

"Yes."

Noelle could barely see his face through the sheen of tears obstructing her vision. "You weren't pretending. You really did fall in love with me."

"Yes," he said once more, and then he brushed away her tears with his fingertips. "I loved you then, and I love you now."

Her heart nearly soared right out of her chest. She stared into his midnight blue eyes, but this time she didn't search them, didn't probe or assess or look for any hint of malice or dishonesty.

Because she knew he was telling her the truth.

"Hey, Jim?"

His gaze never left hers. "Yeah?"

"Will you kiss me?"

He let out a deep growl. "It's about fucking time."

And then his mouth crashed down on hers in a passionate kiss that stole the breath right out of her lungs. His lips were as delicious as she remembered, his tongue greedy and dominant, filling her mouth, coaxing and teasing until she was moaning with abandon.

She clung to his broad shoulders, holding on tight, never wanting to let him go. God, she finally had him back. Her sexy soldier, the gruff, intense man who'd swept her off her feet all those years ago and shown her the kind of love she'd never thought possible.

She kissed him back with everything she had, while her heart pounded against her rib cage, lighter and fuller than it had been in a long, long time.

"You have *got* to be kidding me!"

They broke apart as a shocked voice echoed behind them, both of them spinning around to find Cate standing in the doorway.

"For the love of God." Morgan's daughter gaped at her father. "The picture actually worked? You two have the most fucked-up concept of romance."

"Hey," he said sharply. "Watch your fucking language, young lady."

Cate snorted, then looked over at Noelle. "Welcome back."

Noelle smiled awkwardly. "Thanks."

"Are you going to be my new mom?"

The panic that shot through Noelle almost knocked her on her ass, but then the teenager started to laugh.

"Oh relax. I'm just pulling your leg. I hope we can be friends, though."

"We can try. But you should know that I don't have a lot of friends," Noelle admitted. "I'm not entirely sure how all that friendship stuff works."

Cate flashed her a grin. "I'm sure we'll figure it out." The girl edged back to the door and glanced at her father again. "Is it cool if I go into town with Ash? I need to buy a few more things."

"Sure. Do you still have the gun I gave you?"

Cate rolled her eyes. "Getting overprotective on me already, huh?"

"Hey, I have years to make up for," he protested.

"Ugh. I guess I'll let it slide. This time."

Jim chuckled as his daughter disappeared into the kitchen, then turned to Noelle with a crooked grin. "See what I have to look forward to?"

She grinned. "Don't worry. I'll be around to put out any fires."

His eyes suddenly narrowed, as if her words had sparked

his memory. "By the way, I got a very interesting phone call yesterday."

She slanted her head. "Yeah?"

"Oh yeah. See, I'd sent Sully back to the airfield in Paris to take care of a little rat problem, and what do you know, Sergio was dead in his office when Sully got there. You remember Sergio, don't you, babe? The man who let a contract killer crash our plane?"

"Hmmm. Sounds vaguely familiar."

Jim's lips twitched. "Would you happen to know anything about this little mystery?"

She gave him a sheepish look. "He betrayed you. What else was I supposed to do?"

After a beat, Jim burst out laughing. "God, I love you."

Noelle looked him square in the eye and said, "I love you too."

Keep reading for a sneak peek at the next
heart-pounding novel in
Elle Kennedy's Killer Instincts series,

MIDNIGHT CAPTIVE

Available soon from Signet Eclipse.

"Being a hermit isn't healthy, you know." Bailey paused to shoot a pointed stare at her friend before continuing to wander through the cozy living room of Paige's isolated Somerset country house.

Wall-to-wall bookshelves took up nearly half of the room, crammed with hundreds of titles, which all looked well-read, and the lingering scent of smoke wafting out of the massive stone fireplace hinted that Paige had lit a fire recently. It was obvious that the woman spent a lot of time in this room, which corroborated Bailey's belief that her friend was a total recluse.

"Says who?" From her perch on the overstuffed sofa, Paige sipped her Merlot, unperturbed by the accusation.

Watching the other woman daintily hold the stem of her wineglass was almost jarring. With her slight frame, pale red hair, and fair, freckled face, Paige Grant was cute and delicate—and the last person you'd imagine to be a ruthless assassin. But Bailey supposed all of her colleagues were the same in that way. Sweet and harmless on the surface, hardened and deadly beneath it.

Bailey herself was no stranger to death and violence. Seven years in the CIA followed by five working for a dangerous assassin had definitely hardened her. She didn't see the world as sunshine and rainbows—she saw it for what it was: cold, toxic, and treacherous, with rare moments of warmth, love, and compassion slicing through the darkness like shards of moonlight. *If* you were lucky. She hadn't experienced a lot of warm-and-fuzzy moments in her life, not as an adult, and certainly not as a child.

But right now was one of those moments. Spending the weekend in a beautiful albeit rundown English farmhouse, sipping on deliciously smooth wine and catching up with one of her best friends. Sunshine and rainbows, all right.

"Says me," Bailey announced, returning to the couch and flopping down on the other end. "You're too young and beautiful to be hidden away here. You should be out and about, kicking ass and breaking hearts."

Paige snorted, then set her glass on the weathered oak coffee table and spoke in her crisp British accent. "First, I kick plenty of ass, thank you very much. Second, I'm not interested in breaking any hearts, but if you're hinting that I need a good shagging, then don't worry. I've got plenty of blokes at my beck and call. And third, you say all this as if *you're* a social butterfly, when we both know for a fact that you, my dear, are as big a loner as I am."

Bailey couldn't argue with that. *Loner* was her middle name. But still, her friend's shut-in ways bothered her. Paige's bubbly personality was completely incongruous to a life of isolation.

"At least I attended our boss's wedding," she said mockingly.

"You did not! They eloped."

Bailey grinned. "Yeah, but I flew to Costa Rica after I heard the news and dropped off a wedding present."

Paige rolled her eyes. "Yes, well, I couriered a gift. And mine was most certainly better than yours."

Curiosity flickered through Bailey. "What'd you get them?"

"A ten-book set aptly titled *How to Keep the Sexual Fire Burning After Marriage*." Paige laughed in delight. "Noelle sent me a text message in reply. Two words. *Fuck* and *off*."

Bailey burst out laughing. She would've paid money to see their boss's face when she opened Paige's gift. Poor Noelle had already been annoyed enough that her former-love-turned-enemy-turned-love-again had twisted her arm into marrying him. But Jim Morgan was a stubborn alpha male, and the deadly mercenary had insisted they get married ... or else he would have dragged her down the aisle kicking and screaming. And the icing on the cake—he'd talked No-elle into taking his last name, which officially made her No-elle Morgan now.

Maybe Bailey was a jerk, but she found the whole situation hilarious. She'd met Morgan two months ago in Paris after he'd reconnected with her boss, and she really liked the man. She was glad he and Noelle had finally worked through their decadelong issues.

Though their union did have one drawback.

Noelle and Morgan had joined professional forces. Which meant that Bailey and the rest of Noelle's assassins—chameleons, as they'd been dubbed—now worked for Morgan, too.

"I'm still not sure how I feel about it," she confessed.

Paige furrowed her brow. "My wedding gift? Why? I think it's awesome."

"No, not the gift—it is awesome. I was just thinking about our new working arrangements," Bailey clarified. "We're not mercenaries. We work alone."

"Don't worry. Noelle knows that. She said we'll still be working solo, but if Morgan's team ever needs undercover help, they'll call us in."

Crap.

Crappity-crap-crap.

Bailey quickly swallowed the lump of unhappiness that rose in her throat, but clearly she hadn't managed to mask her expression, because Paige's blue eyes narrowed.

"What's the problem? You've helped Morgan out before. And God knows I get a call from him or Noelle at least once a week hitting me up for tech assistance."

"Which you can do from home," Bailey said, pointing to the insane amount of laptops on the long table across the room.

Cables and electrical bars snaked along the floor, some of them climbing toward the exposed beamed ceiling, all plugged in to power Paige's command central, as she called it. The woman was a wizard when it came to computers, which was why she was on everyone's speed dial. If you wanted information, Paige Grant was your first and only call.

Unless it was the kind of information a computer couldn't find. . . . In that case, that honor went to the Reilly brothers.

AKA the reason Bailey was unbelievably reluctant to call herself a member of Jim Morgan's team.

"I still don't see the issue," Paige said in confusion. "Morgan's a good guy. You said so yourself. Besides, you were the one just talking about breaking hearts—think of all the hot single men you'll be working with. Liam Macgregor is a bloody movie star, that Sullivan guy is smokin' hot, and then there's the scary sexy badass . . . D? Plus there's Sean— Actually, wait. He's off the team. And the cute rookie—"

"Wait. Back up." Bailey had frozen at Paige's last remark. "What do you mean Sean's off the team? Since when?"

"Since a couple weeks ago, apparently. I spoke to Abby the other day and she said he suddenly quit."

"Did he say why?"

"He told Morgan he works better alone and that he was wrong to think he'd be able to function on a team." Paige shrugged. "Or something along those lines."

Bailey's brow furrowed. She supposed that made sense. Sean Reilly didn't take orders well. He was also impulsive to the core, exactly the kind of man who'd join a mercenary team and then abruptly change his mind less than two months later.

A sudden rush of bitterness flooded her chest. Yup, she was well acquainted with Sean's impulsive nature. She'd experienced it firsthand nearly a year ago, after the cocky Irishman had seduced her under the pretense that he was someone else.

And you let him.

It was hard to ignore the internal accusation—especially since it was one hundred percent accurate. Truth was, she couldn't lay all the blame for that night on Sean. The second he'd slid into her darkened hotel room, she'd known he wasn't Oliver, Sean's equally gorgeous twin and the sweeter, more mature of the brothers. She'd *known*, yet she'd still allowed him to touch her. Kiss her.

Fuck her.

Aggravation clamped around her throat as old memories crept into her head—wicked images and seductive words whispered in a deep Irish brogue. Damn him for lying to her. Damn *herself* for letting him.

"I guess he headed back to Dublin to join forces with

Ollie again," Paige was saying, oblivious to Bailey's inner turmoil. "Which is probably where he belongs. The Reilly brothers, information dealers extraordinaire, bona fide Irish heartbreakers." The redhead slanted her head. "Didn't you go out with Ollie a while back?"

Bailey nodded, keeping her expression veiled. "Yeah, we went out a couple of times. We decided we were better off as friends, though."

"Pity. He's quite cute. Sean, too, though that's a given, considering they're identical."

The conversation was veering into dangerous territory Bailey wanted to avoid. She hadn't told any of her colleagues about her night with Sean. The only person who knew about it was Liam Macgregor, who, in the past couple of months, had somehow become one of her closest friends. Figure that one out. Maybe she wasn't as much of a loner as she'd thought.

"Okay, enough man talk. This is our annual girls' getaway, remember?" She grinned at her friend. "What cheesy rom coms did you get for us?"

Paige looked delighted. "Oooh, I ordered a bunch of them from the movie channel on the telly. You're in for a treat."

Bailey laughed as the other woman swiped the remote control from the end table and turned on the television. Back when she'd worked for the CIA, evenings like this hadn't existed in her life. She'd been a solo operative, spending months undercover and executing covert missions on foreign soil. She still did all that for Noelle, except nowadays she actually managed to squeeze in some downtime. Which was kind of comical—two assassins curled up on a couch with popcorn and wine about to watch sappy romantic comedies. Life was strange sometimes.

"I ordered that movie about the chick who loses her memory and her hubby has to make her fall in love with him again," Paige revealed as she clicked the remote. The television was turned to a news channel, the broadcast nothing but a square box at the bottom of the screen as Paige scrolled through the channel list. "Hence the box of tissues on the table. Be prepared to sob like a baby."

Another laugh slipped out, but was cut short when Bailey noticed the line of text running beneath the news report.

"Hey. Stay on this channel for a sec," she said quickly, a frown marring her lips.

Paige stopped scrolling, clicking another button to bring the segment into full-screen view. "Ah, shit," the redhead murmured. "Obviously the world's gone to hell again."

Not the world—just Dublin, according to the screen. Bailey listened in dismay as the reporter quickly recapped the unfolding events to viewers who were just tuning in. There was a holdup in process at a downtown branch of Dublin National Bank. A half dozen masked, armed men had taken the bank employees and patrons hostage, and the law enforcement officers surrounding the bank were attempting to negotiate with the robbers. Apparently the situation was beginning to escalate, with reports of shots fired and hostages screaming.

"Turn it up," Bailey told Paige, leaning forward when a shaky camera image suddenly filled the screen.

Paige raised the volume, and the urgent voice of the female newscaster blared out of the speakers.

"—courageous woman uploaded a video to her social network page. We don't know how she was able to record this, but it's been confirmed that the account belongs to Margaret Allen, a twenty-one-year-old student at Trinity College. Be warned—some of these images are not suitable for young children."

The screen flickered for a beat before the video began to play. Immediately, loud footsteps and angry shouts filled Paige's living room. The two women watched in silence as jerky images flashed on the screen, accompanied by gruff orders from the robbers and muffled whimpers from the hostages. It was difficult to zero in on any one image—everything was moving too fast, and the men in charge wore all black, from the ski masks on their faces right down to the boots on their feet.

An uneasy feeling washed over Bailey as she focused on one of the men. Tall and broad, eye color indiscernible, and voice low and deep as he issued a soft command to someone out of the camera's line of sight.

"Look at these idiots," Paige remarked with a sigh. "Do they honestly expect to get away with this?"

Bailey didn't answer. Something niggled at the back of

her mind, an intangible flicker of familiarity, a sense of bone-deep dread. But she wasn't sure what was bugging her. People robbed banks all the time. People took hostages. People killed other people and did seriously stupid, dangerous shit every second of the day.

So why was this particular armed robbery making the hairs on the back of her neck tingle?

Another anguished sob echoed in the bank, followed by a male response.

"'S okay, luv. It'll be all over soon."

The husky timbre of that voice, combined with the faint brogue, turned the blood in Bailey's veins to ice. A gasp flew out, her heart rate kicking up a notch as she stared at the screen in pure and total shock.

"Oh, shit," she whispered.

Paige glanced over, big blue eyes swimming with concern when she saw Bailey's expression. "What is it?"

"It's Sean." Her finger trembled as she jabbed it in the direction of the television.

"What?" The other woman sounded bewildered. "That's nuts."

Maybe, but Bailey would recognize that voice anywhere. It haunted her dreams every goddamn night.

"It's him, Paige. One of the robbers—it's Sean fucking Reilly." Horror, shock, and confusion clawed up her throat like icy fingers. "It's *Sean*."

Also Available

FROM

Elle Kennedy

MIDNIGHT RESCUE
A Killer Instincts Novel

Adopted by an army ranger, Abby Sinclaire was molded into a master of self-defense. Now, she's an assassin using raw nerve to always come out on top. Her latest assignment is to snuff out a dangerous arms dealer hiding in the underground Colombian sex trade. When the sting goes wrong, mercenary Kane Woodland is recruited as back-up. But their unexpected, primal attraction could put them both at risk. Their only rule: save the kidnapped girls, even if it means they might not get out of this hellhole alive.

"Fans will be eager to see what Ms. Kennedy has in store for her mercenaries."
—Shannon K. Butcher, author of the Edge Series

Available wherever books are sold or at
penguin.com

S0441

ALSO AVAILABLE

FROM

Elle Kennedy

MIDNIGHT ALIAS
A Killer Instincts Novel

An undercover DEA agent has gone off the radar.
Suspecting a mole, the government needs Luke Dubois
and his elite team of operatives to recover their man, and
the New Orleans native thinks he's found his way into the
dark underbelly of Manhattan through Olivia Taylor, the
girlfriend of a mob boss and the sexiest woman he's ever
laid eyes on. His new mission objective? Get past Olivia's
defenses and convince her to take a chance—on him.

"Hard-core romantic suspense loaded with sensuality."
—*USA Today*

ellekennedy.com

Available wherever books are sold or at
penguin.com